# The PRESIDENT'S
# SHADOW

# ALSO BY BRAD MELTZER

## Novels
The Tenth Justice
Dead Even
The First Counsel
The Millionaires
The Zero Game
The Book of Fate
The Book of Lies
The Inner Circle
The Fifth Assassin

## Nonfiction
Heroes for My Son
Heroes for My Daughter
History Decoded
I Am Amelia Earhart
I Am Abraham Lincoln
I Am Rosa Parks
I Am Albert Einstein
I Am Jackie Robinson
I Am Lucille Ball

# The PRESIDENT'S SHADOW

## BRAD MELTZER

GRAND CENTRAL
PUBLISHING

NEW YORK    BOSTON

**Doubleday Large Print Home Library Edition**

**This Large Print Book carries the Seal of Approval of N.A.V.H**

For Jill Kneerim,
my dear friend and trusted agent, for
laughing at the jokes of that twenty-three-
year-old kid who said he wanted to write
novels. You were the first to say yes.
I owe you forever for that.

# Acknowledgments

Every time I write a novel, I convince myself I'm telling you a story about imaginary people. But by the end, I once again realize that the only story I can really be honest about is my own story. We've had a rough few years in my house. We buried both my parents and then, as I thought I was finally over it, I kept struggling through the seismic aftershocks and the inevitable identity quest that went along with it. Today I know: I'll never get over losing my parents. And I don't want to. They deserve to be remembered. These books—and the characters within—taught me that. So once again, I owe you, dear reader, for making these novels possible. On that note, I also owe massive thank-yous to the following: My first lady, Cori, who fought with me and for me, bringing me to the other side. C, you are my true love. I fight for you every day, and your input is felt on every page of this novel. I'm so thankful to have you there. Jonas, Lila, and Theo will always be my best blessings. I keep thinking I'm teaching the three of them, yet no one on this planet has taught me more about myself. I love each of you with everything I have. Jill Kneerim, my friend and agent, this book is for you. When I was twenty-three, you took that first chance. Along the journey of our friendship, you have educated me about writ-ing—and about decency. You challenge me on every draft, and this book is the best of what you taught me; Hope Denekamp, Lucy Cleland, Ike Williams, and all our friends at the Kneerim, Williams & Bloom Agency. Also, an official welcome to the unstoppable Jen-nifer Rudolph Walsh and everyone at WME as they join our family. I so admire what you do, and here's to many more together.

This book is about the power and emotional pull of family, but also about the definition of it. So I need to thank my sister, Bari, the one person who can both laugh and cry with me about our parents' beautiful craziness. Also to Bobby, Ami, Adam, Gilda, and Will, who are always there with us.

Let me tell you who redefined family for

me. Noah Kuttler did. There's no one more loyal, more trusted, more dedicated. I can honestly say, he is **always** there for me. **That** is the definition of family we should all aspire to. I love you for it, Noah. Ethan Kline brings his big literary brain to every one of these books, shaping it for the better. Then Dale Flam, Matt Kuttler, Chris Weiss, and Judd Winick take those early drafts and give me the honesty I need to turn those pages into an actual book.

I could not write my imaginary President without the gracious help of President George H. W. Bush, who always shows tremen-dous kindness by answering my questions. Special thanks to First Ladies Barbara and Laura Bush, along with the amazing Jean Becker, for helping inform my imaginary counterparts. At this point, I hope my love of the National Archives is clear. But my work there could not have been done without Archivist of the United States David S. Ferriero, whose friendship is treasured. He is a host like no other (and I'll admit, makes better pancakes than I do). Also at the National Archives (if you haven't been, go visit), Matt

Fulgham, Chris Isleib, Miriam Kleiman, David Mengel, Trevor Plante, and Morgan Zinsmeister once again helped me conjure my inner Beecher. Whatever the question, they knew the answers. Their friendship means the world to me. Additional thanks at the Archives go to Jay Bosanko, John Fitzpatrick, William Carpenter, and William Cira, who shared with me the coolest new details for the opening chapters. Thanks also to John Laster, Jana Dambrogio, Jon Deiss, and the memory of John E. Taylor.

In every book, there's one person who goes beyond the call of duty. That person is Scott Deutsch. In eighth grade, when I first moved to Florida, I didn't have any friends. Scott was one of the first who was nice to me. When he moved away, we lost touch for years—until a soldier in his unit in Iraq was reading one of my thrillers. That book led to our reunion, and to him being the true military adviser of this mission. Thanks for your kindness all those years ago, and for all you did here to keep the military details right. This book was also forever changed by my friend and hero Rochelle Shoretz, who shared the intimate details of her own illness. As you're reading about Clementine, you're reading about Rochelle. I love you for the trust, Roch. Also thanks to Eljay Bowron, Jim Mackin, Max Milien, Mike Sampson, and Emily Karcher for showing me even more reasons to admire the amazing work of the Secret Service.

Extra thanks to Nancy Russell, Dan Kimball, and Glenn Simpson for the Fort Jefferson details. They put up with every inane question, and in the process gave me my ending; Dan Ariely (go watch his TED Talk) for trusting me with the details of his own burns and hospital experience. I only hope I did it justice; Mike Ressler for Marine Band details; Ruth Martin for the green thumb; Mike Workman for his explosive expertise; my confidants Art DeHoyos and Dean Alban for their historical vision; Dr. Lee Benjamin, Dr. Michael Lemont, Dr. David Sandberg, Dr. Michael Steckbauer, and Dr. Ronald K. Wright for helping me maim and kill with authority.

Even more details came from Cris Alvarez, Kurt Bromund, Alan Brown, Paul Castronovo, David Funder, Wayne Greene, Gary Greenspan Michael Rogers, John

Ryan, Jean Twenge, and Dan Watson; and the rest of my own inner circle, who I bother for every book: Jo Ayn Glanzer, Jason Sherry, Marie Grunbeck, Chris Eliopoulos, Nick Marell, Brad Desnoyer; David Watkins, Mark Dimunation, Matthew Bogdanos, and Bob Gourley. Finally, huge thanks to the USO for introducing me to so many of the incredible members of our armed services. My trips with you broke this whole book open—and gave me even more respect for what you do. And thanks to Don, Dan, and the other folks who anonymously enriched these pages. You know who you are. The books **Dr. Samuel A. Mudd at Fort Jefferson** by Robert K. Summers, **Assassination Vacation** by Sarah Vowell, **Diary of a Predator** by Amy Herdy, **Blank Spots on the Map** by Trevor Paglen, and **Women Who Love Men Who Kill** by Sheila Isenberg were all greatly informing to this process; our family on **Decoded** and **Lost History**, and at HISTORY and H2, including Nancy Dubuc, Dirk Hoogstra, Paul Cabana, Mike Stiller, and Russ McCarroll for giving me so much; Rob Weisbach for being the first to take action; and of course, my family and friends, whose names, as usual, inhabit these pages.

I also want to thank everyone at Grand Central Publishing: Michael Pietsch, Brian McLendon, Emi Battaglia, Matthew Ballast, Sonya Cheuse, Martha Otis, Rick Cobban, Karen Torres, Beth de Guzman, Lindsey Rose, Caitlin Mulrooney-Lyski, Andrew Duncan, the kindest and hardest-working sales force in show busi-ness, Bob Castillo, Mari Okuda, Thomas Whatley, and all my dear friends there who change my life on a daily basis. I've said it before, and I'll never stop saying it: They're the true reason this book is in your hands. Super special thank-you to my fellow dreamer Mitch Hoffman, who never stopped pushing to make this book better. I love what we're building, pal. Finally, I want to thank Jamie Raab. We've been together a long time. But what amazes me most about Jamie is that she always brings a new eye, new ideas, new enthusi-asm. I respect her more than she'll ever know. There's no one like her. Thank you, Jamie, for your faith.

# The PRESIDENT'S
# SHADOW

# Prologue

## Washington, D.C.

Every President has secrets. So does every First Lady.

Today, Shona Wallace was deep into her favorite secret as she knelt in the damp dirt, hiding behind the crabapple trees in the White House Rose Garden. On this cold March morning, she didn't have to look for the cameras. She knew where they were. For now at least, no one was watching.

During the day, just a few steps outside the Oval Office, the garden was used for presidential press conferences and greeting visiting dignitaries. But now—at 5:30 a.m.— the outdoor garden was dark. Desolate. As if the First Lady were the last person left on the planet.

And really, wasn't that the point?

Plunging her fingers into the dirt, Shona took a deep breath, letting the smell of fresh mulch transport her back to those days right after college when she and the President lived in that little yellow rental house in Michigan with the bad toilets and the narrow garden that flooded with every rain. Two weeks after moving in, she got the news that her mother had died. The garden saved her then. She cared for it, and it blossomed: Her matchless burgundy dahlias, which she used to wear in her hair. Three kinds of tomatoes. When they were running for governor, she dug up two hundred tulip bulbs from her mother's garden and planted them in her own.

Even when your mother's gone, and your husband's working so hard he only comes home to sleep, you can count on your garden. You plant it; it sprouts; life blooms. That's not some cheap metaphor for life; it's a basis for sanity. Everyone needs something they can count on, a world they can own all themselves.

**"Dammit!"** the First Lady muttered, down on her knees and tugging with her bare hands on a buried tree root. The root was heading toward her precious bed of English bluebells, set to bloom this spring and perfect for cutting.

Even before Orson's Presidency started, Shona had known she'd need a garden. During the campaign, she'd felt the burn that came with the spotlight of public life. And she'd had it all planned. On her very first night in the White House, she had sought out a little patch of land among the flowerbeds of the Rose Garden. It would be her ground. Her sanity.

Telling only the Secret Service, she'd slipped outside at five in the morning, knelt down in the dark, and planted the seeds of coral bells and morning glories. Many of the seeds came from her grandparents' flowerbed by way of her mother's. Shona had even grown early spring flowers in college, in an inconspicuous patch of ground she commandeered behind the dorm. She'd planted more flowers, even some vegetables, when she and Orson lived in that old rental house, and even later when they were in the governor's mansion. Would she stop now, when she needed it most?

**Please.**

She never told reporters she was a

gardener or tried to use it for political gain. Somehow that would ruin the purpose. No matter where life took her, or what her critics said (they had ripped her apart for gaining weight during the first year of her husband's Presidency: "the freshman-fifteen First Lady"), here was the one patch on the entire planet where Shona Wallace, wife of the President, could run things just the way she wanted to.

**"Gotcha..."** the First Lady whispered, gripping the buried tree root and pulling hard. God, the cold March dirt felt good. And it smelled so fresh, full of promise. Winter had put so much on hold; she loved getting back to work in the earth. With a sharp tug, the root began to yield, though not by much.

Leaning on her left elbow and probing blindly into the dirt, the First Lady felt—

**Tunk.**

Something solid. Not a rock. The root felt weird, almost soft. Spongy. She turned and pulled a penlight from her tool kit, shining it into the hole and squinting down to see what was in there. Under the dirt, it looked light gray, but as she pulled it closer, it was greenish-blue, with a tint of pink. Like skin.

A hiccup erupted from her throat. The spongy root had— Those weren't branches. It had fingers. Four fingers. Squeezed in a fist... An arm... **Oh God!** Someone was buried in—

Stifling a scream, the First Lady dropped the penlight, which fell into the hole. She jumped back, scrambling, crabwalking away from the pit. The press and early staff would be here any minute. Her body was shaking. **Just don't scream.**

"Orson..." she whispered, stumbling toward the West Colonnade of the pristine white mansion. She was gagging and sobbing uncontrollably.

In the Rose Garden, the penlight still rested in the open hole, shining its little spotlight on a dirt-encrusted hand.

**1**

Each morning the nurses watched him.

At 5:45 a.m., they'd see him step through the hospital's sliding doors. By 5:50 a.m., he'd be up among the mechanical beeps and hisses of the ICU. And by 5:55 a.m., the young man with the boyish looks and sandy hair would approach the nurses' station, dropping off that day's breakfast: doughnuts, bagels, sometimes a dozen muffins.

The nurses never made requests for food, but over time the young man had learned that Nurse Tammy liked a pumpernickel bagel with a thin slice of tomato, and that Nurse Steven preferred asiago cheese. Over these past three weeks of hospital visits, they'd gotten to know him too. Beecher White.

"How's he doing?" Beecher would ask as he presented his breakfast offering to the hospital gods.

"Same," the nurses would say on most days, offering kindly smiles and pointing him to Room 355.

The dim room was sealed by sliding glass doors, frosted at the bottom and transparent at the top. For an instant, Beecher paused. The nurses saw it all the time, family and friends picking out which brave face they'd wear that day.

Through the glass was a seventy-two-year-old man with an uneven beard lying unconscious in bed, an accordion breathing tube in his windpipe, a feeding tube snaking through his nose and down into his belly.

"Okay, who's ready for some easy-listening country music from the seventies, eighties, and today?" Beecher announced, sliding the door open and stepping into the room.

Aristotle "Tot" Westman lay there, eyes closed. His skin was so gray he looked like a corpse. His palms faced upward, as if he were pleading for death.

"Rise and shine, old man! It's me! It's **Beecher**! Can you hear me!?" he added.

Tot didn't move. His mouth sagged open like an ashtray.

"TOT, BLINK IF YOU HEAR ME!" Beecher

said, circling to the far side of the hospital bed and eyeing the pale purple scar that curved down the side of Tot's head like a parenthesis. When Tot was first wounded and fragments of the bullet plowed through the frontal region of his brain, the doctors said it was a miracle he was alive. Whether he was lucky to be alive was another question.

Three weeks ago, during surgery, they shaved off half of Tot's long silver hair, leaving him looking like a baseball with yarn sprouting from it. To even it out, Beecher had asked the nurses to do a full buzz cut. Now the hair was slowly growing back. A sign of life.

"You're still mad about the hair, aren't you?" Beecher said, pulling an old black iPod from his pocket and switching it with the silver iPod in the sound dock on the nearby rolling cart.

"Wait till you hear this one," he went on, clicking the iPod into place.

Tot's only response was the heavy in-and-out hiss from his ventilator. In truth, Tot should've been in a rehab facility instead of the hospital, but according to the nurses, someone from the White House had made a special request.

"I brought the Gambler himself," Beecher added, hitting **play** on the iPod as a crowd started to cheer and guitars began to strum. "Kenny Rogers, live from Manchester, Tennessee, then another from the Hollywood Bowl, and a 1984 private corporate concert that cost me a good part of this month's rent," Beecher said, taking his usual seat next to Tot's bed. One of the doctors had said that familiar music could be helpful to patients with brain injuries.

"Tot, I need you to squeeze my hand," Beecher added, pressing his hand into Tot's open palm.

Tot didn't squeeze back. His ventilator coughed out another heavy in-and-out hiss.

"C'mon, Tot, you know what today is. It's a big one for me. Just give me a little something...**anything**," Beecher pleaded as Kenny Rogers began belting out the first verse of "Islands in the Stream."

"By the way, Verona from Human Resources? She said if you wake up and come back to work, she'll wear that tight black sweater she wore to the Christmas party. In fact, she's here right now. In the sweater. You don't want to miss this."

**Huh-hsssss.**

"Okay, Tot, you're leaving me no choice," Beecher said. From his pocket, he pulled out a ballpoint pen, then turned Tot's hand palm-down and pressed the tip of the pen into Tot's nail bed.

At the sharp pain, Tot pulled his hand back.

In neurological terms, it was called withdrawal. According to the neurologist, as long as Tot responded to painful stimuli — like a sharp pinch or a poke with a pen — his brain was still working.

"It's good news," the doctor had promised. "It means your friend's still in there somewhere."

Somewhere.

"C'mon, you chatty bastard—don't ruin my big day. I'm not celebrating alone," Beecher said, again pressing the pen into his mentor's nail bed. As the skin below the nail turned white, Tot again pulled away, but this time... A nurse saw it from the hallway. Tot's head moved sideways, as if he was about to say something.

Beecher shot up in his chair. "**Tot...?** Tot, are you—?"

Tot's head sagged down, a string of drool falling from his bottom lip into his beard as Kenny Rogers—accompanied by Dolly Parton—continued to sing.

Slumping back in his seat, Beecher let go of Tot's cold hand. A swell of tears took his eyes.

"It'll happen. Give him time," a female voice said softly.

Beecher glanced toward the sliding glass door. It was the nurse with the crooked teeth, the one who liked pumpernickel.

"It's a brain injury. It doesn't heal overnight," she added.

"I know. I just wish he could—" Beecher stopped himself and swallowed hard.

"He's fortunate to have you," the nurse said.

"**I'm** fortunate to have **him**," Beecher replied, standing up from his seat and wiping his eyes. He turned to the body in the bed. "Tot, you get some rest. I know you're tired," he added, leaning in and giving his mentor a gentle kiss on the forehead. "By the way," he whispered into

Tot's ear, "if you're good, I'll bring you a photo of Verona in the black sweater."

"If it helps, happy birthday," the nurse called out as Beecher headed for the door.

"How'd you know?"

The nurse shrugged. "I've been doing this for fifteen years. Heard you say it was a big day."

Nodding a thank-you and heading out to the hallway, Beecher glanced over at what bagels were still uneaten at the nurses' station.

Each morning, the nurses watched Beecher.

Each morning, Beecher watched Tot.

But each morning, Beecher and the nurses weren't the only ones keeping tabs.

Diagonally across the hallway, peering through the open door of the visitors' lounge, the bald man known as Ezra eyed Beecher as he trudged down the hallway toward the elevators.

Ten days ago, Ezra had come to the hospital searching for the old man known as Tot. He knew Tot's history. He knew what Tot had done all those years ago. And he knew that with a bit of patience and a side order of good luck, he'd find out everything else he needed just by sitting in this waiting room and studying who else came to Tot's bedside.

A few of Tot's coworkers had visited. There was an old lady who came every few nights and stroked Tot's arm. But more than anyone else, there was the archivist. Beecher.

At the National Archives, Beecher was Tot's protégé and best friend. In a way, he was also Tot's family. And based on what Ezra had heard thanks to the nightlight-shaped microphone that he had plugged into the wall socket next to Tot's bed, Beecher was most certainly a member of the Culper Ring.

"Want a bagel?" one of the nurses called out as she passed the visitors' room. "We've got plenty."

"I shouldn't," Ezra said, his slitted eyes curving into a grin. "I've got a big day ahead of me."

# 2

There are stories no one knows. Hidden stories.

I love those stories. And since I work in the National Archives, I find those stories for a living. Most of them are family stories. This one is too. But it's time for me to admit, as I once learned in a novel, when you say you're looking for your family, what you're really searching for is yourself.

"I see it on your face, Beecher. This is bad news, isn't it?" Franklin Oeming asks, trying hard to look unnerved. In his mid-forties, Oeming's got a thin face that's made even thinner by narrow wire-rimmed glasses and a long Civil War–style goatee. He's a smart guy whose specialty is declassification. That means he spends every day combing through redacted, top-secret documents and reading beneath the black lines. It also means he specializes in people's secrets. He thinks he knows mine. But he has no idea why I'm really here.

"Just tell me how he's doing," Oeming

adds.

"Same as before," I say as I slide both hands into the front pockets of the dark blue lab coat that all of us archivists wear.

He studies every syllable, smelling a rat. Even though he's in a suit, Oeming's wearing an awful Texas-shaped belt buckle that displays the words **Planet Texas** in block letters. I have a matching one in my office. They were old Christmas gifts from the mentor we share, Tot Westman, who gave them to us as an homage to Kenny Rogers. We thought they were gag gifts. To Tot, they weren't. "Planet Texas" is Tot's favorite underrated Kenny Rogers song.

Needless to say, neither of us ever wore the belt buckles...until three weeks ago, when Tot was shot in the head and left in a coma. For luck or superstition, Oeming's been wearing his since. I've been carrying mine in my briefcase.

"Beecher, I know you're at the hospital every day. If the doctors say he's getting worse—"

"He's not getting worse. He's the same. Last week, a nurse said he moved two fingers on his left hand. His right pinkie too."

Oeming watches me carefully. For three weeks now, I've sent him daily updates by email. So for me to suddenly show up on the fifth floor and see him in person...

"This isn't about Tot, is it?" he asks.

I run my hand over the back of my recently buzzed hair, but I don't answer.

"Why're you really here, Beecher?"

He puts enough emphasis on my name that just outside his office, I can hear a few employees in cubicles start closing files and covering papers on their desks. Oeming takes a step back toward his own desk and does the same.

Five floors below us, the National Archives is home to original copies of the Declaration of Independence, the U.S. Constitution, and twelve billion other pages of history, including Lincoln's preliminary draft of the Emancipation Proclamation, the actual check that we used to purchase Alaska, and even a letter written by a twelve-year-old Fidel Castro to FDR, asking for ten dollars. If the government had a hand in it, we collect it, including the downed weather balloon that people thought was a wrecked flying saucer outside of Roswell,

New Mexico. But like that weather balloon, which was classified for decades, when you store America's **history**, you also get America's **secrets**.

And as I said, secrets are Franklin Oeming's specialty.

"I actually need your help with something," I tell him, offering a grin.

He doesn't grin back. "What kind of help?"

"I need a file."

Oeming is a second-generation archivist. His mom used to work in the LBJ Library in Austin, and he grew up playing in the stacks and pulling rusty staples from important documents. That makes him more of a stickler than most, which around here is saying something. "You mind taking a walk?" he says, tilting his head toward the door.

Before I can answer, he's out of his office, weaving around the cubicles and heading out to the Archives' marble and stone hallway. Every person in a nearby cubicle is now staring my way. By the time I join him in the hallway, Oeming's on my left, swiping a security card at a set of locked double doors. As I follow him farther down the hallway, he points to a set of square metal lockers, each one the size of a small safe-deposit box.

I know the rules. Taking my cell phone from my pocket, I slide it inside one of the lockers, slap the small door shut, and take the orange key. He's not talking until he's sure no one's listening. I don't blame him. But if he's taking me **here**—to the true inner sanctum of fifth-floor secrecy—either things are looking up, or I've got a bigger problem than I thought.

**Let's go**, he motions, pointing me to the end of the hallway and stopping at our destination: Room 509. It looks like any other room, except for the thick steel door that resembles a bank vault's.

Oeming swipes his ID through an even more high-tech scanner, then punches in a push-button PIN code, which lets out a low **wunk** as the lock unclenches and the door to this giant safe pops open. In the Archives, we have SCIFs—secure areas to read classified files—all over the building. We also have Treasure Vaults on nearly every floor. None of them hold what we keep in here.

Inside, it looks like any other fancy conference room: long oval mahogany table surrounded by two dozen black-and-tan leather chairs. On the walls are reproduction posters from World War II, including a navy poster that reads **Button Your Lip** and another that reads **Silence Means Security**. It's not just décor. They mean it.

"Watch your hands," Oeming snaps, sounding annoyed as the automatic door with non removable hinges locks us inside. As the door slams, my ears pop. This room isn't just soundproof; it's air-tight. The concrete walls are double the normal thickness and lined with foil and steel to stop eavesdropping, while the ductwork, telephone, and electrical systems are all on their own dedicated grids to do the same.

Around the Archives, this is the home of Ice Cap. The official acronym is ISCAP, which stands for Interagency Security Classification Appeals Panel, which means every other Tuesday, in this fifth-floor vault, some of the highest-level thinkers in the U.S. government come together and take a biweekly vote on which classified documents will get released to the public.

Set in motion by Richard Nixon of all people, Ice Cap has released thousands of blacked-out files, from Cold War presidential briefings, to My Lai massacre details, to top-secret reports of Soviet nukes. For the American people, it adds trust and transparency. But for the archivists who wade though the documents and read what's below the black lines, it adds a whole office of people who have access to what's otherwise top secret and off-limits.

"Beecher, how could you put me in that position?" Oeming asks, circling around to the far side of the table.

"Listen, before you lose your cool—"

"My cool is **lost**! Are you even listening to what you're doing? You're asking me to break the law."

"That's not true."

"It most certainly is true. If you had a high enough security clearance, you'd get the file yourself. But if you're asking me to get it for you—"

"Will you just stop? I'm not asking for myself. This isn't for me. It's for the Archivist."

He stops when I mention the boss. Our big boss. The Archivist of the United States. "You're telling me Ferriero asked for this?"

"He did. Call him," I challenge. "I told him I was coming up here. He asked me to do him a favor."

Back when I first met Oeming, I remember him telling me that when it came to classified information, the only files that had ever haunted him were the ones about the government secretly abducting people who wouldn't be missed—the elderly and homeless—and the human radiation tests that they were subjected to. Oeming said he was sick to his stomach that day. He looks about the same now.

"Beecher, y'know whose chair you're touching?" he asks, pointing to the high-backed chair near the head of the table. "When we vote, that's where the CIA sits. The chair next to that belongs to DoD, representing our entire military and the Pentagon. On the other side, you've got the State Department. Then the NSA. Then the Director of National Intelligence," he adds, pointing out each chair one by one. "The only bad seat in the room belongs to the Justice Department," he adds, motioning to a chair by the door. "And y'know why that's the bad seat?"

"Because it's closest to the door," I say.

"That's exactly right. You have to move every time someone wants to go in or out. And y'know why the Justice Department gets that bad seat?"

"I understand you're trying to make this analogy work—"

"It's because they always want personal favors," Oeming says coldly, pressing his fingertips down on the table. "Everyone else— CIA, DoD, NSA—they all understand how the process works. But Justice, with all its lawyers, always wants to know if we can make a special exception. So once again, Beecher, what's the real story behind this file? And don't tell me it's for the Archivist, because I was in Ferriero's office this morning, and if there was anything he needed, he would've asked me himself."

I take my hands off the back of the chair. "I wouldn't ask if this wasn't an important one."

"So it's work-related?"

I shake my head. "It's personal."

"Is it for Tot?" he adds with enough concern that I start to wonder if he knows our real secret: that three months ago, Tot recruited me to become a member of the secret society known as the Culper Ring. The Ring dates back over two hundred years and was originally founded by George Washington.

I know. It still sounds insane to me too.

Back during the Revolutionary War, Washington created his own private spy ring to help him move information among his troops and beat the British. It worked so well that after he won the war, Washington kept the Ring around to protect the Presidency. To this day, the Ring still exists, and now I'm a part of it. Sounds sexy, right? I thought so too—until Tot was shot in the head and I figured out that the Culper Ring has been whittled down to barely half a dozen members. Tot chose me to help rebuild it. But right now, that's the least of my worries.

"This isn't about Tot," I tell Oeming.

"So if it's not Tot, how much more personal can you—?"

"It's about my father," I blurt.

Oeming's eyes narrow, but not by much. "That's still about Tot, though, isn't it? With him in the hospital, and you all alone, well...looking for some info about your father would—"

"It's not about being alone," I tell him, finally realizing that the tone I hear in his voice isn't anger. It's concern. Franklin may be a second-generation archivist, but he's a first-class good person. He doesn't have a ruthless bone in him, which probably explains why Tot never picked him for the Culper Ring. "Listen," I tell him, "I'm sorry for lying to you."

"I don't blame you, Beecher. I'd lie for **my** dad. Hell, I might even lie for Tot."

"No, you wouldn't."

"You're right. I wouldn't," he says, forcing an awkward laugh and looking down.

I pretend to laugh along with him.

"Y'know, Beecher, when you first started at the Archives and Tot started mentoring you, I was so jealous. Those first years he mentored me were some of the best of my life."

"That's funny, because every time I see him talking with you, I feel like you're that firstborn child I can never measure up to."

We both stand there a moment, the giant table between us. He finally looks up.

"Franklin, my entire life...going back to my very first memories...I was told my dad was a mechanic in the army—that he died when I was a baby, in a car crash on a bridge," I offer, my voice hitching on the words. "Last month, someone gave me proof that there was no bridge...and no car accident. They showed me a handwritten letter that he wrote a week after his supposed death. Now I don't know which story is true."

Anyone else would cock an eyebrow or ask how that's possible, but Oeming spends every day reading the secrets that people keep from each other, including their families.

"You think your dad's still alive?"

"No. I actually don't. But what keeps me turning at night is this one thought: You don't cover up someone's death unless there's a reason to cover it up," I explain. "Pretend it was your own dead father. Before he died, this is the story he couldn't tell you. The bosses at his job said he tripped and took a bad tumble. Then you find out he might've been pushed."

"I assume you've searched through everything at Archives II?" he asks, referring to our facility out in College Park, which holds most of our modern military records.

"There, St. Louis, even out in the Boyers caves. I've spent the last month looking for anything that would give me the full story. Then, a few weeks back, I found **this**," I say, pulling a folded sheet of paper from the front pocket of my lab coat. As I unfold it, there's no mistaking the handwritten file citation at the center of the page.

Oeming reads it for himself. "You said your dad was in the army."

"I did."

"This file, though…the record group…it's from a navy file."

I nod. "Didn't make sense to me either. So you tell me: Still think my dad was just a lowly mechanic in the army?"

Oeming doesn't answer. "How'd you even **find** this file?"

"A friend," I say quickly enough that he knows not to ask any more questions. "The person who gave it to me, her dad was in my dad's unit. She was the one who found their real unit name. Apparently, they used to call themselves the Plankholders."

Oeming frowns.

"You know this group?"

He looks down at the file number, his hand starting to shake.

"Franklin, if you know something—"

"This is really your father's unit?" he says. "He was a member of the **Plankholders**?"

"Tell me what's going on," I demand. "You've heard of them?"

"Not until yesterday."

"**Yesterday?** What're you—?"

"That's what I'm trying to tell you. This group...the **Plankholders**... When I got into the office yesterday, someone had just asked for this exact same file."

I cock my head, totally lost. "If you— If someone— I don't understand. Who would possibly want my dad's files?"

At that, Franklin takes a half-step back. He's standing right in front of the World War II poster that reads **Button Your Lip**.

"Beecher...you're not gonna believe it."

# 3

"So your office said today's your birthday," a Greek fifty-something archivist named Helena says as she angles our navy blue van onto Pennsylvania Avenue.

I nod from the passenger seat, staring out the front window and squinting toward our destination. I could walk if I wanted. But if I plan on pulling this off, the van's my best way in.

"So no big birthday plans?" Helena asks, with no clue as to why I'm tagging along.

"Just the usual," I tell her. "Birthday cake shaped like a book. Strippers dressed like naughty librarians."

"The sad part is, you just described the fantasy of every Archives employee."

"And some women," I add.

"Speaking of, you ever reach out to—"

"I did. I'm going to," I say, knowing who she's talking about. Mina. A fellow archivist I'm friendly with. Helena thinks I should get friendlier, but until Tot's health starts to—

"Please don't tell me you're waiting for

Tot to get better. He'd hate that more than anyone," she says, making me wonder if there's anyone in the Archives who doesn't know my business. It's the occupational hazard of working in a building full of researchers. "Beecher, let me pass you the proverbial folded-up note in class..."

"No one passes notes anymore. They text."

"Then I'm texting you," she says, pantomiming a fake phone in her hand. "Mina likes you. Ask her out."

"We went out. We had a good time. It's just her brother was sick and—"

Before I can finish, my phone vibrates in my pocket.

**"You there yet?"** a text asks, popping up onscreen. It says it's coming from our old hometown church in Wisconsin. That tells me who it really is. Marshall Lusk. Also known as a penetration tester who spends his days breaking into buildings and security systems. Also known as one of my oldest childhood friends and the kid who always had nudie magazines in his treehouse. Also known as the one person I'm hoping will help me rebuild the Culper Ring.

Marshall wants no part of it—or pretty

much part of anything. Years ago, he was burned and disfigured, leaving his face looking like a melted candle. It also left him with an understandable bitterness and a ruthless streak that means I'm still not sure he's 100 percent trustworthy. But since Marshall's dad apparently served in the same Plankholder unit as mine, he's willing to help. For now. As a result, he's the only one who knows where I'm currently going. And who I'm trying to see.

**"Almost there,"** I text back.

Marshall knows what it means. My phone vibrates again, this time with a phone call. It's from a different ten-digit number. I pick it up but never say a word. On the other end of the call, neither does Marshall. But now he's listening. If anything happens, at least there'll be a record of it.

"Y'know, Beecher, even putting Mina aside, I'm just glad you're getting out of the building," Helena adds from the driver's seat, tucking a thick ringlet of graying black hair behind her ear. "I know how hard it's been. I say a prayer for Tot every night."

"I appreciate that. And I appreciate you letting me ride along with—"

The van hits a pothole, sending our cargo in back—half a dozen red plastic collection bins—bouncing through the van. Right now, every one of the bins is empty. Not for long.

"See? Even **he** has pothole problems," Helena says with a laugh. In Washington, D.C., there's only one **he** who gets talked about like that, and it's not God.

Helena makes a sharp right, sending the old van bumping and climbing through a set of black metal gates, stopping at a small security shed.

I lean forward in my seat, looking out through the front wind-shield and finally seeing it: the world's most famous mansion —and the home of the one person who, yesterday, requested the military files that hold information about my dead father.

"Welcome to the White House," a uniformed Secret Service agent says. "Who're you here to see?"

## 4

I'll need to see some ID," the uniformed agent says in a New Orleans accent as Helena hands over our driver's licenses.

In the National Archives, we call it a **gift run**. At least once a week, Helena drives up Pennsylvania Avenue, making trips to the Eisenhower Executive Office Building, to the other executive branch buildings across the street, and even here, to the White House, where she picks up everything from the priceless to the mundane.

All Presidents have the same problem. At each grip-and-grin, every guest, big shot, and visiting dignitary brings you a present. The Russians bring Fabergé eggs, the Australians bring crocodile luggage, the British once brought a Ping-Pong table, and the King of Jordan personally designed his very own motorcycle to give to the President. That doesn't include the hundreds of signed foot-balls, basketballs, baseballs, golf clubs, hockey pucks—plus the countless jerseys with President

Wallace's name on the back— that every Little League and pro team brings, all of them thinking they're being original.

At each event, President Wallace fakes a smile, takes a photo, and hands the gift to an aide, who eventually hands it to us. At the Archives, our job is to store it until Wallace's presidential library is built, but also to keep it nearby—just a few blocks away— in case it has to be rushed back to the White House when the Jordanian delegation suddenly asks to see its favorite jewel-encrusted motorcycle. For Helena, gift runs are part of the job. For me, even Marshall agrees, they're the single best way to get into the White House.

"You're late. Usually, you're right on time," the uniformed Secret Service agent says, glancing down at my ID, then up at the side of the van with its National Archives logo.

"Just one of those days," I say, keeping my smile and trying not to think about who I'm going to see. Back in college, President Orson Wallace plowed a baseball bat and car keys into the face of another man, eventually shattering the man's eye socket, puncturing his face, and driving bits of skull into his brain, causing irreversible brain damage.

That's the man who's currently sitting in the Oval Office. If I could prove it, I would. Though this'll be even better.

"Won't take me but a minute," the uniformed Secret Service agent says in his New Orleans twang, walking our IDs back to his shed and motioning another agent over to our blue van.

"Pop the back," the second agent says as Helena unlocks the back doors and a rush of cold air floods us from behind. On my right, a third agent takes a thin pole that looks like a golf club with a round mirror on the end of it and runs it underneath the van. Bomb search.

"They do this every time," Helena says, reading my expression. "Though usually"— she thinks for a moment—"usually they wait until I get up to West Exec," she says, motioning with her chin to the narrow parking lot that runs along the west side of the White House.

In the security shed, the New Orleans agent takes a long hard look at our IDs. In the side passenger mirror, the other agent extends the pole and slides it even farther underneath the van. Through the open back doors, the last agent examines the empty red storage bins, checking them one by one.

It's all standard White House procedure. No reason for concern.

Behind me, there's a loud **ca-chunk** as the back doors slam shut and the agent gives us the all clear. Faint puffs of smoke roll out of our tail pipe into the cold air.

With a twist of the ignition, Helena shifts the van into gear, hits the gas, and—

**Tuuk-tuuk-tuuk.** The knuckles tap against my passenger window. On my right, an all-too-familiar agent in suit and tie stares back at us. He's got a military crew cut, no winter coat, and a blue-jeweled lapel pin that's worn by all active Secret Service.

Jackpot. That's the fastest service I ever got.

"What're you smiling about, Beecher?" Agent A.J. Ennis asks as he pulls my door open. "Do me a favor and get the hell out of the van."

## 5

"We're old friends," A.J. tells my Archives colleague. I nod enthusiastically.

She actually believes it. As we leave the van behind, A.J.'s right hand grips the back of my arm and his knuckles dig into my armpit. He's moving so fast—forcing me forward and almost lifting me off the ground—I'm practically walking on tiptoe. In the Secret Service, this **armpit carry** is what they use during an emergency to rush the President out of a room. Usually, the President picks up his feet and the agents lift him out. I keep my feet moving. He has no idea this is all I was hoping for.

"You missed me, didn't you?" I ask. No response. "It's okay to say you missed me," I add as we head up the South Lawn toward the White House. "I certainly missed you. At the Archives, there's a real lack of muscular people bursting through their suits."

As we pass the swing set that Obama put in for his daughters, A.J. sticks to the rolling lawn, weaving between trees to keep us out of sight. Wherever we're going, it's off the beaten path.

**"This way,"** he whispers, leading me toward a rectangular patch of grass with the most perfectly manicured garden I've ever seen. The White House Rose Garden.

A.J. pauses, searching my face.

In the corner, a huge blue painter's tarp is tacked to the trees, draping down to the ground and covering a wide swath of flowers and plants. There's yellow maintenance tape and a warning sign that reads:

## BROKEN SPRINKLER HEADS
## GROUND CREW REPAIRS UNDERWAY

A.J.'s eyes continue to drill me. I'm too busy staring past the garden at the tall French doors on the back of the building. The entrance to the Oval Office. There aren't any Secret Service agents stationed outside. That means the President isn't in there. He's somewhere else in the White House.

With a nudge to the right, A.J. steers me past the bright white columns of the West

Colonnade and through a set of doors that take us inside the mansion, toward the Residence. Across the pale red carpet, there's no Secret Service agent outside the President's private elevator. That means he's not upstairs either.

A.J. shoves me to the left, through another set of doors that dumps us in what looks like an outdoor hallway and construction area. The place is a mess. Crates, boxes, and files. Spools of cables and wires. It's all stacked up everywhere. "Workers' area, huh?" I ask, loud enough that Marshall can hear it through the phone in my pocket.

A.J. again won't answer.

Nearly tripping on a crate of hammers and handsaws, I smell French fries and chocolate. We're back by the White House kitchen. Sure enough, as we cut through another door, chefs in spotless white aprons and black hairnets are scrubbing pots and stacking dishes. They don't look up. It's like we're not even here.

With a final shove, A.J. steers me into a narrow hallway that, on the right, has two stainless steel doors and two stainless steel dumbwaiters. This is how they move the food upstairs to the Residence. But as A.J. opens the first steel door...

It makes no sense. We're on the ground floor of the White House—level with the garden. But when the door swings open, there's a dark circular staircase that goes down, down, down.

I freeze, confused. A.J. urges me on. In front of me, the circular stairs are so narrow that we have to go single file. I use the distance to pull out my phone and make sure Marshall's still listening.

No bars. No service. No nothing. My phone's useless. At least Marshall knows where I was when I disappeared.

It only gets worse at the next landing, marked **Basement**. Instead of going through the door, A.J. keeps me on the stairs, which continue going down. There's a second level that goes down even deeper. There're nearly as many floors below the White House as above it.

As we get closer to the bottom, the smell of fries and chocolate yields to the scent of rusted metal, bleach, and warm rain. In Wisconsin, when I was little, I got bitten by a dog on a night that smelled like this.

The stairs dead-end in a narrow hallway that's connected to—

**White House Laundry**, the sign on the closed door says. Yet as A.J. shoves the door open, a heavyset woman with short-cropped hair stands up from her seat at an old card table.

"Francy O'Connor," she says, introducing herself. I know who she is. So does everyone in the White House. "They told me you'd be coming," she adds with a handshake that tugs me into the room. "I just didn't think it'd be this quick."

## 6

"Beecher, I dropped my phone in the toilet this morning. It's that kind of day," Francy says, her pale Irish coloring looking flushed. "Don't make me ask this more than once: Why are you really here?"

"I was about to ask you that same question," I say. "We're pretty far from the press office."

She knows what I'm getting at. The daughter of a law professor, Francy grew up arguing cases at the dinner table, eventually making her way to a Minneapolis newspaper (it shut down). Then she jumped to **Newsweek** (it shut down too). Then she jumped into Wallace's world back when he was governor and a true reformer.

She became a true believer and the ghostwriter for the autobiography that transformed Wallace into a President and Francy into one of those friends who becomes D.C.-famous for being one of those friends. Every President brings a few with him. Scrappy brawlers he can trust.

By the time she reached the White House, Francy had been crowned deputy press secretary to the First Lady, but like almost everything that leaves Wallace's mouth, it's never the full truth. I've never met Francy, but I know that her tightly cropped reddish-brown hair didn't get this gray by dealing with just the press. Last year, when the President's chief of staff happily announced that it was time for him to move on, every wonk in D.C. whispered that Francy, annoyed with his inability to manage staff infighting, had engineered his departure. By flying low as a deputy, tucked away in a quiet office, she's Wallace's hidden eyes and ears. And personal fire extinguisher.

"Y'know, my ex used to think you should go everywhere twice: once for a good time, and once to apologize," she says in a flat midwestern accent that reminds me of home and calms me more than I want to admit. It's the same with her rumpled blue blazer, her never-stylish shoes, and the cheap reading glasses, bought at the nearest pharmacy, that dangle down around her thick neck. Most people around the President start to think they're important.

Francy dresses like she never wants to forget where she came from. "Maybe we got off on the wrong foot," she adds.

I'm tempted to agree, but I see the way she keeps her arms flat at her sides instead of crossed at her chest. Like the best press secretaries, she's a black belt at avoiding conflict and making you feel calm even when you're on fire. If she's trying to make nice—much less hiding in the subbasement of the White House—there's Something important going on down here. And I'd bet money that it has to do with my dad's missing file.

"Why don't you take a seat," A.J. interrupts, pointing me to a nearby chair as Francy shoots him a look and reminds him who's in charge.

"Please, c'mon in," she adds, smile wide. In her fist, she clutches an outdated leather datebook like it's the Bible.

"You seem pretty busy down here," I say.

Neither of them answers.

On my right, a massive ten-foot-wide machine looks like a huge pasta press, though instead of pasta, a long white tablecloth dangles lifelessly from its open mouth. On most days, this is where they press the linens for the state dinners.

As the door closes behind me, I count one...two...three foldable card tables scattered throughout the room. Each one holds a laptop, a printer, and an outdated corded phone. On the far left table, there's a TV with the view from four different security cameras around the mansion. Plugs and extension cords snake everywhere. Whatever this operation is, it was just thrown together. In the Archives, we have the blueprints for the White House. The Secret Service command post is two floors above us. What the hell is this place?

"So you were saying that the reason you came..." Francy offers.

"Actually, I hadn't said anything. If President Wallace wants to know why I'm here, tell him he can ask me himself."

Her smile grows wider at that. "That's not exactly how it works."

"It's not? Because that's how I remember it. He locked me in a room, sat me down, and told me that the next time I saw him, he'd bury me and the Culper Ring."

A.J. goes to say something, but Francy

again cuts him off. More important, she doesn't flinch at the mention of the Ring. "Beecher, I know what your group is capable of. For decades…"

"For centuries," I correct her.

"…the Ring's been a trusted weapon for those who have held this office. But I also know you and the President don't exactly see eye to eye. I don't know why; I don't care why. That's your business. But what'd you think was going to happen when you got here? That you'd sneak inside, and the President would give you a tour of the Oval?"

"Not at all. I assumed that once I handed over my ID, my name would be keyed to some notification system, which it was. Then it'd notify someone the President trusted, like A.J, which it did. And then, I figured that whenever that person came to get me, they'd take me someplace private (though I didn't think it'd be some makeshift hideaway in the subbasement), and that we could sit down and talk like human beings."

"I couldn't agree more. We want the same darn thing."

"You sure about that? Because the way it looks to me, the President of the United States is hiding one of his most trusted staffers in a secret subbasement that's clearly designed to be tucked away from every other person on staff. The only logical explanation is that you're dealing with some nasty bit of news that the President is hoping will go away. Like me. So. If Wallace wants to get rid of me, he can give me my file and send me on my way."

Across from me, Francy and A.J. share another silent glance. It lasts a second too long.

"He's listening right now, isn't he?" I blurt.

They don't respond.

I scan the ceiling, the rolling cart that's filled with cloth napkins, even the top of the tablecloth-pressing machine. There's not a single security camera in sight. No surveillance. No microphones. But for some reason, Francy and A.J. are still standing there silent.

**"Wallace, I know you hear me!"** I call out at the ceiling. **"Tell me why you wanted my father's file!"**

## 7

"The President can't hear you," A.J. says.

"You know how I know you're lying?" I ask. "Because you're talking." Shouting toward the ceiling, I add, **"I know you hear me! If you're trying to use my father—!"**

"Beecher, please," Francy pleads. "Have you opened a paper this morning? We've got a Cabinet member pulled over for a DUI, zinc shortages threatening U.S. Steel, plus this governor in South Carolina who's blaming Wallace for his high electricity rates during the long winter—and that's just **this morning**. He's the President of the United States. He doesn't have time to eavesdrop on—"

"So was it **you**, then? Someone asked for my father's military file. The Plankholder files," I say, pointing to two nearby tables, both of them covered with files. "They told me someone here re-quested it. I want to know why."

Francy's eyes slide toward A.J., then back

to me. "And that's why you came here?"

"Why else would I come here?"

A.J. turns back to the TV with the four video feeds. Every minute or so, the four feeds shift, presenting views from four new cameras. The ones he's staring at now are all exterior shots, including one that shows all the tourists walking along 16th Street and another that shows a close-up of one of the front gates. He's looking for something. Or someone. "You're telling me you don't know about the garden?" A.J. challenges.

Francy holds up a hand, shooting A.J. a stony glare. As she turns, it's the first time I notice that like A.J., Francy's wearing a Secret Service earpiece. I don't care what they say: The President's listening. And giving instructions. If the leader of the free world is making time for this, I've got bigger problems than even I thought.

"So this visit isn't Culper Ring business?" Francy asks, resting her leather binder near the file folder that's on the card table between us.

I shake my head, now confused.

"And it doesn't have anything to do with

the penny? Or the garden?"

I'm still lost. "What **garden**? I don't understand…"

Francy puts a finger to her earpiece. A.J. doesn't. Whatever the President's whispering, he's talking only to one of them. I make a mental note.

"Can someone please tell me what's going on?" I demand.

Across the table, Francy still has her finger to her earpiece. She shakes her head no. Whatever the President's saying, she doesn't have a choice.

"Beecher, yesterday morning," Francy begins, "we found a body part buried in the Rose Garden."

"A **what**?"

"A body part."

"An **arm**," A.J. clarifies, watching my reaction. "Someone's left arm. Sawed off from the elbow down."

The room goes so silent, I hear the buzz from the fluorescent lights. Francy's picking me apart. Her right hand grips the temple of her reading glasses like it's a pen. Her arms are no longer flat at her sides.

"Y'know what's the most important part

of my job?" she asks me.

"Keeping the President safe."

"No. Trusting my gut," she says. "I know you hate Wallace, but I also know what you did weeks ago, to stop the shooter at the Lincoln Memorial. You saved the President's life. So God help me, I trust you, Beecher. I do. For all our sakes, don't make me regret it."

"What're you doing?" A.J. asks.

Francy doesn't even look at him, doesn't care what he thinks.

On my left, she pushes aside an old phone on the card table and opens one of the file folders, revealing a color photo: At the bottom of a dirt hole, a severed arm looks pale green, the color of an old, rotting egg. The skin is starting to slip, the outer layer peeling away from decomposition. As the knuckles peek out from the dirt, the hand is squeezed into a tight fist.

My father's been dead for thirty years. Or at least I think he's been dead. Either way, no way is it his. From the coloring and tightness, this corpse is of someone young.

"What's this have to do with my dad?"

I ask.

"Truthfully, we didn't think anything," Francy says, flipping to the next photo. "Until we pried open the fist and saw what was hidden inside."

## 8

"And this was in the dead person's hand?" I ask.

"He was clutching it. In his fist," Francy says, pointing to the color photo, where the severed arm is laid out on a piece of white gauze. Hunks of tendons and bone dangle from the elbow, along with a cheesy substance, making it look like a prop from a zombie film. All I'm focused on is the way the pale green hand is pried open, palm up. At the center of the palm is an oval piece of copper no bigger than—

"A penny. It's a flattened penny," Francy adds.

I nod, studying for myself. It's one of those elongated pennies you get from a coin-pressing machine at the amusement park. This one's shine is gone. It's nicked and beaten, like it's been through its own war. But as I look closer, I spot the words that're pressed into it. The font's tiny:

## OUR FATHER
## WHO ART IN HEAVEN
## HALLOWED BE THY NAME

"The Lord's Prayer," I say, recognizing it from all the years Mom dragged me to church. I squint to read it all. Not a single word is missing. It ends with a simple:

"I take it you've seen one of these before?" Francy asks, again holding a finger to her ear. Whatever the President's whispering, she's focused more on me than him. I know where her loyalties are, but even former reporters have an irrational addiction to the truth.

"We have a few of these in the Archives," I say, "one or two even from the Spanish-American War. It's an old military tradition. When you get your dog tags and get to your unit, some chaplains may give you a Saint Michael pendant or a pressed coin with the Lord's Prayer on it. You wear it around your neck. For good luck."

"Not just good luck. Like a dog tag, it's also a form of ID. Some even put their unit's logo on the back," Francy says, flipping to a new page and putting on her reading glasses.

Unlike the other photos, this one's a tight close-up of the back of the penny and the small hole at the top of it. It's as weathered and rusty as the front, but instead of the Lord's Prayer, this side's imprinted with a diamond-shaped crest and a waving banner along the bottom.

Usually, you see logos like this on a soldier's shoulder patch. Some units have a lion as a mascot, a few use dragons, and of course, a ton use some version of an eagle. This one has a wide-winged owl clutching a branch. The banner below it reads **HL-1024**.

"Know anything about owls?" Francy asks.

"They used to be symbols of imminent death. Julius Caesar's murder was supposedly predicted by a shrieking owl. Though this one looks pretty content sitting on its branch."

"It's not a branch."

I tighten my squint, pulling the photo closer. Sure enough, the owl's claws aren't holding a crooked branch. They're clutching a flat piece of wood, more like a two-by-four.

"It's a **plank**," A.J. jumps in. "The owl's holding a **plank**."

**Plankholder.**

I look up from the photo. Francy and A.J. are staring back at me. "This penny's from my father's old unit," I say.

"Not just your father's," Francy says, lowering her glasses to the end of her round nose. I thought she was worried I was a threat. She's worried about something far more dangerous.

"There's someone else who was in that same unit with your father," A.J. adds, his face lit by the glow from the security screens.

He doesn't have to say it. We all know who it is. The man who took a shot at the previous President. And who put a bullet in the brain of the previous First Lady. And who recently escaped his padded cell at St. Elizabeths mental institution.

A.J. refuses to say his name. But there's no question who he's talking about.

Nico.

## 9

## Two weeks ago
## Collierville, Tennessee

Nico was down on both knees, mouthing a silent prayer. He had promised he'd say just one, which he did just before he tugged open the screen door, took a final breath of the night air, and picked the locks to sneak inside the small yellow house.

He said another as the screen door snapped shut behind him and he knelt on the cheap linoleum floor. The house smelled of mothballs and old people. Holding his breath, he waited. No dogs. No alarm. No surprise. God was always on his side.

**"Nico, you need to hurry!"** the dead First Lady warned.

Back when he was a patient, Nico knew what the St. Elizabeths doctors would do if they caught him talking to the woman he'd killed a decade ago. These days, the doctors were gone.

"We're fine," he told his former victim.

"I've broken eight different commandments. And still God provides."

The dead First Lady rolled her eyes, but how else could Nico explain these past few weeks? Or the return of his daughter Clementine? A decade ago, Nico had tried to kill a President. Declared insane, he'd been in the country's most famous mental hospital. He'd never thought he'd get another chance at his mission. There was only one person to thank for that.

Closing his chocolate brown eyes, set so close together, Nico knelt down and said another prayer in the kitchen, then another in the living room, then yet another in the hallway lined with family photos and military medals.

**"You're getting worse, Nico,"** the dead First Lady warned as he finished his work in the bedroom. **"It's because your medications ran out."**

Nico knew she was right, but he still did each prayer the exact same way: He mouthed the words. His head bobbed up and down sixteen times, always sixteen. Then he closed his left eye on the word **Amen**.

**"It's the same reason you're seeing the crosses,"** the First Lady added as Nico headed back to the kitchen and noticed the way the seams in the tile floor formed a hidden crucifix. He saw them everywhere now—around the neck of the waitress at the truck stop, on the young girl in the fast-food commercial that kept running on TV, and—like those first few weeks at St. Elizabeths, when they were worried he would kill himself—in those places no one else sees: hidden in tele-phone poles and windowpanes...in intersecting sidewalk cracks and perpen-dicular tree branches...in pens that criss-crossed, extension cords that overlapped, and of course, in the white spaces be-tween the columns of a newspaper, in the blank spaces between the push buttons of a phone, and right now, in the small X's he had carved into the nails of his four main fingers.

Four. Always four.

Four seasons. Four states of matter. Four directions on a compass. Four earth elements. Four chambers of the heart. Four movements in a symphony. And who could forget the four suits in a deck of cards? Nico never forgot the cards.

In chemistry, the valence of carbon—the basis for all life—is four. In religion, Buddhism has Four Noble Truths, Islam has four sacred months, and Judaism has four questions, four cups of wine, and even writes God's name with four letters. Darkest of all were Christianity's Four Horsemen of the Apocalypse. Always four. Indeed, when ancient tribes first wrote the number four—as just a glyph on a cave wall—they did it by joining four lines into a modern plus sign. An actual cross! One, two, three, four pieces. But as Nico stared down at the four X's on his nails, he knew that the true Four Horsemen had already arrived. Throughout history, four Presidents had been assassinated. Again. Four.

It was time for a fifth. There was no choice. All the others were dead. The only way to survive was to move forward! **Liberation!** he told himself as—

**"Nico, don't get fixated!"** the First Lady scolded. **"Forward thinking, not backward thinking!"** she added, stealing the words from the pretty black nurse Nico always responded to at St. Elizabeths.

**"Forward thinking,"** Nico whispered, readjusting his knit cap and tugging open a nearby kitchen drawer. Inside were steak knives, carving knives, even a cleaver. There were also two small measuring cups whose handles overlapped like a—

**"Forward thinking,"** the First Lady repeated as Nico slammed the drawer shut and pulled open the one next to it. Forks, spoons... No, that wasn't it either.

He knew what he was looking for. The house was small; no garage, no work shed. That meant...

He pulled open the last drawer, next to the stove, which clanged as it opened. **There we go.**

Tool drawer.

Nico's fingers dug to the bottom, burrowing past screwdrivers, wrenches, even a hammer. So much to do damage with. But the only thing he pulled out was a pair of small needle-nose pliers with a red rubber grip.

Heading for the bedroom, Nico squeezed the pliers, relishing the small joy in the way they sprang back open in his hand. The nurses would never have let him have a tool like this. It'd been nearly a month since he'd escaped St. Elizabeths. A month since Clementine had snuck him out of D.C. and brought him to the best place to hide.

For the first few days, he couldn't adjust to the quiet. In the hospital, every meal, every shower, even when he was punished in a quiet room, it was all so noisy. He also couldn't adjust to the color. Or the size. A decade of beige rooms, locked doors, and closed fences made even a two-lane street in Tennessee seem blinding and endless. But by now, Nico knew what needed to be done.

Giving a final squeeze to the pliers, he looked down at the four small crosses on his fingernails. Always four. Could any mission be more clear? He'd seen it in his head...plotted it...dreamed it...for years. Four Horsemen had come. Four Presidents were dead at the hands of four assassins. Four assassins. And now that he was out, he could be the Fifth. The one to put a bullet in the President of the United States.

Stopping at the half-open bedroom door,

Nico once again dropped to his knees in prayer. The dead First Lady stayed quiet. She knew what was waiting inside. Nico had earned this one.

"Amen," he whispered, climbing to his feet and slowly elbowing the door open.

Across the room, an elderly man was tied to the headboard of the bed, arms spread wide, knotted in place by the cords that Nico had ripped from the vertical blinds. Nothing was stuffed in his mouth. This far out in Tennessee, Nico didn't care if he screamed.

**"Nico...please...I'm not your enemy!"** the seventy-year-old pleaded, his voice starting to fracture. He was young for his age, still stout in the chest, though his round Santa face had thinned over time.

"Colonel Doggett, I know what you look like when you're lying," Nico told the man who had first brought him into the Plankholders all those years ago. There were four of them back then too. Always four. "That is the last lie you'll ever tell me."

A decade ago, Nico had tried to kill the President. A different President. Now he'd been given a second chance. A chance to finish the mission.

But not until he finished **this** mission.

Holding up the needle-nose pliers with the red rubber grips, Nico headed for the old man's left hand.

"Nico, no…! What're you doing!?" Colonel Doggett begged.

"I told you," Nico said, his voice a dull monotone. "I'm going to ask you about Devil's Island. If I don't like your answer, I'm going to puncture your finger with a pencil and use these pliers to peel away your skin, finger by finger."

**"That's not—! Son, be smart—! You're a good person!"**

"I know that, Colonel. That's why I need you to help me find a cure for my daughter."

## 10

## Today
## Washington, D.C.

A severed arm? A hidden penny with his old unit logo? Plus burying it in the Rose Garden?" I ask. "That doesn't sound like Nico at all."

"Suddenly you're the expert on him?" A.J. challenges.

"Let him speak," Francy warns.

"Remember the last time Nico attacked a President? He walked right up to him at a NASCAR race and pulled the trigger. When he broke out of St. Elizabeths, he put a pen through the orderly's arm and calmly waltzed out a nearby door. He's not the Riddler. He doesn't leave clues."

"We didn't say it was a **clue**," A.J. shoots back from the table on my left. He's hunched in front of the TV with the rotating security feeds. For a second, he turns away from the TV, pointing to the photo of the flattened penny. "But that doesn't mean it's not a message."

"Are you hearing me? Nico doesn't do **messages**. There's no subtleness to him. He sees himself as a knight on a holy mission. If he wants you dead, he'll step into your personal space and put a knife in your eye."

"This is a knife in our eye," A.J. says. "For him to come onto the White House grounds—"

"So you have video of him? I see those security cameras. Was Nico the one you saw in the Rose Garden?"

A.J. looks at Francy, who again is focused on her earpiece. No question, the President's listening, which means there's still something they're not saying. Eventually, Francy nods the okay.

"There are no security cameras in that part of the Rose Garden," A.J. finally offers.

"**What?** Why not? Isn't it right next to the Oval?"

"It is—which tells you why there're no cameras," A.J. explains.

"After Nixon...and honestly, post–Monica Lewinsky...no President wants a video camera recording who's coming and going into his office."

"So whoever buried that arm..." I say.

"Knew our line of sight," A.J. says. "Or maybe got a look at our camera placement last time he was here." He keeps his eyes on me.

"Do you realize how untactful you are?" I ask. "You think last time I was here, I somehow studied where all your cameras are?"

"Beecher, when was the last time you heard from Nico?" A.J. pushes back.

"You're joking, right? Why would Nico care about **me**?"

"You know exactly why. Your girlfriend Clementine—"

"She's not my girlfriend."

"She **was** your girlfriend..."

"She was my first kiss. In eighth grade!"

"She also happens to be Nico's just-as-crazy daughter, who, last I checked, tried to blackmail us and manipulate **you**. What was the lie she told last time? That she was dying of cancer? There's nothing she won't say. And like her dad, for some reason, they both refuse to hurt you."

"That's not true."

"You've been around Nico multiple times, yet he's never laid a hand on you. He looks out for you, Beecher. So it's not a question of **if** they're coming back. It's just a matter of **when**."

I don't argue. Over A.J.'s shoulder, the TV clicks to four new camera angles. To my surprise, someone's staring back. I stay locked on A.J., pretending not to see it. Onscreen, outside the elevator to the Private Residence, First Lady Shona Wallace has her hands on her hips, her smoker's lips pursed as she glares into the camera.

It happens in an eyeblink. The First Lady is unreadable. She can't see us, but she knows who's watching. Message sent, though the more I think about it, there's only one person that message can be for.

My eyes slide toward Francy, whose quick glance at the screen reminds me that when it comes to her placement in the White House, Francy doesn't work for the President. She works for the First Lady.

In a blink, the TV clicks to four new camera angles. Shona Wallace is gone.

"Beecher, we're not accusing you of

anything," Francy says as if the President's wife were never there. "We're just hoping that **if** Nico or Clementine reach out to you, you'll let us know."

My eyebrow starts to twitch. I want to like Francy. She reminds me of that tough high school teacher you don't appreciate until years after graduation. There's nothing fake about her. But to see that look from the First Lady, to see Francy be on my side this quickly, there's something else she's chasing. "Here's what I don't understand," I say. "If that was all you wanted to tell me, why's the leader of the free world personally eavesdropping?"

Francy doesn't answer. She's focused back on her earpiece. "But sir—" she says. "Sir, I can handle this."

Her shoulders fall. Overruled.

Back by the TV screens, A.J. touches his pointer-finger to his ear. Something's coming through his Secret Service earpiece.

There's a quiet click behind me. I spin at the sound.

The door swings open, revealing the most famous gray eyes in the world. No matter how much I hate him, there's still nothing like seeing him.

"Funny, I was just talking about you, Beecher," the President of the United States says as he steps toward me and the door shuts behind him. "Have I got an opportunity for you."

## 11

"Lemon square? You a fan of lemon squares?" President Orson Wallace asks, entering the underground laundry room and holding a plate of fine bone china. At the center of the plate, there's one pale yellow treat left. "Even the French admit... our dessert chef is a marvel."

I watch him carefully, knowing his tricks. Like any politician, he always leads with charm.

"I mean it, Beecher. If a dessert could change your life, this is the one."

"I'll pass."

"Your loss," he says, snatching up the treat and eating it himself. He licks his lips, then sucks the tip of each of his man-icured fingers, one by one, as if it's his first victory. Still, I see the gaps of receding hair pushing back his side part, plus the way the nail on his pinkie is bitten down to the cuticle. He hides it from the public. He's been chewing on it recently.

"If it weren't for the stress of the job, I'd

weigh an extra twenty pounds by now," he adds, flashing a grin.

Francy makes a face. She's heard the joke before. Even better, unlike A.J.—unlike just about everyone—she doesn't take a half-step back as Wallace gets closer. Francy stays right where she is. She's growing on me more and more.

The President's still holding the china plate, which has the Great Seal of the United States on it. But what I'm focused on is the file folder he rests it on top of. The one with the Plankholders penny. From my father's unit. The President knows how bad I want it. But he wouldn't be here if he didn't want something just as much.

"Relax, son. I told you, I'm here with an opportunity. A good one."

"Define **good**. Because last time I saw you, you pounded your big desk and swore you'd stomp out the Culper Ring and me along with it."

His smile spreads even wider as he approaches the table. I'm on one side; Francy and A.J. are still on the other. Wallace steps to the head. "I heard today's your birthday. Happy birthday."

"I appreciate that. Now in the hopes of getting me back to the shredded-paper confetti that they're going to surprise me with in my office, why don't you tell me what you're really after?"

He knots his fingers together prayer-style. His smile's still perfectly in place. "Beecher, you know what your defining characteristic is? You always do what's right. The moment you see someone being hurt, or some sort of injustice, even when it puts you at risk, you can't turn your back to it. You have to help. That's a beautiful trait," the President says, sounding genuine. "As for me, you know what **my** defining characteristic is? I know what people are good at. My defining trait is that I can **find** that defining trait. It's not as beautiful a trait as yours, but it most certainly comes in handy," he points out. "Which brings us to our little gardening problem. I thought you might be interested in helping us clean it up."

I stare straight back at him. "So you want my help?"

"Is that so unreasonable?" the President counters. "Whatever's left of the Culper

Ring, you're the one who leads them now. Isn't that why Tot—"

"Don't mention Tot. I appreciate you calling the hospital so he can stay in the ICU instead of transferring him, but that doesn't mean we owe you anything."

"I agree. You owe me nothing. But isn't that the purpose of the Ring: protecting the President?"

"We protect the **Presidency**," I clarify. "Besides, don't you have hundreds of Secret Service agents already investigating all this?"

The President and Francy both go silent. A.J. turns back to the TV, which clicks, as if on cue, to four new camera angles. I glance around the laundry room, with its foldable card tables and hastily assembled computer stations. We're two stories below the White House. A tiny windowless room that few people know about. "You think the Service had a hand in this?"

"It's too early to point fingers," the President says. "But to bury someone's arm in the Rose Garden... to get that far without being seen... You don't just hop the fence and make a mad dash. To pull off a trick like that..."

"You need help," I say with a nod. Only way to bury that arm is with an inside job. "You think it was someone on staff?"

"Maybe it's staff; maybe it's the Service," Francy says as I again picture that angry look on the First Lady's face. For the first time, I start wondering if maybe this isn't just about the President. "The point is, however they pulled it off, it was nearly flawless."

**"Nearly?"**

The President gives a nod to Francy, who flips to a new photo in the file folder. Unlike the sterile close-up of the flattened penny, this is an outdoor shot of dozens of people on the South Lawn of the White House.

"Looks like a party," I say, studying the smiling crowd, which is being entertained by the Marine Band, all decked out in their scarlet coats with white shoulder knots and three rows of brass buttons. A time stamp in the corner tells me it was two days ago. 4:27 p.m.

"It's our annual St. Patrick's Day event," the President explains. "We invite the Irish ambassador, plus every Irish reporter and congressional staffer in town, plus the Marine Band, which leaves everyone in tears with a heartrending version of 'My Wild Irish Rose.' They moved it outside since the weather had finally turned." He flips to a new photo, where the Marine Band members are mingling with the crowd, their instruments and musical sheets tucked under their arms.

"Recognize **him**?" the President asks, pointing to the bottom right of the photo, where one of the band members, a trumpet player, cradles his instrument like a football. We see him only in profile, frozen midstep as he exits the right side of the photo. He's a red blur as he heads past a group of suit-and-tie staffers and the head of AmeriCorps enjoying their green beer. The First Lady is there too with her usual perma-smile. In the far background of the photo, two other trumpet players are talking to fellow band members holding French horns, trombones, flutes, and piccolos.

"There were forty Marine Band members at the White House that day," A.J. explains, turning away from his TV with the surveillance feeds. "Twelve clarinets, two oboes, four saxophones, and naturally, since there's that nice trumpet duet in 'My Wild Irish Rose,' two trumpets. Same in the band photos: **two** trumpets."

The President points back at the profile shot of the trumpet player rushing to the far right. Then he points to the two other trumpet players in back. One, two...**three** trumpets. It's one trumpet too many.

"So that's how he snuck in? As a Marine Band member?"

"We can't tell if he came in uniform, or changed once he was here. All we know is, according to this photo—and it's the only one where he's caught on film—there was suddenly a third trumpet player roaming the grounds of the White House."

"I don't understand. For him to get inside the gates, doesn't he still have to sign in and go through security?" I ask.

"Of course," A.J. says. "But when there's a big event like St. Patrick's Day, since security's dealing with so many check-ins, we'll bring the band's bus straight to the Southeast gate, then march them up the lawn with a less rigorous check-in.

Whoever our trumpet player is, he knows our playbook."

I look down at the photo. Even if he weren't in profile, his white Marine Corps hat obscures his face. "So no ID, no prints, no name-plate on his chest?"

"Marine Band members don't wear nameplates. But that doesn't mean we didn't get the name he wanted us to see," A.J. adds. "Look at his music folder."

Without a word, Francy flips to the final photo in the file. It's a close-up of the music folder our mystery man is cradling. In thick black magic marker, he made it easy to read:

**A. Hidell.**

My face goes cold.

"You recognize the name?" the President of the United States asks.

I nod, finally understanding what they're really worried about. This isn't about me. Or the Culper Ring.

"On the day John F. Kennedy was shot, Alek Hidell was the name on the fake ID carried by Lee Harvey Oswald. It's the name Oswald ordered the gun with."

## 12

**Two weeks ago
Ashford, Virginia**

She was bleeding. Again.

She tasted it in her mouth—the salty metallic taste of her own blood—as she plowed through the lobby of the office building, keeping her head down to avoid the lone security camera in the corner. She knew the risk in coming here. The Secret Service had her picture all over the news. For two weeks, the **Washington Post** had put it on its home page in place of the Editor's Pick. But at this point, she had no choice.

Readjusting her brown bobbed wig and giving one last glance outside, she checked the building's directory and slowly, carefully, picked up speed. She never ran. If she ran, her teeth would literally rattle and shake in her mouth. Then the blood would really come.

Having cancer was bad. This was worse.

Worse than losing her hair. Worse than the smell of her own burnt skin during radiation.

It'd started with a simple toothache. The pain was tough, but she could deal with pain. The old white mess of scars on her elbow was proof of that. Plus, going to a doctor meant questions, insurance, and the risk of being seen.

It wasn't until two weeks ago, eating microwave popcorn in her motel, that she reached for a kernel stuck in her teeth and instead pulled out a hunk of...something. Grayish and smoky in color. It was a piece of her gums. Underneath, she could see her exposed, dead jawbone.

In medical terms, it's called osteonecrosis of the jaw, a by-product of her oral chemo. The blood supply to her jaw was blocked, so the bone in her jaw was dying.

Soon, her gums were bleeding at every meal. When she ate, it was like chewing on her own teeth. She still didn't go to the doctor. Her first solution was lots of yogurt. Once, she even ate baby food. Her second was to stop chewing on the left side of her mouth. But ten days ago, when an infection took hold and got so bad she could smell her own rotting flesh, that was the end. Replacing her blond wig with an outdated brunette bob, she'd practically crawled into the emergency room.

The surgeon who saw her gave her antibiotics to stop the infection. To make sure it didn't get worse, he also wanted to cut out a big piece of her jaw.

"Will I look like Roger Ebert?" she'd asked.

The doctor wouldn't face her. "We'll do our best."

He turned to make a note on his clipboard; she swiped his prescription pad and disappeared. As a cancer patient, she knew that pain can cause you to make decisions you wouldn't otherwise make. She wasn't letting it take her face.

Today, both the pad and the infection were gone. But as she headed through the lobby, the real disaster was just getting started.

"Need me to hold it?" a man called out from the building's sole elevator.

Shaking her head and avoiding eye contact, she darted for the less crowded stairs. Anything to stay out of sight. For two weeks now, that was her new routine. Every few days a new office building, a new set of stairs, a new set of strangers.

"Anybody home?" she called out, tapping the translucent glass in the magazine-covered waiting room. It was a few minutes before two. Just as lunch was ending. The best time to cut the line and drop in for an emergency appointment.

"I'm surprised it took you this long," a voice announced behind her.

She spun at the sound, finding a short, bald, muscular man in a messy-prep polo shirt. Collar popped, which already made her hate him. He was young and looked wealthy, his slitted eyes burning with the cockiness that comes from being in your late twenties. Even his black herringbone overcoat had an expensive-looking polish. His hand was tucked into the front. Like Napoleon.

"In the flesh. The real Clementine," he said.

"You have the wrong person," she said, trying to duck around him.

He stepped to the side, blocking her path. "I'm not Secret Service. I'm here to help," he promised. "Though you need to be smarter. Once you start jumping from dentist to dentist, you're easy to track. That's how I found Beecher: when he was in the hospital, visiting Tot."

Inside her cheek, her four lower left teeth wiggled like a row of loose children's teeth, twisting and floating on her dead jawbone.

"You look like you're in pain," he added. He was standing so close, she noticed his stark white eyelashes.

"I didn't catch your name," Clementine challenged.

"Ezra," he said, taking another small step closer. "We need to talk to you. About history."

"Ah. Creepy, stalky, and obsessed with the past. You must be looking for my father."

"Nico. We have a proposition for him."

"You keep saying **we**. Who's **we**?"

"Who else?" Ezra said, smiling through his slitted eyes. "The Knights of the Golden Circle."

## 13

## Today
## Washington, D.C.

"If someone's copycatting Oswald—" I say.

"We don't think it's a copycat," A.J. interrupts. "Whoever our trumpet player is, this wasn't an attack. He knew we'd see this. He **wanted** us to see this...just like he wanted Mrs. Wallace to find that arm with the penny in it." As A.J. says the words, Wallace's shoulders pitch in anger. I don't care how strong Presidents have to be. No one likes having his family threatened.

"So you think whoever did this—"

"I think **Nico** did this—and I think **Clementine's** helping," A.J. interrupts.

"I'm not arguing with you," I say as I pick up the photo of the trumpet player. "All I'm asking is, based on Nico's last victim, do you think they're after the First Lady?"

A.J. looks to Francy, who looks to Wallace, who again offers a silent nod. There's no question of the hierarchy.

"We're not sure. We tried moving Mrs. Wallace out of the eighteen acres first thing yesterday morning," A.J. finally says, using the Service's slang for the White House. "She wanted to wait for the President; they'll both be going off-site today. In fact, we were in the midst of that when we got the call that you were suddenly at the front gate."

"What about the medical examiner? Can they get DNA from the arm, maybe tell us who it is?"

"Beecher, if we call in the D.C. police, they work for the mayor, not us. If we call in the FBI, they'll bring it to the press and we'll lose control of the entire investigation."

"You're telling me the President can't have his own secret—?"

"Are you paying attention?" A.J. asks. "Right now, the Rose Garden is covered with a blue tarp and a sign that says **Broken Sprinkler Heads**. It'll let us preserve the integrity of our crime scene without every reporter in the country sticking their nose in the dirt while playing Woodward and Bernstein. Then, two hours from now, the Usher's Office will announce that up on the third floor of the White House, the wallpaper in the billiard room is starting to peel, and therefore the room needs a paint-and-carpet renovation. Bringing in those workers gives us the perfect excuse to move the President and First Lady out of the White House and to a safe lo-cation until the work is complete."

"And the press won't think that's suspicious?"

"The press'll do what it does with every White House renovation: They'll say we're building a new secret underground bunker. But trust me, President Obama renovated the Treaty Room; Bush renovated the Briefing Room; Clinton gave us a new Music Room. You won't believe what we've investigated here under the guise of 'home improvements.'"

"What he's trying to say," the President adds as A.J. turns back to his surveillance cameras, "is that **this** is what the Culper Ring was designed for. It's a small circle we're standing in, Beecher. I'd like to keep it that way."

It's a flawless pitch, delivered by the flaw-less pitchman. Best of all, if I make nice, it's the cleanest way for me to get what I came here for. But c'mon. When is anything ever that easy with Wallace? I know he's full of crap. He's always full of crap. Even worse, big bears always hide big claws.

It all comes from his hatred of the Ring: We know what he did back in college, when he used a baseball bat and car keys to put that kid into a coma. If I let him inside, it gives him a perfect chance to nuke the Culper Ring from within. But right now, he has what I want. And I—thanks to the Ring and its ability to keep a secret—have what he wants. In this town, lifelong relationships have been built on less than that.

"You're smart to be cautious. We haven't done much to earn your trust," the President adds. I know it's his job, but sometimes I forget how uncanny he is at reading people. And mobilizing them.

"Beecher, have you ever heard of the Courtyard Café?" he adds.

I shake my head.

"During the Cold War, when the Russians had their nukes aimed at us—and we at them—the exact bull's-eye for their missiles was actually a small shack, a little hot dog stand, in the center courtyard of the Pentagon. It's called the Courtyard Café. Of course, it's no surprise they were aiming at the Pentagon, but for years, we wanted to know: Why'd the Russians pick that little shack? And are you ready for the answer? It's because on all their satellites, every single day, they'd see our top generals going in and out of that building. In and out, in and out. Moscow spent millions studying it, eventually deciding it was the entrance to an underground briefing area below the Pentagon. But all these years later, you know the real reason those generals kept heading for that shack? Because that café had cheap coffee and the best hot dogs."

"So sometimes a hot dog is just a hot dog?" I ask.

"Or sometimes, when someone says they can use your help, they really are just looking for your help," the President says, glancing down at the empty plate that had held his lemon square. It's now covered by the photo of the flattened penny that came from Nico's unit. My father's unit.

They're the ones who know how my dad really died. And why.

"When those files...the Plankholder files...get pulled from storage, I want them. I need to see them," I insist. "If you want my help, you need to promise me that."

"I understand. You know so much about history, but you don't know anything about your own," the President says. "No matter what you think, though, we all want the same thing," he adds, trying to be reassuring.

It doesn't help. I don't trust him. Not a bit. But right now, if I want my father's files and want to know how they're tied to this buried arm, there's only one way to get them. Does that bring its own risks? For sure. Though aligning myself with the President also brings unique opportunities, especially when it comes to showing the world who he really is. Under Tot, the Culper Ring was eviscerated. This is our chance to rebuild, to make it more effective than ever. The Ring deserves no less than that.

In my hands, I'm still holding the photo of the trumpet player in profile. It's blurred so much, I can't even tell if it's a he or she, much less their hair color. But I still read body language. "That's not Nico. Or

Clementine."

"For all we know, it's someone they hired to sneak inside," Francy says.

"Or maybe Nico and Clementine have nothing to do with this," I say.

"You really believe that?" the President asks. "After all Nico's talks of destiny, and history, and how God chose him to kill a President? Three weeks ago, Clementine went to visit him; within two hours, he escaped and disappeared. Now, what a surprise, we've got body parts showing up in the White House. C'mon, Beecher, there's coincidence and then there's—"

"Francy, check this out," A.J. announces, waving her over to the TV.

Francy joins him quickly, both their faces glowing white as they lean toward the monitor with the surveillance camera feeds. For a full thirty seconds, they just stand there. A.J. hits a few buttons on a keyboard so only one of the four camera angles is now showing onscreen.

"You may want to look at this," A.J. says, turning back to us.

"Not now," the President scolds.

"I didn't mean **you**, sir. I meant **him**," A.J.

says. He's pointing at me.

"We've definitely got a problem," Francy adds, her reading glasses swaying as she taps a finger on the TV.

Onscreen, across the street from the White House, a lone figure lingers by the front gate on Pennsylvania Avenue, hands stuffed in his pockets. He's wearing a wool cap and keeps his head down, but there's no mistaking who it is.

Aw crap.

What's he doing here?

## 14

Bursting out from the East Wing entrance and weaving through a crowd of visitors waiting to start their White House tour, I make a sharp left on East Exec and nearly collide with a middle-aged woman trying to take a cell phone photo of the White House. The President didn't say a word as I left; they want to know why he's here too.

"**Sorry**...!" I call out, waving an apology as I swim upstream on East Exec.

"**Watch yourself!**" a dad with two little kids barks as I cut past him and almost plow into someone else. But what catches me off guard is when that someone else grabs my wrist. And squeezes.

I fight to pull away.

He squeezes tighter, digging his thumb into my wrist. A jolt of electricity zigzags to my elbow. My arm goes numb. "**What're you doing!?**" I hiss, finally turning to face him.

His drooping gold eyes, the color of white wine, lock on me. His whole face sags, and his putty-like skin appears extra waxy in the sun. Still, even without his burns, I know that look since our childhoods in his treehouse. Not here. Be smart, Marshall insists with a burning glare.

**"Look, check him out!"** someone whispers next to us.

I turn just as two overweight teenage girls quickly look away. On our right, an older woman tugs her husband's arm, trying to steer his gaze toward us. This is Marshall's life every day: pretending not to notice all the stares.

He lowers his head and steers me through the throng, back toward the public part of Pennsylvania Avenue.

I again try to pull free; he again squeezes the pressure point on my wrist.

"What're you doing here!?" I demand.

He shakes his head, glancing up toward a nearby lamppost. A round security camera stares back down. I almost forgot. Marshall breaks into buildings for a living. Of course he knows where the cameras are.

As he leads us through the crowd, he doesn't duck and weave; he plows forward in a straight line. Some people see him, others just feel him coming. It's why he's so good at his job. The man with the boiled face is here. Whether it's from fear or pity, everyone gets out of the way.

"You know they saw you, right? They caught you on camera inside," I tell him as we cross Pennsylvania Avenue and head across the street to Lafayette Square. He stops at a nearby bronze statue. It's not the big statue at the center of the park— of Andrew Jackson looking glorious on horseback. It's the smaller statue—of General Lafayette himself, his arm raised in mid-speech—that's tucked in the corner of the park.

"They shouldn't care," Marshall says, his voice grinding like crushed glass. His military posture is perfect as he scans the area, ever the wolf.

"Of course they care. They know what you are!"

"And what am I, Beecher?"

I pause, choosing each word carefully. Until a few weeks ago, he'd been gone from my life. In one of my first cases with the Culper Ring, he came back, even helping me solve an old murder and stop a serial killer. "They've seen what you do. At the Lincoln Memorial...you may've been trying to protect the President, but you're still the one who killed that shooter. Last I checked, they don't like suspected murderers hanging outside the White House."

"I'm not the one they should be worried about," Marshall says, looking down and kicking at a spot on the sidewalk. "Six o'clock. Directly behind me."

I glance over his shoulder. On the left: a homeless man tugging a rusted toy red wagon filled with old newspapers; on the right: a bald tourist with an old-fashioned camera around his neck.

"The tourist," Marshall says. "When A.J. took you out of the van and into the White House, the tourist was watching from across the street. Took photos of the whole thing."

"**What?** I thought you were—?" I look back at Marshall. "I told you to stay out of sight...that you should just listen through the phone. Why'd you come early?"

"I was looking for someone like him," he says, still keeping his back to the tourist.

"But don't you see? Now that the

President's seen you...now he knows we're working together—"

"C'mon, Beecher, how dumb do you think Wallace is? He knows we saved his life last month. He knows that my dad served with your dad and Clementine's dad in the same unit—that's what ties us all to Nico. You really think he doesn't know I'm helping you?" He shakes his head, but his skin's so stiff, his face moves like a solid mask. "Just tell me, did you get the files or not?"

"That's the thing. I don't think this is about the files." For the next few minutes, I bring Marshall up to date, telling him about the First Lady and the buried arm...the flattened penny that was stashed inside its grip...even the part about the trumpet player with the name Alek Hidell.

For a full thirty seconds, he just stands there, his gaze jumping between me and the bald tourist who's still across the park. Marsh readjusts his black gloves. It's not that cold out. He uses them to hide the burns on his hands.

"They think it's Nico?" he finally asks.

"They do."

"You don't agree?"

"You tell me. Y'think Nico and Clementine could make their way into the White House and bury an arm in the Rose Garden?"

"Not without assistance."

"Exactly," I say. "Now you see the problem."

"So Wallace doesn't trust his own Service?"

"He trusts some of them. He definitely trusts A.J.—and this woman Francy. But the way Wallace tells it..."

"He wants some help from the Culper Ring," Marshall says skeptically.

"Trust me, I didn't believe him either."

"But now you do?"

"How long have we known each other? Wallace lies. He always lies. And he does it in a way that makes you feel like he's doing you a favor."

"So you think he's after you?"

"I'm not big enough."

"Don't be so sure," he says. "You're the one who found his secret: on that night with the baseball bat."

"I still can't prove it."

"For now."

I nod in agreement. "That's why the

President wants the Ring; he knows the damage we can do. Especially to him." Marshall understands. For over two hundred years, the Ring has had a hand in every battle from the Revolutionary War and Gettysburg, to Hiroshima and getting the hostages out of Iran. Even the way it's splintered today, its remaining members can pull off a miracle. Wallace doesn't want that miracle being turned on him.

"So he's doing this to bring you on his side," Marshall says.

"Or maybe he's trying to squash us altogether. All I know is, we want the files about our dads' unit, and he's got the files about our dads' unit. At least this way, we get what we want **and** we get to keep an eye on him. It's the one thing even Tot couldn't pull off. This is our chance: to add strength to the Ring and rebuild it right."

Marshall looks down at his gloves but doesn't readjust them.

"Beecher, what're you really looking for in those files?"

"I'm not sure what you mean."

"In the Plankholder files. With our dads. My father came back with no legs. Now that he's dead, I want to know what happened to him in that unit. And I get that you want to know how your own dad died—"

"Or if he was killed."

"Of course. Anyone would want to know that. But these risks you're taking..." He stops a moment. "This isn't just about these files, is it? There's something else you're searching for."

Sometimes I forget how long he knows me. And how quickly he spots my lies. "I don't know what you're talking about."

Marshall stands there silent, once again eyeing the bald tourist with the camera. "Do you think the President is being up-front about the arm?"

"Like I said, he's not up-front about anything. But you should've seen the First Lady's face. It's a severed arm. They didn't even like looking at the photo. Plus when Wallace was talking about his wife finding it...the rage in his voice... There're some things even a scumbag politician won't lie about."

Marsh is still eyeing the bald tourist. "Do you know the real secret of how Presidents become Presidents?" Before I can answer, he explains, "It's because they're good at getting people to do things for them. In fact, they're not just **good** at it. They're maestros. Virtuosos. To get that title of President, you need thousands of people doing thousands of different things, all for your benefit. It's a massive churning machine. And y'know what feeds that **machine**?" he asks. "People like **you**, Beecher. It's fed with your life, and your family, and your reputation. Because when things go wrong...and they **always** go wrong...the President isn't allowed to have that skunk smell around him. So when that happens, he doesn't just replace you. He crumples you up, tosses you out back, and...chomp goes the woodchipper."

"You have a very graphic view of politics."

"A realistic view. You need to be smart here."

"I am being smart. You think I don't see the magical coincidences? This arm just happens to have a penny in it that just happens to come from our dads' unit? The woodchipper isn't just coming, Marshall. It's already here. Whoever set this up—whether it's Nico, Clementine, or whoever they're working with at the White House—I know they're waiting to grind us, and by **they**, I mean Wallace too. He'll take our help and throw us in the trash faster than anyone."

"But the way you're talking, the President has you—"

"Wallace doesn't have me doing anything. I'm exactly where I want to be. The only way I'm finding out what happened to our dads is by being right by his side. So you tell me which is smarter: walking away with nothing, or ducking a few spinning blades while we pick his pocket?"

Marshall stands there, unreadable as ever.

"So what do we do about **him**?" I ask, motioning to the bald tourist.

Marshall doesn't hesitate. Forever fearless, he turns around and marches straight at the tourist. "You!" he calls out. "Can I help you with something?"

The tourist looks our way, confused. **"Me?"**

"Don't insult us," Marshall warns. "I saw you on the south side of the White House, then I saw you here. So. For the last time," he adds, plowing at the man. **"Can I help you with something?"**

The bald man's confused look shifts to anger. He's short and muscular, built like a rugby player, with the crooked nose to prove it. But as we get closer, the most haunting parts of his face are his slitted eyes and stark white eyelashes. He looks like the ghost of Andy Warhol.

He reaches for something from his chest pocket.

**If that's a gun...**

Marshall's all over him. He grips the bald man's wrist. With a squeeze, Marsh goes for the same pressure point that made my arm numb. But without even batting a white eyelash, the bald man whips his arm free and jams a thumb into Marsh's neck.

"Hkkkk!" Marshall gasps, grabbing his own throat and stumbling backward. I've never seen anyone move that fast. Not even Marshall.

"Secret Service!" the man announces, pulling out his wallet and flashing a badge.

I shouldn't be surprised. For years, the Service has used the same trick as Disney World, dressing their agents as tourists so they can blend in and eavesdrop on the crowd. But as I look over at Marshall, he's bent over, more pissed than ever. His eyes narrow at the agent. He sees something he doesn't like. I don't blame him. It's been barely ten minutes since I left the basement hideout where the President told me there was a rotten apple in the Service. And suddenly, here's someone in the Service who decided that the best use of his time was taking my picture as A.J. led me inside.

"Let's see some ID! Both of you!" the bald agent barks. He's younger than both of us.

As I hand him my ID, I spot the orange-jeweled Secret Service pin on the lapel of his jacket.

"Take it easy. We're on the same side," Marshall says coldly, pulling out his own driver's license plus the government ID that he uses when he breaks into a public facility and gets questioned. "Next time, though, maybe you should identify yourself a little earlier," Marshall adds, getting face-to-face with him. "Otherwise, you may get your arm broken."

"I was going to say the same about your

neck," the bald agent replies.

Within seconds, they're chest to chest, dueling egos. Most people look away when they're this close to Marshall. Andy Warhol doesn't seem to be bothered.

"Okay, everyone put your macho away," I interrupt, pushing them apart and stepping between them. For a moment, Marshall pushes back, looking for a skirmish. But just as quickly, he lets it go.

The bald agent stands there, studying our IDs. Eventually, he has no choice. "Next time, think about where you are," he warns, motioning to the White House and tossing back my ID. Without another word, he follows the path back through the park.

We both stand there, watching him from behind.

He's headed toward 17th Street.

"You don't think he's Secret Service, do you?" I eventually ask.

Marshall doesn't answer. "I saw you steal his pin, Beecher."

Of course he did. Marshall doesn't miss anything. From my pocket, I pull out the agent's orange-jeweled lapel pin that I swiped off his jacket.

In the world of the Secret Service, every agent who guards the President wears the same-color pin so, among the dozens of people in business suits, they can easily spot each other. "A.J. was wearing one with a **blue** jewel," I point out. "This one's **orange**."

"That a problem?"

"Last year at the Archives, we did an exhibit on the history of presidential staff. We featured these pins and all the shapes and sizes they've been over the years."

"So this orange jewel tells you something?"

"I don't care about the orange. I care about **this**," I say, turning the pin around. On the back of the pin, there's an engraved six-digit number. "Each pin is numbered and accounted for. When we trace it, it'll tell us if he is who he says he is."

"You think he's our missing trumpet player?"

"The photo was too blurry. But he could be."

Marshall presses his burnt lips together, nodding his approval.

"So you ready to see where he's headed?" I add.

Pulling out his cell phone, Marshall swipes to an app, and a map appears onscreen. A rectangle with an oval in it shows Lafayette Square. A bright green dot represents us. A red dot represents the bald Secret Service agent who's been watching me since I first got to the White House.

When Marshall came back into my life and helped me save the President, I invited him to join the Culper Ring. He told me no. But it didn't stop him from asking for one of the tiny silver beacons that, during his little shoving match, I saw him tuck into the bald agent's jacket pocket.

It's the simplest of Culper Ring tech. And among the most effective.

"Can I ask you one last question?" I say to Marshall, who's locked on his screen, watching the agent's red beacon make its way through the park. "I know you saw me go in through the south entrance of the White House—but when A.J. brought me out, it was through the **north** entrance, where you seemed to be waiting. How'd you know that's the exit I'd be coming out of?"

"It's the public entrance. I took a guess," Marshall says.

In the distance, the bald agent is long gone. On Marshall's phone, the red beacon is racing toward 17th Street. As fast as it's moving, he's definitely running. "Away from the White House," Marshall points out.

"And away from Secret Service head-quarters," I say as we take off after him.

I don't care how fast you run, Andy Warhol.

We see where you're going.

## 15

## Twenty-nine years ago
## Lawton, Oklahoma

Some people think they know when they're going to die. Alby White was one of them. Naturally, he wasn't so sure of the **how**— whether it'd be by fire, car crash, or heart attack—but at twenty-two years old, he believed one thing: that he would die when he was young.

Today was Alby's first time on an airplane (which he liked). It was also his first time in first class (which he liked even more). It would also be his first time in a plane crash.

"...should be touching down in the next ten minutes for an on-time arrival in Oklahoma," the pilot announced, his voice calm as a grandfather's. "Current weather shows light winds, temperature a gorgeous eighty-five degrees. Flight attendants, please prepare for arrival. Welcome to a beautiful day in—"

"—the United States Army!" the loud-mouthed Irish kid with a mop of rust-colored hair called out across the aisle. Alby had met him when they were boarding—or rather, tried to meet him. The Irish kid brushed him off, choosing to make small talk with the square-shouldered all-American recruit who was standing first in line at the boarding gate. Both looked a few years younger than Alby. Just kids out of high school. But some things never changed. Cool kids always found cool kids. And cool kids never found Alby.

From twelfth grade, to junior high, even down to his first years in grade school, Alby had never been bullied. He was relegated to the even lower rung of unpopularity: He was **ignored**. Worse, he **knew** he was ignored. Whenever kids were reminiscing in his Minnesota school, someone would say, "I didn't even realize you were in that class with us."

In Alby's mind, that was life—until he met Teresa, the first girl who ever really noticed him. On the first day of school, pinned to her jean jacket, was a Charlie Chaplin button with two arts-and-crafts googly eyes glued to Chaplin's face. By the tenth day of school, the button was on Alby's chest. Teresa knew Alby was shy, but as she told him, Chaplin was proof that even the quiet ones can still be stars. Alby laughed at the sappiness. But he kept wearing the button.

Alby's mom had told him to be careful, but like so many small kids from a small town, he and Teresa had big plans— until right after prom, when she peed on a plastic pregnancy test and saw a plus sign. Minnesota was a liberal state. Teresa's family wasn't. Within four years, Alby and Teresa had two girls and a newborn. A little boy named Beecher.

It wasn't until one of Alby's daughters broke her collarbone and Alby's mother was hit with Parkinson's that Alby thought about the army. Most jobs let you add your wife and children as dependents; the military lets you add your family **and** your diaper-wearing mother whose tremors are getting so bad she can no longer hold a fork. But that wasn't Alby's only reason for becoming an army man.

"So off to basic training, huh?" a gate agent with a pointy face and equally pointy breasts had called out from the check-in kiosk.

"How'd you know?" Alby asked.

"Envelope," the gate agent said, pointing to the wide manila envelope he was clutching to his chest. There were three other recruits on the flight. All were doing the same: all pretending to be calm; all dressed in T-shirts; all four hugging the envelopes with their enlistment orders for Oklahoma's Fort Sill. "My brother served for two years," the gate agent added, handing Alby a surprise upgrade to first class. "Enjoy the extra legroom."

As Alby said his thanks and headed down the Jetway, he felt in his pocket for the googly-eyed Chaplin button. He had brought it with him when all three of his kids were born. You better believe he was bringing it here.

He was supposed to be sitting in the window seat on the left. Instead, the Irish kid known as Timothy Lusk slid into Alby's seat, taking the prime spot next to his newfound friend, the all-American boy whose black hair was already buzzed in a perfect crew cut. In the game of life, there were winners and losers. Alby knew the crew cut kid was a winner. He read the name on his envelope. Nicholas Hadrian.

"Call me Nico," All-American said, extending a confident hand-shake to Alby. "Am I in your seat?"

"He's actually over **there**," the Irish kid— Timothy—interrupted, pointing Alby across the aisle, to the window seat by himself.

Alby was about to argue. He wanted to argue.

But he didn't.

"Sorry, can I squeeze past?" the fourth and final recruit—a pale redhead with faint freckles and a worried face—whispered as he took the window seat in the row behind Alby. According to his folder, the redhead's name was Julian, though when the plane eventually burst into flames, Alby would barely be able to remember it.

"Once again, thank you for choosing to fly with us," the pilot added two hours later as the plane began its final descent. "We appreciate having you on board. We'll be on the ground momentarily."

Still feeling the novelty of his stomach lurching and his ears popping, Alby pressed his forehead against the window, mesmerized by the approaching Oklahoma landscape.

**"JesusMaryandJoseph,"** Timothy said across the aisle. Like Alby, he had a flat midwestern accent. And like Alby, he had a young son. Named Marshall. **"Our new home,"** Timothy added.

As Alby glanced over, Timothy was staring out his own window. But his seatmate—Nico—was just sitting there, perfect posture...shoulders back...his arms draped across the armrests like they were part of his throne. At first, Alby wasn't sure what Nico was doing. **What was he looking at?** Nico was staring straight ahead, a gold cross dangling from his neck and a satisfied grin on his face.

It was a grin Alby would never forget.

On any plane, most people need to keep themselves busy. They read a book, flip through a magazine, or do **something**. But as Alby looked across at Nico... Nico's chest was out, his chin was raised, his lips curled into that contented grin. Some people are so self-assured, they don't need anything. They can just...be. Nico's

grin was a grin of thankfulness. Of eager-
ness. Of **confidence**.

No question, Nico was a winner. And no
question, as Alby stared across the aisle,
he couldn't help but sit up straight and
stick out his own chest. In high school,
Alby's history teacher had told him that
every life is built like a monument. Alby had
hoped that in the army, he'd put down his
first piece of granite. But as his shoulders
and posture sagged back down, Alby knew
—he could feel it: Like his marriage, like
parenthood, like everything else in his mess
of a life, there's no magical transformative
moment that turns you into the person you
want to—

**Ka-duuunk.** The plane shook and jerked
as its wheels met the runway. Alby glanced
outside. The plane lurched forward, brakes
biting. Bumpy landing.

Nico opened his eyes and the Irish kid
next to him offered a soft high-five.
"Welcome to the rest of your life," Nico
said, whispering to himself.

Twisting around, Alby peeked through
the gap between seats, trying to make eye
contact with the redheaded recruit—Julian

—behind him. No luck. Julian was staring out the window. Instead, the only welcome Alby got was a cordial nod from the elderly couple sitting across the aisle diagonally behind him. Besides the four recruits, they were the only passengers in first class. As he smiled weakly at the couple, Alby couldn't see what was just outside his window, off the runway. Indeed, with the plane rolling toward its gate, he never saw the silver gasoline truck— being driven at high speed by a man in the midst of an epileptic seizure—until it swerved toward the side of the plane, just below the wing. From the back right-hand side of the plane, words and screams tumbled together in that picosecond before impact.

**"LOOK OUT!"** a woman shouted.

It didn't help.

The crash of truck into plane sounded like metal teeth being smashed together. The impact created a ruthless shear as the truck sliced through the plane's belly. For Alby, it was as if he were moving forward in one moment, and in the next was weight-less, floating like an astronaut. Every strand of his sandy hair swayed and swerved like he was underwater. A flick of spit hovered in the air, and then, as gravity and momentum returned, he was violently jerked sideways, to the left.

The seat belt bit tight against his side, and he opened his mouth to scream. The sound was still stuck in his throat.

**"The truck—! Gasoline!"** someone yelled. **"It's gonna—!"**

An explosive burst mushroomed upward, engulfing the back half of the plane. Smoke punched though the cabin, stampeding up the main aisle in a black wave. The cockpit door stayed shut. No one came out. The screams were deafening, coming from behind them.

In moments of crisis, the reason people say that things move in slow motion is that the brain is struggling to process too much in-formation at once. As a result, the brain slows it all down to digest each bit of emotion, pain, and reality.

Choking on smoke, Alby didn't see anything in slow motion. For him, it was all happening too fast.

He was twenty-two years old. This was it. The moment of his death. The only image in his brain was of the airline worker with the pointy breasts.

Across the aisle, there was a metal snap. Ripping open his seat belt, Nico shot out of his seat and dashed for the front door. Alby couldn't see much. There were sounds of kicking, pounding. Nico was trying to jimmy the latch with his fingers. There was a loud click as the lock unclenched and the door...

A burst of daylight stabbed through the smoke, which spun in a tight swirl—a beautiful tornado—which was sucked outward from the change in cabin pressure.

Nico jumped outside, disappearing. Right behind him, Irish Timothy was yelling as he ran full speed to the door and did the same. Barely twenty seconds had passed. There were sirens in the distance, plus a rumbling from the main cabin as the rest of the passengers fought to get free.

Behind him, there was another click as the redheaded recruit undid his seat belt and ran to the door. **"Good God! The flames!"** Julian called out, staring outside. He turned back to Alby, their eyes locking. **"Get out...! The gas...! You gotta get** out!" With a jump, he was gone.

Alby's lungs burned with heat. He couldn't see anything through the black smoke. He was clawing at his seat belt, but it wasn't working. It was stuck. The sirens outside were screaming full blast, but nothing was louder than the screams coming from behind him, in the main cabin. **Were they burning back there?** He smelled gasoline and smoke.

**"Jonathan...!"** the elderly woman screamed behind him. Out of the corner of his eye, through the smoke, Alby saw the older couple across the aisle. She held her husband's shoulders, shaking him. He wasn't moving.

Tearing at his seat belt, Alby lifted the buckle, but the tongue of the belt wouldn't come undone. He lifted it again. And again. The impact from the crash... **Why wasn't it working!?**

**"Jonathan, please...!"** the elderly woman begged.

A well of tears blurred Alby's eyes. He was coughing so hard from the smoke, a burst of snot shot from his nose. His lungs were burning. As he pulled on the buckle again, he couldn't help but look at the elderly woman. She wasn't crying anymore. Her eyes were closed. In defeat. She had given up.

Some people think they know how they're going to die. Thrashing in his seat, all Alby could think of was what his wife had said at the bus station. The tears were running down her face as she whispered it in his ear: She said he wasn't coming back. The saddest part was, when the words left her lips, he knew she was right.

Outside the window, a final black mushroom cloud belched into the air. Alby gripped the buckle with his fingertips, slowly  the strap and working his way out of its grip, climbing up on his seat until—

**Zzzzt.**

He had enough slack. He was **free**!

**Get out!** he told himself.

Frankenstein-walking into the aisle, he stumbled forward…to the front of the cabin …to the sunlight…The sound of sirens and screams was drowned out by his heartbeat, which thundered and shook his teeth. He looked back at the old couple, sitting silently in their chairs. The woman looked up at him with wide, begging ice blue eyes. Her face was the color of bone. He wanted to howl...wanted to help them, but if he did—

**"Jump!"** someone yelled. It wasn't anyone from outside. It was the voice in his head. It barely registered with Alby. Without thinking, he obeyed.

Too frightened to jump, Alby clenched his face and took a blind step into the swirl of smoke outside.

Tumbling from the plane, as the world went black, all he could think about was the elderly woman clutching her husband.

## 16

## Today
## Washington, D.C.

**"Marshall, wait!"** I shout.

He doesn't. Sprinting full speed, he has one eye on his phone as he studies the red beacon we've been following for blocks now. I'm starting to breathe heavily as we search for the supposed Secret Service agent with the white eyelashes who was watching me outside the White House. But when the red beacon doubles back down H Street and makes a right on 9th, I know the pain is only starting.

Reaching the wide berth and whizzing cars of Pennsylvania Avenue, Marshall stops running. He's winded, but not perspiring. I used to think it was because of his military training, but the truth is whatever burned him, burned his sweat glands too. As a result, he only perspires from his back and his crotch, which means his body can't regulate itself, which also means he can't stand being in the sun. But Marshall being Marshall, he doesn't say a word. Even about who we're chasing.

"You think he's here?" I call out.

He glances again at his phone, but I don't need a digital map to know where we are. Across the street, stretching two city blocks and guarded by enormous Corinthian columns, is the granite-and-limestone building that I've called home for my whole working life. The National Archives.

"Don't tell me he's inside," I say.

"He's not," Marshall says, plowing across the street and weaving between cars crawling in the heavy traffic. None of them honk. Despite what people think, Washington hates conflict. As he reaches the curb, Marshall's no longer looking at his phone. Whatever he smells, he knows where he's going.

"You see him?" I ask.

Marshall picks up speed, storming for the main entrance. He definitely sees something.

I scan the area by the revolving doors. There's the usual mix of lingering tourists, but no one who looks like White Eyelashes.

"Marsh, if you see him..."

He passes the front entrance, heading toward the bus stop. The rest of the block is empty. It makes no sense. On his phone, the red beacon's still blinking.

I look down. There's no subway running below us. I look up, checking the columns and windows that face this side of Pennsylvania Avenue.

Still barreling forward, Marshall stops at the limestone statue that sits to the left of the main Archives entrance. The sculpture shows a young woman looking up from the pages of an open book.

Wedging his foot into the base, Marshall scales the front of the statue and reaches upward. Patting along the woman's carved toes, he picks up something. Tweezed between his thumb and pointer-finger is a small silver beacon. **Our** beacon.

"Eyelashes found it?" I ask.

"He didn't just **find** it, Beecher. He knew where to **return** it." Motioning back at the building, he adds, "This guy knows exactly who you are, Beecher."

"Then why'd he ask to see our IDs?"

"Because he didn't know who I was. Though now we gave him that too."

Still catching my breath, I shake my head. "I'm not so sure that's the only reason he picked this spot," I add, motioning to the base of the statue. The face of the limestone is inscribed with a line from Shakespeare:

## WHAT IS PAST IS PROLOGUE

There's only one sociopath I know who leaves overdramatic spooky messages like that. The sociopath they think is somehow looking out for me.

"**Now** you think Eyelashes is working with Nico?" Marshall asks. "I thought you said Nico doesn't leave clues."

"This isn't a clue. It's Nico's mantra. In his crazy-ass head, he thinks he's been chosen by history—that he's part of the same secret club as John Wilkes Booth and Lee Harvey Oswald. For him, killing a President is destiny."

"That doesn't mean Eyelashes is working for him."

"I agree. Eyelashes could be someone inspired by Nico, or maybe he's a nutbag who happens to like burying body parts in the Rose Garden."

Marshall doesn't reply. He just stares over my shoulder.

"What're you doing?" I ask, following his gaze.

He continues scanning.

"You think Eyelashes is still watching us?" I add.

"That's what I'd do." For a full two minutes, he stands there, picking apart every car, tourist, and bus that passes.

"I don't think he's here, Marsh."

"I can see that, but unless you have a better solution—"

"Actually, I do," I say, pulling out the orange lapel pin that I stole from White Eyelashes's jacket. "If we wanna know who he is, here's the best way to track him. Now c'mon, you coming?"

Marshall doesn't move.

"What's wrong?" I ask. "This is our chance."

"Our chance for what? I told you, this isn't the old treehouse. I didn't ask to be part of your club. I don't want a membership."

"Then why'd you come to the White House this morning?"

"Because you said it might help us find out what they did to our dads."

"And it will."

"You keep saying that. Just like you keep saying that this is just about yours and your dad's history."

"It **is** about our history!" I say, feeling my temper rise.

"And that's the only reason? I know you since kindergarten, Beecher. Tell me what you think is in our dads' file."

"I told you, that's what I'm looking for!"

He shakes his head, still scanning the street. "I have a reporter friend who plays this game with his fellow reporters: Would You Eat a Shit Sandwich? They pick a big story and ask, **Would you eat a shit sandwich to get the missing eighteen-and-a-half-minute Nixon tapes?** Then they all decide if they'd do it."

It's an unsubtle point. Some stories aren't worth the cost of getting them. "This one's worth it," I tell Marshall. "It's my dad."

"You sure it's just your dad? You're now tracking down a murderer and personally putting your neck in presidential places where it shouldn't be. Is that really worth finding out whether your dad died on this Tuesday or the Tuesday after that?"

"It's about **how** he died—and who took him from me! Can't you see that!?" I explode as a few tourists turn to stare.

Marshall stares right back, scaring them off. "I buried my dad. So I know it feels good to think this is bringing you closer to your father," he tells me. "But it's also bringing you closer to the other person you're chasing: the only person who can make all those reporters eat shit sandwiches on a daily basis."

I know who he's hinting at. The big man himself. "That's why you think I'm helping the President? That I'm hoping to find something else to nail him on?"

"Have you asked yourself that question?"

I look away, watching a puff of black exhaust swirl from a bus's tail pipe. It clouds everything in front of me.

"I know you hate him, Beecher. And I know you still blame him for Tot being shot."

"This isn't about Tot."

"Sure it is. With you these days, everything is. But what you're doing here... You can keep telling yourself it's out of kindness...

or an investigation about your dad. But all these risks you're taking...the hunt you've so quickly and recklessly turned this into... You're not just looking for answers. You're looking for a fight."

"You don't know what you're talking about."

"Says the person who's now closer to Wallace than you've ever been—and with the whole Culper Ring standing behind you. That certainly makes it easier to put the knife in, doesn't it?" he asks, his voice slowing down. "I know it's hard being in charge, but from personal experience, listen to me on this: Blind, heated vengeance is the easiest way to get yourself and everyone else killed."

"That's really how you see this? That this is my vendetta? What about doing something simply because it's **right**?"

He stares at me, his waxy face unmoving. "Sometimes I think we're from very different worlds, Beecher."

"We grew up two blocks from each other. It can't be that different."

"What do you want me to say? I'll stand by you because we're **friends**?"

"I didn't realize that was such a silly concept for you."

"Beecher, this isn't me, you, and Clementine eating Halloween candy in her backyard hammock. Those days are gone."

"That's my worry: Are you my friend here, or is this just about your own self-interest?"

His glare tightens, but as always, he's unreadable. "Last month, when you finally found me again, do you remember the very first question you asked me?"

"I asked where you got your burns."

"And do you remember my answer?"

"You didn't give one."

He lowers his chin and presses his lips together, making me feel his silent threat. This is the reason Tot doesn't trust him. I don't know Marshall. I don't know what he's been through. And if Tot weren't lying unconscious in a hospital bed, he'd kill me for inviting Marsh into the Culper Ring. In fact, this is the exact moment where he'd remind me that Marshall's real expertise is finding weaknesses in things. Including me.

"You watched me bury my mother," he finally says. "But I've also buried my father;

I've buried my aunt; I've buried a woman who gave me more pure happiness than I ever thought I'd be allowed to have—"

"I get the picture."

"I don't think you do. What I'm really trying to say is—when it comes to White Eyelashes, and this arm in the Rose Garden, and the President himself—I don't want to be burying **you**."

On my left, another city bus pulls into the bus stop, hissing and belching as the doors swing wide and a few passengers step our way, toward the Archives.

"I appreciate you worrying about me," I tell him.

Marshall's silent as the crowd flows past us. Latching on to their momentum, he follows them up the block.

"It's tempting when that power comes, Beecher. But y'know the fighter who's in the most danger? The one who doesn't realize he's slowly starting to like it."

I look down at the orange Secret Service pin and the six digits engraved in the back of it. Considering where I'm now headed, I know he's right.

## 17

## Twenty-nine years ago
## Fort Sill, Oklahoma

Alby always thought he would die when he was young. His death was coming. Soon. But it wouldn't be in an airplane crash.

"...there you go, son. Need you to squeeze my fingers," a scratchy voice with a Tennessee twang said.

Blinking awake, Alby squinted up at the fluorescent lights. There were two men—one white, one black—standing over him. Both were wearing light blue button-down shirts. No white coats. No stethoscopes. But everyone knows a doctor when he's hunched over them.

"He's awake!" the white doctor called out to someone outside the room.

"Albert, can you squeeze my fingers?" the black doctor with the Tennessee accent repeated. He had a thin but kind face with two snaggly bottom teeth. As he leaned down, a set of dog tags swayed from his neck like a tire swing. This was a military hospital. "Albert, are you—?"

"Alby... My name's Alby," he sputtered, his throat feeling tight. As he squeezed the doctor's fingers, his right leg pulsed in pain. Two of his fingers were taped together in a metal finger splint.

The fall. He remembered jumping, falling from the plane. And the smell. That bitter black smoke. Like a human barbeque.

**"He's awake!"** the white doctor shouted for the second time.

Yet as Alby lay there motionless, sinking down into the hospital bed, the one memory he couldn't shake was of the elderly couple — the woman with the ice blue eyes begging for help—that he'd turned his back on.

"You know what a miracle it is that you got out of there!?" the white doctor asked.

"Not just a miracle," the black doctor said. "The quick thinking...his reflexes..." He shook Alby's hand, pumping it like a politician. "That was impressive, son. And I can tell you right now, it didn't go unnoticed."

"I'm not sure I understand," Alby offered.

"You will, son. I promise: Men like you are exactly who we're looking for."

## 18

## Today
## Washington, D.C.

"White eyelashes? What is he, a super-villain?" she asks through my phone.

"You asked for distinctive features," I tell her, keeping my voice down as I weave through the lunchtime crowds and local food trucks on 7th Street.

"No, Beecher, I asked for a name. A department. Even whether he was uniform or suit-and-tie," a mechanical robot voice says in my ear. She uses it as a disguise, but I know who she is. Immaculate Deception. Also known as Mac. Also known as the Culper Ring's resident hacker.

"So you couldn't find anything?"

"It's the Secret Service, Beecher. I can ask around, but there's a reason the word **Secret's** in the title. This isn't like looking for twenty-four-hour locksmiths in the yellow pages."

She shows her age with that one. In

reality, Mac's a seventy-two-year-old former navy officer named Grace Bentham. During her time at Harvard, Amazing Grace invented the term **debugging** when she found a moth in a Harvard Mark II computer. Since then, she and Tot have been the heart of the present-day Culper Ring. And its fiercest protectors. Decades ago, when the Black Hawk helicopters went down in Mogadishu, Mac was one of the first ones notified—and helped find spare local copters and jeeps to send in for the bloody rescue.

"By the way," she adds, "as long as we're on the topic of missing people who're pissing me off, where'd your boy Marshall race off to?"

"What's that supposed to mean?"

"It's the second time. Three minutes after he left you at the Archives, his cell phone went **poof**."

**"Poof?"**

"No signal. Untrackable."

"Wait, are you—? You're **spying** on him?"

"I spy on you too. It's my job, Beecher. You told me Marshall was helping us. I always look out for those who help us,"

Mac says. "But when someone's cell signal goes dead, y'know what that means?"

"He shut his phone off."

"No. Shut phones still bleed a traceable signal. If I needed to, I could track a shut phone on a plane. But if the signal goes black like Marshall's, it means he took out his battery or placed it in one of those lined bags that block all transmissions. Wherever he's going, he doesn't want to be seen."

"Or maybe he just doesn't want to be seen by **you**. Don't forget, with the job he has, people aren't supposed to see him coming."

"That's exactly my fear," she says, her mechanized voice slowing down. "That you're not gonna see him coming."

As I turn on H Street, my destination's halfway down the block: the tan-brick, nine-story building. There're no food trucks allowed around here. No trash cans either, so no one can leave a bomb. Plus, they don't keep a sign out front. They don't want anyone knowing what's in there.

"I appreciate the concern, Mac. But I've known Marshall my whole life—"

"No, you knew him in junior high. Then you both grew up, and he happened to come back into your life, oh that's right, just as you were getting involved with us."

"Now you're simplifying."

"Beecher, I've had seventy-two birthdays. I appreciate the emotional tug and swell of youth that comes from seeing an old child-hood friend, but let me tell you what Tot would tell you—"

"That I don't know this man anymore. I've heard the speech."

"Then start listening to it," she says as I reach the front of the brick building and spy the eye-in-the-sky security cam hidden under the overhang. "This isn't just about you. Every time you invite Marshall inside, you're also giving him a free look at **us**."

She won't say it out loud, but I know who **us** is. The Culper Ring.

As I open the glass door and step into the dark lobby, there's no ignoring the shiny silver writing in giant block letters along the brushed silver wall:

**WORTHY OF TRUST AND CONFIDENCE**

I turn away, preferring my metaphors a bit more subtle.

"Mac, I will never, ever do anything to hurt what you and Tot have built."

"You're missing the point. This was built two hundred years ago, long before the two of us. And you want to know why it's lasted this long?" She pauses to make sure I'm listening. "Because from the very first days that George Washington put it together, he had two rules: First, even **he** wasn't allowed to know everyone in the organization. That way, no one person could ever take us all down. And second, when you get tapped for membership, you put the needs of the organization before your own."

She pauses again, leaving me staring at the word **TRUST** on the lobby's silver wall. On my right, two burly men with thick military necks pull off their IDs and hide them in their jacket pockets as they're about to leave the building. In most of D.C., people keep their IDs on as a way to professionally brag. Here, they take them off, so no one knows where they work.

"Beecher, during my early years in the military, I was lucky enough to work with three different astronauts. All three of them made it to the moon," Mac explains. "And the thing about being an astronaut is they train their whole life to do this one thing. Then when it's over, they all react the same way: The moment they leave the moon, they know they're never going back again. Even worse, they know they can't talk to anyone about it since no one can truly appreciate the full scope of what they've seen. It's the same here. If you're committed to the mission, we'll give you a breathtaking, once-in-a-lifetime view. But like those astronauts, you need to understand: It's a **lonely** view."

I think of Tot lying there in the hospital over these past few weeks. Besides me, Mac, and two coworkers who dropped off cookies shaped like little Declarations of Independence, he hasn't had a single visitor.

"It'll save your life," Mac says in my ear. "Speaking of which, you think I don't see where you're headed right now? That's a dangerous fight you're picking."

I hadn't told her where I was going, but I'm not surprised. She's always watching.

**"You Beecher White?"** a man with a flat

nose calls out from the security booth across the lobby. He's behind thick ballistics glass— bulletproof and bombproof— in a seat that makes him a full two heads taller so he can look down at me. Better view to see whether I'm hiding a weapon.

"They'll never let you in," Mac warns.

Usually she's right. On a daily basis, every threat that's made against the President of the United States comes through this building. On 9/11, it's where they hid the First Lady. It has multiple armories, a joint operations center, and thousands of agents who aren't afraid to take a bullet. But if you want to sneak into the headquarters of the United States Secret Service, like anything else in life, it all depends who you know.

"I'm Beecher White, from the National Archives," I tell the guard. "I have an appointment with your Archivist."

## 19

Marshall didn't smell it at first. He knew it was coming, though.

Flashing a fake ID and a matching smile, he blew past the young security guard who clearly bathed in Axe body spray.

As he headed past the hospital's gift shop, it was the whiff of Mylar balloons and fresh flowers.

Even as he followed the crisp white hallway past the visitor waiting area in George Washington University Hospital, all he could smell was the usual mix of old couches, bleach and disinfectant.

But again, he knew it was coming. Every hospital smelled of it, even if most patients didn't know where the smell was coming from.

Sure enough, as he reached the entrance for the emergency room and its automatic doors slid wide, there it was.

Silverol.

At just a whiff of the ointment's harsh antiseptic and metallic smell, Marshall's throat went dry and his brain raced back to those first days in the burn unit when they'd lie to him and say that by rubbing Silverol into his red-and-yellow open flesh and the skin hanging off it, the pain would go away.

It wasn't their only lie. When they first brought him in, Marshall's left arm was so swollen, blood stopped flowing to his hand. A doctor appeared at his bedside with a dozen different scalpels. He told Marshall that he needed to cut into his skin so he could drain all the liquid and reduce the swelling. The catch was, since Marshall's lungs were so damaged, they needed to do the operation in his hospital bed. No anesthetic.

"Don't worry," the doctor had reassured him. "All the nerves in your arm are dead. You won't feel it."

He was wrong.

Two male nurses held down Marshall's arms and legs.

His nose was charred away. One of his eyes was so off-center from his face, it looked melted. Out of the other, Marshall watched as the scalpel cut into his arm, starting at his shoulder, down to his wrist. Each slice looked precise, but felt like it was being done with a rake.

**"This is my death! No more!"** he screamed, the pain so raw he couldn't breathe.

"Marshall, listen to me," the doctor insisted. "Count from ten to one for me. That's all. Count from ten to one, and I promise we'll be done."

It wasn't much of a consolation, but at least the end was in sight.

"T-T-Ten..." Marshall began, slowly counting and screaming as the scalpel dug into his skin. **"Ahuh**...n-nine..."

"There you go..." the doctor said, halfway down Marshall's biceps.

"E-E-Eight...oh God..."

Slowly, over the next few seconds, the doctor sliced downward, finishing the last of his five incisions. Sure enough, the counting helped. The end was finally approaching.

"T-Two..." Marshall said. And then... "Wh-Wh-One."

At the time, Marshall's face was burned so badly no one could tell he was trying to smile.

The doctor didn't smile back. "Okay, Marshall," he said, grabbing a new scalpel. He glanced at the nurses, who quickly tightened their grip. "Now to your fingers."

Marshall screamed so loud, and the pain was so electric, he eventually passed out.

Looking back, Marshall knew the doctors and nurses were only doing their best. If he had known they'd be slicing his fingers, he'd have never made it through the first part. And as he found out later, that operation was the only thing that'd stopped them from amputating his arm.

Still, today, as Marshall took his first step into the emergency room and the metallic smell of Silverol invaded his airways, his head went light and the rakes dug back into his arm. All around him, curtained rooms were filled with the sick and injured. He was walking so fast, the curtains on each passing room followed in his wake. But even with his candle-wax skin, he didn't attract attention. There's always a rush in the emergency room.

"Dr. Lemont, please call your office," the intercom announced from above. There was no Dr. Lemont at the hospital. Marshall knew what it meant.

He still didn't run. Panic only brought attention.

In the back corner of the room, past the graveyard of spare wheelchairs and gurneys, Marshall ducked into a narrow corridor, following it around to the right. It dead-ended at a beige metal door with a bright red sign that read **Authorized Personnel Only**. Unlike most doors in the hospital, this one had no glass in it. Instead of a PIN-code lock, it had a black, square proximity-reader just above the doorknob. A little sticker in the corner read DOC.

**Department of Corrections.**

In select city hospitals, there are designated rooms in case the local prison has an inmate who needs surgery or has a life-threatening illness. In Washington, D.C., that room connects to the emergency room—and, if the Secret Service needs it, can also be commandeered for a far more private patient.

Pulling a key fob from his pocket, Marshall pressed it into place. The door popped open.

"You're **late**," Francy announced, clutching her datebook at her side.

Marshall didn't answer. As the door shut behind him, he was still focused on the fading Silverol smell...and the familiar figure standing just behind Francy's shoulder.

"Trust me, we're having one of those days too," the President of the United States said, stepping forward and wringing his own hands. "Now can we talk about our friend Beecher?"

## 20

**Two weeks ago**
**Arlington, Virginia**

Clementine knew she wasn't safe. She had that feeling in the back of her throat, the same feeling from when she was twelve years old and the older men would come check on her in the dressing room while her mom was singing on-stage. Back then, those men had a hungry look in their eyes. A look of inevitability.

It was the same look Ezra had today. Not for Clementine. For their mission. For what he promised her here, in the empty strip-mall parking lot off Wilson Boulevard.

"Don't. Not yet," Ezra insisted, grabbing her wrist as she went to open the door of his gray rental car. His slitted eyes homed in on the digital clock of the car's dashboard. 3:54 p.m. "These are people of precision," he warned. "You walk in early, they'll walk away."

Pulling free of his grip but still scanning

her surroundings, Clementine didn't like this corner of the lot, where every passing car on Wilson Boulevard could see what they were doing. Yet as she readjusted her brown wig, she knew that was the point. The best place to hide was usually in plain sight.

"Can I ask you a question?" she said, staring straight ahead at the only storefront with a bright red **Closed** sign. All the other stores were open. "Why're you doing this?"

"I told you. The role of the Knights—"

"No, forget the Knights. I'm talking about you. Why're you doing this?"

Sitting up straight, Ezra followed her gaze out the front wind-shield, his white eye-lashes glowing in the sun. He had the posture of a private-school boy, and that haughty cockiness in his voice that said he wasn't ashamed it was private school. From his breast pocket, he took out a fine leather wallet. Like his black overcoat, suede shoes, even his belt...it was all brand-new. It took money to look this effortless.

"See this picture?" he said, handing an old photo to Clementine. "That's **me**," Ezra explained, pointing to a little boy, barely three years old, who you could only see from behind. In the photo, young Ezra's tiny hand reached upward, excited, as he shook hands with an older man whose leathered skin and slicked pompadour Clementine recognized instantly.

"Ronald Reagan," she blurted.

"I was three years old. Reagan was out of office by then. This was taken at the opening of his library."

Clementine stared down at young Ezra shaking Reagan's hand. "Don't tell me you're doing this for the Gipper."

"You asked why I'm committed to this. There's my reason. For **him**," Ezra said, pointing to the side of Reagan, at a salt-and-pepper-haired man standing by young Ezra's side.

Clementine had missed the figure at first. But there he was, in mid-laugh, his graying hair defying gravity as he bent sideways, holding a proud hand on young Ezra's shoulder. He was beaming.

"This your dad?" Clementine asked.

"My grandfather, Tanner Pope. Taught me how to saddle a horse properly, served twenty-five years with the Secret Service, and was on President Reagan's personal detail, including the day Reagan was shot." Looking over at Clementine, he added, "He was also, like his father, and his father before him, a member of the Knights of the Golden Circle."

Clementine looked back at the photo and the way the old man's mouth curved open in mid-laugh. Her own father—Nico— had told her stories of the Knights. From John Wilkes Booth to Lee Harvey Oswald, all four presidential assassins had supposedly been Knights. Nico saw himself as a self-made Knight too. Truth is, she'd thought it was her father's typical ravings, but to hear Ezra tell it... "Does that mean your dad was also—?"

"I don't think my father even **heard** of the Knights. He never had a chance," Ezra said. "Twenty-two years ago, long before my father could join, the last generation of Knights were hunted down. Slaughtered like dogs. I'm guessing they spared Grandpa Tanner since that's when he had his first stroke. But his legacy...the work of the Knights..."

"I get it," she interrupted, spotting the hunger in his eyes. "You want my father to help you rebuild."

"Something like that," he said, calmly plucking the Reagan photo from her hand. He propped it up on the steering wheel, his thumb over Reagan's face so it was only him and his grandfather. "Don't look at me like I'm crazy, Clementine. Haven't you ever wondered, when you're lying there in bed, after you shut the TV and the house goes quiet, and you're just staring at the ceiling—don't you ever wonder if you're meant for something **greater**?" His eyes stayed on the picture. His thumb now covered his grandfather too. "When I was three years old, my grandfather took me to meet the most powerful man in the world. Don't tell me it wasn't for a reason."

Feigning agreement, Clementine stared at the old photo on the steering wheel. She didn't like Ezra. Didn't trust him. But what bothered Clementine most was the simple fact that she **understood** him. The way Ezra's eyes so desperately begged at the photo, was it any different from the emotional undertow that had caused Clementine to spend the last year searching for her father? These last few months had cost her her soul. She'd become a murderer—she'd taken someone's life—all in the name of finding answers from Nico, making a connection with Nico, and of course, finding a cure for herself from Nico.

Even now, as her father ran off yet again, promising that he'd return with a solution for her cancer, Clementine knew she shouldn't believe him. But she couldn't help herself. It was a basic rule of life: Parents are full of promises; children are full of needs and longing. The perfect ingredients for disappointment.

As she sat there in the passenger seat, Clementine came face-to-face with another basic rule of life: It's far easier to judge others than to judge yourself. Indeed, the more she heard Ezra talk about his grandfather, the more she saw her own misplaced expectations for her father. No, not just **misplaced**. They were hopeless. Even ridiculous. For months now, Clementine had thought her father would have answers. It was time to admit, Nico didn't—and never would.

"You're really in pain, aren't you?" Ezra asked.

Clementine didn't move. She gulped down a swirl of blood as her back teeth floated in her mouth. If she wanted help, medical or otherwise, Nico couldn't help. He wanted to. But she'd need to get that help herself.

And she would. If nothing else, Ezra was at least good for that.

On the dashboard, the digital clock blinked to exactly 4:00 p.m. Across the parking lot, through the glass door of the closed store-front, a pale figure in a white doctor's coat appeared, then disappeared just as fast.

Clementine closed her eyes and swallowed the pain, along with another pool of blood.

"Just remember," Ezra added, popping the door and heading outside. "Once we're done here—"

"Don't worry," Clementine shot back. "In my family, we always keep our promises."

# 21

## Collierville, Tennessee
## Two weeks ago

It took three fingers before Nico believed him.

**"Nico, please...on my granddaughter's life— Fahhhh!"** Doggett screamed, twisting in his bed as Nico squeezed the needle-nose pliers and peeled a thin ribbon of skin from the colonel's thumb.

**"That was smart, starting with the thumb,"** the dead First Lady pointed out, knowing it was the least sensitive of all the fingers.

Nico nodded, holding tight to the colonel's wrist. If he went too big, too fast, Doggett would pass out.

**"I swear to God, Nico! If I knew the answer, you think I wouldn't—? Guhhhh!"** Doggett screamed again. And again. A swell of snot and tears rolled down his face. It got particularly loud when Nico moved on to Doggett's ring finger.

"You don't wear a wedding band, but I see the indentations," Nico said, using the tip of the pliers to grab a sag of loose skin. "Did your wife die or did she leave you?"

Doggett was sobbing now, barely hearing the question.

With another sharp tug, Nico raised the pliers above the colonel's chest, like a kid playing the game **Operation**.

Slowly releasing his grip, Nico opened the pliers just enough to add another thin ribbon of finger-skin to the bloody pile he was building on the colonel's chest.

**"I think he just said his wife's name,"** the dead First Lady said.

Nico nodded, eyeing the original wedding photo on Doggett's bedroom wall. The bond between husband and wife could be profound. But it was nothing like the love for one's own child.

**"I-I-I don't know how to save your daughter,"** Doggett pleaded, his voice barely a whisper.

By the time Nico started peeling Doggett's pointer-finger—the most sensitive of all the fingers—there was no mistaking the tart smell of urine that pooled in the seventy-year-old colonel's bed.

"Our Father, who art in Heaven, hallowed be thy name...!" Doggett cried.

Nico smiled at that. The Lord's Prayer. He glanced down at the carpet, tempted to kneel and—

**"Don't do it,"** the First Lady warned. **"Finish the job. There'll be time for praying later."**

Of course she was right. And sure enough, as Nico continued to peel the skin from the colonel's third finger—as Doggett begged and prayed and continued to insist that he didn't know how to save Clementine—Nico finally did believe him.

"A-All these years...I knew you'd come," Doggett muttered, barely conscious. "I knew it'd be you."

"Who else?" Nico asked. "Who else knew the details of what you did to us?"

Colonel Doggett clenched his eyes, refusing to look at the pile of skin on his chest. His body was shaking, his arm a bloody mess. "Tabatchnick. Dr. Adrian Tabatchnick."

**"Who?"** Nico asked, not recognizing the name.

"Dr. Moorcraft. From the island. Tabat-chnick is the new name they gave to Moorcraft..."

Nico sat up straight, chin out, nearly dropping the pliers. **Hnnn.** All those years in St. Elizabeths, he'd never even considered it.

Dr. Moorcraft was still alive.

## 22

### Today
### Washington, D.C.

"Phone and metals on the belt," the agent with the flat nose says, pointing me to the X-ray. We have an X-ray at the Archives. But not like this one.

As my keys and cell phone roll away on the conveyor, I pull open a heavy plastic door and step into a narrow chamber that has a closed door at the opposite end of it. Sally port. The door ahead of me won't open until the back one closes. The chamber is the actual magnetometer.

There's a soft **click** behind me. X-rays… chemical scan…I don't even want to know what radiation I'm being bathed in, but in Secret Service headquarters, you don't get inside unless you're clean.

**Click.**

"Push ahead," Flat Nose calls out.

As I give the second door a shove, the modern hallway widens and the ceiling rises, revealing an exposed glass stair-case that heads to the upper floors. On my left, groups of agents, all big and burly, head to a room labeled the Silver Star Café. The Service's cafeteria.

"Beecher, over here," a female voice behind me says, her voice clipped and hurried.

I spin to find a tall woman—late twenties—with olive skin and hair the color of honeycomb. As always, she wears it in a jogger's ponytail, but she's all business suit as she pumps my hand with a com-manding handshake. I've known her since my first days in the Archives. Mina Arbogast.

"I owe you for this one," I tell her.

"You owe me nothing," she says with that accent I can never place. Sounds almost European.

"By the way, how's Michael?" I ask, referring to her boss, the Service's longtime Archivist.

"They didn't tell you? I mentioned it to your office when they called. Michael took retirement a few months back. I've been running it since."

Turning to face her, I crane my neck back. I always forget how tall she is. She's built like an athlete. "So you're the new Archivist?"

"Wow," she laughs. "Thanks for trying so hard to hide your shock."

"Nonono...that's not what I— I just meant that you're so— you're just—"

"I have to say, I cannot **wait** to see how you complete this sentence." She crosses her arms but never loses her grin.

I feel the blood rush to my face. "I'm going to stop talking now."

"Smart. You must be an archivist," she teases, grin still in place.

I like this woman. I've always liked her, back since the first day I met her, years ago, at a conference when we were both on a panel about preserving classified documents. To open the panel, a sweet elderly female moderator announced that at the dinner that night, there'd be **parking in the rear**. I know. Judge me all you want. The best part was, she kept repeating it, over and over. "Don't forget, for the dinner... **there's parking in the rear**."

Mina tipped back on the hind legs of her

chair, looking for someone to share a juvenile laugh. She found me. With a quick exchange of eye-smiles, we were instant friends, though truth be told, every time I saw her at a conference, I'd tell myself to ask her out. But I didn't. The first time, I blamed it on the fact that my fiancée was dumping me. I did the same the time after that. A few weeks back, I finally asked.

It was kinda a date—a private tour of the Archives for her and her older brother, an army vet who'd been severely injured in Afghanistan and sick since he'd returned. A week after I showed them around, just as I went to ask Mina out again, I heard that her brother had died. Mina had known it was coming, but I didn't want to be the guy who capitalized on that.

"You see they moved next year's conference to Arizona?" she asks. "Don't these dummies know archivists are like vampires? People with pasty white skin don't like the sun." When I don't laugh, she takes a closer look at me. "Wow, not even nibbling at my cheap archivist jokes. You're in real trouble, aren't you?"

"I just want to know..." I say, following

her to her office and reaching into my pocket, "if you can tell me more about **this**." Tweezed between my pointer-finger and thumb, I hold out the orange-jeweled Secret Service pin that I swiped from White Eyelashes's jacket.

From the look on Mina's face, my problems are just starting.

## 23

"This man who attacked you and Beecher..."

"He didn't attack us," Marshall said.

"Who **approached** you. Who **got away from you**," Francy clarified, reaching for the TV remote connected by a thick cord to the hospital bed. "What'd he look like?"

"Bald. Younger than me. White eye-lashes," Marshall said.

**"White?"**

"Looks as odd as it sounds. He's also got a wealthy veneer. Shows it off. New money," Marshall added. "I figured you had him on camera."

"A.J. tried," Francy said, pressing a button as the TV sparked to life. She turned the volume up loud in case anyone was eaves-dropping. But as the picture bloomed into view, showing Fox News talking about last week's DUI for the secretary of education, she quickly switched to ESPN. "Whoever this man with the eyelashes is, even when he was fighting with you and Beecher, he stuck to the side of the statue where we don't have eyes."

Marshall nodded. White Eyelashes wasn't stupid. "You think he's the one who buried the arm?" Marshall asked.

"Who the hell else would he be?" President Wallace interrupted. "Two days ago, we've got a Marine Band member sneaking inside and using the alias of Lee Harvey Oswald. Two hours ago, we've got this guy lurking across the street and somehow also knowing how to stay out of sight. And on the way here, they told me that right now, the country of Brazil is on the verge of financial collapse and threatening to sink the whole region unless we step in and figure out a creative way to help. But yes, beyond all that, at five o'clock this morning, I got pulled out of bed by my terrified wife, who found a body part buried in our Rose Garden. This is the job, Marshall. You're the one who saw him. We need you to find out who he is."

"I thought the job was taking down Beecher and finding you the members of the Culper Ring," Marshall challenged. "Isn't that why you asked me to weave my way back into his life?"

At that, the President went silent, pretending to watch ESPN. Marshall wasn't surprised. During the past few months, when it came to Beecher-duty, Marshall had met solely with A.J. The moment he saw the President—and saw that Wallace had looped in his longtime friend Francy— he knew something was clearly wrong.

"Why're we in a hospital?" Marshall asked. "Are you sick?"

"I had a colonoscopy scheduled for this morning. All standard," the President said, still eyeing sports highlights. "No one knows we canceled yet, but barring calls from the Brazilian president, the heads of Congress who don't want to give them a dime, and whatever other disaster is already on my schedule, I've got about fifteen minutes to catch you up to date."

Marshall stood there, his eyes narrowing. The President didn't need to be here to catch him up to date. "What about A.J? Where's he?"

"At the White House. They want to move the President as soon as we get back," Francy said, sounding genuinely helpful as she pointed a hitchhiker's thumb toward the room's outer door, where Wallace's bulletproof limo was waiting.

Marshall made a mental note. It was one thing for them to be worried someone in the Service had let White Eyelashes in. It was another for them to be keeping A.J. **out**.

"I've heard only good things about you," Francy added. "Thanks for all the help as we readjust."

Marshall cocked his burned-away eyebrow. **"Readjust?"**

Francy glanced at Wallace, whose dark gray eyes were still locked on ESPN.

"I need you to stay away from Beecher," the President said.

**"What?** You told me—"

"Don't tell me what I told you. Listen to what I'm telling you now: It's time to leave your friend alone."

"Why the change of heart?"

The President just stood there, watching highlights from last night's basketball games.

"Is it because he's suddenly helping you?" Marshall asked. "You think if this is all an inside job by the Service, now you need the Culper Ring to protect you?"

The most powerful man in the world continued to watch basketball.

"Or maybe you're playing long ball," Marshall continued. "That by bringing Beecher closer, you think you'll have more control over him? Or better yet, that by the time Eyelashes is caught, the Ring will be right there for you to pick off however you like. Any of those sound right?"

"Watch this shot," the President of the United States said, motioning up to a long three-pointer from last night's Celtics game.

"Does Beecher still have the phone you gave him?" Francy asked. "The one that supposedly lets him listen in on A.J.'s calls?"

Marshall nodded, but before he could say anything—

"I appreciate your still keeping us updated, Marshall," the President interrupted as Francy shut off the TV. "If you touch a hair on Beecher's head, there won't be even a stain of you left to identify. Are we clear?"

Marshall bit at the chapped bits of skin on what used to be his lips. As the President turned to the door, Francy pulled a tri-folded sheet of paper from her datebook and handed it to Marshall.

"What's this?" Marshall asked.

"What we promised you. For helping with Beecher," the President said. "Despite what you think, I'm a man of my word. Whatever happened to Beecher's father and yours, that's the ship they were on," the President explained. "Nico too. We're trying to get the rest for you now."

Looking down, Marshall read the words on the page, then read them again. Here's where all their fathers' lives changed.

**The SS Needle's Nest.**

"It won't work," Marshall blurted.

"Pardon?"

"What you're planning with Beecher. Whatever you're scheming—"

Francy shot him a look.

"I'm not trying to insult you. I'm just telling you, even if you think he's your new best friend, when it comes to Beecher, don't mistake niceness for weakness. He's licking his chops for this fight."

"We appreciate the advice," Francy said.

"I don't think you do. Right now, you're in a chess match. But do you know who the world's best chess masters play against to test their skills? Not seasoned vets. Seasoned vets always make the same rote moves. Instead, they practice against amateurs. And y'know why? Because amateurs are **unpredictable**. When you play an amateur, when you play someone as motivated as Beecher...?" Marshall's voice became a whisper. "That's who'll make the move you'll never see coming."

At the corner of the President's mouth, a small crease deepened like a parenthesis. "Have you heard a damn word I said? We finally got Beecher playing for my side, which is where he should be. When we catch this prick who broke into my house...this guy with the white eyelashes...? This isn't chess, Marshall. It's war."

## 24

## Twenty-nine years ago
## Charleston, South Carolina

They flew Alby out first thing in the morning. There was no warning, no heads up. Right before the hospital's 4 a.m. shift change, two men in brown-and-green fatigues entered his room, handed him his own camo field jacket, and told him it was time to leave Oklahoma. "Where we going?" Alby asked.

"You've been reassigned," one of them replied.

Within two hours, their C-130 four-prop plane touched down at the army airfield in Walterboro, South Carolina. Not counting the pilots and his two guides, Alby was the only one on board.

"So you're White? You're the last one, son," a guard at the front gate said, making a note on his clipboard as Alby and his guides pulled into the Charleston Naval

Shipyard, into the area known as Weapons Station.

As the car made its way toward a two-story, cross-shaped building, Alby glanced out the side windows, then the back. It was just past nine in the morning, on a weekday, yet there was no one in sight. Every sidewalk and parking lot was empty. Still, Alby could feel it. Everyone knows when they're being watched.

"C'mon, you're late," another guard called out as the car bucked to a stop in front of the building. Like everyone else in this section of the base, his fatigues had no nametag, no patches showing rank or branch of service. "You better hurry. Ship's about to leave."

**Ship?**

As they began to run, Alby reached into his pocket, feeling for the googly-eyed Charlie Chaplin button. It didn't help. He knew his history, so he knew that when the military wanted to brief FDR, or Truman, or even modern Presidents, it put them on military boats as a way to guarantee privacy. But it also kept prisoners on ships, since out there, the laws didn't protect them.

"Can someone please tell me what's going on?" Alby pleaded as he saw the name on the back of the ship. **Needle's Nest.**

Once again, he didn't get an answer.

## 25

**Today
Washington, D.C.**

"It's definitely one of ours. I think from the eighties," Mina says, pinching the orange lapel pin in her own fingers.

"Is that bad?" I ask.

"Depends where you got it. If it's stolen…"

"I didn't steal it."

"I'm not accusing you, Beecher. I'm just saying, sometimes these pins come up in estate sales. An agent accidentally pockets one, then after they die, their relatives find it," she explains as I follow her up the hallway, toward her ground-floor office. "For the most part, though, we try to keep the pins under pretty tight control."

On our right, I see why. I've never been here before. Along the wall is a glass display case labeled **Fallen Heroes**. It's filled with thirty-six headshot photos, some color, some black and white. Below each photo is a star-shaped badge. These are the thirty-six men and women who gave their lives to the Service. I can't help but read as we walk. The first agent died in 1902 in a streetcar accident while protecting Teddy Roosevelt; the most recent died in a field office during the Oklahoma City bombing. I get the message. Every day, these people risk their lives.

As she reaches the end of the hallway, I'm still trailing behind her. "Can you tell me about the serial numbers on the back of the pin?" I eventually ask.

She glances over her shoulder. She was holding back on that. I can't tell if it's a test or something else.

"Can you first tell me where you **got** the pin?" she challenges.

It's a fair question, but my brain flashes back to the White House this morning. To bury that arm in the Rose Garden...to sneak it past security... The President wouldn't say it, but I saw the look on his face. You don't get that far without someone in the Service. I take another look at Mina and her honeycomb hair. I don't care how well I know her, I'm not ruling out anyone yet.

"Don't look so suspicious, Beecher. If

someone showed up in your office holding an old document they shouldn't have,
you'd be asking the same questions."

She's right about that too. I clear my
throat. "If I tell you where I got it, can you
keep it to yourself?"

"I'm an archivist. You think I have any
other friends but you?"

"Mina, I'm serious."

"So am I. Last month, what you did for
James," she says, refer-ring to her brother.

"I heard what happened. I hope you got
my note."

"...and the donation to Wounded Warrior.
You didn't have to do that, Beecher. Just
that tour of the Archives... You'll never
know what that meant to him."

"C'mon, you brought me a disabled vet
whose dying wish was to see the Declaration of Independence. Like I could really
say no to that."

"You'd be surprised what people said no
to. You tell me what you need and I'm on
it."

At the end of the hallway, I take a final
look over my shoulder and whisper, "The
pin came from one of our big supporters."

"Big donor?"

"More like a big mouth. A few years back, he donated three different Benjamin Franklin letters to the Archives. Two were forged. So before we accept any more of his 'gifts,' even if it's just a pin like this, we like to double-check the authenticity."

"Time. **That's** why you were playing all cryptic? You think we don't have crazy donors here?" she asks, turning the corner into a long rectangular room. "A few years back, a Texas millionaire tried to donate the Book Depository window that Oswald shot JFK from. Turns out, he had the wrong window. Another Texas guy had the real one, which shows you how crazy Texas is."

She says something else, but as I look around, I see that the far wall has a mural of a presidential motorcade with the U.S. Capitol behind it. The rest of the room is lined with photos of Presidents and archival exhibit cases filled with Secret Service artifacts. Old counterfeiting machines. A newspaper with a "Kennedy Dead" headline. Oswald's rifle (definitely a replica). The pistol used to try to kill President Ford (definitely real). They even have documents from the very first assignment where the Secret Service was called in to protect a President: stopping grave robbers who were trying to steal Abraham Lincoln's dead body.

"Where do you go when you do that?" Mina blurts.

"The what now?"

"Wow. You don't even realize it, do you? For two minutes you were just standing there, mouth gaping open like some Old World immigrant walking into Disney World."

I squint at the case on my right. "Is that the actual door from the limo when Reagan was shot?"

"Kick-ass, right? Rumor is it was Reagan's idea. The Gipper was a black belt in bad-assery. When he was President, did you know he used to carry his own gun?"

"A thirty-eight," I answer. "He'd hide it in his briefcase. Even take it on Air Force One."

She turns my way. "How'd you know that?" she asks, her voice lifting with excitement.

I stare down at an antique pencil sketch showing the layout of a long hallway with instructions for where every agent should stand to protect President Wilson when he signed the Treaty of Versailles that ended World War I. "It's our **history**."

As I turn to face her, Mina tilts her head, eyeing me with a look I've never seen before. "You know anything about antique guns?"

"My dad was in the military."

"Then you should love guns."

"I dunno. I'm a reader, not a fighter."

She half-smiles. "That's cute. You're a cute guy. Why have I never asked you out again?"

"I've been wondering that myself. You should."

She stops at that. "I might. C'mon, Booksmart," Mina says, turning back to the orange pin. "Let's see if we can connect your old serial numbers."

## 26

### Twenty-nine years ago
### Charleston, South Carolina

"No. No way," Alby said emphatically, standing on the dock right next to the boat. The Needle's Nest.

"You're late, Private," the guard said. "You better move with a purpose."

"If you want me to go down there, you need to tell me what's down there." He pointed to the bottom of the stairs, to the metal door that led to the boat's lower cabin.

When he'd first spotted the water and the long cement dock be-hind the cross-shaped building, Alby had expected a submarine, or even a coast guard cutter. Instead, bobbing at the end of the dock was a deep-sea fishing boat. It was huge, at least eighty feet. But it was old and rusted. "You're crazy if you think I'm—"

"Private, you really think this volunteer army is voluntary?" Grabbing Alby by the biceps, the guard dragged him down the stairs.

At the bottom, the guard twisted a knob and opened the metal door, practically tossing Alby inside.

"...as we officially welcome you to—" At the front of the room, a man with a round Santa Claus face was standing there like an exclamation point, his hands cupped on a podium. He looked like he had a great laugh, though he wasn't laughing right now.

Matching Santa Claus's posture, Alby stood up straight and hesitantly stepped inside. A dozen heads turned his way. All young men, all Alby's age. Fresh recruits. Half were in uniform, and the rest were in jeans and black pullovers. They were sitting at three rows of desks, like in a classroom.

Unlike the boat's exterior, the quarterdeck down here had been recently finished. New blue carpet, new coat of paint. And a brand-new student.

"You must be Private White. Colonel Doggett," the exclamation point with the Santa face announced. "Welcome home."

As Alby headed to an open seat in the back, a familiar face with a perfect crew cut nodded a silent hello from the front row. The all-American from the plane crash. Nico was here.

So was the Irish loudmouth, Timothy.

But it wasn't until Alby slid into his seat that he spotted the red hair on the kid directly in front of him. The fourth musketeer from the plane. The nervous redhead. Julian.

Twisting in his seat, with his eyes dancing more nervously than ever, Julian glanced over his shoulder at Alby, but not for long.

"As I was saying," Doggett continued, hands still cupped on the podium, "when I first joined the military, I was told that when you enlist, it's like driving at night without lights, without brakes, and you know that there's a fork coming in the road. You don't know where it is. But it's there. It's **coming**." Staring out at the dozen young recruits, he added, "You all just hit the fork. You're on it right now. And in these coming months, it'll take everything you've got to steer through it. But the good news? These people you're surrounded with? These're the best brothers you'll ever have," he said as Alby glanced from Nico's perfect posture to Julian's sagging shoulders.

A skinny black man with thick Arthur Ashe glasses stepped up to Alby's left, knelt down on one knee, and motioned for him to roll up his sleeve. In his teeth, he held a loaded syringe like a dog's bone.

"Tetanus shot," the man known as Dr. Moorcraft whispered.

"I already got my tetanus," Alby whispered back.

"Just to be safe," the man with the thick eyeglasses said, jabbing the needle into Alby's arm.

"Y'hear what happened to the others?" Julian asked, again glancing over his shoulder.

Alby cocked a confused eyebrow as he held a cotton swab to his arm.

"On the plane. The old couple," Julian whispered, chewing his thumbnail.

"No," Alby said. "You?"

Julian shook his head. His eyes danced back and forth. "I keep thinking about 'em."

Alby nodded, thumbing the Charlie Chaplin button in his pocket.

At the front of the room, the colonel was looking right at them, his Santa eyes tightening.

"Over these next few months, not everyone will make it through the program," Doggett insisted. "But if you persist and push forward, if you can see where that fork takes you, we won't just make you better soldiers. We—and you—will make **history**."

With the shot of verbal adrenaline, every young soldier was sitting up straight. Julian was no longer biting his thumb. Alby was no longer fiddling with Charlie Chaplin. And in the front row, as the boat slipped away from the dock and set a course for its destination, Nico and Timothy were no longer the only ones convinced they would change the world.

## 27

**Two weeks ago
Arlington, Virginia**

"这样会伤害," the chubby Asian dentist insisted,
a surgeon's mask covering his mustache.

**"This will hurt,"** his female assistant
translated as the doctor lowered his scraping tool into Clementine's open mouth.

"Ah uh-huh-hann," Clementine replied
from the dentist's chair. **I understand.**

She knew the alternative: cutting out her
jaw and disfiguring her face. This way, she
at least had a chance.

Outside, the sign on the closed storefront
read **Happy Jade Herbal Shop**. Inside, it
smelled the part—sandalwood incense—
and looked the part: The far wall was lined
with small glass cookie jars, giving it a
candy store feel, though the jars were
filled with ginseng, dried ginkgo, dong
quai, plum flower, and every Chinese
herb imaginable. On the left-hand wall, a
bamboo bookcase held teapots, rice wine,

and medicated honey. There were even Himalayan salt lamps and fingerless gloves up by the register for the local potheads who always wandered in.

Still, only certain customers were invited to the breakroom in back.

"This way," a young Chinese woman had offered when they first stepped inside. She wore a sage green uniform top with a logo of a lotus. A white cat lay asleep on the counter by her desk.

"I don't understand," Clementine whispered to Ezra, starting to panic as they followed the woman behind the counter and into the back.

**You'll see**, Ezra said with a glance.

Three seconds later, she did.

Reaching the small breakroom, the young assistant made a beeline for the huge refrigerator and tugged it open...

Then climbed in and kept going.

Inside, the fridge had no shelves. No back.

"This way," the young Chinese woman repeated, ducking her head and stepping into the hollowed-out refrigerator, which led them into the sterile beige room that was hidden so carefully behind the storefront.

A chubby Asian doctor in a white lab coat was waiting for them. Behind him was a medical rolling cart.

For the Chinese, the Russians, the North Koreans, and any other spy willing to pay cash, when an appendix ruptured or a broken arm needed to be set, Happy Jade Herbal Shop was less than ten miles from CIA headquarters, and just a phone call away. In-deed, as Ezra explained, even the very best of us sometimes need a doctor, a surgeon...or a dentist.

"我可以将它保存," the Asian man told Clementine, stuffing the tips of his fingers deep into her open mouth as she lay flat on her back on a massage table that was draped in a white sheet.

"He thinks he can save it," his assistant said, though neither of them sounded convinced.

Staring up at the swivel light above her—and trying to pretend that, through his surgical mask, she couldn't smell the whiff of eggs on the dentist's breath—Clementine nodded a hesitant thank-you, her mouth still wide open. There was no dental vacuum or little sink to rinse in. Every few minutes, she'd spit blood into a bucket. But based on the carefully set-out array of mouth mirrors, dental picks, and various-sized scrapers, the dentist seemed to know what he was doing. At least he was equipped.

Turning to the rolling cart, he reached for what looked like a narrow pair of pliers. **Pliers!** Clementine thought as he twisted the implement into her open mouth. Thanks to the Novocain, she didn't feel anything, but as he pulled the pliers out, she saw the grayish-white lump of flesh that came too. More dead gum.

"它看起来很糟," the dentist said in a low voice.

This time, the assistant just nodded.

Glancing sideways, Clementine saw that Ezra was no longer there. She knew he'd be back soon. Once his part of the bargain was done, Clementine had promised she'd make an introduction to Nico.

Over the course of the next two hours, the dentist drilled a groove behind Clementine's back left teeth, inserted a thin metal wire into that groove, and with a bit of cement to hold it, used the wire to tie her four back teeth together so they wouldn't fall out of place.

As he knotted the wire, he was pressing so hard on Clementine's mouth that tears spontaneously erupted from her eyes as her body tried desperately to protect itself.

**As long as I get to keep my face**, Clementine told herself, staring with determination at the blinding swivel light. When it came to what had happened on the island all those years ago, Beecher was searching for his father. Clementine was searching for something far more selfish. A cure. Or at least a treatment.

From the soft grin in the dentist's eyes, she thought all was probably going well enough. But the longer Clementine lay there on the table...and spit into the blood bucket...and felt the tears blur her eyes...she knew, even in the best of circumstances, this victory was nothing more than temporary.

Fighting cancer was hard enough. But fighting a rare cancer no one's ever heard of?

"她再次出血," the dentist said to his assistant. The assistant nodded, and this time didn't even look down at Clementine.

Staring up at the swivel light, her mouth open wider than ever, Clementine fought to keep her head still as the dentist knit the last knots together. With a final tug, he stood up straight, pulling his hands from her mouth.

"打开你的手," the dentist told her.

"Open your hand," the assistant said.

Before it even registered, Clementine felt the dentist uncurl her fingers and press a small white object into her palm. A tooth. Her back molar.

"From tooth fairy," the dentist said with a huffy laugh.

Lying there on her back and forcing her own shaky laugh, Clementine raised the fat tooth to her face. It weighed nothing.

She studied the two bloodied divots where the roots used to be. There was a metaphor in there somewhere: From her mother to her father, so many roots had been ripped from her life. And as she tried to save herself, she'd ripped so many roots from others.

As Clementine held the tooth up toward the blinding white swivel light, it seemed to disappear above her...and right there, for the very first time, she knew what the ending of this story would be. Had to be. For all the running around she was doing, for all the pain she put up with, there was only one way she was getting out of this.

"Tooth fairy. You know tooth fairy, yes?" the dentist repeated.

Clementine just lay there, staring up at the light.

Any minute now, Ezra would be back. By bringing her here, by getting her help... She knew it came with a catch. He'd want her decision: About her father. About their involvement. And of course about the Knights.

"Spit please," the dental assistant said, holding up the blood bucket.

Clementine blinked, but didn't move.

During near-death experiences filled with white light, some people find God or see lost loved ones. Today, in a make-shift dental office in Arlington, Virginia, Clementine stared up at a blinding white swivel lamp and found something else entirely.

There was no mistaking it. Her whole

body felt lighter as months of pain and fear lifted from her chest.

"You okay?" the dental assistant asked.

Clementine nodded, her eyes burning from the light.

Finally. She knew exactly what to do.

## 28

# Today
# Washington, D.C.

"Can we just agree there's no such thing as a good computer?" Mina asks, standing over her desk and squinting at her monitor.

"Can't find it?" I ask.

"No. Chill. It's here. Just in a different—" She's already moving, sidestepping me and headed to a small storage closet in the corner of her office. As Mina passes, she smells of old books and lavender shampoo. God, how good that smells. The fact that that excites me shows just how long it's been since I had a proper date.

"So now that you're in charge, what's the head Secret Service Archivist do?" I call out, trying to make small talk as I notice how neat her desk is. Funny. Most archivists are pack rats.

"Same as you," she calls back from the other room. I can see her through the door, her fingers walking along the spines as she scans a large bookshelf. "Preserving and cataloguing our current items, plus we get a lot of collectors. Every day, there's some guy saying he's got an old gun, or old metal baton, or a 1960s vehicle that was used in the LBJ administration, and could we please check the car's VIN number to verify authenticity."

Above Mina's desk, there're no diplomas, no vanity pics like you see in most D.C. offices. Instead, there's just a single framed poster from World War II, warning GIs about the dangers of malaria. **This Is Ann... She Drinks Blood!** the headline reads, pointing to a bright red cartoon mosquito with a crooked nose. But as I look closer at the mosquito and the crooked nose...

"Is this Dr. Seuss?" I ask.

"Kick-ass, right?" Mina calls back from the other room. "He and Walt Disney did tons of cartoons and posters during World War II. I know most people prefer Disney, but c'mon, Dr. Seuss didn't have to kill off the mother to make a solid plot line."

"Still, cartoonists fighting Hitler."

"Amen," she says. "Though still doesn't make up for Epcot."

I laugh. "You blame that on Walt? He died sixteen years before it opened."

"I blame so much on Walt," she tosses back.

As I scan the rest of her work space, I see it's pretty sparse. This is her new office. In fact, besides the Dr. Seuss on her wall and a pair of running shoes tucked beneath the desk, the only evidence of her actual life is a framed four-by-six photo with a newer, similar-sized photo propped against the frame. The newer photo is from the Archives. Her brother, in his wheelchair and with oxygen cannulas at his nose, holds up both hands in victory and flashes a frail but glowing smile. He's sitting right in front of the Declaration of Independence.

"Sorry...you weren't supposed to see that," Mina calls from the storage closet.

I keep staring at the photo. As an archivist, she knows the rules. When it comes to the Declaration, no pictures allowed. By anyone.

"We took it when you were in the bathroom," she explains, already apologizing. "You saw what kinda shape James was in. He barely lived another week. He just wanted the photo so bad—it made him so stupidly happy."

I nod, still focused on his proud smile and the way his crooked arms are up in victory. It's like looking at the photo of a kid you just heard was abducted. All you see is the lost potential.

"Christ on toast. You **knew**," Mina calls out.

I stay silent.

"You went to the bathroom on purpose, didn't you?" she says. "You **knew** what we were doing."

I still don't answer. On the day I gave them the tour, James said the Declaration was why he'd fought for this country. He deserved far more than just me faking a dumb bathroom break.

Still kneeling at a file cabinet in the storage closet, Mina stares over her shoulder at me.

"You would've done the same," I tell her. "In fact, right now, you kinda are."

Unwilling to argue, she turns back to the filing cabinet, more determined than ever to help. I turn back to the framed photo on her desk. It's of Mina.

I lean close. It looks like it was taken years

ago, at a school track meet. I remember
her mentioning that she liked to run, but
I've never seen this. In the photo, she's
in pain, crouched down on both knees,
head bowed. This isn't the thrill of victory.
It's young Mina meeting the agony of defeat.

**"And jackpot was his name-o!"** she
calls from the storage closet. Through the
door, I see her flipping through a stack of
old ledgers.

Wasting no time, I pull out my phone,
open a browser, and enter Mina's name,
along with the words **AT&T Indoor
Championships**, which are printed just
above the bib number pinned to her back
in the photo.

According to Google—and some track-
and-field website—Mina wasn't a runner.
She was a long jumper, a high school
and college star. The photo's from the
Olympic trials eight years ago. From what
I can read, she was the underdog, but
when she took second place in something
called Flight 1, she made it all the way to
the finals.

She lost by .02 meters.

Less than an inch.

I look back at her photos. In one, she's crouched in defeat. In the other, there's her dead brother. Most people keep their life's highlight reel on their desk, but these —the longer I look at them—something tells me they're the two worst moments in her life. For Mina, **this** is her motivati—

"Wanna tell me what's going on?" she asks behind me.

I spin, starting to apologize. But as Mina towers over me, she's holding the orange pin in one hand and an old, open ledger in the other.

"Where'd you find it, Beecher?"

"The **pin**?"

"Yes, the pin. Now answer my question."

"I already told you—"

"Tell me again. And this time, try including some truth. I appreciate what you did for my brother, but according to these serial numbers, this isn't just some random find."

"Mina, if you're accusing me of something, you have my word, I have no idea what it is."

She shifts from one foot to the other, digesting my reaction. "From what it says here, this pin went missing—and might've been worn by someone else—on a very specific day."

"And that day is?"

"March 30, 1981."

My face goes white. A chill spreads out from my chest.

March 30, 1981.

The day President Ronald Reagan was shot.

## 29

## Camp David

Every Secret Service agent has a day that's the most important day of their life. For Agent Scottie Koller, that day was today.

Looking back, Scottie could blame it all on a movie. When he was twelve years old, back in Hopkinsville, Kentucky, he was sick with diarrhea and home from school. His mom was the one who put it on: **In the Line of Fire**.

His mother had a crush on Clint Eastwood. Scottie fell in love with something else entirely: Brave men willing to take a bullet. Watching history from a front row seat. And of course, Rene Russo with a gun.

Scottie didn't rewatch the movie until years later, but like the best dreams, once they take root, they have a way of digging in. Even back then, it was so clear: wearing that crisp black suit; running alongside the

President's bulletproof limo; joining the Secret Service.

A decade later, when Scottie arrived for his training at the Service's Beltsville, Maryland, facility, six other agents in his recruiting class told the exact same story. To this day, **In the Line of Fire** remained one of the Service's best recruiting tools, which explained why, soon after it was released, the army and the rest of the military created entire departments to engage Hollywood.

At the time, for Scottie Koller, it was day one in the Service.

Today was day 1,927. Just over five years.

"Koller, from Command Post," a voice crackled through Scottie's earpiece as he lugged a bag of golf clubs down the outdoor slate steps and to the backyard of the President's elegant, California-style Camp David bungalow. "How're things looking? Are the golf clubs safe?"

"That's funny, Command Post," Scottie shot back through his hand mic, readjusting the golf clubs and approaching a wide patch of grass where the marines had already melted away the snow. The

President's private driving range. Didn't matter that it was always ten degrees colder at Camp David. Wallace was on his way; everything had to be ready. "By the way, I took a piss in your thermos yesterday," Scottie added.

"I know. That's why I switched my thermos with yours," Command Post replied as Scottie dumped the golf bag in the back of an all-terrain golf cart.

During Scottie's first couple of years on the job, he'd been one of the youngest at the White House…until the U.S. women's national soccer team came to visit and Scottie got caught hitting on one of the assistant coaches. The worst part was, he wasn't even hitting on her. That much.

These days, Scottie sat in the Baltimore field office, doing back-ground checks on new Service applicants. **The Rubber Gun Squad**, they called it. The only bone he was thrown was when the President came out to Camp David and they needed extra help doing perimeter checks. Usually, that had Scottie ruining his shoes as he walked through the surrounding woods. Today, though, they wanted him inside the fence.

"Homerun and Hyacinth are fifteen minutes," Command Post added, using the Service's code names for Wallace and the First Lady. Fifteen minutes until arrival. Time to clear out. Especially at Camp David, the First Lady hated to have agents lingering.

"Almost done," Scottie told Command Post, following his training and scanning the golf range from left to right, then up and down. The golf clubs were in place. Same with the cart. On his right was an extra sled for the kids. Everything was—

No. Everything **wasn't** in place.

At the foot of the slate stairs, just between two clumps of mountain laurel, two dull golf balls sat together on top of the dirt. Like they were meant to be noticed. For half a second, Scottie just stared at them, tempted to let them be. It was the marines, not the Service, who were supposed to keep Camp David clean. Besides, it's not like a few stray golf balls could do any harm.

Yet as he turned to leave, one thought rushed to the front of Scottie's brain, making him miss his dead mom and laugh in the same breath: No way would Clint Eastwood let those golf balls be.

"Koller, you clear?" Command Post asked in his ear.

"Almost," Scottie replied, kneeling down and angling his outstretched arm between the bushes. Stray branches poked at his face. "Lemme just—"

Like a skill crane with stuffed animals, Scottie squeezed tight, plucking the balls from the dirt. To his surprise, they weren't the only thing that came up.

Just beneath the loose soil, his fingers gripped what felt like a thick pipe. It was cold, frozen, and from the size of it, far wider than the irrigation pipes that ran through the backyard. It also felt crooked and slightly...hairy. Jumping back but still holding tight, Scottie thought it was a dead animal. Whatever it was, it wasn't buried deep. Clumps of dirt leaped in the air as it tumbled toward him. It landed hard. Scottie squinted through the shadows. At the very tips of it... Were those...? He leaned in closer.

Fingernails.

"What the f—!"

"Koller, you okay!?" Command Post barked in his ear.

Every Secret Service agent has a day that's the most important day of their life. For Agent Scottie Koller, that day was today.

**"Wave off!"** Koller shouted into his hand mic. "Wave Homerun off! He is **not** cleared for arrival!"

# 30

**Athens, Tennessee
Two weeks ago**

Nico was usually smarter than this.

**"What're you waiting for? Make a pick,"** the dead First Lady said.

Nico just stood there, scanning the vending machine that he'd been eyeing for two minutes.

**"Ooh, they got sunflower seeds. Full of healthy fats and only a dollar. Make a pick,"** she added, knowing that the longer he lingered, the more likely he'd be seen. Even in these small highway rest stops, there were always cameras.

Nico still didn't move, the brim of his Washington Redskins cap tapping like a woodpecker against the vending machine glass.

**"You're still thinking about Colonel Doggett, aren't y—?"**

Nico turned abruptly toward the main doors.

The First Lady knew that look. She also knew that Nico had more acute hearing than the rest of us. He was listening to something outside.

**"What's there? Police?"** the dead First Lady asked.

Nico shook his head, walking slowly as he eyed the front door. Whatever it was, it was still out there.

Again, Nico was smarter than this. Smart enough to eat at vending machines since it helped him avoid human contact. Smart enough to choose the smaller rest areas that had just bathrooms, rather than the big ones that had restaurants and tons of tourists. But as he pushed his way out of the faux-log-cabin building, he wasn't being smart.

**"What? You hear the people around back?"** the First Lady pleaded.

McMinn County, Tennessee, was a dry county, which explained the half a dozen cars that filled the narrow parking lot. With no place to drink, even on cold nights like this, locals used the picnic tables around back to create their own outdoor bar.

**"Nico, if someone recognizes you..."**

Picking up speed, Nico cut around to the back of the building. A few local high schoolers were scattered around picnic tables, nursing cheap beers. Weaving among them, Nico headed straight for the last table in back, by the edge of the woods.

**"Ephraim, don't!"** a girl with straight blond hair and a far-too-short skirt insisted. "They're private!"

"But you look so good in 'em," Ephraim teased back, holding a phone over his head as the girl jumped up, trying to reach it. Behind Ephraim, two other boys—red-headed twins—cheered him on.

**Four of them**, Nico thought. Of course there were four.

"C'mon, just a quick peek," the redhead on the left goaded.

"Ephraim, those were for **us**!" the girl yelled, her face growing red with rage, her beer spilling as she yelled.

"Baby, I just wanna show you off," Ephraim promised. "Didn't you say it turns you on? It'll be even better than—"

"Give her the phone back," Nico said.

The girl stopped jumping. All four turned

Nico's way. They weren't high school kids. They were older than that. Dumber too, judging by the Bud Light Lime beer they were drinking.

**"What'd you say?"** Ephraim challenged, taking a step toward Nico.

**"Nico, please don't do this,"** the First Lady begged. **"If they recognize you—"**

"Your girlfriend asked for the phone four times," Nico said, still locked on Ephraim. "Why aren't you listening to her?"

Ephraim stood his ground. Behind him, his two redheaded friends got up, all of them sticking their chests out and giving the international sign for **we're more than happy to beat your ass**.

Nico glanced at the girl. She had freckles. Just like Clemen—

A can of beer flew through the air, clipping Nico in the forehead. The girl. The girl threw it.

**"Who you think you are, bitch!?"** she shouted, running fast and shoving Nico hard in the chest. He stumbled backward, caught off guard. **"Answer me, you dickless runt!"**

Within seconds, the two redheads were

holding the girl back, making room for her boyfriend to—

Ephraim's punch came full speed, hitting Nico in the center of his face. A flash of black, then bright stars, took his vision. It was a fine punch, Nico thought. But he'd spent a decade in an insane asylum. He'd taken far worse than that.

**"Nico, you have my permission,"** the First Lady said. **"Eat them alive."**

Nico stood up straight, nodding a thank-you. The nearby crowd was already running, forming an instant circle around them.

"Lookit who's decided to fight back!" one of the redheads teased.

For Nico, old instincts kicked in, buzzing him with adrenaline and making him feel as charged and awake as that first night outside the hospital. His ears and teeth tingled. Above the cheers and yelling, he heard a hummingbird in the distance.

Yet as Ephraim stampeded toward him, fist raging like a freight train, Nico took a deep breath and simply...closed his eyes.

Ephraim's punch was a shovel across Nico's jaw, sending blood and spit flying as Nico spun, staggering sideways.

**"What're you doing!?"** the First Lady yelled. **"I know you saw that coming!"**

Ephraim wound up again, planting his next punch in Nico's gut, nearly lifting him off the ground.

**"There you go!"** the other redhead shouted, circling around and waiting for Nico to fall.

Nico stayed on his feet, swaying slightly, arms flat at his sides. He knew the way out of this. Jab his thumbs in Ephraim's eyes. Or use the pliers in his pocket to puncture Ephraim's windpipe. There were plenty of options.

**"Throw a punch! Do something!"** the First Lady demanded.

But again, Nico stood there, his bottom lip already swollen as an odd smile took his face.

"What's wrong with you? Stop smiling!" Ephraim shouted. He punched Nico again in the face. And again.

Behind them, Ephraim's girlfriend grabbed a nearby beer bottle, smashing it across the back of Nico's head. Nico weathered it. Last time he was tackled, it had taken half the orderlies on staff to bring him down.

**"Why aren't you fighting back!?"** the First Lady screamed.

Nico took another punch to the gut. He could've taken that too, but he decided to let gravity take hold. As Nico crumbled to the ground, Ephraim's friends rushed in and the kickline began. Within seconds, the mini-mob turned Nico's face, his body, any open area, into a soccer ball. Nico curled into fetal position, his hands clamped over his ears. But what the crowd couldn't see was that, even through the kicks that drilled his liver and made him nauseous, Nico was smiling wider than ever.

"That's enough. Let him be," someone finally announced. Ephraim's girlfriend spit in Nico's hair. Someone else poured beer on Nico's back.

As the group dispersed and the beer ran off him in a thin waterfall, Nico lay there, breathing heavily in the cold, wet dirt.

**"You happy now? Get what you want?"** the First Lady challenged.

Still grinning, Nico muttered something no one else could hear.

The First Lady rolled her eyes. Nico said it again. The same thing he'd said as Ephraim and his crew were kicking at his face. Nico was still whispering it now. A prayer. Always a prayer.

**"That girl was right. You're a sick bitch,"** the First Lady added.

And a lucky one, Nico agreed, feeling like his chest had been punctured. God had brought him so much lately—the blood of Colonel Doggett...and soon of Dr. Moorcraft. But as any good Christian knows, once sin shows its face, there can be no redemption—and certainly no salvation—until there's penance.

**"By the way, genius, they just put a switchblade in your tires,"** the First Lady added. **"And have you looked at your face? You put the whole mission at risk. You're not getting anywhere without help."**

Nico continued fighting for each breath, bloody saliva drooling from his mouth. He was barely able to move as his body trembled from the beating. "C-Call her," he muttered, pointing a dirt-covered finger to the pay phone by the rest stop. "We need to call her."

The dead First Lady knew who he meant. Not Clementine. He'd never ask more of Clementine.

Her.

The one who would help.

# 31

**Today
Washington, D.C.**

Mina, I promise you, I got the pin from a wealthy donor," I tell her.

"And I promise **you**, I don't care how nice you were to my family, if you don't take out the make-believe part of your make-believe story, I'm gonna pick up the phone, call the eighth floor, and we can have this same conversation in a locked room with half a dozen pissed Secret Service agents who would love nothing more than to work out their anger issues on your face."

I don't budge.

She reaches for her phone.

I still don't budge.

She starts pressing buttons.

"I took it off someone who threatened me," I concede.

Mina's eyes narrow. She doesn't believe it. But at least she's stopped pushing buttons.

"I swear to you," I add. "I was in the park... across from the White House. This guy approaches and flashes a badge, says he's Secret Service."

"His badge was real?"

"Looked real."

"But you didn't catch his name on his ID?"

"He did it fast. Trust me, the whole thing smelled. The only good news was, I knew about the pins and their serial numbers. Remember? We had a pin exhibit at the Archives."

"So you stole an agent's pin?"

"Fifty bucks says he's not an agent," I explain. "I figured if I could trace the pin, I'd find out more about him, or at least where he got it."

A soft beep-beep-beep erupts from her phone. It's been off the hook too long. She rests it back in the cradle, still holding the orange pin in her hand. "What'd this supposed agent look like?"

"Bald. Short." I look up at Mina. "Way shorter than you," I add. "Plus he had these eyelashes. Stark white."

"White?"

"I'm telling you. **Very Flowers in the Attic**."

"**What's Flowers in the Attic**?"

"Old scary book. Like **Children of the Corn**, but instead of corn, there's an attic. The point is, it's the truth," I insist. "But when it comes to the pin, what'd it have to do with the day Reagan was shot?"

"Oh, so even though you admit that you were lying, now I'm supposed to help you?" she asks.

"Mina, how long do you know me...?"

"That doesn't mean I know you well."

"...but I'm telling you, we're on the same side. I know what the Service does here. I **respect** what you do here. But if you don't tell me what's going on, I think you might be putting people in danger."

She lowers her chin. "Define **danger**, because if you know of an imminent threat—"

"I don't know anything. That's why I'm here. If you want, call...call A.J. Ennis," I say, already regretting the words. Bringing A.J. in creates its own risk. But right now, it's all I've got. "A.J's one of yours. Works at the White House. He'll vouch for me."

Her hand's still on her phone, but she doesn't pick it up.

"Mina, if I was the one you had to worry about, do you really think I'd be here asking these questions? Please. Tell me how the pin ties to Reagan."

She eyes the photographs on the corner of her desk. Her losing at the long jump. Her brother in front of the Declaration. The only thing worse than remembering the past is the fear of reliving it. She doesn't need any more regrets.

"Y'ever see the footage when Reagan was shot?" she finally asks, her voice sharp as ever. She won't face me; she keeps staring at her photos. "Reagan had just finished giving a speech at the Washington Hilton, and as he's leaving the hotel, about to get back in his limo, John Hinckley steps out of the crowd. Six shots are fired, the President goes down, and of course it's instant chaos. But y'know what also happens in that moment?"

"The Secret Service do their job," I say.

"That's exactly right. Bullet number one hits James Brady in the head. Bullet number two hits a local police officer,

Thomas Delahanty, in the neck just as he's spinning to protect Reagan. Then, as the President is completely exposed and the third and fourth shots ring out, Agent Timothy McCarthy spreads his body over Reagan, making himself the target as he takes a bullet in the belly, while Special Agent in Charge Jerry Parr quickly shoves Reagan into the limo, preventing what could've been a head shot. From there, it's the definition of pandemonium. More shots ring out. The crowd starts attacking Hinckley, pulling the hair from his head. And we're already blaming ourselves for screening everyone inside the hotel, but not screening anyone outside, including Hinckley, who made his way to the front of the rope line. But do you know why we can all live with it in the end?"

"Because the President didn't die."

"That's exactly right again," she says, finally turning away from her desk to drill me with her look. Most archivists are terrified of confrontation. Mina isn't terrified of anything.

"If Reagan had died," she says, "the investigations would still be going on. But since he lived, everyone was invited to the White House, where all the agents got a hearty handshake and a shiny new set of presidential-seal cuff links."

"So what's all that have to do with the orange pin?" I ask.

"On the morning Reagan was shot, our Protective Division issued forty-two special-admission lapel pins to our agents who were working the Hilton event. At the end of that same day, as Reagan was being operated on and the stock markets were closing to prevent a financial meltdown, forty-**one** lapel pins came back."

"You're saying the final pin was stolen?"

"Maybe it was stolen. Maybe it just fell off during the struggle with Hinckley. Don't forget, once the shooting started, agents were running through the crowd, getting knocked in every direction."

"So this pin..."

"Was assigned to an agent named Tanner Pope, who did presidential detail for nearly a decade. His dad was Secret Service too, long history. Anyway, when the Reagan shots were fired, the crowd turned on Hinckley so fast, some agents had to start throwing punches to protect him and take him into custody. Agent Pope was one of them."

I see the look on Mina's face. "But you don't think that's how Pope lost his pin, do you?"

"Here's the thing: Agent Pope was in the crowd; the crowd went crazy; the pin went missing. But. When you look at the actual evidence, there's a photo—just one photo—of Agent Pope earlier that day. It was taken inside the Hilton ballroom, before President Reagan even arrived. Pope's in the far background. And maybe it's the blurry picture...maybe it's the old, grainy film from the eighties...or maybe it's just a Secret Service fairy tale. But in that photo—taken three hours **before** Hinckley fired his shots—it looks like Agent Tanner Pope's pin was already missing from his lapel."

The room goes quiet as the heat in her office cycles off.

"I'm not sure I follow," I tell her. "You're saying John Hinckley used Agent Pope's pin to cut through the crowd and get to the front of Reagan's rope line?"

"That's one theory, though I'm not even sure it matters. In the end, Hinckley didn't need a pin at all. Thanks to our own security screw-up, it was open season on the rope line. But for the past three decades, Agent Pope's pin has been missing. Until you show up with it. Today."

"Can I ask a more basic question? Why's that so suspicious to you?"

She's watching me more carefully than I've ever seen her. "You really don't know, do you?"

"Know what!?"

She crinkles her nose like the Dr. Seuss mosquito on her wall. "Beecher, I've been in the top job for barely a month. So why do I know so much about Tanner Pope?" Before I can answer, she adds, "I recently got a call from his family. They were looking for his credentials as a keepsake."

"I'm not sure I follow."

"I'm trying to tell you," she says impatiently. "The owner of that pin—Tanner Pope... He was found dead three weeks ago."

The chill in my chest spreads outward, gripping my shoulders. As I close my eyes, I still see the photo that the President showed me this morning, of the arm they found in the Rose Garden. It was thin and gangly, which made me think someone young. But maybe it could've been this old man, Tanner Pope.

"Have you ever seen this before?" I ask, pulling a folded sheet of paper from my pocket. It's two color photocopies— both sides of the flattened penny they found in the corpse's hand.

"I just told you a man was dead," Mina says testily.

"I heard you. That's what I'm trying to help you with. Now have you seen this?" I ask again.

Mina eyes the Lord's Prayer on one side, then the other with the owl clutching the plank, plus the banner that reads **HL-1024**. "I know they're worn for good luck," she replies.

"What about the owl or the HL-1024? That mean anything in the Secret Service world?"

"What would this have to do with the Service?"

Before I can answer, my phone vibrates in my pocket. I shouldn't pick it up. The thing is, it's not my regular phone. It's the old flip phone that Marshall gave me two months ago—a clone of the one A.J. uses to make private calls. It's supposed to let me listen in, but over the past few months, the phone hasn't rung once. Until now.

"I need to take this," I tell Mina, flipping it open and hitting the **mute** button.

There's a click on the other line and I press the button to take the call. For the first few seconds, there's nothing but silence. Until...

"We got another," A.J. says in his familiar Tennessee drawl.

"Stick number two."

**Stick?** What's he mean by stick?

"You sure?" a familiar female voice asks. Francy.

"They just waved off his copter. He's headed back. You need to get here," A.J. adds.

Francy goes silent. There's a click as he hangs up. Message received.

"Beecher, did you hear what I just said?" Mina asks. "If you know something about Tanner Pope..."

In my right pocket, my other phone

vibrates. My real phone. Caller ID shows King's Copiers, a copy shop in Maryland that closed three years ago, if it was ever really open.

"Two phones?" Mina challenges as I pick it up. "Since when are you so popular?"

I hold up a finger, focusing on my cell. "Beecher here."

"It's me," A.J. says in my ear, careful to never ID himself. "We found another."

"Another what?"

He pauses, annoyed. "Another body part. Get your ass here now. We found a second arm."

# 32

**Twenty-nine years ago
The Atlantic Ocean**

I know where we're going," Julian said, his stomach pressed against the back rail of the boat as he coughed the last bits of vomit out into the ocean. "I know…"

No one heard him.

That's not true. They heard him. But in any group of kids, the first thing they found was weakness. Whatever Julian said, they weren't listening.

"I'm telling you: Cuba. It's Cuba," Timothy said, holding what looked like a spyglass to his face. It wasn't a spyglass. It was the scope they'd pulled from a rifle.

Ten minutes ago, Timothy, Nico, Alby, and the rest had pooled their money and bought a half hour of time with the scope from the guard, a marine who couldn't have been two years older than they were. It let them see six hundred yards, but at this time of night, there was nothing to see but black ocean.

"Cuba? It's the Bahamas," said an Arkansas kid with an oval face and a mullet that he didn't think was a mullet. "This far south, only thing here is the Bahamas."

"And Cuba," Timothy countered.

"They're not sending us to Cuba," Nico said, his strong baritone ending the argument. Kids found weakness first. They found leaders right after that.

"There's still the Cayman Islands. And Haiti," Alby called from the back left corner of the deck, where he was practicing the knots Colonel Doggett had taught them.

No one replied. Not even the ones lying on their backs next to him, trying to get some sleep. They hadn't thrown him in with Julian yet, but as they crowded around Timothy, still fighting for a look through the rifle scope, Alby knew it was just a matter of time.

Forty hours ago, when the trip first started, the young recruits had been guessing Hilton Head and Savannah. A recruit from Atlanta said there was a submarine base in Georgia. All they knew was the land on the right meant they were headed south. It wasn't until noon, when the burn of the salt water had them licking their lips and they saw the scaffolding for the rockets at Cape Canaveral, that they realized they were in Florida.

"Miami," Timothy had said, reigniting the speculation.

"There's an air force base south of Miami," Nico agreed.

It was a good guess too—until they zipped past the Miami skyline and the boat didn't slow down. On their right, as a late-summer darkness took the sky, ports, bridges, and white beaches became island after unidentifiable island. By midnight, they were in the Florida Keys, licking their lips harder than ever.

At 2 a.m., spotting the lights of Key West—the southernmost tip of the United States—they knew they had to be close. There was nothing south of that. They were tired and hungry, and most hadn't slept in nearly forty hours.

Yet as they blew past Key West and the lights of the docks faded into the wavy ink, the twelve newest members of the Plankholders fell silent.

"Have a nice night," the marine guard said, heading down to the galley and leaving them his rifle scope.

"Can someone tell me what the eff is going on?" Arkansas Oval-face asked, feeling the sway of the boat and glancing around at the black sky. The only thing darker was the ocean. All around them, there was nothing in sight. No lights. No landmarks.

"This is bad," Nico added, staring down at the compass on his watch. "It says we're still going southwest."

"Can't be," Arkansas said.

"Toldja," Timothy said, happy to have the rifle scope to himself.

"Cuba."

"It's not Cuba," Julian yelled out, though again, no one turned his way.

"Why do you keep doing that?" someone called behind him. Following the sound and keeping his grip on the boat's back rail, Julian turned to find the only kid skinnier than himself.

"You know they don't care what you say," Alby added, sitting Indian-style on the deck. "Why keep trying?"

"Because I'm **right**."

"Fine. Then tell it to someone who's actually **listening**," Alby said, tossing his rope up across the back rail and continuing to practice his knots.

As Julian's red hair whipped into a swirl, he didn't say anything. Next to him, Alby tied another knot.

"Julian, that's the cue that I'm listening."

"Yeah...no...I know," Julian stuttered, kneeling down, but still studying Timothy and the others.

Julian clicked his two front teeth against his two lower ones. "They think it's Cuba, but there's something else out there," he whispered. "This isn't the first time the government's made this trip."

"What're you talking about?"

"It's true. I read it in one of my books. The first time they came here was a century ago. They brought all the prisoners with them."

"Whattya mean **prisoners**?"

"The greatest of them all," Julian said, his red hair matted by a burst of wind as the boat continued to slice southward. "The men who killed Abraham Lincoln."

# 33

## Today
## Crystal City, Virginia

Elbowing open the door of his SUV, Marshall scanned the underground garage. He was the only one here. By design. Most people parked on the first basement level, or the one below that. Marshall always rode down to the fifth sublevel, until there were no other cars in sight. No one to stare at him or see him coming.

By now, anyone else would be celebrating. In his gloved hand, he held the sheet of paper the President had given him back at the hospital.

There it was in fat black letters: **The SS Needle's Nest**. The name of his father's ship, the first clue in figuring out what'd happened all those years ago, and the real reason Marshall had spent these past few months trailing Beecher for the President.

For sure, Wallace had given Marshall everything he wanted. Yet as he shoved open the red fire door, entered the fluorescent-lit concrete room, and headed for the dull silver elevator, he also knew that U.S. Presidents, and especially Presidents like Wallace, aren't in the business of giving people everything they want. In fact, what they usually give you is the very opposite of that, presenting you with just enough to make you feel like you owe them something in return.

Marshall knew the danger that came with debt. Especially when that debt was to a President. It was that exact thought that stopped him in his tracks as he spotted the call button for his loft on the twelfth floor. Every morning before he left, Marshall wiped the button clean. Now it was marked with a muddy smudge. Like a fingerprint.

In his right pocket, he put a hand on his switchblade. From his left, he pulled out a key fob, waving it at the small black rectangle set just above the call buttons. There was a reason he'd picked this building. No doorman to walk past, few tenants to stare at you...and a simple way to tell if anyone had dropped by while you were gone.

As the elevator rose, Marshall calmly bit off his gloves with his teeth. A jigsaw of light purple scars marked his hands. He extended all ten fingers in a wide stretch. For burn victims, as the healing begins and scabs shrink, the skin tightens. To counter the stiffness, every few hours Marshall stretched the skin on his knees, elbows, and fingers.

**"Fuuuuh,"** he growled, fighting the stiffness and pain that would never go away. It hurt even worse when he punched something.

Still eyeing the fingerprint, Marshall tried to tell himself it'd been the diplomat's kids from the seventh floor. They were always playing games and pushing buttons. But as the indicator above the door climbed from the ninth floor, to the tenth, to the eleventh, Marshall didn't let go of his modified switchblade.

At the twelfth floor, the elevator doors rolled open, revealing a small carpeted entryway and Marshall's front door. The door was slightly open.

He checked the lock. Still intact. Pro job.

His breathing slowed. Marine training

took over. Pulling his knife, Marshall popped the four-inch blade. He'd had it modified years ago, adding two grooves that ran down the center of both sides. When a normal knife entered someone, skin and muscle sealed around it. With the grooves, the blade was now what they called a bloodletter.

Inching forward, Marshall didn't arch the knife up by his shoulder. He held it at waist level, pointing outward, where it would do far more damage to vital organs. With the tip of the knife, he edged the door open.

Something moved on his right.

There. From the kitchen.

Her hair was brown now. Clearly a wig. But there was no mistaking those eyes. Ginger brown. And as crackling as her father's.

"Nice to see you too," Clementine said with a crooked grin.

## 34

"Where're you going!?" Mina calls out as I stride toward her office door.

"It's my boss. Work emergency," I tell her, halfway into the hallway as A.J. barks an address through my phone. He wouldn't call me unless he absolutely had to. That alone tells me there's more going on than another found body part. "Thanks for the help with the pin!" I call back to Mina.

She yells something, but as I pass the display case of Fallen Heroes, a galloping noise echoes above me. I follow the sound up—eight flights up to be exact—to nearly the top of the modern glass staircase, where a group of suit-and-tie agents plow down toward the lobby.

They move in a quiet, tight unit. As they get closer, from their ages, I'm guessing senior staff. No one's panicking, but in Secret Service headquarters, if you're taking eight flights of stairs instead of waiting for the elevator, someone's pulled the emergency cord.

"Believe me, I agree completely," a voice with a warm Virginia twang says. I can't see him at first. He's blocked by the group, but as they circle down the stairs and reach my floor, he pulls out in front, an enormous dark-skinned black man, clearly in charge.

Fine pinstriped suit. Gold pen that he grips like a sword in his left hand. Round tortoiseshell glasses soften the fact that he's a walking, lumbering mountain. Except for the American flag pin on his lapel, he looks like a linebacker, but his calm, commanding presence makes me want to jump in line behind him and follow him down the final flight of stairs.

"Director Riestra, your car's this way," one of his aides calls out as they cross through the lobby.

**Director.** No surprise. If A.J. found another body part, the biggest of big guns are getting called in. The head of the Secret Service. That still doesn't explain why he's calling me. There's something they're not saying.

At the sight of the big boss, two agents leaving the cafeteria freeze in place. So do the others walking the hall. Agent by agent, they all play Red Sea as Riestra plays Moses.

From where I'm standing, diagonally behind him in the corner of the lobby, Director Riestra can't see me, but I see him. He's about to leave the lobby, just a few steps past the cafeteria. Lifting his gold pen, he scratches his neck. And then, for no evident reason, Director Riestra glances over his shoulder, looks my way... and locks eyes.

My chest caves. It happens so fast, I'm not even sure I saw it right. Does he know me?

"Making friends with the boss now?" Mina asks behind me.

I jump at the sound. I didn't realize she'd followed me.

"What're you talking about?" I say. "He doesn't know who I am."

"I'm starting to think I don't know who you are either—or what you're really doing here," Mina says. "But let me tell you... **I'm going to find out**." Mina looks back at her director, staying silent. "I'm trying to help you, Beecher. I really am. But maybe it's best if you leave now."

She has no idea how right she is. I dart through the lobby. The director's already gone, but if what A.J. said is true—if they found a second body part and this is another inside job—I'm betting Director Riestra and I are headed to the exact same place.

## 35

"Please, before you say anything…" Clementine began.

"Get out of my house," Marshall said loudly.

"Can you please just—?"

"Why're you here? What're you doing?" he shot back, still holding his knife as he headed toward her in the kitchen.

"What's it look like? I'm **dying**."

Marshall heard the break in her voice. She was gaunt and pale. Her words sounded garbled, as if her tongue was swollen. Something was wrong with her mouth. He didn't care. "Do you think that what works on Beecher works on me?"

"Marshall, can you please just put the knife down?"

"Where's your father? He here too?" Marshall asked, striding through his 1990s-era IKEA living room like he was hunting. Shoving open the door to his bedroom, he went through to the bathroom, where he slapped open the shower curtain to make sure the apartment was empty. He never ran. Never panicked.

"Marsh, it's just me," Clementine said.

"**Marshall.** They call me Marshall now," he said, rejoining her in the kitchen, still scanning the apartment. "I haven't been Marsh since seventh grade."

"That's fine. But whatever you're thinking, this isn't—"

"Last time you came to help, your father escaped from the insane asylum and you disappeared with him. The time before that, you killed an Archives employee."

"That was an accident!"

"You also shot one of the President's aides in the neck. Want me to go on?" he challenged. "Are you with White Eyelashes?"

"Who?"

"Bald. Has an air of private-school jackassiness. White eyelashes."

"Ezra. His name's Ezra."

"Ezra. I see." Marshall glared at Clementine. Unlike most people, she looked him right in the eyes. Not at his candle-wax skin or his face. He'd been stared at enough to know the difference. He still didn't lower his knife. "Ezra's working with your father, isn't he?"

"Marshall, you have no idea what's going on."

"Just tell me why you're here. I know you always want something."

"I want you to put the knife down."

The knife stayed where it was.

"I get it. You have no reason to trust me," Clementine said. "I just need you to listen."

"Whatever you're about to say, I don't believe a word of it."

"You will. Please. Just two minutes," Clementine pleaded. "I think they're about to kill Beecher."

## 36

Most people walk right past it. The storefront door is boarded up, all the windows are covered with news-paper. There's even a sign taped to the glass that says

**CONTRACTORS
USE LEFT DOOR,
RING DOOR BELL THERE**

In this trendy newly gentrified neighbor-hood, it almost fools me into thinking I have the wrong address.

But here's the thing: One, I know this address. And two, I know what used to be located here two hundred years ago.

Back in 1996, this building at 437 7th Street, NW, was set to be demolished, until a local carpenter was sent inside to make sure no homeless people were lingering. As he walked into the front room, some-thing fell from the ceiling onto his shoulder. Looking up, he noticed a letter sticking out from a crack in the ceiling.

In the attic, he found stacks of Civil War–era newspapers, piles of old files, and thousands of mottled letters. There was also a sign for **Barton's Missing Soldiers Office**.

Over a hundred years ago, this redbrick building held the third-floor office where legend Clara Barton helped track down missing soldiers from the Civil War, long before she founded the American Red Cross.

Back then, Barton got over sixty-three thousand requests from families looking for lost loved ones. She and a small staff helped find twenty-two thousand of them, just by writing letters. It's one of the main reasons that, to this day, the army issues dog tags to people like my father.

For nearly two decades, promises were made to restore this building, but it's been sitting here since.

I lean toward the **Contractors** sign and see that in the corner, there's a tiny GSA logo. General Services Administration, the agency in charge of all U.S. government buildings and real estate.

I take that back. This structure hasn't

been sitting here at all. It's designed to look like a shuttered storefront, but this is an official—and officially hidden—government building.

I glance over my shoulder. Across the street, in the front window of the restaurant Jaleo, two men in suits sip coffee. Neither looks my way, but even from here, I see their earpieces and blue lapel pins. Secret Service.

It's the same when I ring the bell. The newspaper-covered door pops open. The lights are off. I can't see much. A shadowy figure grabs me by the arm.

"Let's go, Beecher. Quickly," A.J. says, tugging me inside and scanning the street for himself. "They're waiting for you upstairs."

## 37

She was breaking the first rule of the job. It wasn't a small rule either. It was a big one—the very first rule she was taught on her very first day: **Do the job you were hired for.**

Mina had nodded as her predecessor said it. When it came to the Secret Service, even the secretaries and support staff quickly got caught up spotting imagined threats. A few years back, the guy who washed towels in the Secret Service gym followed a suspicious-looking Saudi man for six blocks before realizing he was a diplomat.

So since the day she started, Mina Arbogast had always kept to the mission: **Be the Archivist. Do the job. Leave the investigating to others.** She'd never broken that rule.

Until today.

Was it a mistake? She was still asking herself that question, but when it came to Beecher, no matter how much she wanted to doubt him, all she kept seeing was that photo of her brother—crooked arms up in victory—and that nice guy who'd excused him-self to go to the restroom.

**Ping**, the elevator rang as it yawned open, revealing the ninth-floor hallway.

On 9/11, when the first plane hit, the head of the Secret Service ran up to the ninth floor. Years ago, when a ricin letter was sent to the Oval Office, that investigation was brought up here too. The ninth floor was the home of the director's Command Center and the Intelligence Division. Not the offices of the Archivist.

**Do the job**, Mina told herself, ignoring the Command Center and plowing toward the door marked **ITU**. Internet Threat Unit.

"Sign in," the receptionist announced as she buzzed the door open.

"How dare you show your face up here!?" a female voice called out.

To the right of the receptionist, from a nearby cubicle, a Hispanic female agent with mossy green eyes tipped back her chair, giving Mina a playful grin. Raquel Dominguez. Fellow female. Fellow mara-thoner. And based on the receptionist's stare, the perfect distraction.

"How's your knee?" Mina asked as she printed her name in the sign-in book.

"Better. How's your hip?" Raquel countered.

"Hurts when I run. Or walk. Crawling feels good, though."

"You should give it a rest before the marathon."

"I know," Mina said.

"But you won't."

"I know," Mina said, faking a limp and hobbling past the receptionist, who spotted Mina's ID and didn't even bother asking who she was here to see. With a wave to Raquel, Mina headed deeper into the maze of cubicles that was filled with so many young agents, they called this office the **Food Court**.

Throughout American history, the number one way to threaten the President has been via handwritten letter. Today, God bless Facebook, 80 percent of threats came through social media, which explained why every desk in the office was staffed with a clean-cut, fresh-faced agent clicking at a computer screen. Almost all of them were men, all of them in their twenties.

Except one.

"Mr. Goddard?" Mina asked as she approached the double-size cubicle in back. She called his name again before he finally turned around.

"Do I know you?" the older man asked, lowering his reading glasses. He had the sharp eyes of a professor and the well-trimmed gray goatee of someone trying to look younger than his sixty-three years. It didn't help.

Well known as the oldest agent on staff, Harlan Goddard should have retired a decade ago, but after taking time off to launch a failed private investigation firm, and then calling in favors to come back, he had less than a year to earn his full pension.

"I'm Mina Arbogast," she said, extending a strong hand. "From the Archivist's office."

Goddard looked at her hand but didn't shake it. "I thought the Archivist was that boring black guy with the wire glasses."

"He was. We upgraded."

Goddard rolled his eyes. "Is this something quick, or is it gonna be a pain in my ass?"

"Depends if you know your navy memorabilia as well as everyone says you do."

Goddard rolled his eyes again. "Listen to me, Mina Arbogast. I've been charmed by better than you. Just tell me what you want."

"I already did," Mina said, pulling a sheet of paper from her folder, slapping it against Goddard's desk, and revealing a photocopy of Beecher's flattened penny and the owl that was clutching a plank. "What can you tell me about this?"

## 38

## Two weeks ago
## Athens, Tennessee

Nico used to have dozens of them. Most were women; a few were gay men. All of them, back when he first pulled the trigger a decade ago, claimed to love him. Or at least wanted to help him.

When you try to murder the President of the United States, 99.999 percent of the country hates you. But infamy also brings you a few fans.

They start by sending letters. The desperate ones add photos. The naïve ones add gifts: brownies and homemade cookies that quickly get confiscated. Doesn't matter how bad the crime is. When the Boston Marathon bomber was arrested, dozens of young women built adoring webpages to get his attention.

It was no different for Nico.

Still, after year one, most of the groupies had faded away, especially when the trial ended and the circus lights disappeared. By year five, that number had been cut in half again. By year ten, only the dedicated were still writing a daily or even weekly letter. Four of them. Again four, Nico noted.

One of them was AnnaBeth.

She fit the profile: unmarried, slightly overweight, and a ton of love in her heart for strangers and for God. She wasn't weird or deranged. She was a bookkeeper at a local insurance agency and ran the canned goods drive for her church.

Nico? It was simple: Lifers made the greatest, most devoted boyfriends. Whether AnnaBeth admitted it or not, Nico wouldn't reject her, and he certainly couldn't leave her. When you factored in Nico's own commitment to God, he burrowed to the core of her dreams and vulnerabilities.

Years ago, at her church's summer camp, a counselor whose breath smelled like chocolate licorice had snuck into her bunk, held her down, and changed her life forever. She muttered prayers to herself as it was happening, but that didn't stop it. It continued for the next six summers she was at that camp.

When AnnaBeth was a child, no one saved her. But she could save Nico. And tonight, at nearly four in the morning in a grassy field behind a Tennessee rest stop, she would.

**"Nicky! Nicky, can you hear me!?"** AnnaBeth called out, bending down over Nico, her bulging eyes at full salute as her wiry black hair dangled in his face.

**"Nico, tell her I hate when she uses that pet name,"** the dead First Lady said.

Blinking back to consciousness, Nico glanced around to make sure this wasn't a dream.

"Mother of pearl, you scared me!" AnnaBeth added. "And your face—! Who did this t—?"

"You have a car, yes?" Nico asked.

"First tell me who—"

"You have a car. I need you to take me somewhere."

AnnaBeth sat up straight. Her eyes went even wider with excitement, like she wasn't capable of blinking. "Whatever you need. You know I'll take care of you." Over the past decade, AnnaBeth had visited Nico at least once a year. To finally be able to touch him, she still couldn't believe it. "I'm just so glad you called me, Nicky."

There were three other girlfriends Nico could've called. AnnaBeth was from North Carolina, closest to Tennessee.

**"You realize you'll have to snap her neck when we get there,"** the First Lady pointed out.

As AnnaBeth pulled him to his feet, Nico stayed silent. AnnaBeth slid an arm around his waist, and the two walked together to her car.

## 39

## Twenty-nine years ago
## The Atlantic Ocean

"Is this some made-up ghost story?" Alby asked, sitting Indian-style at the back of the boat.

"It's not a ghost story," Julian promised, licking salt water from his lips and kneeling on one knee for balance. It wasn't just exhaustion, or that it was the middle of the night. The water was choppy, shoving against the boat that sliced southwest through the darkness.

"Look it up yourself," Julian said. "John Wilkes Booth was the one who pulled the trigger, but back in 1865, in the months before he shot Abraham Lincoln, Booth plotted with a group of coconspirators. He wasn't working alone. He was—"

**"Guys! Guys, look at this...!"** Timothy whisper-hissed from the side of the boat as he peered through the rifle scope. **"I think I see something!"**

Like twelve-year-olds fighting over a nudie mag, the small group swarmed Timothy, elbowing for a view.

"Julian, you with me?" Alby asked, noticing how transfixed Julian was by the crowd.

Kneeling down on both knees, Julian had been picking at a sharp but narrow fragment of fiberglass on the boat deck.

"You were saying about John Wilkes Booth," Alby prompted.

"Yeah....no..." Julian said, now staring at the crowd, but knowing the consequence of joining it. "For me, it goes back to—Last week, when we all met on the plane, I was coming from Fort McNair. In Washington, D.C."

"What's that have to do with—?"

"Can you please stop interrupting? **Please**," Julian begged, picking at the fiberglass and wedging it under his fingernail to bend it slightly upward. "I'm trying to tell you: A hundred years ago, on what's now the tennis courts of Fort McNair, there used to be a penitentiary and wooden gallows. In the months after Lincoln was killed, that penitentiary held the eight coconspirators who plotted to kill Lincoln. Seven men and one woman—"

"Mary Surratt," Alby said.

"Mary Surratt. She was the only woman," Julian said with a nod. "On a sweltering July in 1865, after their sentences were handed down, a Union Army captain named Christian Rath marched four of those prisoners—Lewis Powell, David Herold, George Atzerodt, and Mary Surratt —out to the gallows and put nooses around their necks. He made the other four prisoners watch. Then, while Mary was screaming that she was innocent, Rath clapped his hands three times. On that third clap, his fellow soldiers kicked out the supports and Powell, Herold, Atzerodt, and Mary Surratt fell down through the gallows.

"Mary's neck snapped instantly, the first woman executed by our government. One of the other men wriggled there for a solid five minutes. Soon, all four were dead. And y'know what Atzerodt's last words were? **May we meet in another world**," Julian said. The words hung in the warm air.

Glancing to his left, toward the crowd, Alby noticed a fellow recruit trying to eavesdrop, though he was working hard not to look like it. The Boy Scout. Nico.

"What happened to the other four prisoners?" Alby asked.

"That's the question, isn't it?" Julian said as he continued to pick at the fiberglass deck, digging at it with his fingernail and bending the fiberglass upward. "Those four who weren't hung—Samuel Arnold, Ned Spangler, Michael O'Laughlin, and Dr. Samuel Mudd—were scheduled to be transferred to a federal prison in Albany. But in the middle of the night, a soldier woke them up, taking them out to a boat on the Potomac River."

"A boat?"

"Like this one. Unmarked. Meant to be unseen. Theirs was a medical ship. Mudd wrote about it in a diary. He figured they were being transferred to the prison in Albany..."

"Julian..."

"...but when the ship started heading south, he knew they weren't going to Albany anymore."

**"Julian, your hand!"** Alby said, pointing down to the gush of red blood pouring from Julian's finger onto the deck. He'd been pressing so hard, the shard of fiberglass had pierced his skin.

Nico and a few others started to stare. None of them came to help.

**"Guys, I swear to God I see something!"** Timothy called out, still looking through the rifle scope.

"See, it's already starting," Julian said as the crowd again began to rumble.

"What're you talking about?" Alby asked.

Julian sucked the tip of his bloody finger. "Don't you see?" Julian asked. "It's the same as a century ago. There's something bad about this place."

"What place? What're you even—?"

There was a loud pop. A bright magenta flash arced like a rainbow through the black sky. Flare gun.

**"There! You see it!? There it is!"** Timothy shouted as the light from the flare headed toward the water and revealed the outline of…something.

**"Holy… I see it!"** the kid from Arkansas joined in. So did an-other. Within seconds, a dozen young recruits were all pointing into the distance. They were in the middle of the ocean, but there was definitely something out there. Something big.

**Hukkkk**, the boat belched, jerking violently and slowing down.

**"On your feet. Here we go!"** the marine guard called out, racing up from the downstairs cabin. Behind him, Dr. Moorcraft with his Arthur Ashe glasses carried a rack of syringes holding malaria vaccines.

Hopping up and joining the line, Alby was still gripping his knotted rope. Next to him, Julian was still sucking his finger. There was another bright flash as the boat's white spotlight spun out toward the water, revealing what looked like...

**"That a castle?"** someone asked.

"Julian, where the hell are we?" Alby whispered.

**"A perfect hell.** That's what the Lincoln conspirators called it," Julian explained as a brick fort, wide as a city block, came into view. One of Uncle Sam's best hiding spots. "For four years, here's where the government hid them: seventy miles from Key West, on the edge of the Bermuda Triangle. Devil's Island."

## 40

## Today
## Washington, D.C.

At the top of the steps, carved into the closed wooden door, is an uncovered mail slot. This is where Clara Barton used to receive letters about missing soldiers. As I duck down to peek through it, the door swings open.

"You must be Beecher," a massive black man with round eyeglasses says. I recognize him from headquarters. Leonard Riestra, director of the Secret Service. Standing behind a short nineteenth-century dining room table, he's even bigger up close—a wide pitted face, deep-set eyes, and the thickest hands I've ever seen.

I brace for a fight. Instead, I get this:

"How're Tot and Mac?" he asks in a warm Virginia drawl.

"You know Tot and Mac?"

"I'm in charge of the Secret Service, Beecher. You think I've never worked with the Culper Ring before?" he asks, throwing in a generous laugh. He takes a seat on my right, leaving the head of the table empty. "Ever since I heard what happened, Tot's been in my thoughts every night."

His kindness comes on so fast, I can't help but doubt it.

In the corner, as I approach the table, presidential friend Francy O'Connor nods a respectful hello, like she's truly happy I'm here. What catches me off guard is, I believe her.

The only other person there is a trim but tired-looking Hispanic man who motions for me to sit next to him. He's in his late forties, with the receding, cul-de-sac hair-line to prove it. I'm guessing Riestra's right-hand man. He shoots a look to his boss. Whatever's going on, he's nervous.

I scan the rest of the room, searching for the President. There's a closed door in the corner, but it looks more like a closet. Other-wise, the room's been restored to its former Civil War glory, right down to the antique carved oak bookcase and the pale, vine-patterned wallpaper that fills the place with the smell of glue. Out of the corner of my eye, a shadow flickers through the carved mail slot, then disappears just as fast.

I can't help but think of Wallace listening in during our meeting in the White House basement. Despite all their saferooms, this is the second time they've picked a place off the beaten path. They keep telling me they need me, but I know who I'm dealing with. There's something they're still hiding. Maybe they're trying to stall me, keeping me away from somewhere else. Still, if they're working this hard to keep us off campus, they don't want their colleagues knowing. That alone is reason enough to see why I'm really here.

"This's who we're waiting for? This's him?" a voice calls out from what sounds like a speakerphone.

It's coming from Riestra's laptop at the center of the table. As Riestra spins it around, there's an older man with a gaunt face and a flattop of white hair. From his posture, he's military. At the bottom of the screen, it says **Cactus**.

Even without the Secret Service code name, I recognize the wood-paneled walls and the array of high-tech monitors behind him. I was there two months ago: the Service's command post at Camp David.

Now I know why they're nervous. Guarded by both the marines **and** the Service, Camp David has even better security than the White House—so if they found a second arm and it was somehow there...

"Len, you ask him yet or not?" the old man barks onscreen.

"Thanks for the subtlety," Riestra says, forcing a chuckle, this one more strained. He has a laugh like a drain sucking.

"Ask me what?" I say.

"Beecher, meet Dr. Malcolm Yaeger," Riestra says as the doctor snaps on a pair of light blue rubber gloves. "Dr. Yaeger is the medical examiner for Virginia's Tidewater district. He's also a Great Patriot."

I've heard Tot use those words before. **Great Patriot.**

Back in the eighties, when the hostages came back from Iran, a Great Patriot put them all up at the posh Greenbrier resort, so they could finally have a place to privately relax. More recently, after the CIA's annual retreat, a Great Patriot flew the top CIA chiefs to the small town of Cuero, Texas, so they could have their own private meetings and an off-the-book vacation. Sometimes, Patriots are former members of the government. Other times, they're simply regular citizens who step up when they're needed. Either way, who-ever Dr. Yaeger is, the President and the Service trust him more—and think he'll keep far quieter—than the regular D.C. medical examiner who would normally be assigned to this case.

"A.J. told you we found a second arm, yes?" Riestra asks, though I'm starting to realize he doesn't ask a question unless he already knows the answer. As I nod, he picks up his gold pen and glances over my shoulder at the open mail slot. I turn, expecting to see another shadow. Nothing's there.

"This second arm was buried in the garden, just behind Aspen," Riestra explains, referring to the President's private cabin at Camp David. "We brought in Dr. Yaeger to see if we have a match."

"Which we can't know yet," Yaeger shoots back, his voice high-pitched and meticulous. "Nothing's conclusive until we run DNA, but when you dismantle a person... Whoever dismantled this..." He puffs out his cheeks and holds up a wide towel that looks like gauze dotted with dirt. He doesn't have to say it. Whoever did this is a monster.

Sagging at the center of the gauze is a pale green arm, severed at the elbow. Like the one they found in the Rose Garden, its outer layer of skin is slipping and peeling away from decomposition. Unlike the other, the fingers are open, each slightly black at the tip.

"He went for the hard cut too," the doctor adds, pointing to the elbow. "Sliced between the radius and ulna, then tore the elbow joint. If you ask me, the shoulder's a far easier one to hack through. Other than that, the digits of both hands are similar in size and appearance. Ungual surface too."

"Ungual?" I ask.

"Nail bed. His fingernails," the doctor explains, cradling the arm like he's a pageant winner holding roses. "Both hands were . Either the victim was from money or liked to look like he was."

"And how old do you think the deceased was?"

"Late twenties, early thirties," he says, pinching the sagging skin. "Based on decay and disintegration, I'd say he's been dead two weeks tops," he adds as my mind flips back to Tanner Pope, the Reagan Secret Service agent who supposedly died three weeks ago. Pope was an old man. This corpse is someone young.

"That mean something to you, Beecher?" Riestra challenges. As I turn his way, I realize he's never taken his eyes off me.

I shake my head; Riestra keeps it friendly, deciding not to push. Once again, he glances back at the door's open mail slot. If he's waiting for someone, they're still not there.

There's a low buzz as Francy's phone vibrates. She pulls it out, checking who it is. When Riestra shoots her a look, Francy holds the phone up, trying to keep me from seeing it. Too late. Caller ID simply says SW. Riestra nods. Shona Wallace. When the First Lady calls, you don't ignore it.

"Malcolm, tell him what you said about the actual cut," Riestra prompts, though

I'm still eyeing Francy. Her call doesn't last long. Covering her mouth for privacy, Francy whispers something, then quickly hangs up.

"See for yourself," the doctor says on-screen, turning the elbow toward us. "Clean cut. Not ragged. He used something sharp like a butcher's knife. But when you look close, the multiple nicks in the cartilage and bone suggest it was probably something small, like a scalpel."

"Tell him abou—" Francy interrupts.

**"I wasn't finished speaking,"** Yaeger growls. "And just so we're clear, as far as I'm concerned, we don't need you here."

Francy starts to speak, but Riestra shuts her down with a cold glare. It reminds me of our time in the White House basement. If what Francy said is true, she's not entirely sure why Wallace hates me—or what he did all those years ago to put that kid into a coma. It's a detail worth holding on to.

"Malcolm, you were saying..." Riestra adds.

"What I was saying," the doctor continues, "is that when you look at the margins where the arm was severed, the skin is yellow and waxy at the edges. No bruising whatsoever."

"Which means?" I ask.

"Means it was done post-mortem. Whoever chopped the victim's arms off, he waited until he was dead," the doctor clarifies, his voice slowing down as he turns his gaunt face toward me. It's the same around the table. On my left, both Riestra's balding deputy and Francy are watching my reaction closely. On my right, Riestra's clutching his gold pen tighter than ever.

I stare back at all of them. "What's really going on here?" I challenge.

"I'm not sure I follow," Riestra says.

"I appreciate you inviting me here—and especially for catching me up to date. But considering I don't know the first thing about forensic science...and that the director of the Secret Service probably doesn't ask for much help from local archivists...and that there are a few hundred more reasons I shouldn't be here, I can't stop wondering: Why'd you bring me here?"

Riestra taps the side of his glasses with the back of his pen.

"You found something in the second

hand, didn't you?" I challenge.

Still no answer.

"I heard what Dr. Yaeger said," I continue. "The cuts were the same, the blades were the same, even the polished fingernails were the same. So considering that when I spoke to the President this morning, he told me that the Rose Garden arm was clutching a flattened penny that traced back to my dad, let me just ask: What'd you find in the new arm, and what's it have to do with my father?"

Looking over my shoulder, Riestra eyes his deputy. The deputy shakes his head.

Ignoring him, Riestra turns to the computer screen and throws a silent nod at Dr. Yaeger. "Tell him, Malcolm."

"Len..."

**"Tell him,"** Riestra says in a tone that reminds everyone he's in charge of a multibillion-dollar fighting force that could take out most small countries.

Onscreen, Dr. Yaeger again puffs out his gaunt cheeks. He holds up a white index card, aiming it at the camera. It's no bigger than a baseball card, but with vertical and horizontal creases, like it's been folded and folded again. "When they dug up the new arm, this was found in his fist," the doctor explains.

"I don't understand."

"Neither did we," the doctor says. "It's blank on both sides. Francy said you've seen that before."

He flips it over, then back again. It's definitely blank. But the instant I see it, I'm reminded of the one suspect they're always looking at—the person who used to live in St. Elizabeths—and the one subspecialty where I'm the true expert.

Nico.

"You need to pee on it," I blurt.

## 41

## Twenty-nine years ago
## Devil's Island

Today, it was bricks.

"Six more?" the marine guard named Dominic asked.

"Yes, sir," Timothy agreed as the guard stacked another six bricks onto the double-wide stack that Timothy was struggling to carry.

"Six more?" Dominic said to the next person in line—Arkansas Ovalface—who was already carrying nearly twenty.

A single bead of sweat rolled down from Arkansas's freshly buzzed brown hair. This time of day, it had to be at least 110 degrees. "Yes, sir," he replied as Dominic added six antique redbricks from the messy pile on the edge of the island's beach.

As Nico stepped up, he was carrying a triple stack. On day one, when the new recruits were moving rocks for a retaining wall, Nico had carried the most. Same for day two. Today was day nine.

"Eight more or ten more?" Dominic challenged.

Staring down at the pile of bricks he was balancing against his still-new camo uniform, Nico stayed silent. His legs were swaying. His eyes started to flick back and forth. He thought it was because of the heat or the lack of sleep. Just like he thought his constant diarrhea was from something he'd eaten.

"You know best, sir."

"Good for you. You're learning, Nico."

"But Sergeant, if we could just use the wheelbarrow, our speed would—"

"A full dozen it is," the guard said, gathering up another twelve bricks and dropping them one by one on the pile for maximum effect. "Alby, six more?" Dominic added, turning to the next person in line.

Alby had seen **The Karate Kid** enough times to know that when they tell you to sand the floor, you **sand the floor**. "Yes, sir," he said as Dominic gave him six new bricks.

"What about your friend? Where's he?" Dominic asked.

"Julian? He's on his way."

"You sure? Because by my count, he's been gone twenty minutes. Now, let's try this again: **Where's your friend?"**

Alby didn't answer, feeling that familiar pinch in the back of his neck. He didn't like lying.

"Alby, do you have any idea why this place was built?" Dominic asked, pointing over Alby's shoulder at the island's only real feature: the six-sided redbrick fortress known as Fort Jefferson. "Back before the Civil War, our government was worried about foreign enemies invading the southeastern tip of America. So they spent decades shipping in sixteen million bricks and building these massive walls. They put in a moat that ran all the way around... and the cannons that you see up top?" he said, pointing up to the twenty-five-ton Rodman cannons, a few of which still pointed out over the parapet of the fort's outer wall. "At one point, those were the most powerful guns in the world, making this place the most impenetrable and expensive coastal fort ever built. It rivaled the biggest and best castles in

Europe. Nothing could get through it," he explained. "And then the steamship was invented, along with artillery that plowed through brick like it was a pillow fort. By the time the Civil War began, no government in the world was building forts like this anymore. The whole place was obsolete. Abraham Lincoln turned it into a prison for Civil War deserters, and it was quickly overrun by mosquitoes and malaria."

"I'm not sure I understand, sir."

"Alby, our job today is to build that next steamship, that next tank, that next type of soldier that no one sees coming. That's why we brought you here. If we build you right, we'll plow through our enemies. If we build you wrong, they'll be plowing through us."

"And by **us**, you mean Julian."

"By us, I mean **all of us**. Including Julian," the guard said, grabbing four bricks and adding them to Alby's stack. "We all know Julian's struggling. Help him help himself. You need to find him.

Now."

"I am... I'll find him, sir," Alby said, fighting to cradle his bricks like a lumpy bag of groceries. Alby had always been a nervous per-son, but after everything he'd been through—from the plane crash to a week on the island—he was starting to feel it physically. The ache in his neck had swelled into a thick knot at the top of his spine. He told no one. Like Nico, Alby never let on he was in pain.

"I'll find him right now," Alby added, tripping through the sand as he sped back toward the main entrance to the fort.

As Alby headed through the shaded brick archway, he stared at the four narrow vertical slits on either side of him. **Loop-holes.** Three centuries ago, if an enemy approached the castle, archers would stand behind the walls and point arrows through the slits, killing the attackers from a protected space. Once arrows became obsolete, they did it with guns. Over time, the word **loophole** came to mean **something to exploi**t.

"You seen Julian?" Alby called out to the tall kid from Texas who was racing past him in the fort's grassy courtyard, a sixteen-acre plot that was dotted by date palm trees and patches of windblown sand.

The tall Texan ignored him. No one wanted much to do with Julian. Or Alby, for that matter.

"Bricks **here**!" another marine guard yelled, pointing Alby to a nearby pile, where Nico and Timothy were dumping their own. Next to them, two other recruits were laying the foundation of a small rectangular structure about as long and wide as a racquetball court. At first, Alby had thought it was going to be a retaining wall or a drain, but the walls were getting too high.

"Anyone seen Julian?" Alby asked. Again, they ignored him.

Adding his bricks to the pile, Alby scanned the wide courtyard. On his left were the concrete barracks. On his right was the New Orleans–style redbrick house with a square porch that served as officers' quarters. Otherwise, most of the fort was empty and abandoned, except for the section that was...

Of course.

The prison cells, where Dr. Mudd and the rest of the Lincoln conspirators had been locked up a century ago. Yet just as Alby started to run, a flash of orange caught his eye. There, on his right. By the sliding yellow pine door marked:

## MECHANICAL AREA—DO NOT ENTER.

From the angle and the way the sunlight pried though the open door, Alby knew that flash of orange anywhere. Julian's red hair.

**What in the hell's he doing?** Alby thought, making his way to the door. Behind him, Nico and Timothy were headed back for more bricks. The other marine guard and his fellow Plankholders were back to building the brick structure. As usual, nobody was looking at Alby.

Tugging the pine door open, Alby snuck inside and slid it shut. He was hit with a whiff of stale rainwater and the even staler smell of urine. Along the back wall were three rusted generators. On the left wall were milk crates filled with rusty tools. Julian was down on his knees, hands at his chest, his back to Alby.

"Julian, you okay?"

Julian didn't answer.

"Why're you—?" Alby cut himself off, stepping closer. "Are you praying?"

Still nothing.

"Julian, can you please not be crazy for once? They're gonna crucify you. Sarge knows you're not working!"

Julian turned, but just barely. He smacked his lips. "Alby, how've you been feeling?"

"What're you talking about? C'mon, we gotta go!"

"Answer my question. Since we got to the island...have you felt well?" Julian asked, turning some more. There was something in his hands. A thin paperback book. Julian wasn't praying. He was reading. "Alby, I think I found it."

"Found what?"

"What we're making. All this work...all these bricks," he said, smacking his lips again. "Do you know what we're building out there?"

"A retaining wall...an outhouse... Doesn't matter what it is. It's training—they make us work until—"

"An oven," Julian blurted.

"A what?"

"A furnace. That's what **these** are for," he said, pointing to the corner of the dark room where there was a messy pile of iron rails, thick like pool cues, but each one at least twenty feet long. Next to them was a neat stack of black metal grates, like you'd see on a barbeque.

"Julian, when was the last time you had something to eat? You don't look so—"

"It's in this book. I found this book," Julian said, his eyes dancing faster than ever as he held up an old paperback. It had a white cover and a black-and-white photo of a nineteenth-century balding man with an overgrown, pointy beard. **Dr. Samuel Mudd**, it read in thick letters. One of Lincoln's famous killers. "The structure we're making...it used to be here back when he was here...back when the fort was first built. It's called a **hot shot furnace**."

"Let's get you out of here. You need water."

"You're not listening to me, Alby. This is technology from ancient Rome. It was one of the world's first super-weapons. The Romans would build a long brick furnace, like two lanes of a bowling alley. Then they'd take cannonballs and roll them down these sloping iron rails which sat above the flames. When the cannonballs came out the other side, they'd be heated to over a thousand degrees. Then they'd fire them at attacking ships, where the balls would skip across the water. A regular cannonball does enough damage. But these heated ones would set your ship on fire. Instantly."

"Julian, maybe you should—"

"So elegant, isn't it?" Julian asked, gripping one of the black grates and resting it in his lap directly on top of the book. "Sometimes I wonder if that's our real specialty as a people: We forever get better at killing ourselves."

"Not **ourselves**," Alby said. "An enemy. All this training is to fight an **enemy**."

"Yeah, no..." Julian said, staring down and letting his open palm hover above the black grate in his lap. "That's what I meant."

# 42

## Today
## Washington, D.C.

A.J. counted the steps. There were sixteen in all.

In the world of the Secret Service, the agent closest to the action—the one whose shoulder practically touches the President as he moves through a crowd—is said to be **an eyelash away**. The agent who rides shotgun in the presidential limo is said to be **an arm's length away**. And the one who sits in the back of the ambulance, trailing the motorcade and guarding extra pints of the President's blood, is **thirteen cars away**.

Right now, as Agent A.J. Ennis stood heels-together on the gray-and-rose-colored needlepoint rug at the base of Clara Barton's refurbished staircase, that number was **sixteen steps**. Not bad, really. Unless, of course, you're used to being an eyelash.

"How's it going?" A.J. texted to Francy, who was upstairs in the room with Beecher and Director Riestra.

A.J. stared down at his phone. Ten minutes passed. Francy didn't text back.

Glancing up the sixteen steps, A.J. had a clear view to the second floor. There was a closed door and a glow of light coming from the open mail slot. It'd be easy to climb up and eavesdrop through it. But even A.J. wasn't that paranoid.

He didn't blame Francy for being inside. The President and Francy had spent decades together, come into power together, and even sat at the deathbed of Wallace's mother together. To the First Lady especially, Francy was family.

But A.J. was family too. Thirty years ago, A.J.'s father had been one of President Wallace's dearest law school friends. They were in each other's wedding parties. In fact, during their last semester together, when money was so tight that the school wouldn't let the future President register for classes until he paid his tuition bill, A.J.'s father had called his own father. The next day, an anonymous donor wrote a

check that settled Wallace's law school bill.
It was never again discussed. But like in
any family, it was never forgotten.

Years later, A.J. didn't use his connection
when he applied for the job. The Service
knows talent when it sees it. But as he
rose through the ranks and made his way
to the President's Protective Detail, it did
explain why Wallace began asking for him
personally. During those first few months,
the President put his life in A.J.'s hands—
and after those trips to Blair House and
Lake George and of course that off-the-
record trip to Ohio that tested his loyalty,
A.J. began to put his life in the President's.

Yet despite everything he'd done for
Wallace and all the secrets he was keeping,
A.J. was still here, standing heels-together
on the needlepoint rug, staring up at the
closed door, sixteen steps from the action.

**Not a big deal**, A.J. told himself, though
he couldn't help but think that the same
thing had happened earlier at the hospital
when the President and Francy met with
Marshall. They were in. A.J. was out.

Once again squinting up at the mail slot,
A.J. put the tip of his foot on the first step.

Then took it off. Every day, he saw staffers vying to fight their way into the President's inner circle. But as everyone in that circle knew, the worst smell of all was desperation.

**All is fine**, he insisted to himself, well aware he was still wearing the blue-jeweled lapel pin that signaled his proximity to the President. **They'll tell you everything when it's done.** Just having Beecher up there—not to mention his direct boss, Hurricane Riestra— Francy already had enough to deal with.

It was good advice. It was the right advice.

But as A.J. stood at the foot of those sixteen steps, that didn't mean he believed it.

## 43

**"Pee?"**

"Trust me. Urinate on it," I tell Dr. Yaeger through the computer teleconference.

"Invisible ink," the director of the Secret Service says.

Riestra knows what he's talking about. Two months ago, I caught Nico using invisible ink to hide secret messages on a set of playing cards. It was a magic trick he stole from George Washington himself, who, as head of the Culper Ring, used invisible ink to hide his own Revolutionary War secrets. It wasn't a new trick. Invisible ink dates back thousands of years, from Egypt to China, using the juices of leeks, lemons, and limes. But as every science fair winner knows, if you write something in lemon juice, all you need to do is hold a hot candle to the paper, and presto—you bring the secret message to life.

For that reason, George Washington decided to replace the **heating** process with a **chemical** one. Washington wrote his notes in an invisible ink, called the **agent**. Then when the recipient applied a different chemical, called the **reagent**, the hidden message would appear. As long as the British couldn't find the reagent, they'd never crack the code. It's a trick our government still uses today.

"You think we didn't know it was invisible ink?" Dr. Yaeger asks. "I tried every reagent we have—from the Service's private formula to the CIA's...even MI5."

"You're forgetting who you're dealing with," I point out. "Nico was locked in St. Elizabeths for nearly a decade with no chemistry set. The only liquid he used there was the one he always had immediate access to."

Onscreen, the doctor stares down at the blank index card they found clutched in the hand at Camp David. Next to me, Francy and Riestra's deputy are so silent, you can hear the wallpaper glue hardening.

"Go piss on the paper," the head of the Secret Service says.

## 44

"Where'd you get this?" Agent Goddard asked, hunched at the desk in his cubicle, his tongue flicking the stray hairs of his gray goatee.

"A friend," Mina said, staring down at the photocopy of Beecher's flattened penny.

"And your friend's sure this was a navy unit?"

"That's what he said."

"Then why didn't you bring your friend with you?" Goddard asked.

"He's not a fellow employee."

Goddard looked up, his professor eyes simmering and starting to boil. "Mina, I'm Danny Glover in every **Lethal Weapon** movie. I've got 133 days until retirement. So if you're bringing me a tornado of feces…"

"This isn't a tornado. It's nothing bad. It's official Service business," Mina promised, watching Goddard again look down at the image.

"You see something, don't you?" Mina

asked. "The owl and the Lord's Prayer. They're not just…they stand for more than just an owl and the Lord's Prayer?"

"Actually, I think they're pretty much exactly that: The Lord's Prayer is always on these pennies…and the owl with the plank is clearly the mascot for whatever unit this is. But what I'm more interested in is this…" he said, stabbing a papery finger at the inscription below the owl: **HL-1024**.

"That's not their unit number?" Mina asked.

"That's not how unit numbers run," Goddard explained. "Navy units are usually single or double digits—like Squadron 7… or the **Nimitz**, which is CVN-68—but I can't think of a single navy squadron that has three digits, much less a four-digit one like 1024. Even army units usually only have three digits. I think the only four-digit ones are reserve units or medical ones. Like the 4077."

Mina stared at him.

"From **M\*A\*S\*H**," Goddard explained. Still nothing.

He rolled his eyes and turned back to the

image of the penny. "What's even more hinky is this so-called **HL** part," he added. "In the navy, we have HS squadrons like the HS-10, which does helicopter anti-submarine work, or the HSC-3, which does helicopter sea combat. There's even **HSL** and the newer **HSM** squadrons. But I can't think of anyone that's an **HL**."

"So HL-1024..."

"It's not a unit number. In fact, if I had to guess..." Goddard leaned in closer, squinting to see the tiny writing. He studied it in silence.

"I think it's a map," he finally blurted.

"A what?"

"A map. Look at the format—HL-1024—two letters followed by four digits. That's the standard format on nearly every military map in existence: two letters, four digits."

"So this is someone's map?"

"Or the whole unit's map. Maybe it's where they were founded, or had their first battle. Whatever it is, if I'm a betting man, and I'm always a betting man, I'd wager that what you're looking at are **coordinates**."

As Goddard handed her the photocopy,

Mina reread the **HL-1024** for herself. "Can you tell me where this map is pointing?"

"Nope," Goddard replied, tonguing the corner of his goatee. "But I know someone who can."

## 45

## Ten days ago
## Carter Lake, Iowa

"Mother of pearl, what a neighborhood," AnnaBeth said, ducking down to peer out the car's front windshield.

"It will be on our left," Nico said from the passenger seat, staring straight ahead and showing no interest in the upscale homes of Shoreline Estates.

It was still dark, so early in the morning the newspapers hadn't been delivered yet. It'd taken longer than they'd thought to reach Iowa. To hide, they'd traveled only at night, plus an extra day just to deal with Nico's injuries. In the motels, AnnaBeth and Nico never slept together. Never kissed. Barely even touched, which AnnaBeth took as a blessing. Courtship first. Sometimes she put her hand on top of Nico's, and he wouldn't pull away.

**"When you tear her throat out, you think you'll be able to see her in ghost**

form, like me?" the dead First Lady asked.

Nico didn't answer. He'd been thinking about it. Usually he continued to see his last victim, but with Colonel Doggett, nothing had happened.

**"Maybe it only works with women,"** the First Lady added with a laugh. **"Though let's be honest: What would you do without me?"**

**"Here.** This one," Nico told AnnaBeth, pointing at the outdated, stone-fronted ranch house with the Christmas wreath still on the front door. The home belonged to Dr. Moorcraft, who used to give Nico, Alby, and Timothy all those vaccinations on the island.

"Your friend is going to be so excited to see you. So thrilled," AnnaBeth said, her round face beaming, her voice so excited it popped like fireworks. She reached over to the center console and put her hand on top of Nico's. "And when he helps you clear your name— He must be a lawyer, a big lawyer—"

"If I wanted to tell you about him, I would," Nico blurted.

AnnaBeth shrunk in her seat, but not by

much. On the center console, Nico still hadn't pulled his hand away.

**"How do you think she'd react if she knew what you were about to do in there?"** the First Lady asked.

Nico's eyes slid sideways, up the long driveway, to the overbuilt beige house with the Christmas wreath. For all these years, this was where Moorcraft had been hiding, in Iowa.

"Don't park in front," Nico said, pointing her toward the house next door.

Halfway up the block, AnnaBeth shut the car off and unclicked her seat belt. Nico shot her a look.

"I can wait here if it's easier," she offered.

"That'd be better," Nico said, staring at her until she reclicked her seat belt. If something went wrong, at least she could drive him out of here. Kicking open the door, he added, "This way I can surprise him."

## 46

## Today
## Crystal City, Virginia

"You don't believe me, do you?" Clementine asked from the kitchen.

"I told you I wouldn't," Marshall shot back, still holding his knife as he glanced back toward the living room. "I don't believe anything you say, Clementine."

"But if they go after Beecher—"

"No. Enough lying," he said, turning toward her, then back to the living room.

"Why do you do that?" Clementine interrupted.

"Do what?"

"That thing with your head. Every time you talk, you turn away. Are you—?" She went to say something, then decided against it. "You're worried about your looks?"

Locking back on her, Marshall took a deep breath through his nose. Like an ox. "Don't play the burn card with me," he warned.

"Wait, wait, wait...or are the burns— Is that why you live like **this**?" she continued, pointing toward the living room starter sofa, glass-and-metal coffee table and matching glass-and-metal entertainment center. "That came right out of the catalog, including the little candy dish and the candlesticks, didn't it? You've got no photos, no picture frames, there's not even a single book in the whole apartment. C'mon, the only personal effect here is that painting," she said, motioning toward the far right wall, at the elegant painted canvas barely bigger than an iPad. It was of a woman with blurred eyes and no mouth. As she enters a soothing, turquoise body of water, her arms and torso dissipate, spreading outward and becoming part of the water. The signature at the bottom read **Nuelo Blanco**. "I looked Blanco up, Marshall. That's a forty-two-thousand-dollar painting. So let me ask: Is this even your real life, or just another front where, if something bad happens, you can grab the painting, run off, and rebuild the way your dad did after your mom died?"

"Don't talk about my parents either. I know how you fight: gouging and biting down through whatever emotion takes you inside. You're like a termite."

"And you're a mule," she shot back. "I just told you they're trying to kill your pal Beecher, and you just stand there with no reaction, turning away and worrying about what I think about your sad burned face?"

Marshall refused to take the bait. "Y'know what I remember about you, Clementine? Your earrings."

"My **what**?"

"Back in seventh grade, there was this girl from the high school who you picked a fight with."

"Kathy Stankevich."

"Whatever her name was. She was waiting in the schoolyard, and when they came running to your locker to tell you, I was right there in the hallway. They said this girl was waiting outside to fight you, and I'll never forget, when you heard those words, you took off your earrings, stuffed them in your pocket, and stormed, fists clenched, out to the schoolyard. Always looking for a fight."

"You know what I remember about you,

Marshall? When we were in third grade, everyone at church pitched in to buy you a bunny. They said you wanted a pet."

Marshall didn't react.

"We all know why the town did it. You were the poor kid whose dad was paralyzed in a wheelchair. Every Christmas, they felt the need to buy you something, and that year, it was a bunny."

"What's your point?"

"The point is, later that year, when the church made all of us go to your birthday party, my mother took that bunny home with us. Y'know why? Because when she saw it in your house, that bunny hadn't been played with in so long, its nails actually grew and curved around the outside of the metal cage."

Marshall's stiff posture never wavered. "I was allergic. My mother kept it in her room."

"I didn't say you did it on purpose, Marshall. I said you did it **years ago**." She kept her eyes locked on his. "When you know of an old disaster in someone's life, all you see is who they were. But none of us are who we used to be."

Glancing down at the floor, Marshall

extended all his left-hand fingers, stretching the skin. He knew who Clementine was. He knew her disasters. And he also knew she was right. "Who's **they**?" he finally asked.

"Pardon?"

"Before, when you first mentioned Ezra, you said they want to kill Beecher. Always **they**. Who's **they**?"

Walking over to the sink, Clementine spit out a mouthful of blood. It wasn't a quick spit like a baseball player in a dugout. It was a slow-motion one, gathered by her lips, then dangling down like a tear on a shiny spider's web. "Ever hear of the Knights of the Golden Circle?"

## 47

## Twenty-nine years ago
## Devil's Island

Today, it was cannonballs. Or at least it was supposed to be.

At 4:40 a.m., Alby's alarm ripped him from a dream where he was doing that trick he used to do in the kitchen: walking with his three kids—his two daughters and young Beecher—wrapped around his ankles, dragging them playfully along. In the dream, though, he was walking into the ocean, all of them sinking from the weight and drowning.

For the past week, as they were finishing the brick furnace, he'd spent his breaks on the edge of the island, staring out at the blue-green ocean and telling himself the work was making him stronger. On some days, he believed it.

This morning, as he rolled out of bed and joined the line for the bathroom, Alby still felt the soreness in his arms, his back, and especially his blistered hands.

"That was too late," Arkansas said, referring to last night, when the guards had kept them working on the brick furnace until one in the morning.

Alby nodded, stepping into the shower and keeping the water cold. Except for the officers' quarters, there was no air conditioning on the island, so the instant Alby turned the shower off, warm beads of sweat pooled across his forehead, poised to run into his eyes.

His diarrhea was getting worse, which he blamed on the food. So was the throbbing at the base of his skull, which he blamed on his lack of sleep. But the morning's roughest hit came when Alby got back to his cot and noticed that next to him, Julian's bed was already made, like it hadn't been slept in.

**"Julian, you here?"** Alby called out, glancing around the room, which was a blur of young men pulling on tank tops and tying boot-laces. The heat was so ruthless, the sergeant had stopped making them wear full uniforms.

No one answered. Where the hell was

he? Alby replayed last night. Julian had been in the barracks, reading, as always.

"Anyone seen Julian?" Alby said to no one in particular.

**"Let's go—barracks empty!"** Timothy shouted as the group of young Plankholders began to scramble down the aisle that separated the two long rows of beds. They knew the consequences if they didn't arrive as one unit.

Fighting with his bootlaces, Alby hopped to the door, noticing that one person wasn't moving at all.

"Nico, you coming?" Timothy called out.

Nico didn't look up. He was sitting on his cot, elbows on his knees, boots still untied.

"What're you doing? What's wrong?" Timothy asked.

"Something bad happened," Nico whispered.

"Nico, I know it's early. We're all tired—"

"You're not listening," Nico said. "My hearing. I can hear things. Something bad happened. Outside."

"What're you talking about?" Timothy asked.

Alby didn't hear the exchange. He was

already halfway out the door, still scanning for...

**"Julian! You out here...?"** Alby shouted into the morning darkness.

A blast of hot salty air sent the first flood of sweat down his brow to his eyes. Alby ran down the concrete steps and glanced across the grassy courtyard. Over by the furnace, there were flickering blades of light. Flashlights.

Three days from now, the official report would say that Alby should have waited for the rest of his unit. But he didn't. Instead, he started running. Slowly at first, just a jog.

He tried to convince himself that all this was normal. Last night, they'd used flashlights while lugging bags of coal into the furnace's firebox. They used flashlights again when they lit the oven for the first time, just to be sure it worked. A black cloud of smoke had wafted upward as all the Plankholders cheered.

Today, at 4:56 a.m., no one was cheering.

**"Julian, that you?"** Alby asked, squinting through the dark and counting three different shadows by the back of the brick furnace.

A blast of white light blinded him as a flashlight turned his way.

**"I told you to keep 'em inside!"** a deep voice shouted.

**"Get him out of here!"** another barked.

Alby knew that voice. Colonel Doggett.

Squinting and putting up a hand to block the light, Alby couldn't see anything. But he smelled it.

When Alby first left the barracks, the warm air had blown it the other way. But as he got closer, he tried to place the smell. It was putrid and sweet, so lush it punctured his nose and went straight to his tongue. He couldn't put words to it, but everyone knows when they smell something foul.

A belch of black smoke spiraled up from the redbrick chimney.

**"Julian..."** Alby whispered, running toward the furnace.

**"Take him out of here! Now!"** someone shouted.

The flashlights twisted and turned, adding a dull glow to the black smoke that was now pouring from the furnace's back door as well as its cross-shaped windows.

Whatever was burning inside, it was big.

**"Julian...!"** Alby shouted as a set of strong hands grabbed him by the biceps. Alby's arms were so slick with sweat, he managed to slip free, running forward for a better view. He nearly tripped over a discarded army boot. It was charred and burnt.

**"Julian... Oh, God... What'd you do...!?"** Another set of hands grabbed him. Then another.

**"Get off me! He's my friend!"** Alby shouted, thrashing wildly, the smoke pouring over him. They were all starting to cough.

Alby was close to the furnace. The coal door was still vomiting smoke from the back as a familiar and wide shadow turned Alby's way. A glint from the flashlight lit his Santa face. Colonel Doggett didn't say anything else.

With a final tug, Alby was jerked backward, his boots dragging through the garden of loose leftover bricks.

**"Lemme go!"** Alby screamed, still coughing, still thrashing, still determined to get a look inside.

It never came.

The black smoke spun and twirled, dissipating as it reached the ocean. Across the dark courtyard, the guards yelled, forcing the Plankholders back into their barracks. And for the rest of his short life, Alby White never forgot the putrid and sweet odor that filled his nostrils that night.

48

## Today
## Washington, D.C.

"Doc, how's it look?" Director Riestra calls out at the screen.

We're all staring at the laptop, crowded around like kids in a dorm room. Onscreen, there's nothing but an empty chair in the command center. In the background, there's the faint flush of a toilet.

"Doc?" Riestra repeats.

From the right, Dr. Yaeger appears, his gloved fingers pinching the edges of the damp white index card. His white eyebrows knit together, still confused.

"What's it say?" Riestra asks.

"You tell me." As the doctor turns the sheet around, the once-white index card is now marked by a pale purple...

"Are those letters?" Riestra asks.

Everyone leans in. Onscreen we see:

`/ • / • | | ʃ`

"Morse code?" Francy says.

"It's not Morse code," Riestra says definitively.

"Hebrew?" his deputy asks.

"Not Hebrew either."

"It's not even English. Except for the S," the doctor adds.

"It's a code," I blurt.

"A code!? Thanks for that, Langdon," Riestra challenges.

I ignore him. Francy is looking my way. I'm locked on the screen as my eyebrow starts twitching.

"You recognize it, Beecher?" the doctor asks.

I barely move.

"Is it something Nico's used before?"

"Not Nico. Though I bet Nico knows it," I say, leaning in closer. "It's an old substitution cipher, from the Civil War. It came from the papers of a man named George Washington Bickley."

Francy turns my way. It's a ridiculous name, and one hard to forget. "In the late 1800s, Bickley was the leader of..."

"The Knights of the Golden Circle," Francy says.

I nod, my eyes still locked on the cipher.

Francy takes out her phone, motioning to help me look it up online.

I shake my head. Like I need a phone.

"You can read it then?" Riestra asks. "What's it say?"

I squint, seeing my own reflection on-screen. Symbol by symbol, I replace each with a letter. With just seven spaces, I'm guessing it's a name. Or, knowing Nico, some cryptic, obscure location. But as the letters fall in place and I read the word for myself, my wind-pipe constricts.

"It looks like a message," I say, thinking about the President.

"Beecher, tell us what it says!"

"It's a single word: **goodbye**."

## 49

**Ten days ago
Carter Lake, Iowa**

Still in his bathrobe as he stepped out into the cold, the doctor wasn't thinking about his high blood pressure. He wasn't thinking about his daughter's divorce. He wasn't even thinking about his recent battle with acute pancreatitis, which had left him a diabetic with a whole new set of problems.

Instead, as the doctor left his front door and strolled down the long driveway in his daily hunt for the morning newspaper, he was thinking of the girl with fake boobs who always flirted with him at the dry cleaners.

It was hard enough getting old. Even harder doing it in the suburbs. Maybe he'd drop off another rumpled shirt today just to see how much she'd lean over the counter.

Reaching the foot of the driveway and

pushing his sturdy Arthur Ashe glasses up on his face, the doctor was so lost in the thought of her chest, he didn't even notice the man who was waiting for him, standing next to the mailbox.

"It's better for the environment if you read online," Nico said in his steady monotone, handing the doctor his morning **Wall Street Journal**.

The doctor locked glances with the man whose life he had destroyed all those years ago on the island.

Nico stood there, posture perfect, chin out.

Dr. Moorcraft swayed slightly, then fell sideways, fainting and crumbling onto the asphalt.

Nico dragged him inside by his ankles.

## 50

# Today
## Crystal City, Virginia

"The KGC," Clementine said, standing at the sink and wiping the blood from her lips. "Ever hear of the Knights of the Golden Circle?"

"I know your dad's obsessed with them," Marshall said. "He thinks John Wilkes Booth was a member. And Lee Harvey Oswald."

"John Wilkes Booth apparently was a member. So was Jesse James. But forget my dad a second. After Ezra approached me, I looked them up. Back during the Civil War, dozens of groups like the Knights sprang up all over. People across the South were enraged, and they needed an outlet. But unlike the Freemasons and other secret societies that focused on centuries-old traditions, the Knights of the Golden Circle wanted something far more practical: They wanted the Union to lose so they could preserve slavery. That's basically their story: They were a bunch of racists who wanted their own "golden circle"— a chunk of land including Mexico and the Caribbean—to call their own. When the Civil War ended, some say the Knights disbanded. Others say..."

"That they escaped and went underground. Beecher told me about your dad's obsession."

"Forget my dad! You think I don't know how crackpot his theories are? Mental illness doesn't just run in my family. Its prints. But I'm telling you, Marsh..."

"Marshall."

"I'm telling you, Marshall, here's an unarguable historical fact: After the Civil War—after John Wilkes Booth fired that bullet into Abraham Lincoln's brain— the Knights of the Golden Circle disappeared. Maybe they regrouped in the sixties; maybe they didn't. But here's one thing I know for certain: If Ezra has his way, they're coming back—and they're coming for the Culper Ring."

Marshall didn't move as she said the words.

"C'mon, Marshall, you think you're the

only one who spent time with Beecher? I know about the Ring."

Marshall still didn't react. He didn't trust her, but he could still get information. "Why did Ezra send you here?"

"Have you listened to a word I said? Ezra wants nothing to do with me. He only helped me so I'd make the introduction."

"Introduction to what?"

"Not to **what**. To **who**." Reading Marshall's confused expression, she added, "Pretend your personal mission in life is to rebuild the Knights of the Golden Circle. Who's the number one—and hardest to find—presidential assassin you want on your side?"

Looking down, Marshall lowered his knife and retracted the blade. "Nico," he whispered. "Ezra wants to recruit your dad."

Clementine spit more blood into the sink. She didn't have to say another word. There was only one reason Ezra and the Knights would want a big gun: They were hunting big game.

"They're going after the President," Marshall said.

"Not just the President. Think about Beecher and the Culper Ring. Their job is to protect Wallace—"

"You think Ezra cares about Beecher and the Ring?"

"Marshall, **all** Ezra cares about is the stupid Ring! He blames the Culper Ring for hunting down the Knights. He thinks they're lawless animals who robbed his family of its rightful legacy. You should see the picture he carries with him—the haunted look in his eyes when he shows you the photo of him and his grandfather in the Oval Office meeting Reagan. The scariest thing about Ezra is he wants to be remembered. He wants a place in history. So whatever Ezra's got planned—whether he's hitting the President or Beecher or all of them at once—he's not going for something small. He wants Hiroshima."

Still trying to make a picture from the pieces, Marshall was tempted to ask her about the arm buried in the Rose Garden, but something told him not to. Instead, he eyed the way Clementine gripped the edge of the counter, like she needed it to hold herself up. "That still doesn't tell me the real reason you're here," he said.

"I already—! Look at me...I'm **dying**!"

He stared at her. "I believe you when you say that." They held each other's gaze. "What I don't believe is your sudden concern with the welfare of Beecher or Wallace or pretty much anyone but yourself."

"And so, **what**? You think I made this all up? Do you have any idea what I've been through? Look at this—! This is— This is—" She reached into her front pocket and held out a small white object in her open palm. "This is the tooth I lost in the elevator when I sneezed on the way up here. I've got half a dozen of these things at this point. I've been keeping them in the ashtray of my rental car, and if I take too wide a turn, I hear them rattling like dice."

"Clementine, I know you're—"

"You don't know anything! And you of all people **should**!" she yelled, pointing to her own face. "My gums are gray! I spent the last two weeks in a makeshift dental chair trying to keep my jaw from collapsing! And you know what I finally realized? I can't stop it. No matter how much I pray or

beg or try to pretend this is all God's will—"
She took a breath, still holding on to the
counter. "We all have our mountains to
climb, don't we? This is the end of mine.
And if that's the case...I don't know...
When the curtain comes down, don't you
want your last act to be something good?"

Marshall stood there, noticing for the first
time the red tint on her teeth. "That's an
excellent speech. It really is," he said. "But
don't insult me with the I'm-just-trying-to-
earn-my-angel-wings talk. I've taken a
man's life before. I know you have too.
And once you're a killer...once you give
away that part of your soul...some dirt
won't ever come off."

"That doesn't mean I'm lying about Ezra,"
she shot back. "You know that's true."

"So why'd you bring this all to me instead
of taking it to Beecher?"

"Because I need to stop hurting him."
From the palm of her hand, she dumped
her tooth on the counter. "When I was lying
there in that dental chair, it's the one thing
I realized in my moment of clarity: Every
time I get near Beecher, I cause him pain.
If this is the end of my mountain, I need to

do better by him."

"That's the first true thing you've said today."

"You're wrong," she insisted. "And you were wrong about Kathy Stankevich too. I didn't pick a fight with her. She told everyone my mother slept with Craig Andrade's dad."

"I thought your mom **did** sleep with Craig Andrade's dad."

"Of course she did. But c'mon...it's still my mom," Clementine said, picking up her tooth and sliding it back in her pocket. "I can help you get Ezra. Let me prove it to you."

"I thought you didn't know what he was planning."

"I don't," she said, glancing down at her watch. "But if we hurry, I know where he'll be."

## 51

"We need to move him," Francy insists, referring to the President.

Riestra holds up a pointer-finger, never taking his deep-set eyes off me. "Beecher, are you sure that's what it says? **Goodbye?**"

"Check the code yourself." I hold up my phone, where I pulled the code up to make sure I got it right. "Back during the Civil War, the Knights of the Golden Circle—"

"I know who the Knights are. And I know the Culper Ring took them apart. But if Nico thinks he's part of them—or is trying to rebuild some new version..."

"Len, we really need to move him," Francy repeats.

"What if this isn't a threat, though?" I ask. "What if Nico's trying to tell us something different?"

"He buried an arm in the Rose Garden, then one in Camp David with the word **goodbye** in it!" Francy shoots back.

"She's got a point, Beecher," Riestra agrees. "In our line of work, that's a very particular threat."

"Or maybe it's simply someone sending a very particular body," I say, pointing back to the screen. "One arm—sure—that's a message. But when it's two arms from the same person—"

"What makes you say it's the same person?" the doc interrupts, suddenly suspicious.

"You saying I'm wrong?" I challenge. "I saw the corpse's fingertips...the black ink...Are you telling me you didn't finger- print both arms and run them through your system? Testing DNA takes a few days; running a fingerprint takes two minutes."

The doctor's—and Riestra's—silence gives me the answer: The two arms definitely came from the same body. No doubt, the buried body parts trace back to a particular person...though the top medical examiner and the head of the Secret Service wanted to keep that fact to themselves.

"Why didn't you tell me the arms were from the same body? Does that mean you have an ID too?" I finally ask.

"You do realize this isn't **your** investigation, Beecher? It's **ours**." Riestra adds a quick laugh. He's got his smile back in place, like we're old pals. "I mean, it's not like I'm asking you to share what you found with any other archivists you might've run into."

He never mentions Mina's name or the fact that I was inside Secret Service head-quarters, but as he flashes his white picket teeth, there's no doubt in my mind. He's head of the Service. He knows I've been in his building.

"Ever hear the name Kingston Young?" Riestra challenges.

I shake my head.

"You're sure? **Kingston Young**," Riestra repeats, lowering his chin and staring at me over the rims of his glasses.

"I'd remember a name like Kingston. Who is he?"

Riestra stares at me for another solid twenty seconds. "Apparently, someone who's missing both arms," he eventually says, the lightness in his voice telling me I've passed his test. "According to the fingerprints, Kingston is the man those arms trace to. Police say he died two weeks ago," he explains. "Now in the spirit of reciprocity, Beecher, have you got anything you want to share with me?" He puts on a frozen smile.

I can't help but think that this is just another test. Maybe that's the reason Riestra brought me here. I didn't think Mina would rat me out, but maybe she did. Maybe he already has all the details about White Eyelashes, the orange lapel pin, and of course the Reagan Secret Service agent named Tanner Pope, who also apparently died a little over two weeks ago. If that's the case, it won't hurt to share. Still, I hear Tot's voice in the back of my head repeating the very first lesson he taught me when he invited me into the Ring: **Always trust my gut.**

Across from me, with his white picket smile in place, Riestra readjusts his round glasses. They're still a little crooked.

"You know everything I know," I tell him.

Leaning forward, Riestra rests both elbows on the table, which shifts from his weight. "Darryl, move him," he says to his deputy, referring to the President. "And to the new place we discussed."

"But sir—"

"To the place we discussed," Riestra

growls, low enough that the room goes silent.

The same thing happened the last time someone took a shot at President Wallace. After the 9/11 attacks, when President Bush was chaotically hopscotched across the country, the Secret Service learned its lesson. Since then, protocols have been put in place for terrorist and other assassination scenarios. Today, the Service doesn't just randomly decide where to hide the commander in chief. Those decisions were made years ago, based on thoughtful research and careful threat analysis. When there's a threat at the White House, they move the President to Camp David; when there's a threat at Camp David, they know the next spot too. But from what I can tell, Riestra's carving a new path.

"He's not gonna be happy. Mrs. Wallace either," Francy warns.

"Y'know what'll make them even less happy? Having their heads separated from their bodies," Riestra says.

Francy grits her teeth. Riestra's assistant heads to the corner and starts whispering something into his wrist. But based on the infighting—and the fact that the White House and Camp David have already been compromised—this isn't just about how Nico, or White Eyelashes, or who-ever's doing this, broke in. It's that this person has the Service's private play-book, and he knows where the President—and First Lady—will be next.

"You sure you're not doing exactly what this killer wants you to do?" I ask.

Riestra turns back to me.

"Think about it," I tell him. "Last time Nico attacked—and used the invisible ink—he knew I'd break his code. He was count-ing on it. In fact, when we chased after him—Francy, I know you know this—that's when someone **else** took an open shot at the President. For all you know, they're doing the same thing here."

"That's the beauty of being spontan-eous," Riestra says. "No one knows where Wallace is going but us."

"That's not true! Just to move him, your agents know!"

"He's got a point. Listen to him," Francy says.

"Francy, Beecher...I appreciate both your advice. But we're done here."

"Don't do this! When it comes to Nico, he's not— For all you know, his whole goal is to get you out of your protocols! Maybe that's what he—!"

"I said we're done." Behind me, his deputy puts a hand on my shoulder, lifts me from my seat, and shoves me toward Francy and the door. As I stumble, Riestra again readjusts his glasses, his smile wider than ever. "Don't worry, Beecher. As long as I'm taking care of Wallace, he'll be perfectly safe."

## 52

The door slams behind me like a thunder-clap, leaving me alone on the second-floor landing.

When I caught Riestra staring at the mail slot, I thought President Wallace might still be in the building. But as I trudge down-stairs, I finally see who it really was. I forgot he was here, always listening.

A.J. glances up, then quickly looks away. Body language says he's pissed, maybe at me; maybe at his boss. Either way, it's Something to exploit.

"I'm surprised they kept you down here instead there," I say, hoping to put him on my side.

He looks me square in the face, nearly a full head taller than me. "Eat a bag of shit, Beecher."

With a shove on the door, he points me into the bright cold. But just before the door closes, I glance back, catching A.J. staring my way. He doesn't say a word, doesn't make a face. But he's watching.

And thinking.

I don't care how tough he is. Y'know what they call the person who does all the work but gets none of the credit? An opportunity.

Three steps from the storefront, my phone vibrates over and over again. Seven voicemails. Upstairs, they were blocking my cell, and yes, even for them, that's illegal.

Caller ID shows seven different randomly generated numbers. I know who that is. As I call her back, she picks up on the first ring. "They give you anything good?" Immaculate Deception asks.

"First things first. Please tell me you found something."

"Of course I found something. Tanner Pope," her robot-generated voice says, referring to the Reagan Secret Service agent who owned the orange lapel pin and who, like the owner of the missing arms, died just a few weeks ago. "When you look at Tanner's death at the ripe old age of ninety-two, the poor guy didn't even have an obit, much less anyone to come to a funeral."

"So no family?" I ask.

"I didn't say that. No wife. No kids. But according to the overly talkative receptionist at his nursing home, Pope apparently has a twenty-nine-year-old grandson. Name is Ezra."

"You think that's White Eyelashes?"

"It would explain how he got Grandpa Tanner's Secret Service pin."

I nod to myself. According to the medical examiner, the severed arms trace back to someone who's a similar age. **Late twenties, early thirties.**"What do we know about Ezra?" I ask Mac.

"Bright guy. Grandpa Tanner was giving him money too: private school at Andover; undergrad at Yale; now doing graduate work at GW's Elliott School, studying international security policy. No loans, no debt."

Across the street, the two Secret Service agents are still sitting in the restaurant window, pretending to sip coffee. "Mac, why do I feel like there's something you're not saying?"

"Because, Beecher, those schools are the only places where Ezra's left a trail.

Other than a campus email, he's got no driver's license...no bank accounts... a P.O. box for his tax returns... I can't even find a cell number. Living in the twenty-first century, the only time you see anonymity like that is with major wealth or witness protection."

"So you couldn't find anything?"

"What kind of computer genius do you take me for? Of course I found something: According to the registrar at GW, Ezra's been on academic leave for the past two weeks."

"Y'mean since his grandfather died?"

"Not just his grandfather," Mac says, her robot voice starting to creak. "Apparently, poor Ezra's roommate died too. Some kid named..."

**"Kingston Young,"** we both say simultaneously.

My windpipe constricts tighter than ever.

"How'd you know Kingston's name?" Mac asks.

"The buried arms...that's who they belong to," I say, already running down the block, back to the Archives. "Mac, I need Ezra's home address—"

"Already checked it out. Landlord said he hasn't seen Ezra in weeks."

"What about the victim? Does Kingston have family? Someone we can talk to?"

"Got it. On it."

"By the way, your old pal Riestra sends his best."

"Who?"

"Leonard Riestra. He said he worked with you and Tot."

"Riestra? As in **director of the Secret Service**?" Mac asks. "He's barely been on the job six months. I've never met Riestra in my life."

## 53

## Twenty-nine years ago
## Devil's Island

There was no funeral for Julian. On the island, there wasn't even a coffin.

Instead, they tied his charred body to a field gurney and covered it with an American flag held in place by bungee cords. That was it. The body was there one day, gone the next. According to one of the guards, they put it on a coast guard cutter that took it to Homestead Air Force Base back in Florida.

It all happened so fast, Colonel Doggett didn't even do the , rifle, and boots service that's done in every branch of the military. Whether you're army, navy, air force, or marines, when there's a fallen soldier— even a suicide—they display the helmet, rifle, and boots, giving everyone a chance to say a final prayer. But out here, Julian hadn't had a helmet or a rifle. None of them did, Nico pointed out.

On their own, the remaining members of the Plankholders gathered in the dilapidated chapel on the second floor of the fort, where the red brickwork was most ornate. Joining hands, they lowered their heads. At the center of their circle was a handwritten note that someone had found among Julian's belongings. Julian had written it to his older sister. From what they could tell, both their parents had died when they were young, and Julian wanted to thank her for all she'd done, and apologize for how he'd failed.

From that day forward, every member of the Plankholders, from Nico to Timothy to Alby, carried a pre-written goodbye note everywhere he went.

Colonel Doggett gave them the next day off, letting them fish and snorkel around the island, while Dr. Moorcraft gave each of them an extra pill to take at bedtime. "To help you relax," he promised.

For the better part of a week, it seemed to work.

Then one night, Alby awoke at 2 a.m., sweating from the heat and holding his chest like someone was standing on it.

Bolting up, he frantically looked around. No one moved. Every-one else was asleep.

Out of habit, he checked Julian's cot. A few days back, Timothy had swiped the pillow, but otherwise the bed was perfectly made. Yet as Alby glanced across the aisle to the other row of cots, he noticed a second bed was also empty.

Nico's.

Probably just in the bathroom, go to bed, Alby told himself as he squinted through the dark. Unlike Julian's bed, Nico's was unmade, the covers thrown aside. The pillow still had a dent in it. But something on the top sheet caught Alby's eye: a paperback book.

**"Nico, you here?"** Alby whispered toward the bathroom.

No answer.

Alby glanced back at the bed, and the paperback. Without even seeing the cover, he thought he knew what book it was, but there was only one way to know for sure.

Throwing his own top sheet aside, he scuttled across the aisle. The laminate floor puckered with each step. Halfway there, he could see the black-and-white photo of Dr. Mudd on the cover. For sure, it was Julian's old book. The book he was reading the day before he—

The laminate floor puckered again. This time, on Alby's far right. Not by the bathroom, by the door that led outside.

Alby spun toward the sound. The room was dark, and the door too far away to see anything clearly. Just muddy shadows.

**"Nico, that you...?"** Alby whispered. No answer. He looked down and noticed... Nico's boots were gone.

Alby raced toward the bathroom, checking every stall. All empty. He glanced back at the main door. It was after curfew. If Nico had snuck out—

A flash of light flickered through a nearby window. By the time Alby turned, it was gone. Whatever it was, it had come from outside.

For the second time, Alby told himself to go back to bed. But he knew the rules. If Nico was caught out there this late, they'd all be paying the punishment.

Rushing for the door, Alby was still barefoot as he shoved it open. **"Nico, if you're out there, get back!"** he hissed.

Something with a tail scampered under the barracks. There were rats all over the island. The grassy courtyard...the brick furnace...all of it was dark silver, glowing faintly in the moonlight. In the distance, ocean waves played their metronome. The only bright light came from Alby's left, past the grove of date palm trees. A single window was lit in the red-brick New Orleans–style house that served as the officers' quarters. Home to Colonel Doggett.

**No. Please no. Nico, you're smarter than that.**

Of course, a week ago, Alby would've said the same thing about Julian.

Feeling the grass bite between his toes and hearing another small animal skitter through the darkness, Alby took off, rushing toward Colonel Doggett's glowing window.

**"Nico, you dumbass, where are you...?"** he hissed again, ducking down and running low, passing palm tree after palm tree. Even at night, the hot island air burned his face. Sand was scattered through the grass, sticking to his feet. A mosquito bit his ear.

**"Nico...!?"** he whispered to his left, into the fort's arched brick storage areas known as **casemates**. A century ago, the casemates had been designed to hold weapons and gunpowder. A few still did, holding barrels of gunpowder for the cannons. But most were just for storage, filled with tools, industrial spools of cables, and milk crates full of canteens and supplies.

A loud **thud-thud-thud** echoed up ahead, like someone coming down a flight of stairs.

Alby stopped, ducking behind a dying date palm tree with a cracked trunk. Up by Colonel Doggett's house, a bright light flickered on the front porch. The screen door opened. Someone was coming out.

Peering out from behind the tree, Alby squinted into the dark. He could hear another mosquito orbiting his head, buzzing with a steady hum.

Doggett's door opened wider. There were men talking, though from this distance, Alby couldn't hear much. Couldn't see them either. They were still inside.

"—much harder than you think," one of

them said, giving the door a final shove. Alby knew that voice. A bright fluorescent glow rolled across the front porch as Colonel Doggett stepped outside. He turned slightly, holding the door for someone behind him.

Fifty feet away, still crouched in the darkness, Alby gripped the date palm hard.

"Boat should be waiting for you," Doggett added, glancing around as Alby ducked lower.

There was a hollow **thunk thunk** as two loud boots joined Doggett on the porch. At first, Alby assumed it was a guard...or even Dr. Moorcraft. Whoever it was, they were dressed in fatigues with no nametags or patches. Same as the first guards who'd found Alby after the plane crash and brought him into the Plankholders.

"So I'll see you on the other side?" the stranger asked Doggett.

As Alby heard the voice, he balled his bare feet into the grass. He knew that voice, though it was happening so fast, Alby's brain still hadn't placed it.

It wasn't until the stranger stepped

outside—and the fluorescent lights lit his face…and his familiar red hair—that Alby realized it wasn't a stranger at all.

**Mother of God… How can that—?**

Alby's stomach sank to the dirt. The stray mosquito took a final orbit around his head. And right there, on the square porch of the redbrick house, was a man with pale freckles and a confident smile.

His red hair was buzzed, but it was starting to grow out. His shoulders were straight now, not slumped. And his skin was perfect: no burns, no bandages, not a single mark on him.

**It… It can't— It's not possible. He died in the furnace eight days ago.**

Julian.

That's Julian.

## 54

## Today
## Baltimore, Maryland

I press the chipped, circular button, feeling it vibrate on my fingertip.

**"Who's there?"** an older woman's voice crackles through the intercom.

"My name's Beecher White. I have a delivery. Needs a signature."

There's a pause, followed by a loud, metallic roar that no modern building would ever permit.

"How's it look?" Mac asks through the phone in my ear. When I don't reply, she adds, "Why're you being so quiet?"

Pushing my way inside, I still don't answer.

"Beecher, what're you seeing? Something wrong?"

I'm in an area of Baltimore called Pigtown, which pretty much lives up to its name. A few blocks away, some of the apartment buildings and row houses have been refurbished. This four-story walk-up hasn't.

It's not a terrible area. "It just reminds me of my neighborhood in Wisconsin," I explain. "Working class. In another life, I've lived here before."

"Welcome home, huh?"

I nod to myself as I climb the narrow staircase. The hallway smells of fresh paint, but there's no missing the frayed gray carpet, loose banister, or missing metal treads on every third or fourth step. Our landlord used to do the same: adding new paint, hoping it would cover all problems.

"You can leave the package on the mat," the woman yells through the door at apartment 4D.

"Sorry, ma'am. Needs a signature," I call back, working extra hard to sound friendly.

She lives in a rough neighborhood; she's no sucker. She opens the door a half inch, chain still in place as her narrow bloodshot eyes stare up at me. "Where's your package?"

"Mrs. Young, I'm sorry to bother you—"

She slams the door in my face.

"Ma'am, please," I say. "I'm here to ask you about your son."

The door stays shut.

"Your son is Kingston Young, yes?" I ask, using the name of Ezra's former roommate who died from a suicide two weeks ago and, according to the Secret Service, is the owner of the severed arms that were buried in Camp David and the Rose Garden.

"If you're not police, I'm calling them right now," she threatens.

"Tell her you're FBI," Mac says in my ear.

I shake my head. "Mrs. Young, you don't know me, but let me tell you the most important thing about me: I will never lie to you."

"You lied about delivering a package," she shoots back.

"Time to stop being nice," Mac scolds in my ear.

"Ma'am, I care about what happened to your son."

"Did you even know him?" she challenges.

"I didn't, but here's the absolute truth: I don't think Kingston committed suicide."

I stare at the peephole. A solid ten seconds go by. The chain rattles and clinks, then the door swings open, revealing a sixty-year-old pudgy woman with elegant silver hair and a mouth that curves downward at the corners. She looks like she hasn't slept in a month.

"You won't regret this, Mrs. Young. I promise you that."

## 55

## Arlington, Virginia

Marshall couldn't put his finger on it. But he could feel it coming.

"Three more minutes," Clementine said from the driver's seat, gripping the door handle but waiting to open it.

Marshall barely noticed. In the passenger seat, he was scanning the strip-mall parking lot, focusing on the lone BMW motorcycle parked by the dog groomer's. The only thing worse than a Harley snob was a fool on a BMW.

"That motorcycle's always there," Clementine reassured him.

On his left was a dinged-up black Honda Prelude, with an old **Elliot in the Morning** bumper sticker.

"The Honda belongs to the nurse. The doctor parks around back," Clementine added. "Trust me, this is how it always is."

Marshall couldn't argue with that. So far, every detail was exactly as Clementine had described. The parking lot was perfectly empty. The passing traffic on Wilson Boulevard was perfectly far away. Even the way the plaza curved around meant that the Happy Jade Herbal Shop was always perfectly out of sight. But as Marshall knew, when everything was going right, and especially when things were going right with Clementine, something was about to go wrong.

The winter sun slipped from the sky as the digital clock blinked to 3:58 p.m. Two more minutes.

From the passenger seat, Marshall studied the storefront. A bright red **Closed** sign kept most people away. Tinted windows scared away the rest. If Clementine was right and Ezra was inside, there's no way they'd know it.

"This is a bad idea," Marshall said.

Clementine shook her head as the clock blinked to 3:59. "Then why'd you come?"

"What're you—?"

"Why're you here? If it's such a disaster, why'd you bother?"

"You said he was going after Beecher."

"No. If this was about Beecher, you

would've called Beecher and told him everything. You didn't. You didn't even try. We all play our personal games, Marshall. I'm not judging you for it, but how'd you put it again? 'You're a killer just like me. Some dirt won't ever come off'? So. For the fourth and fifth time: Why're you really here?"

Marshall studied the girl in the brown wig whom he'd known since second grade. She had crow's-feet at her eyes, a deep worried crease between sharp eyebrows, and shiny, waxy skin from all the chemo. These past few years had taken their toll. But to him, she looked exactly the same. Just as fiery.

"I came here for Ezra," Marshall finally offered. "He buried those arms. He knows what happened to your crazy father; he knows what happened to my dead one."

"Your dead one, huh?"

Marshall sat there, unmoving.

"Is that the story you told Beecher? Or did you tell him what really went down?" Clementine asked. "Don't worry. I understand. We all have our secrets, right, Marshall?"

His gold eyes studied her. Nico. Only Nico could've told her that truth.

Clementine went to say something else, but as the clock blinked to 4:00 p.m., she shoved open the car door, charging forward.

Following behind her, Marshall kept his pace slow and steady, studying the storefront and the front door. "You're sure he doesn't know we're coming?" he called out.

"He doesn't. I know how he works. I've been coming here for weeks," Clementine insisted, spinning around and crossing defiantly into Marshall's personal space. Her single-mindedness was what Beecher loved most. Beecher saw it as fearless. Marshall saw it as reckless. Either way, as Marshall knew, the most dangerous person to follow is someone with nothing to lose.

"Whattya think, he's got a sniper on the roof, ready to shoot at us?" Clementine challenged as Marshall slowed down even more.

"Sniper on the roof makes no sense. If he misses, it'd take too long to climb down and chase us."

"You really can't turn it off, can you? You always see the world as trying to take your head off."

"You're still not listening. This whole approach—trying to surprise him—it's a mistake," Marshall said as they moved toward the storefront. "We don't even know if Ezra's here."

"Of course he's here. He doesn't miss my appointments. I don't even think they'd let me inside if he wasn't there."

Marshall stopped, refusing to follow.

"What? What's wrong now?" Clementine asked.

"When you come here, is Ezra usually with you?"

"Why would—?"

"Just answer the question: Is Ezra with you or not?"

"So far, he's been. He's usually my ride."

"But now you're suddenly coming by yourself?"

"Relax. I told him I was running late, that I'd meet him here."

Clementine continued toward the herbal shop. Marshall stayed where he was. On their far left, a loud horn blasted from Wilson

Boulevard. Perfectly normal for rush hour.

"I'm out. Gimme your keys," Marshall said.

"What're you talking about?"

"You and Ezra had an understanding. A pattern. Now you're changing it. Gimme your keys. I'll be in the car."

"Will you just—?"

"Keys. **Now.**"

Rolling her eyes, Clementine tossed Marshall the keys. He headed back toward the parking lot. She kept walking toward the storefront.

Both refused to look back, so neither saw what was coming.

There was no loud screech of tires. Just a low guttural rumble, like the sewer below was clearing its throat. Marshall was halfway to the car as he heard it. Before he even turned, he knew what it was. And who it was headed for.

The black Dodge Charger tore around the corner, picking up speed. Its engine burbled with an angry snarl.

**"Clementine...!"**

She nearly jumped out of the way as the car clipped her, the nose of it biting her legs and grazing her thigh. Her movement saved her life. But like a human seesaw, her legs flew up, her head crashed down.

Marshall was frozen in place, still in mid-yell as the sound of bone and crushed glass twirled together in a haunting ballet. Clementine's arm bounced against the windshield, her limbs flailing like they were filled with rubber bands as she spun to the ground. Her shoulder skidded across the asphalt.

The driver of the black Dodge hit the brakes. Even with the sky growing dark, there was no mistaking his bald head. Or his slitted eyes and white eyelashes.

Ezra didn't say a word as he leaned out the window. He simply glared at Marshall, pulled his gun, and fired.

## 56

# Baltimore, Maryland

"You're sure this is his handwriting?" I ask.

Mrs. Young nods. As she passes me the letter, her body's shaking, like she's been hollowed out and filled with bits of glass.

I'm still in the hallway, just outside her apartment, which reeks of an overdose of potpourri. Over her shoulder are the torsos of three tailor's mannequins, all without heads or arms. On her wrist is a tomato-shaped pincushion bracelet.

"The police kept the original," she explains, motioning to the letter, but refusing to look directly at it. "They said I'll get it back when... I-I don't even know when."

I nod like I understand. And I do. Last month, Clementine gave me a similar note by my father. A suicide note from what I'm still not convinced was a suicide.

"He did it on his birthday. Read it," she adds.

**Dear Mom,**

**Here's my reason: I've lived on this planet for twenty-seven years, yet there aren't twenty-seven days that I would live over again. When you wonder why I've done this, read that sentence again.**

**I know you'll blame yourself. I love you for that. But this is my choice. I know where I'm going. I know what I'm doing. I'm not afraid of where this takes me.**

**Thank you especially for that day out by the piers after Dad died. Also, please tell Ezra I'm sorry for the mess.**

**Your son,**
**Kingston**

"He used a shotgun," she says. "Put the barrel to his chin, aimed straight at the ceiling, and—" She takes a breath, reliving the moment. "The police wouldn't let me in. They said the shotgun blast blew his entire face..." As I glance at Mrs. Young, she doesn't look away. Her dead eyes beg me, searching for something that can't be replaced. My mother has that same look when she talks about my dad. The light in her face isn't just faded. It's gone.

"I-I know that's his handwriting... I know those're his words..." she adds, her voice unraveling. "But no matter how many times I read it—**I've memorized it at this point**— okay, he carried his darkness around, but I still don't understand why he's **gone**! Do you know what that feels like? To have the person you care about most plucked from your life, and you don't even know **why**!?"

I stare straight into this woman's hollow face. When I was twelve, our local pastor was the one who gave me the birds-and-bees talk. When I was thirteen, our next-door neighbor taught me how to shave. And for as long as I can remember, I've celebrated every Father's Day remembering the Father's Day all those years ago, when I opened my mom's medicine cabinet and found a shakily handwritten Post-it she'd written to herself: **You have all the strength to make it through today.**

She still doesn't.

Today, I tell myself I do.

"Mrs. Young, your son was wrong about one thing: I know you gave him more than twenty-seven good days. Now please, let me help you help him one last time."

Nodding violently, she pinches the bridge of her nose to hold back tears.

"In the letter, your son mentioned someone named Ezra. Did you know Ezra well?"

"The police asked the same thing. Ezra was his roommate. He's a good boy, though. From a good family. If anything, he's exactly what Kingston needed."

"I'm not sure I follow."

She pinches the bridge of her nose tighter than before. She's not fighting back tears. She's thinking.

"When my husband died, everyone told me stories of how wonderful he **was**. And he was. Like any of us, he had moments of pure greatness. But he could also be petty. He was bad with money. And most of the time, he couldn't see that his biggest problems were usually his own doing."

"You're saying Kingston—"

"Look at the neighborhood we live in. Ever since Kingston was little, I knew he wasn't meant for this place. He was a workhorse too. Driven to get out. But when he met Ezra...to see someone from money ...someone who had taste, and knew how many years to wait until you opened a certain bottle of scotch... Ezra's grand-father apparently worked for President Reagan. When Kingston met Ezra, his whole world became **bigger**. It wasn't just the connections, though. Ezra showed him restraint. And kindness."

"Kindness?"

She takes a half-step back, giving me a good look at her apartment. "Son, I get ten dollars to hem a pair of pants. Fifteen dollars to shorten the sleeves on a dress shirt, though in this neighborhood, most people roll up their sleeves. Even with grad school loans, you know what it costs to have your own apartment plus meals down in D.C.?"

I nod, well aware of why I live in the Maryland suburbs.

"Kingston never said it, but when it came to paying for groceries, meals, and every-thing else, I know Ezra stepped in to help. Even gave Kingston a winter coat when he saw the ratty old jacket my son was wearing."

"That doesn't sound like our man with white eyelashes," Mac blurts in my ear. I almost forgot she was there. "You think we have the wrong guy?" she adds.

"Ma'am, can I ask you one last favor? Do you happen to have a picture of Ezra? Just for our records."

"Like a photo? Of my son's roommate? I don't think I— Wait. That's not true— Here... **C'mere**," she says, waving me inside. As I follow her toward the living room, she flips through a stack of pictures piled up on top of a nearby end table. "When the boys first moved in, I took a picture to show my sister the hardwood floors. Anyway, as I snapped it, Ezra was— **Here**," she says, pulling a single picture from the stack and handing it my way.

The photo's grainy, from an old camera, and shows an apartment that's typical grad school: futon, coffee table made from a wide plank of wood on stacked cement blocks, even a guitar. In the far left corner, a young man wearing a faded green-and-yellow plaid shirt enters from the kitchen, his mouth half-open, midsentence. He's definitely bald. But as I zero in, he's got sleepy and handsome features, thick eyebrows, and the preppy, untucked style of a J.Crew model.

One thing I know for sure: This isn't the guy with white eye-lashes who was spying on us outside the White House. My stomach twists. It makes no sense. How can this be the wrong guy?

"You're sure this is Ezra?" I ask.

"Who else would it be?" Mrs. Young asks, getting nervous.

I look back at the photo, still picturing the slitted eyes of the guy who looked like Andy Warhol.

"Beecher, send me a copy," Mac barks in my ear.

"Ma'am, you mind if I use your restroom?"

Mrs. Young points me toward the kitchen. "Second door on your left."

Moving quickly, I hold tight to the photo, getting ready to text it to Mac. Halfway down the hallway, I notice the array of framed photos on either side of me. They're from decades ago, Christmas shots taken at Sears, each one of Mrs. Young and Kingston, each with a different outdated sweater. I almost run right past them until —

Oh God.

I squint to make sure I'm seeing it right. There's no mistaking it. In every

Christmas photo, year after year, her dead son... Kingston...has a bowl cut of white-blond hair and an awkward smile. He's also got thin slitted eyes and stark white eyelashes.

Son of a bitch.

"What's wrong?" Mac asks.

"Ezra's not Ezra."

"What're you talking about?"

"The guy we're chasing—the guy with white eyelashes. He may be calling himself Ezra. He may've shaved his head like Ezra. But I'm telling you right now, he's a man who supposedly died two weeks ago. His real name's Kingston Young."

## 57

"**Gogogo! Get out of here!** Marshall told himself. Scrambling into Clementine's rental car and hearing the pop of a gunshot, he kept his head down and turned the keys in the ignition. **Put it in reverse! Get away from here!** It was the only way out. Fight smart. Fight later.

Across the parking lot, there was another loud pop from the front seat of Ezra's black Dodge. A second gunshot. Putting the car in reverse, Marshall saw Clementine's trembling body, twisted awkwardly across the concrete. Her wig had fallen off her head. She was lucky the car hadn't been moving full speed.

Of course he didn't want to leave her. But as Ezra fired again, Marshall had no choice. In situations like this, you have to get away.

Yet as he looked back at Clementine and her exposed bald head…

**Dammit.**

Throwing the car into drive, Marshall stomped the gas. The tires swirled, kicking bits of rock and melted snow through the air.

As the car barreled forward, Marshall pulled his own gun, firing out the window with his left hand and holding the steering wheel with his right. At this speed, he knew he wouldn't hit Ezra. But he would distract him.

Sure enough, Ezra ducked down in the front seat, no longer firing.

Pressing the gas even harder, Marshall picked up speed. The car blazed like a missile toward its target: straight into the side of the black Dodge, to that sweet spot midway between the front and back doors.

The impact was a violent gnashing of metallic teeth. At that speed, Marshall's car T-boned the black Dodge, which practically bent around the hood of the gray rental. Marshall knew what he was aiming for. Now the Dodge was undrivable. Ezra wasn't getting away.

Still skidding sideways, the Dodge snapped through one of the strip mall's stucco support columns and sent a metal trash can flying. The skid stopped just short of the herbal shop's plate glass window. Ezra flew from the driver's seat to the passenger seat, hitting with a thud.

**"Clementine, you hear me!?"** Marshall shouted, fighting the airbag from his face and searching for his gun, which had gone soaring during the impact.

Outside, Clementine was still on her side, still trembling.

Kicking open the car door and ignoring the burning pain where the steering wheel had smashed into his chest, Marshall raced to her.

**"Clemmi, open your eyes!"** he yelled, grabbing her nearby wig. He didn't like seeing her bald. It reminded him of his mother's funeral.

Clementine didn't move, but her stomach was— She was breathing. One of her cheeks was scraped raw. Blood poured from her mouth along with something wiry and metal. Marshall pulled it out to keep her from choking on it. It looked like a retainer, but with two fake teeth on each side. A bridge.

He held the bridge in one hand and tried to put the wig back on her head. It wouldn't stay, sliding to the ground like lifeless straw.

**"Clemmi, please—if you hear me, I need you to nod."**

Still no response. If it'd been anyone else, he'd call for an ambulance. But this was Nico's daughter, still at the top of every most-wanted list.

Turning Clementine over and crouching down on one knee, Marshall scooped a hand behind Clementine's neck and another below her knees. He put the wig on her belly, so focused on not dropping it, he didn't even feel the barrel of the gun that poked him from behind and wedged its way into his armpit.

**"What in the f—!?"**

Behind him, Ezra again didn't say a word. He just pulled the trigger.

**Pop.**

## 58

"Beecher, get out of there," Mac blurts in my ear.

"When was the last time you actually saw your son's roommate?" I ask Mrs. Young, who's either the greatest liar of all time, or clearly has no idea that her dead son Kingston is not only very much alive, but has recently gone all **Talented Mr. Ripley** with the real Ezra's life.

"I don't know," she says, sounding wary. "I last saw Ezra… maybe sometime around Christmas. Why?"

"You need to leave there. **Now**," Mac insists.

"Was he at your son's funeral?" I ask, staying with Mrs. Young.

"I-I didn't see him there, but I know he signed the guestbook and was—" She starts to sway, nearly knocking into a nearby sewing mannequin. "Can you please tell me what's going on?"

I look over at another photo of her and Kingston on the wall, a high school graduation pic where he's in full cap and gown. I don't know what's worse: this white-eyelashed bastard letting his own mother think he's dead...or killing the real Ezra, and then showing up at his own funeral just to sign the guestbook to throw folks off the trail. Whatever the case, White Eyelashes clearly wanted Ezra's life in more ways than one. "Two minutes," I say to Mac in my ear.

"Who're you talking to? You know something about my boy?" Mrs. Young stutters, tears flooding her eyes.

"Beecher, if White Eyelashes is as smart as we think he is, he's got someone watching his mom's place!" Mac insists.

A loud buzzer shrieks through the room, punctuating the point.

"Don't answer it," I tell Mrs. Young.

Panicking, she lunges, pressing the button. I don't blame her. She doesn't know me.

"Ma'am, my name is Leonard Riestra—from the United States Secret Service."

As soon as I hear his deep voice, I fish through my coat pockets to see if they traced me here. Both are empty. I know they can't track my phone. Mac takes care of that. That still leaves my car, though there's nothing I can do about it right now.

"They don't bring the director for house calls," Mac warns as Mrs. Young buzzes him in.

For Riestra to be here, they're not screwing around. Neither am I. For centuries, the Culper Ring has worked outside the system, safeguarding the United States against whatever abuses inevitably show their faces. For the past few hours, the face that keeps showing up is Riestra's. Maybe he's just trying to protect the commander in chief. Maybe he and White Eyelashes are in this together. Either way, here's the one thing I can't shake: Whatever message those body parts are sending, the only way to bury them that close to the President is to get help from someone inside.

"Why's the Secret Service here? What's going on?" Mrs. Young asks.

I glance out the window, toward the alley behind the building. Right now, I'm half a step ahead of the Service. I've done nothing wrong; it doesn't matter if they find me here. But if they do, I'll be sitting in this living room for the next three hours as they pump me with questions.

"Where's your fire escape?" I ask Mrs. Young.

"There's isn't a—"

"Please. I know you have one. Is it off the bedroom or the living room?" I owe Marshall for that. He taught me never go in a place unless I know how to get out.

Mrs. Young doesn't answer. Outside, a thundering herd echoes up the stairwell. Riestra's not alone.

"You have nothing to hide," I say to Mrs. Young. "You can tell them you spoke to me. They know who I am. Give them all the details. Tell every agent that's here."

I take off for the bedroom, a cramped little rectangle that sadly reminds me of my own room. Alarm clock on only one of the night-stands. Creased pillows on only half the bed. This is how I've lived for too long.

Through the window, I spot the rusty grating of the fire escape.

"You know what happened to my son, don't you? You don't think it was suicide," Mrs. Young calls out behind me as I tug at the closed window. Years of old paint crack and fall as the window gives way and the cold twirls across my torso.

Back in the living room, there's a loud knock on the door. Riestra's here. Mrs. Young doesn't move, staying with me.

"Ma'am, I promise you one thing," I tell her, straddling the windowsill with one foot outside. "I want to catch the person who did this. I know what it means when you don't know why your loved one is gone."

She nods tearfully at me.

The knocking on the front door gets louder than ever. **"Mrs. Young, please open up!"**

I duck out onto the fire escape, scrambling quickly down the metal stairs, bits of rust biting at my hands. Third floor...second floor... I kick at the metal pin that frees the final ladder and sends it dropping to the ground. Rung by rung, fist below fist, I clamber down, leaping off the final perch as my soles smack the pavement.

Before I can even stand up, there's a quiet click behind me.

"We're the Secret Service," A.J. says. "You think we don't cover the back exit?"

## 59

The gun was an antique, releasing a small black musket ball that blew out the front of Marshall's armpit, taking hunks of muscle, skin, and blood with it. Back during the Civil War, guns like this needed to be reloaded, and the gunpowder repacked, after each shot. Instead, this modified six-shooter gave Ezra multiple shots.

For a half-second, Marshall just stood, staring down at the shreds of skin of his blown-out armpit like he was staring at a bruise he didn't remember getting. As training took over, he reached into the bloody hole, which swallowed his fingers up to the knuckle. If the bullet was there, he couldn't find it. His heart took a long, aching beat. Then the burning pain arrived.

His legs wouldn't work. Crumpling to the ground and gripping his own armpit, Marshall clenched his teeth, refusing to let himself scream. A sound still came out of him, a guttural wail that sounded like the howl of a dying dog.

"Y'know, another inch over and I would've collapsed your lung," Ezra said, standing over him. "Don't worry, though. In that part of your armpit, there're no major vessels, no critical organs. Though eventually, the blood loss will certainly be a problem."

"Y-You should've put that bullet in my head," Marshall growled.

Ezra smiled at that. "You think I came to kill you? I did my homework, Marshall. I know who you are."

"You know nothing about me."

"That's not true. There's a reason I want you on my team. So here's your chance," Ezra said, squatting down next to him and putting a hand on his shoulder. "Would you like to join the Knights of the Golden Circle?"

## 60

**Twenty-nine years ago**
**Devil's Island**

It was just another breakfast. And since it was Friday, the cooks had put little bits of bacon into the eggs as a treat. Ever since Julian died, the Plankholders had been tossed a few extra indulgences.

For most of the troops, it was an appreciated gesture. For Alby, it would've been too. But as he sat there at his cafeteria table, replaying that moment last night when he saw Julian—**alive and doing just fine**—Alby didn't care much about breakfast, much less bacon-infused eggs.

"You eating your biscuit?" the kid from Arkansas asked, sitting across from him.

"Not really," Alby replied, sliding Arkansas his tray and working hard to keep everything looking normal.

"You look like hell," Arkansas added. "What's wrong with you anyway?"

"Wha? No, I'm fine. I just— Crappy night's

sleep."

Arkansas nodded. So many of them had been fighting diarrhea. "That mean you're not eating your eggs?" Arkansas asked.

Alby spun his cafeteria tray, sliding the eggs across the table. "By the way, you seen Nico?" Alby asked.

"Right behind you."

Alby turned, just in time to spot Nico standing there, silent as could be, with his own tray of bacony eggs.

"Mind if I sit?" Nico asked, sounding congested.

"Sure. Yeah. Of course," Alby stuttered, pointing next to him. He hadn't seen Nico come in, much less get in line or get his food. It was almost as if he'd appeared from nowhere. But what unnerved Alby more than anything else was the simple fact that Nico was now sitting at Alby's table. Except for Arkansas Ovalface and...well, Julian...almost no one ever sat at Alby's table.

Otherwise, like any morning, everyone was in his usual place. Timothy and the meatheads were at their regular table. The marine guards were at their regular table.

And at the front of the room, Colonel Doggett sat alone at the head of his own regular table.

"You eating your biscuit?" Arkansas asked Nico.

"Leave me alone, Ovalface," Nico threatened, putting a hand on his biscuit and pulling out a familiar paperback book. The same book that had been on Nico's bed last night. Julian's old book. **The Diary of Dr. Mudd**, one of Abraham Lincoln's killers.

When Alby woke up twenty minutes ago, of course he'd wanted to tell someone— to tell **anyone**—what he'd seen last night. But as he watched Nico sit there, hunched over and lost in the pages of the last book Julian was seen reading, something told Alby to keep his mouth shut. At least until he had more info.

For a while, Alby sat there, eyeing Colonel Doggett at the head table. Doggett didn't look at Alby, didn't even glance in his direction. If Doggett knew that Alby had been there last night, ducking behind the date palm tree, Alby wouldn't even be here this morning, right?

**For sure**, Alby decided. **Had to be.**

Ten minutes later, the colonel wiped his mouth and bused his tray. Leaving his table, Doggett nodded a hello to the marine guards, and another to Dr. Moorcraft. But as the colonel slid his dirty cafeteria tray into the rolling rack, Alby realized that Doggett was doing the one thing he never did on **any** morning: He was headed for the Plankholders' tables.

"Everybody get a good night's sleep?" Colonel Doggett asked, stopping midway between the meatheads' table and Alby's.

"Yes, sir," Timothy shot back along with a few others. Nico didn't react at all, didn't even look up from his book.

For a half-second—no more than that— the colonel's dirt brown eyes turned to Nico, then to Alby. Nico still didn't look up. It was just a half-second. It felt like an eternity.

"I like the bacon in the eggs. Makes it good, right?" the colonel asked to another round of **Yes, sirs**.

That was it.

Doggett didn't look at Nico again. Didn't look at Alby either. But Alby was looking at him, studying the colonel's face, his exclamation point stance, and the only thing he was carrying: a manila file folder tucked under his arm.

No big deal. Every colonel has files. But as Doggett nodded goodbye and pivoted toward the door, Alby couldn't help but think that somewhere on this island there had to be other files. Records that could explain what was really going on.

"Mind if I eat the hash browns too?" Arkansas asked Alby.

Without a word, Alby got up from his seat.

As the colonel shoved the screen door open and left the cafeteria, Alby followed directly behind him.

Alby knew what he had to do, and where to find what he was looking for.

## Today
## Arlington, Virginia

"G-Go screw yourself," Marshall said, fighting to take a breath and feeling like there was a thorn in his lungs.

"Before you say no—" Ezra began.

"I already said no. If you want to keep fighting...I-I told you where to put your next bullet," he said, crawling away from Ezra, away from the barely conscious Clementine. Marshall's body was in shock. His armpit was burning. He cupped the bullet wound with one hand as blood seeped between his fingers, leaving a trail of droplets behind him. Based on his breathing, the bullet hadn't gone clean through his armpit. Something internal was hit.

"Where you going? To your car?" Ezra asked. "Don't be such a martyr. You know you're not leaving Clementine behind. And you're certainly in no shape to move her. It's really a teachable moment: At times like this, wouldn't it be nice to have someone you can call for help?"

"Eff you. You shot me."

"Would you've talked to me otherwise? Should I have just texted you a quick note instead: **Wanna hear about the Knights? Smiley face!?**"

Crawling on his belly, Marshall looked down at his shirt, where a small spot of blood was growing next to his nipple. The bullet had ricocheted off his ribs. "You're a sick person, and you don't even know how sick you are," Marshall said, coughing the words as his lungs tightened. "Your so-called Knights—"

"You have no idea what the Knights are!"

"I know **exactly** what the Knights are! You think we don't know about the buried arms? Or that Clementine didn't tell me about the maudlin little photo you carry around of you and your grand-father meeting Ronald Reagan? Y'know how many grip-and-grin photos a U.S. President takes? Reagan probably took—**ahuh**— he probably took eighty **just that day**! It doesn't mean you're special! And it certainly doesn't mean you're on some holy mission! You're a child who's chasing the Culper Ring for nothing more than imagined revenge."

Ezra stood there, posture square as ever, licking his own busted lip from the car crash. "You put a lot of faith in the Culper Ring considering how little you know about them."

"Whatever you're about to say, you're a liar," Marshall insisted, still belly-crawling to the car, each new breath bringing new pain.

"Ask this: Do you have any idea who's in charge of the Culper Ring, or what they really stand for? Or are you just as naïve as Beecher?"

Marshall stopped, glancing back over his shoulder. Ezra's clothes were brand-new. Herringbone coat. Polo shirt. Over-priced dark jeans. But the way his jeans were bunched at the waist, held in place by his belt... They didn't quite fit. Like he was wearing someone else's clothes. It was the same with his belt. The prong of the belt pointed left, like you see with some-one left-handed. But Ezra was holding his gun with his right. Something was off. Why would someone dress like someone else?

"Unsettling thought, right?" Ezra asked. "You think you're playing for the Culper Ring angels, but what if you picked the wrong side?"

"Tell me why you put that coin in the buried arm."

"You really are lost, aren't you? When someone sends a message—"

"Tell me about my father."

"First things first. I want you to join us, Marshall. And I think you will...once you hear the real mission of the Knights of the Golden Circle."

## 62

## Baltimore, Maryland

A.J. studies me, arms crossed over his tie, not saying a word. He always plays pissed when he sees me, but as he stares down at me, his thick ribcage rising and falling, it's like he's breathing different.

"I figured you'd be with Francy and the big man," I challenge.

Casually, he glances up at the tall brick building, studying the fire escape, but not answering.

"Riestra must be pretty invested to come here and do his own legwork," I add.

A.J. glances around the L-shaped alley like I'm not there.

"A.J., did you hear what I—?"

His eyes slide sideways toward me. He chews on some imaginary gum in his cheek. "No sign of Beecher back here," he says into his hand mic, eyes perfectly locked on me.

I take a step back, confused. The blue-jeweled lapel pin is gone from his chest.

He's no longer on Wallace duty.

Still in shock, I head toward the side of the alley that leads out to the street.

A.J. shakes his head, then catches himself. This isn't easy for him. Before he can talk himself out of it, he points with his forehead to the other end of the alley, which cuts behind a neighboring building.

**This way...?** I ask with a glance.

He turns his back to me.

I take the hint, running slowly at first, then faster as I hear a window open four stories above us.

**"She said Beecher came this way!"** Riestra shouts from the fire escape.

"I'll check again!" A.J. shouts back. "You sure he didn't go up to the roof!?"

I'm running so fast, I don't hear the answer.

Shooting out of the alley and reaching the street, I make a quick left, back toward Tot's—

**Screeeech.**

The car appears from nowhere, bucking to a stop in front of me.

"Don't look so surprised. C'mon, get in!" an older woman with a wide nose, outdated horn-rimmed glasses, and a silver bob calls out. Usually, her voice is in my ear, coming through a voice modulator: Amazing Grace aka Immaculate Deception.

"Mac, what're you—?"

"The Service traced your car. That's how they knew you were here."

"Who told you that?" I ask, tugging open the door and sliding into the passenger seat.

She shoots me a look over the brow of her horn-rims. On her wrists are two carpal tunnel Velcro braces. She undoes the Velcro, then redoes it again. "What's my job, Beecher? You think I don't have some-one in the Service?"

She hits the gas. I'm staring in the passenger rearview, watching the building shrink behind us.

"Why didn't you tell me you were here?" I ask.

"I just got word about the car on the way here. My hope was, you'd be out of there before they came."

"You were wrong about that."

"But you know what I'm right about?" she asks. "Riestra isn't just looking for White Eyelashes anymore. He's also looking for **you**."

## 63

"To understand the Knights," Ezra began as he tucked his antique gun back in his coat, "you first need to understand the Culper Ring."

"I already know about the Ring," Marshall shot back, still down on his belly, gritting his teeth to get a deep breath. If he was lucky, the crash was loud enough that someone called an ambulance. He closed his eyes to listen. Nothing was coming.

"You know the story Beecher told you... and that Tot told him."

"Just get to the point. If you think the Ring is evil—"

"Evil? You think this is some childhood game? What George Washington built with the Ring...I admire it more than you know. In fact, for those first few years, the Ring worked beautifully. But there are some things the Culper Ring can't do. Ever hear of Thomas Hickey and William Tryon?"

Marshall shook his head, keeping his chin

down. He was finally in position. He had a clear view under the gray car. During the crash, his gun had gone flying. It should be here somewhere.

"Back in 1776, Thomas Hickey was in charge of protecting one of the military's biggest generals. Hickey's friend Tryon was the governor of New York. Together, along with the mayor, they plotted to kill Hickey's boss, a man named George Washington." Ezra waited for Marshall to look up, but when he didn't, he added, "Can you imagine where we'd be today if they succeeded? Forget Benedict Arnold. Thomas Hickey is the name we should remember. But lucky us, the Culper Ring did their job, rounding up Hickey and everyone involved. That's their mission: to protect the President."

"They protect the **Presidency**," Marshall gasped. The thorn in his lung felt like it was slicing downward.

"They **try** to protect the Presidency. But everything has its limits. In the end, Hickey was found guilty and became the first person to be executed for treason in what would be these United States. To send a clear message, George Washington made every member of the military attend the hanging. Twenty thousand men watched as Hickey swung by his snapped neck. Fair punishment, right? Except for this: Hickey was the **only one** punished. The other conspirators—the mayor, even the governor—all the big shots—walked free. As usual. Some say it's because there wasn't enough evidence, others say Washington didn't want another political fight."

"If you have a point, make it."

"I looked you up, Marshall. Three years in the marines, then dismissed for not following orders and conduct unbecoming an officer. They asked you to do something you didn't like, didn't they? Is that how you got those burns, or did they come from civilian life?"

Still on his belly, Marshall held tight to his wound, his heart beating through his armpit. He scanned around for the gun, but he saw nothing but broken glass.

"The military trained you well, though. So let's stick with that training," Ezra added. "What's the most important punch in a fight?"

Marshall didn't answer.

"You know this: the first one," Ezra said. "So when Governor Tryon's group tried to kill George Washington—**and got to walk away scot-free!**—let's just say not every member of the Culper Ring thought they should be so forgiving. Don't forget, this was 1776. The height of the Revolutionary War. Think of the stakes. They took a potshot at our leader. If you're trying to keep our country safe, do you turn the other cheek...or do you answer them back and let them know they can't do that again? Within the Ring, the men began to talk. And as with any group, it's like a plate glass window—once there's a fracture, it slowly begins to spread...until eventually, there's a break."

"I get it," Marshall grunted through gritted teeth, trying to re-member his training. "That splinter group became the Knights of the Golden Circle."

"You make it sound so simple. I'm not sure they even had a name back then. They were just a few men in the back room of a tavern. Then they added a few more men. Then they had their own meetings, their own discussions. And finally, their own solutions.

"A few years later, Governor Tryon was found dead from an unmanned illness. And y'know who else was found dead? His son, then his daughter. Tryon's group never threatened our country again."

Down on the ground, Marshall stared at the stain of blood that was widening across his shirt. "There's no victory in murdering children."

"There's also no victory in having your enemies slit your throat in the middle of the night. Don't act like you don't understand. As a marine, you took an oath to keep this country safe. For over two hundred years, the Knights have done the same thing— by staying in the shadows and taking on the battles no one else wants," Ezra explained, his voice picking up speed.

"Look at...look at...look at the end of World War II. The U.S. government was spending millions recruiting the Nazis' top scientists to keep them from working for our enemies. At one point, four of the Nazis' senior bomb-builders were trying to sneak into the Soviet Union. Three others were making their way to our then-enemies in Egypt. Thanks to the Knights, none of them made it. Was that a hard decision? Absolutely. But was it the **right** decision? The safety of two hundred million Americans versus seven back-stabbing Nazis determined to kill us? What would you have done, Marshall?" he asked. "The only reason this country's been able to live in peace for so long is because someone's out there making those tough choices."

"I liked your speech better when Jack Nicholson was up on that wall, shouting it at Tom Cruise."

"Don't pretend you're not who you are. Soldiers are always soldiers. They need the fight."

"You're wrong."

"I'm right. I see the way you're no longer searching under the car, trying to find your gun. You're no longer picking apart what I'm wearing. Look me in the eye and tell me you're not thinking about the Knights' mission. Right before 9/11, in the hours **before** those planes flew into the World Trade Center, hundreds of Saudi families left the U.S. in the middle of the night, like they knew what was coming. The Saudi government, with all their oil, walked away scot-free under sovereign immunity. You think that's the right reaction by our leaders? Is that the country we're supposed to be?"

Marshall's only answer was the huffing of his breath.

"I know you've wrestled with those same hard decisions. You brought that gun with you today," Ezra said. "When you came here with Clementine, were you planning to put me under citizen's arrest, or a solution grounded in a bit more justice?"

For a full minute, Marshall stayed silent. He rolled onto his side, feeling the thorn in his lung. "You said the Culper Ring hunted the Knights. Why?"

"Jack Ruby."

Marshall scowled. "You're officially insane."

"Trust me, when I read the diaries, I was just as doubtful. But you need to understand, for over two hundred years, from John Wilkes Booth to Lee Harvey Oswald, there have always been those who have used the Knights' name for their own benefit. Booth claimed to be a Knight, though most think it was just a distraction. Oswald was rumored to be one too. Neither of them were true Knights. But in those days after JFK's death, while our country was still reeling from watching the President's head explode, LBJ didn't turn to the Culper Ring. He turned to the Knights and called on a man who would become one of our most famous members."

"You're saying Jack Ruby was a Knight?"

"He did what had to be done to keep this country safe. Look at the facts: If Ruby hadn't fired that famous shot, young communist Lee Harvey Oswald would've had a trial that dragged on for months, where he'd rant against our government and pull our attention away from the Soviet threat. Can you imagine putting Jackie Kennedy on the witness stand, where the sleaziest defense lawyers in the world would've turned her into a sobbing mess as they forced her to watch, along with the rest of us, the exact moment when her young husband's brain was spit across her bright pink suit? C'mon, Marshall, answer me honestly: With the Cold War at stake, what was truly better for our country: spending another year reliving JFK's assassination and being emotionally torn apart, or putting the entire incident squarely behind us?"

Down on the ground, Marshall stared at Ezra, not saying a word. But he still heard the advice his captain had given him when he first enlisted: **I'd rather be judged by eight of my peers than carried in a coffin by eight of them.**

"We can't change who we are," Ezra added. "You're different than Beecher. You see what he'll never see. My grandfather saw it too. The Culper Ring is a perfectly designed shield. And sometimes the President needs a shield to protect him. But sometimes he needs something more aggressive. Something from the shadows."

Silent, Marshall managed a small grin.

"I know you see it. I **knew** you would. So let me make it official," Ezra said, reaching his hand out to help Marshall up. "Will you join me as a member of the Kn—?"

The gun erupted with a pop, and a burst

of blood catapulted forward. Ezra never saw it coming. He was in mid-turn as Clementine stood behind him, swaying and fighting to stand as she pulled the trigger. The bullet should've hit Ezra in the back of the head, but as he spun, it blazed through his right cheek, splitting the skin and taking some bone with it.

**"Ahhhh! My face!"** Ezra screamed, stumbling forward and trip-ping over Marshall, who could barely hold his head up. **"You crazy bitch! I'll kill you!"**

As Ezra continued to stagger, Marshall rolled onto his back, revealing a wide pool of blood below him.

"Please tell me you know he's full of shit," Clementine stuttered, limping toward Marshall.

"S-Shoot him again. Don't let him go," Marshall insisted. His face was gray. Each breath was a hard wheeze.

Struggling to keep her balance, Clemen-tine pulled the trigger again, her bald head shiny with sweat. The shot missed, and a neighboring storefront's glass window shattered. An alarm screamed. That would bring the police.

She stumbled over to Marshall, kneeling at his side. "Oh God— what'd he do to you?" The blood kept coming, pouring from his armpit.

"Don't...don't let him go!" Marshall yelled, trying to move, but getting nowhere.

In the distance, Ezra turned the corner, still clutching his face as he ran from the plaza. Clementine's own legs were throbbing. Her face and arms were dotted with cuts. She could either give chase or help Marshall. It was no choice at all.

Hobbling and darting for the herbal shop, which had bandages and medical supplies, Clementine yanked on the door. But as she stepped inside and was embraced by the smell of sandalwood incense, there was no sign of the nurse in the sage green uniform. Or her white cat.

"Please, I need help!" Clementine screamed, tasting her own blood in her mouth. Don't pass out, she told herself. "Someone's been shot!"

No one answered.

Wasting no time, Clementine speed-limped, doing her best to run to the break-room in back. The refrigerator door that hid the sterile area was wide open. Yet it wasn't until Clementine stepped inside that she remembered: **That door's never open.**

**"Mrrrr,"** the skinny white cat murmured from the far left-hand corner.

Clementine jumped at the sound, spinning to find the chubby Asian doctor hunched facedown over the rolling medical cart. The nurse in the sage green uniform was right next to him, facedown over the make-shift dental chair. A thin but crooked dark line ran down both their spines, seeping though the back of their shirts like a skunk stripe.

Blood. From the wet black holes in the back of their heads, neither had known what hit them.

**"Prrrd,"** the cat called out in a trilling sound that was more insistent. At the nurse's left foot, there was a splatter of blood. The cat kept circling near it, trying to get closer to her owner, yet avoiding the blood.

Sirens sounded in the distance.

**Run!** Clementine told herself. But instead, her first instinct was...

"C'mere!" she called out, her whole body

aching as she scooped up the cat and held him against her chest. Behind her, the drug closet was locked. She rummaged through a few open cabinets, grabbing bandages, gauze, and anything else that looked helpful.

"Don't fight me, cat!" she warned. As she hobbled back through the herbal shop and out the front door, the sirens doubled in intensity.

"Marshall, we need to go," she called out, reaching down and grabbing the metal bridge with her fake teeth. She tossed everything, including the cat, into her rental car's open window.

Marshall didn't move. His face was pasty, his half-open eyes looking waxy and wet, like he wasn't in there.

"Marsh, don't do that! Don't leave me!" Clementine shouted, grabbing him by his good arm and trying to drag him toward the car. He was too heavy.

The sirens were only getting louder.

# 64

## Baltimore, Maryland

"And you're sure you didn't see him?" Director Riestra asked.

"You think I don't know what he looks like?" A.J. pushed back. "I checked the alley myself. Both of them," he added, pointing to each of the empty brick alleyways. Truth is, A.J. was still surprised at his decision to let Beecher go. He hadn't planned it. Like any hasty choice, it'd been more gut than brains. "If Beecher was here, he already got away."

"You keep saying that. But when I got in the apartment, Mrs. Young's bedroom window was still open. She said Beecher had just run out."

"And again, maybe he went up to the roof. Maybe he's faster than we thought. I don't know what you want me to say."

Riestra readjusted his round eyeglasses, then made a little popping noise with his mouth. "For me, y'know what the greatest feature of the Secret Service is, A.J? Our exactitude. When you're on protective detail, it's a perfectly oiled machine. You do eight-hour shifts, then you get to go home for a rest, then, to make sure you're always fresh, you come back and rotate to a new position where you start all over and do it again. Morning shift, afternoon shift, midnight shift. It's like a Model T Ford. Whatever part you're plugged into, the machine works exactly the same.

"Of course, we have to keep an eye on the rotation system. So sometimes you work the one-spot and get to be on the left shoulder of the President, sometimes you do advance work before he gets there, and sometimes you're stuck babysitting the press or watching monitors in a basement," Riestra added. "But when I looked at the past few weeks, you know what I found? You, A.J., always seemed to pull that one-spot. Day after day, week after week, you always got that same assignment: left shoulder of the President. And when I dug a little deeper, do you know why you got that spot?"

A.J. stood there, his posture stiff as oak.

In a corner of the alley, a swirl of dead leaves spun in a mini-whirlwind.

"I looked it up; it was fascinating," Riestra said. "You got that spot because the chief of staff **personally** put in a request for you. But y'know what I also know? The chief of staff doesn't know you all that well, which tells me that that request came from someone even higher up the totem pole. And considering how high the chief of staff sits, well...who else does that really leave to make a re-quest like that?"

"Sir, I'm not sure what you're—"

"You're in my damn way, asshole. I know you're lying about Beecher. I know you saw him come off that fire escape. So whatever private thing you've got going with the President—I don't care if he keeps you around so you can go down on him every day—"

"Sir, that's not—"

Riestra grabbed A.J.'s shoulder, pinching the skin on his neck hard. Pulling him close, Riestra whispered, "You have no idea how close you are to having the very worst day of your life. I don't care if you know God Almighty. When I ask you something, don't lie to me. We clear?"

A.J. nodded. He smelled cigarettes on Riestra's breath.

"I'm putting you back on training duty," Riestra added, storming toward the front of the building. "If Wallace wants you, he can come get you."

Standing there in the alley, mentally replaying the slow-motion end of his career, A.J. wasn't surprised. This day had been coming. From the moment the President had asked him for that first favor back in Ohio, A.J. had known he was out on a moral tightrope. It's hard to say no when the most powerful man in the world asks you personally. But with each passing request, that rope was slowly twisting into a noose.

A.J. was tempted to call Francy, or former White House doctor Stewart Palmiotti, or even the private number that would connect him to Wallace himself. Instead he stood there, drenched in the alchemy of loss and embarrassed relief that follows the death of someone who'd been suffering for too long. In the corner, the whirlwind of leaves continued to swirl.

At the far end of the alley, Director Riestra headed for his black sedan.

It was that annoying little detail—of Riestra ducking into his car—that floated there, nipping at the back of A.J.'s brain. If Director Riestra cared about the buried arms, shouldn't he be upstairs, talking to Mrs. Young? Shouldn't he be getting more details about the victim? Instead, the director of the Secret Service got in his car—alone, without his own chief of staff—and drove away.

**Huh,** A.J. thought. **There's one other person who would really want to know that.**

## 65

## Twenty-nine years ago
## Devil's Island

Today it was the cannons. Just as it had been the day before, and the day before that.

"Here, use this," the marine guard named Dominic said, handing Alby a long metal pole with a moon-shaped metal scraper at the end of it.

For three days now, the Plankholders had been in charge of cleaning and restoring the island's twenty-five-ton Rodman cannons. Back during the Civil War, only 320 of these massive cannons had been produced. Fort Jefferson had six—all still intact—one at each of the six bastions, pointed out from the roof of the six-sided fort.

Back then, each cannon could fire a cannonball over three miles, all the way to Loggerhead Key, making these the most powerful guns in existence. During the 1900s, the iron carriages that they were mounted on were sold off as scrap metal by the military. But since the cannons themselves were too heavy to move, they'd been sitting here, rusting in the salty, sandy terreplein for decades.

Three days ago, Alby and the Plankholders had used hydraulic jacks to prop each cannon up, one by one, then wedged stacks of wood under them so they could roll them onto granite blocks and point them even farther out over the parapets.

Two days ago, they'd used hammers and putty knives to scrape away the rust pustules and half-inch-thick corrosion that coated the exterior surface of each cannon, especially where it'd been lying in the sand.

Today, six of them, including Alby and Nico, were armed with long moon-shaped scrapers, which they'd use like giant Q-tips to reach into the fourteen-foot-deep mouth of each cannon. One cannon was filled with dead birds and crabs. Another had ancient bottles in it. All had thick coats of rat droppings and plant debris. For six hours, Alby baked in the sun, fighting to scrape it all away.

According to the guard, when they finished, a small electronic device the size of a shoebox would be inserted into each cannon, then the muzzle would be covered. Supposedly, it'd help them track any changes in the cannon's temperature or humidity, for preservation purposes. They'd know if an animal got inside. Or even a dead body, Dominic explained with his panting laugh.

But right now, Alby was still scraping at layer after layer of rat droppings, and sweating so hard his fingers were starting to prune. Up here on the roof, there was no shade; this close to summer, there was also no breeze. "102 degrees exactly," Nico muttered to no one in particular.

Still, for the Plankholders, there was one benefit to being on Fort Jefferson's roof: the view. For three days now, they'd stared out at the ocean, mesmerized by the aqua-marine horizon. During those moments, this island really was the only place left on this earth. For Alby, though, it wasn't the ocean view that captured his attention. It was a different one.

Throughout these three days, while his

fellow Plankholders looked **up and out**, Alby stared **in and down**, with a perfect view of the fort's open hexagon-shaped courtyard. From up here, Alby could see it all: the top of every tree, the roof of every building, and of course, where everyone was going.

For three consecutive days, Alby watched. And eventually, he became certain of this: Every day, after Colonel Doggett left breakfast and headed back to the officers' quarters, within ten minutes, one person always followed.

Dr. Moorcraft.

## 66

## Ten days ago
## Carter Lake, Iowa

Dr. Moorcraft bolted awake, thinking he was in bed. He was seated in his kitchen, hands locked with plastic zip ties behind his back.

"Whabuh— **Why am I—!? My finger!?**" he howled, thrashing around, bucking his chair against the Mediterranean tile, fighting like a dog trying to see its tail.

"I peeled the skin from your pinkie," Nico explained, sitting across from the doctor, palms flat on the antique farm table. The open needle-nose pliers lay between them.

**"Look how wide the pliers sit when they're open,"** the dead First Lady said. **"It looks…"**

**"…like a cross,"** Nico and the First Lady said simultaneously. Nico smiled. There was nothing better than being understood.

"Why're—? Who're you talking to?" the doctor asked.

"No, I agree," Nico said to the First Lady.

"I'm doing his ring finger next."

"Nico, whatever you're seeing... I don't know your history, but you've been on antipsychotics and neuroleptics for years. If you're off those, your hallucinations will start getting wor—"

"You don't have a wedding band," Nico said to the doctor. "It was the same with Colonel Doggett."

"You saw Doggett? Is that how you—?"

"Did your wife die, or did she leave you, like Doggett's did?"

"Son, you're not hearing me. I'm trying to help you."

"That's your second lie. All these years, they told me my sickness...that God chose me for this. That He— That He— That He made me this way...that He put this sickness in me. I know now that's not true."

**"God made you good,"** the First Lady said.

"God made me good!" Nico agreed, hands still flat on the table, like he was cupping something under his left palm.

"What's in your hand?" the doctor asked, still twisting to free his own arms. He was clearly in pain, but like the specialists in St.

Elizabeths, he fought hard to keep control.

"Do you know why we all wear wedding bands on our left hands?" Nico challenged. "It dates back to the ancient Romans and Egyptians, who thought that the fourth finger on your left hand connected with a vein that led directly to your heart. Vena amoris, they called it. The vein of love."

"Son—"

"It's idiocy really. They were proven utterly wrong. But that's how medicine is, isn't it? Sometimes it makes the gravest of errors," Nico said, leaning forward, his face darkening.

"Nico, I'm sure that speech sounded perfect in your head, but whatever you're after, this venture is pointless. Why would—?"

"I went through your drawers, Doctor. I found **this**." Nico slid his cupped hand forward and lifted it, revealing a pile of over two dozen tiny white...

"**Baby teeth,**" the First Lady explained as Nico brushed a few of them from his hand and they bounced across the table.

"You've been in this house a long time, haven't you?" Nico added. "That many teeth... You raised your kids in this house.

You hid here all these years when the government gave you a new life. But not everyone—"

"She's your daughter, isn't she?"

**"Don't answer him,"** the First Lady insisted.

"The girl on the news. The one who they say helped you escape. I know she's your daughter."

Nico froze, blinking over and over. "Who told you that?"

"She's sick, yes?" the doctor asked. "Is that why you came here?"

**"Cut his other finger,"** the First Lady said. **"Take the knife. Slice him where his wedding band used to be. Don't trust a word he says until you peel his skin like a grape and he—"**

"Tell me her symptoms," Dr. Moorcraft added. "How's she presenting? Is it cancer?"

Nico nodded as the First Lady continued to yell.

"How far along? Any idea of her staging?" Moorcraft asked.

Nico's voice was a whisper. He glanced down at the table. "Her teeth are falling out."

Moorcraft's face didn't shift. He barely moved. But Nico had been around enough doctors to know when the nightmare was worse than even they'd anticipated. "I'm sorry she's suffering."

"You need to help her," Nico insisted.

"I don't think you underst—"

**"You. Need. To. HELP HER!"** Nico exploded, leaping from his seat, pouncing across the table and scattering all the teeth as his hot breath blasted Moorcraft's face. As he collided with the doctor, Moorcraft's chair tipped back.

Twisting mid-fall, Moorcraft landed on his side. There was a pop at his elbow, where it was pinned by the chair.

**"My arm...!"**

Kneeling down, Nico shifted the doctor's arm so it was no longer pinched by the chair. But he left him on the floor. "You need to help her!" Nico again growled.

"You're not listening! I wish I could save her. I wish I could give you everything you need and get you out of my—"

"You put something in us! You know what it was!"

**"It doesn't matter what it was!"** the

doctor shot back, the side of his head still pressed to the floor, arms behind his back. "You were part of an experiment. There were side effects no one ever anticipated, and now your daughter's experiencing an uncontrolled division of abnormal cells, the likes of which we've never seen before. You know what the cure for that is? **Nothing.**"

Still down on both knees, Nico shook his head.

"With you—and your daughter—we were trying to do Something noble, something grand. But for you to come here and think that if you skin me alive, I'll pull out a magic test tube filled with a magic green elixir... This isn't a spy movie. There's no secret antidote that you pour into her mouth just as she's about to die. If your daughter's disease has progressed this far, I'm sorry, but there's nothing left to do."

Nico shook his head faster than ever. The First Lady knelt next to him, putting an arm around him.

"Your daughter needs you now. More than ever. But if you truly want to help her..." Lying on his side, down on the

Mediterranean tile, Moorcraft craned his neck and turned toward Nico. "...the best thing you can do is make sure she doesn't suffer."

A pit opened in Nico's throat, a twisting, elastic crater that stretched down his chest, past his stomach, tugging from within, hollowing him out. Next to him, the First Lady whispered that it was part of God's plan, but as Nico knelt there, replaying the past few weeks—

Every father has dreams for his child. For decades now, Nico had kept those dreams buried, locked away. Indeed, for most people, the biggest dreams usually stay hidden. Then, two months ago, Clementine had returned to his life. Nico was doubtful at the time. He didn't know this woman, and so many wanted so much from him. Yet one night, back when they were still sleeping in the car, Nico was startled awake, hearing something outside. Glancing out the back window, Nico followed the sound. It was Clementine, head bowed low. **Please, God, keep my dad Nico healthy and safe.** She was saying a prayer. For him.

A lump clenched his throat. Nico never mentioned it to her. But in that moment, as a father, Nico opened that old box and carefully, curiously, cautiously, returned to those old dreams. For these past few weeks, those dreams were his fuel, his purpose. And now, down on his knees in the kitchen, no matter how hard Nico grabbed at those dreams, they were nothing but wisps of smoke. To have Clementine return was life-changing. But Nico knew, he should've always known: In life, especially for him, some things can't be changed.

**"Nico, talk to me,"** the First Lady insisted.

"The doctor's telling the truth," Nico said, his voice back to its flat monotone.

"I am! I swear on those baby teeth, I am!" Moorcraft pleaded.

**"You need to kill him,"** the First Lady said.

Nico didn't hear her. He was still staring at the doctor. "How'd you know who Clementine was?"

**"Clementine?"**

"My daughter. When you mentioned her before, how'd you know she was my daughter?"

"Nico, you know how much money was invested in you? You really think we didn't keep track of everything you did?"

Nico nodded. "And the files from back then, where are they now?"

"I-If I had to guess? Right where we left them. On the island."

Nico nodded again, this time a bit slower. "I appreciate that." Climbing up from his knees, he glanced around the rustic and enormous Spanish-style kitchen. "This room is bigger than our day room at St. Elizabeths," Nico added.

"I'm sorry they locked you up there," Moorcraft said, still bound in the chair, lying on his side. "I never wanted—"

The doctor never got the words out.

Nico grabbed the needle-nose pliers from the table and stabbed them deep into Moorcraft's throat. Flecks of blood hit Nico's chin and lips. Arching his arm back, he stabbed the doctor again. And again. And again.

**"There you go, sweetie. We can't change who we are,"** the dead First Lady said with a grin.

Nico was in a frenzy now, gripping Moor-craft's hair and stabbing the doctor in his neck, his face, his cheek. **"You stole my daughter! You stole her life from me! I WANT IT BACK!"** he roared, blinking tears from his eyes, spit flying from his mouth. **"GIVE IT BACK! GIVE ME HER—!"**

**"N-Nico...?"** a brand-new female voice called out from across the room. A younger woman's voice.

Nico turned, following the sound. In the doorway, the over-weight woman who'd driven them here—AnnaBeth—was frozen in place, a thin curl of her wiry black hair twirling down her cheek. "Mother of pearl... Nico, what's happening?" she stuttered, starting to wobble.

Bits of blood spotted Nico's face. One fist still gripped Moor-craft's hair; his other held the pliers, which were deep in the doctor's cheekbone.

**"Nico, she's a witness now,"** the First Lady blurted. **"You know what to do."**

"I-Is that the lawyer?" AnnaBeth said, tears swelling. She looked like she wanted to run, but her legs didn't move. "I thought you were— You said you were coming to speak to him."

"I told you to wait in the car," Nico said, gripping the doctor's hair.

**"You're supposed to be speaking to him,"** AnnaBeth pleaded. "Why're you—? What have you done?"

**"Nico, if she tells anyone you're here..."** the First Lady began. She didn't have to finish the sentence.

"I believed in you!" AnnaBeth cried. "I told everyone you were gentle!"

**"You know what to do with witnesses,"** the First Lady added.

Nico nodded, already hating himself for it. He let go of Moor-craft's hair. The doctor's body slumped to the floor, making a splash in the puddle of his own blood. Nico's free hand held the needle-nose pliers, which had bits of flesh in their tips. He headed toward AnnaBeth.

"Nicky, please," AnnaBeth sobbed. "We're supposed to be to-get her! Please don't do this!" She closed her eyes as Nico got closer. "We're supposed to be together!"

**"This is her own fault. Not yours,"** the First Lady added. AnnaBeth clamped her eyes shut. Nico was so close—almost nose-to-nose—she felt his breath on her face. The last thought in her head was about her dog, and who would pay for him at the kennel.

For a long moment, there was nothing but silence.

When AnnaBeth opened her eyes, the kitchen was empty. Nico was gone.

**"Are you stupid!? What're you doing!?"** the dead First Lady yelled as Nico walked calmly through the living room, back toward the front door. **"You need to get back there and take care of this!"**

Nico ignored her. In life, some things could never be changed. But some things had to be.

**"This is the moment you'll regret,"** the dead First Lady warned. **"When you're lying on the ground and they lock you away for the last time, this is the part where you screwed it up!"**

Pushing the front door open and heading for the car, Nico again didn't answer. He knew what he had to do. And where he had to go—the last place he wanted to be: back where it all started.

## 67

## Today
## Washington, D.C.

A.J. sat in his parked gray Dodge, staring down at the flip phone he used only for private calls. He knew the number on the screen, he knew it by heart: Beecher's number. He just didn't know whether to hit the call button or not.

For two more minutes, he played out the various scenarios. Beecher would definitely appreciate the info. And if the Culper Ring was as good as the President thought, it might even be able to protect him.

But as A.J. sat there in his cold car, his feet getting even colder, he couldn't help but picture what would happen tomorrow morning, when he returned to the Secret Service training facility out in Beltsville. The exact same place where, all those years ago, he'd first started as an agent.

For A.J., that was it. There're two choices

in this world: going forward or going back. It's really no choice at all.

Hitting **end** on his phone, A.J. dialed a brand-new number. It rang once before someone picked up.

"I thought we talked about using this line," Francy said.

"I know. I was just—" He caught himself, refusing to beg. "I wanted to make sure you got there okay."

He could hear Francy rolling her eyes. "Is that your way of trying to find out where we are?"

Of course it was. Over the past few weeks, ever since Palmiotti left the White House, and Francy was brought into the President's circle, A.J. could feel himself being squeezed out. But there was always a way back in.

"I think you may have a problem," A.J. said, careful to use the word you. Not **we**. He'd learned that early: The only way out of the doghouse was to acknowledge you were in it.

"What kind of problem?" Francy asked.

"Riestra." He let it hang there in the air.

"Can you please stop playing coy and

mysterious? It's annoying," Francy said. "I'm listening."

"He's already gone."

Francy stopped at that. "Define gone."

"As in, **got in his car and drove away**. By himself. He didn't talk to Mrs. Young. Didn't ask her any questions. Didn't even stop to find out why her son's arm might've been buried in the Rose Garden. Far as I can tell, the only thing Riestra's hunting is Beecher."

Once again, Francy was silent. "You think Riestra's a Knight."

It was a statement, not a question. "All I'm saying is, I know it's been a rough few days. And I know how hard it is when it feels like one of your own might be working with the other side. But I swear to you, Francy, you know me. You know my family. That's two generations. We'd give our lives to keep Wallace safe...to keep this country safe."

There was nothing but silence. In the background, he heard Francy whisper, "Yes, ma'am." She wasn't just with the President. The First Lady was there too.

"Just tell me what you need me to do,"

A.J. added, well aware that he was begging.

Again, silence. Until…

"Actually, there's one thing we could really use your help with."

"You name it, I'm there."

"This one you need to hear from the man himself."

A.J. squeezed his cold toes into a victorious fist. Those were the words he'd been waiting for. "Just tell me where you are."

# 68

## Washington, D.C.

Mac stays quiet as we ride up in the elevator. Her head is down, away from the camera. She doesn't want to be here. Neither do I. But sometimes, there's no choice.

"Beecher, this is foolish," she whispers as the elevator doors roll open and I head out into the bright white fluorescent-lit hallway of the ICU. "With everything going on—"

"I know what's going on. But you were there when the nurses called. They said something happened with Tot. If you were the one in the coma, wouldn't you want us coming in for you?"

Mac's seventy-two years old. She knows the answer. "Promise me we'll be quick."

"We'll be quick." Nodding a hello to the Jamaican nurse who's always on the night shift, I ask, "How's he doing, Jocelyn?"

"Same," Nurse Jocelyn says, like nothing's wrong.

"**Same?** Someone said that something

happened, that he was sick. They called us from a hospital phone."

Nurse Jocelyn shakes her head. "We don't call anyone. Not unless—" She cuts herself off, trying to keep us calm as we race for Tot's room. "Your sister's in there with him now. I never met her be-fore. That was nice of her to come."

Mac and I both freeze, trading a glance. I have one sister who lives in Wisconsin and takes care of our mom. The other moved to Philadelphia and hasn't visited me a single time since I've been in D.C.

Whoever's in there with Tot isn't my sister.

Racing for the sliding glass door of Room 355, I yank it open.

The lights are dimmed. Tot's in his usual spot, head tipped sideways, mouth sagging open, palms facing up like he's pleading for death. In the corner, in a wood-and-vinyl hospital recliner, sits a tall woman with olive skin and honeycomb-colored hair.

The Archivist from the Secret Service. My pal Mina.

"Y'know, Beecher, for a smart guy," Mina offers, "you don't always do the smart thing."

## 69

How many places can you can hide a U.S. President?

Surprisingly, a lot, A.J. had learned during his first few months on White House detail. In Washington, D.C., there were hiding spots all across the city: in obvious places like bomb shelters below buildings, but also in basements of hotels, in underground mechanical rooms that connected to national monuments, even in the basketball court of the FBI building, a steel-lined room in the Library of Congress, and a docked submarine by the Vice President's house.

Still, all those were short-term spots, in case the President had to be hidden fast. If nothing was nearby, the Service could create one in an instant: In every city the President visits, massive C-17 cargo planes arrive the day before—always at 1 p.m.— delivering ready-to-build octagonal safe-rooms to the hotel. In the President's room, the Service shoves all the couches and chairs against one wall, builds the saferoom panel by panel, then rolls in wide pieces of ballistic glass to cover each window.

If the President has to be moved, helicopters stand ready at Andrews Air Force Base to take him to more long-term facilities, like the White House bomb shelter. If the shelter's compromised, he'll go to Camp David. If that's compromised... The list goes on and on.

Yet as A.J.'s car elbowed through the late traffic on Route 50 and rolled slowly past the Iwo Jima Memorial, he knew that every one of those hiding spots was no longer an option.

Turning up the radio, A.J. tried to lose himself in an old Red Hot Chili Peppers song that reminded him of when he graduated college and moved to D.C. He could smell his first apartment with the carpeting that reeked of perfume and dog pee. But the song wasn't having the calming effect it used to.

Whoever was now leading the Knights, they'd already been inside the White House. The buried arm at Camp David had panicked the Secret Service even more. So if A.J. was guessing about where the President was currently being hidden, he assumed it'd be somewhere like Mount Weather, the self-contained city out in Maryland. Every year, as the President delivered the State of the Union address to the assembled power players in Congress, the Supreme Court, and the full Cabinet, Mount Weather was where they'd hide the one member of the Cabinet who was forced to stay behind in case a terrorist group set off a bomb at the speech and slaughtered the rest of our government.

A decade ago, when too many reporters found out about Mount Weather, it was taken off the list of presidential safehouses. But after 9/11, Homeland Security secretly rebuilt it to serve as the base for the rest of the government in case of terrorist attack. The President had an underground bunker below Building 409. And to this day, directions to the facility were on the back of the IDs for top White House staff. No doubt, it was a reliable choice.

But according to Francy, a predictable one.

Indeed, as A.J. pulled off at the exit from George Washington Memorial Parkway, he still wasn't sure he was headed to the right place. But according to Francy, this was it.

At the end of the ramp, A.J. made a left at the multiple stop signs. No surprise, the wide street was empty, blocked off by yellow metal barricades with signs that read **Gate Closes At 7 p.m**. The street was also cobbled, so cars were forced to slow down. No strangers out here. And no speeding.

In the distance, there was no missing the curved memorial with its tall neoclassical archway. But what made A.J. turn down the radio and kill the Chili Peppers bass solo was the sight of the two guards just in front of the barricade.

They were dressed in fluorescent orange vests to make them look like standard late-night security, but A.J. saw the earpieces they were wearing. Secret Service.

For the average visitor, this was a place to find dead Presidents—not a live one.

The sign read **Arlington National Cemetery**. As A.J. lowered his window, the guard said, "You must be A.J."

## 70

"What're you doing!? Get away from him!" I demand, rushing into Tot's room, past his hospital bed.

"Beecher, I'm not here to hurt anyone," Mina insists. "I just want to talk to you."

"Then do what everyone else does. Call me! Pick up a phone! Or do what your boss does and track my car!"

To her credit, she doesn't take the bait. She sits there evenly, legs crossed. My mother fights like that. It drives me just as crazy.

I turn to check on Tot and it's the first time I realize Mac is gone. She never even came in the room. I don't blame her. The reason she's so good at her job is that, for decades now, she's made sure people like Mina don't know she exists.

"Who was the old lady?" Mina asks, eyeing the sliding glass door.

"Fellow archivist," I insist.

Mina shifts her weight. She doesn't believe it, but she lets it go.

"Why didn't you just call me?" I challenge.

"Would you've come?"

I don't answer. "How'd you know I'd come here?"

"Gina from your Legislative Affairs office. We got our masters in library science together. She says you come here every day anyway. I just needed you a little faster."

I don't say a word. The red blinking life-support machines offer their usual chorus of beeps and hisses.

"So this is Tot. The one you always talk about. He means a lot to you, huh?" she adds.

I stare at her, staying quiet.

"Beecher, I get it. There's not a single good reason for you to talk to me, so let me share this: If Director Riestra really did track your car, this is the very first I'm hearing about it. And if you think that's a lie too, well...if this were all some Riestra ploy, do you think you'd be talking to me right now...or would you be sitting here talking to **him**?"

Rolling the question through my own head, I turn back to Tot, instinctively pulling the edge of his covers over his feet. He's wearing blue anti-embolism socks to make sure he doesn't get blood clots from being bedridden for so long.

"Listen," Mina says, "I didn't come here to intrude. I'll get out of your way, but efore I do..." She opens her purse. "That coin you asked me about, with the owl on it," she says, pulling out a folded sheet of paper. "I figured out what the HL-1024 means. They're coordinates. They point to a place on a map."

She holds out the paper, waiting for me to take it.

"Why're you doing this?" I ask. "Because I let your brother sneak a photo?"

"You really don't see it, do you? James was buried with that photo. It's in his coffin. His request," she says, her voice catching on the words. "You're a good person, Beecher. If you're chasing something, I know you wouldn't ask if it weren't important."

I take the paper from her, still not unfolding it. "I appreciate that."

She stares over at Tot, picking him apart with an archivist's eye. "Is that why he's here? Something with that penny?"

I don't answer.

"Beecher, when you needed help, you called me and I came running. More important, you wouldn't have made that call unless you trusted me. So please don't treat me like I'm some newbie pushing the book cart in the reference room. Whatever you're after, it's clear it goes back to that jeweled Secret Service pin you asked me about. And since the owner of that pin died three weeks ago, and is somehow tied to President Reagan being shot—and for some reason, my boss, Director Riestra, apparently cares enough to track your car, well, as my Nana used to say, when you're knee-high in manure, you can roll up your trousers or roll up your sleeves."

"I'm not sure sleeve-rolling is the real solution here."

"Then let me tell you what is: You can either tell me what's really going on, or you can wait for my bosses to track you down and you can tell them. Personally, I think I'm the far safer option. And one who's already proven herself to you."

Another hollow hiss echoes through Tot's breathing tube. I look at his hands to see if they're moving. Nothing's changed. Not for weeks.

"How'd your brother get injured?" I finally ask.

"What's that have t—?"

"I spent three hours with him. We made small talk about baseball, old documents, and even how the oxygen tube kept giving him nosebleeds. But he never told me how he got hurt."

She pauses, but not for long. "It was years ago."

"Afghanistan?"

"Iraq. I wish I could say we were super-close, but James was almost a decade older than me. It was me, him, and our mom, who was always working, always doing for us. James didn't get the best grades, but he was the one who cooked dinner and made sure the laundry was done. He joined the army because he thought it'd be a cheap way to train doing vehicle maintenance, then he'd send money home so that I'd be able to have more options than he did. Pretty amazing for a loudmouth Red Sox fan."

"So he was injured while serving?"

"Everyone thinks soldiers die by jumping on grenades, but it's rarely that cinematic. James was at the front gate of the base when a red car pulled up driven by a six-teen-year-old kid who leaned out and asked for directions. By the time James got close enough to talk to him, he spotted a yellow jug in the kid's lap, packed with plastic explosives. **Boom**, that was it. By some miracle, James survived, but the shrapnel shredded his lungs, bit into his spine, and even jammed a thin sliver into his brain. Even after years of surgeries and therapy, he was never the same. You saw: He fought to put full sentences together, and when he did, it was to tell you how much he hated the wheelchair and the colostomy bag, or how a Red Sox lineup from five years ago might pull it out today. That's why I wanted just one good day for him. When he started repeating himself and rooting for those old teams, the doctors told me he was having mini-strokes in his brain. They said this might be it. They were right," she says, leaning forward in her chair and staring through me as she replays the memory.

"I'm sorry."

"And I appreciate your instinctive need to console me. But if James's loss taught me anything," she says, motioning over my shoulder, back toward Tot, "it's that when you don't get the father you want, you find the father you need."

I stare down at the man who took me into his life from my very first day at the Archives. A raspy hollow hiss echoes through Tot's breathing tube. I already lost one dad in my life. I don't want to lose two.

"That's not awful advice," I eventually admit.

She laughs at that. "Thanks for setting the bar so low. It really helps tamp down my pesky self-esteem."

"You know what I mean."

"I do. Just like I know this is about more than a flattened old penny with the Lord's Prayer on it. This isn't just some work project, is it? It's cutting pretty deep with you."

I keep staring at the bits of blood on Tot's feeding tube, still holding the folded paper with the map coordinates. If Riestra knew she was here, he'd never let her hand those over. Better yet, Mina knows her boss is tracking me. By offering to help, she's risking her job, risking her life. Tot would tell me never trust anyone. But Tot's not really here. Mina is. And no question, to dig out of manure, sometimes you need an extra hand.

"It's where my father's unit was stationed," I say.

She looks at me, eyebrows crinkled and confused.

"The coordinates you found. On the penny. It's where my dad was—and where I think he died."

"So I was right. This is family," she says, nodding over and over, like she's reliving her own battle. "You won't regret this, Beecher."

"Sure I will. You will too. I'll tell you the rest on the way. Are the coordinates far?"

"Depends," Mina offers. "You got a plane?"

"I actually do." Sliding open the glass door, I peek out into the hospital hallway. Empty. Mac is long gone. I take out my phone to call her. The screen's already lit up. **Call in progress.** "Mac? That you?" I ask into the phone.

"Don't do what you're about to do," Mac warns.

I stop where I am, pointing Mina ahead of me, toward the elevator. For this, I need privacy. "You turned my phone on?" I hiss at Mac. "You've been listening the whole time?"

"And I need you to listen to **me**, Beecher. This woman's being far too helpful for a Secret Service agent, especially when we're worried that the only way White Eyelashes pulled this off is because he was working with a Secret Service agent."

"She's not an agent. She's an archivist. And a friend."

"You have no idea where she's taking you."

"Sure I do—and y'know what else I know? That when it comes to my father, she's the **only** person who's brought me a single answer—and she put herself at risk to do it."

"That doesn't mean she's on your side."

"If she wasn't on my side, you really think Riestra wouldn't be here right now?"

Even Mac can't rebut that. Back in the Rose Garden, there was a reason the

Plankholders penny was being clutched in the buried hand. That penny was a message. And now a location. Finally, we're about to find out where it's pointing—and most important, who sent it. "She's taking me to where my father died," I explain as I start running toward the elevators. Mina's already holding one open. "Now can you get us a plane or not?"

## 71

Ezra was leaning toward the bathroom mirror, so close he could see the pores in his nose, as his phone began to ring. He didn't pick it up; he couldn't. He held a threaded needle in one hand; his other pinched the skin on his cheek, clamping the two layers shut.

The bullet wound looked worse than it was, a fleshy charred line that burrowed diagonally across his cheek. Of course it'd been Clementine. From the moment he first decided to approach her, he'd known she was an animal, no different from her father. But Ezra had thought her self-interest would get him closer to his goal.

Gritting his teeth, Ezra pressed the needle to his face. A sharp stab sent it into his skin, then he looped it around, pulling the thread tight as his skin cinched shut. Truth was, he didn't mind the pain. Great movements required great sacrifice.

Ezra's phone rang again. He still didn't pick it up.

He'd learned from some extreme nature show on cable that you needed to braid five strands of thread for homemade stitches. A local CVS supplied the rest: needles, beige thread, and an alcohol-smelling bathroom where he could lock the door and find privacy for the past twenty minutes.

With another pierce, another loop, and another tug on the thread, the stitches pulled tight and the wound squeezed shut. For a final touch, Ezra added a dab of Krazy Glue to hold the knot in place, still thinking how much easier this would be if he hadn't done what he did to the doctor and the nurse at the herbal shop. He didn't regret it; he had no choice. They knew him too well, and for the Knights to finish their mission, everything had to be—

Ezra's phone had just stopped ringing. Now it was ringing again. Whoever it was, they were calling back.

"Talk," Ezra said, picking it up.

"Sorry, I was— This is Jocelyn. Nurse Jocelyn. From the hospital. You said...uh... you said you'd pay a reward if we saw Something in Tot Westman's room."

"Depends what you saw."

"The guy you asked about. Beecher. He was here, at the hospital."

"He still there now?"

"That depends if you've still got that thousand dollars you offered. I know for sure Beecher's headed to an airport. You give me what you promised, I'll give you where he's going." When Ezra didn't reply, she added, "Listen, I got a daughter in Special Olympics who wants to go to the national games. She ain't getting there unless I find the funds. Now, you want to know where Beecher went or not?"

Ezra glanced at his reflection in the bathroom mirror, feeling the pull of the stitches as a smile took his face. "Nurse Jocelyn, I'll be there in ten minutes."

## 72

A.J. had been to the cemetery before.

His great-great-aunt—an army nurse in World War II—was buried here. Nobody in the family liked her, but they all respected her service, which explained why every trip to D.C. brought them to Arlington National Cemetery.

A.J. had seen the perfectly arranged headstones. He'd seen JFK's eternal flame, and the graves his father liked even more: those of Joe Louis and Lee Marvin. And of course he'd seen the sentinel who stood guard at the Tomb of the Unknowns, and who was there right now, in the darkness with his polished M14 rifle on his shoulder. The sentinel didn't turn, didn't move, as A.J. followed the twisting path past the tomb.

Heading up the hill and following the moonlight and Francy's directions to Section 3, A.J. reached into his pocket, feeling for his phone. He was still tempted to call Beecher. He couldn't explain why.

The President was inviting A.J. back into the family, trusting him enough to bring him here. But the more A.J. climbed the hill, the more headstones he passed, and the more his thumb kept prying open his flip phone and then letting it snap shut.

Up ahead, his destination stood out, even in the darkness. Of over three hundred thousand graves at Arlington National Cemetery, there were only two mausoleums. One was this, a white marble house with a pointed roof and two meatball shrubs in front. Above a tarnished metal door was the engraved name **Miles**.

As a young Civil War hero, Lieutenant General Nelson Miles had risen to the top command of the U.S. Army. But when he criticized our policy in the Philippines, he earned the anger of President Teddy Roosevelt, who, when Miles retired, wouldn't even send him the standard congratulatory note. From that alone, A.J. was well aware why Wallace had picked this place. As with any U.S. President, everything came with a message.

In the end, Miles had lived out the remainder of his life as a nobody. At the age of eighty-five, on a trip to the circus with his grandchildren, as the band began playing the national anthem, Miles stood at attention, saluted the flag, and dropped dead of a heart attack. The new President, Calvin Coolidge, made amends by offering a first-class burial.

Nearly a century later, A.J. stepped across the damp dirt, toward Miles's reward. Planks of rotted wood covered each of the mausoleum's windows and clanked in the wind. A squirrel skittered up one of the building's carved columns, then raced down again as A.J. approached.

Weaving his way among nearby graves, A.J. never took his eyes off the dark mausoleum. There were no lights on inside. No nearby cameras—and most oddly, knowing the Service's protocols for any presidential visit—no guards either. For the first time, A.J. wondered if the mausoleum led to someplace farther underground. Getting closer to the meatball shrubs and the front door, he didn't know whether to knock or just—

**Rrrrrrrrr.**

The metal door swung open, scraping

against the stone floor. A familiar face poked out from the shadows.

"Don't worry, there're no ghosts," Francy O'Connor called out.

"Is he—? He's in **there**?" A.J. asked, referring to the only **he** who ever mattered.

Looking over A.J.'s shoulder, Francy made sure they were alone. "He's not happy about it either. Now c'mon. Before we let all the heat out."

A.J. strode toward the open door just as a light went on in the mausoleum.

## 73

It's nearly midnight as we pull up to the locked chain-link gate. Outside, a gangly, middle-aged man in a cheap sport jacket and no winter coat squints into our headlights, undoing the single padlock. Not much of a security system.

I lean out the passenger window. "We're here to see—"

"Mr. Mulligan is waiting for you," the man says, pointing a long elegant finger toward our destination: the wide airplane hangar on our right.

"Mr. Mulligan?" Mina asks, shooting me a look as she hits the gas and pulls forward.

I nod, knowing it's a fake name. Mr. Mulligan is Hercules Mulligan, an Irish tailor who, two hundred years ago, had the single greatest name in the Revolutionary War, and also saved George Washington's life (twice!) by passing British plans to the Culper Ring. Mulligan wasn't an official Ring member, but he was there when they needed him. Like the man waiting for us now.

"I didn't even know there was an airport out here," Mina says as we pull into a canopied parking spot that keeps us hidden from prying eyes.

That's the whole point of coming out to Manassas, Virginia. If we fly out of Reagan or Dulles, even on a private charter, we're subject to an array of camera surveillance. But out here, Manassas Airport allows the wealthiest people to fly in and out of our nation's capital without ever being seen.

"You're Beecher," a Southern voice insists, more Kentucky aggressive than Virginia calm. Tall and fit in a black, nononsense pea coat, he has short cropped hair dyed blond to offset his seventy years. His belt buckle and shirt buttons form a perfect line. No question, former military. Mac said he works for one of the big government contractors; she wouldn't say which.

"Mr. Mulligan," I reply, extending a handshake.

Mulligan doesn't take it. His right hand stuffed in his pocket, he motions for us to follow him to the back of the hangar.

"You're younger than the last one," he says over his shoulder.

**Last one?** Tot told me it'd been years since they asked anyone to join the Ring.

"Tell Mac if my wife dies, Mac's still the first one I'm calling," he adds, making sure to always stay a few steps in front of us.

He stops at the back of the hangar, giving us our first good look at what we're really here for. Mac gave me three things for the trip. This is the first: a private jet with two thin black stripes running along the side. Most companies prefer a low profile and won't put their logo on their private planes—though they sometimes hide it in the plane's tail number. This one reads **N619LM**. LM. Lockheed Martin. Uncle Sam's top contractor. "Do me a favor," Mr. Mulligan adds as the pilot sticks his head out. "Don't wreck my plane."

## 74

The crypt was warm inside—they had a heater and a light.

Following behind Francy, A.J. scanned the mausoleum as he stepped inside. There were bodies all around him, hidden behind ancient marble slabs, each one marked by an engraved nameplate draped with spider-webs. Along the back wall stood a round iron table that held a vase of dried flowers and two goblets that hadn't been touched in decades.

"Dinner for none," Francy joked, her steps scratching against the floor's dried dirt and mortar.

As the heavy door shut behind them, A.J. cocked an eyebrow. Still no guards, no cameras, and no hidden staircase that led to an underground bomb shelter.

"The President isn't here, is he?" A.J. asked.

Francy sat on the edge of the wrought iron table, arms flat at her sides.

"So the reason you brought me here..."

A.J. began. He thought about it a moment. "This was a test. You were checking my loyalty."

"We needed to know who you were talking to."

"Then ask me; I'll tell you! You know I'm not with the Knights!"

"What about Beecher?" Francy challenged. "We know you let him go, A.J. Truthfully, I'm okay with that. We need Beecher and the Ring in this one. But when things like that happen...and you don't tell us...we need to know who you're really playing for. And who else you're talking to."

"Are you high? I haven't called **anyone**! **Not even my dad!** Tap my phone! Run my phone records **right now**!"

Francy rubbed her middle finger against her thumb, severing a nearby spiderweb. "Already did."

"What?"

"Your phone. We tapped it hours ago." She spread her five fingers wide, like a magician finishing a trick. "You passed, A.J. You could've called anyone and told them we were here. You didn't."

A.J. stood there, now burning from the

heat. "You really think that little of me?"

"Don't sulk. You know what's at stake here. You saw how close the Knights got. Answer me honestly: If you were me, and Wallace asked you to double-check **everyone**—including swiping **his daughter's** phone to see if they were tracing us through that—you're telling me you would've done anything different?"

Now A.J. was the one who was silent.

"Exactly," Francy said. "By the way, want to tell me what Beecher knows about Wallace's past, because last I checked, sitting Presidents shouldn't be spending this much time thinking about lowly archivists, even Culper Ring ones?"

"If Wallace wants to tell you, he'll tell you."

"Fair enough," Francy said. "Now you ready to help me find where Beecher and Ezra are really headed to?"

A small grin took A.J.'s face. "You have no idea how long I've been waiting for you to ask me that question."

## 75

## Somewhere in South Carolina

**"Did it work?"** Marshall whispered in his sleep.

"Did what work?" Clementine asked.

Blinking awake, Marshall squinted up at the fluorescent light. Fluorescent lights meant hospital rooms and operations. This wasn't a hospital, though. The smell was wrong. It smelled of black tea. And cats.

Marshall was flat on his back. A thin polyester blanket, like from a cheap motel, covered his chest. Clementine sat at the edge of his pulldown bed, watching over him. Her cheek was scraped raw, though a scab was forming. The room was moving back and forth.

"We're on a train?" Marshall asked, trying to sit up as a deep pain in his armpit argued otherwise. Now he remembered. He'd been shot. Ezra had used an antique, retrofitted revolver, probably to make some awful historical parallel that only Beecher would appreciate. This was why he hated—

"Did **what** work?" Clementine repeated. She was feeding a piece of cheese to a skinny white cat in her lap.

Marshall didn't like cats. He felt like they knew the truth about him. "You took their cat?"

"It needed a new owner. But what you said: You asked if it worked," Clementine explained. "What were you talking about?"

Marshall stared back at her and the cat. "No idea." Looking around, he saw that his shirt was off. Strips of white medical tape covered his wound. Now he remembered the black tea. Clementine had grabbed boxes of gauze from the dentist's office. Marshall had her soak the gauze in black tea, then wring it out. The real pain came when she had to shove the gauze **into** the wound at his armpit. He'd passed out from the pain, but the tannins in the tea had helped shrink the blood vessels and encourage clotting. No doubt, it's what'd saved Marshall's life.

"Why're we on a train?" Marshall asked.

"You think I could've gotten you through an airport? You couldn't speak, much less stand. The auto-train left before dark. The porter helped me get you into a wheelchair. I told him you had a tough day of chemo, so if you see the guy, pretend you have my cancer."

Marshall lifted his arm, gauging the pain in his armpit. Clementine had dug out the musket ball with tweezers. The throbbing would be there for a while. He'd been through worse. Marshall's breathing was still heavy, though. Harder than it should be. Through the oblong window, the sky was dark. It was the middle of the night.

"You need sleep," Clementine said.

Marshall nodded. Wedged against the headboard of his bed was the stub from the train ticket. Destination: Florida. "What's in Florida?"

"The one person who can help us," Clementine said. "We're going to see my father."

## 76

## Twenty-nine years ago
## Devil's Island

"Gotta pee," Alby said.

That's all it took. The marine guard barely turned as Alby raced down the brick staircase, from the roof, toward the barracks. He didn't enter the barracks, though. Instead, as Alby reached the ground floor, he unbuttoned his shirt and pulled out an unread week-old newspaper, **Stars and Stripes**.

They didn't get much news on the island. Papers came once a week, shipped from abroad in a separate delivery from the one that brought food and fresh water. If Alby got caught, this was his excuse, that he was delivering the new issue to Dr. Moorcraft.

By now, he knew the pattern. Every day after breakfast, Dr. Moorcraft carried a set of file folders to the colonel in the officers' quarters. A few hours later, Dr. Moorcraft left the offices, carrying those files deeper into the fort's brick labyrinth.

Just as he'd planned, Alby walked as calmly as he could, pretending to read the Stars and Stripes. Sure enough, up ahead, Dr. Moorcraft was exiting the colonel's quarters. Like clockwork.

Still holding the **Stars and Stripes**, Alby kept his pace, walking evenly. A hundred feet ahead of him, Dr. Moorcraft weaved through the fort's connecting brick rooms. According to what Julian had said, during the Civil War these rooms had held cannons and guns. Today, sand and rat droppings were everywhere.

As the hallway bent to the left, the true labyrinth began. There were barely any windows, barely any light. With a sharp turn, Dr. Moorcraft disappeared. Alby didn't panic. For a week now, he'd been wondering where Dr. Moorcraft disappeared to. Now it made sense. Straight ahead, a metal plaque was bolted to the wall:

## DR. MUDD'S CELL
## AROUND TO THE LEFT

From the very first day the Plankholders had arrived, this was the place with the best ghost stories: the old dungeons where they locked up the men who tried to kill Abraham Lincoln.

As Alby turned the corner, he didn't hear anything. No footsteps. No running. No shuffling in the sand. Just the usual rhythm of ocean waves in the distance. He squinted down the dim hallway. An orange crab walked sideways along the stone floor. But otherwise...

Dr. Moorcraft was gone.

Confused, Alby headed around the corner. The **Stars and Stripes** was now damp where he clutched it. The ceiling was lower down here, the hallway narrower. Ahead of him was an archway that framed a metal jail door, like you'd see in an old Western. Above it was a plank of wood that held a hand-carved message:

### WHOSO ENTERETH HERE
### LEAVETH ALL HOPES BEHIND!

This was it. The entrance to the dungeon and Dr. Mudd's cell.

As Alby got closer, he saw that the door with the metal bars was still shut, locked with a chain.

It didn't make sense. Where was...?

**Fwuuup.**

The sound came from behind him, from the main hallway, like a door scraping against the floor. Alby spun. As he raced back to the hallway, he heard the click and thunk of a lock.

There. On his left was another narrow corridor, this one with white-painted bricks. At the end of the corridor was an old wooden door. Alby had been here before, during their safety orientation. It used to be one of the fort's old gunpowder rooms. Now, because it had an interior location that didn't face the ocean, it was the go-to hurricane shelter in case another storm hit.

Now it made sense. Every day, Dr. Moorcraft met with the colonel. Every day, when that meeting was done, the doctor came here. The perfect hiding spot for his files.

Alby walked away, still pretending to read **Stars and Stripes**.

Soon enough, Dr. Moorcraft would be gone. And then, later tonight, Alby would get what he wanted.

## 77

# Today
## Somewhere over North Carolina

"This is it?" I ask, leaning over the private jet's eucalyptus-wood desk and staring down at the oversize, mottled sheet of paper. The map Mina found. It'd been rolled up for so long, we put my two shoes on it to keep it open. "Anything special about it?"

"All maps are special," Mina explains from the opposite side of the desk as she redoes her ponytail. It's past one in the morning, though even with the jet's dimmed lights and reclinable caramel leather seats, neither of us can sleep. "Think of the maps Magellan used to circle the globe. They were filled with trade routes that every rival country wanted. But for centuries, as someone smarter than me once said, the Portuguese controlled the Indies because they controlled the maps."

I study our own map, which features an old aerial satellite photo that looks like it was taken during the Cold War. At the center is a black-and-white hexagonal building, surrounded by water on all sides. Fort Jefferson, aka Devil's Island, aka the prison that held Abraham Lincoln's killers —and, for some reason, my father and his Plankholders unit. If my hunch is right, it's also where my dad died.

"You okay?" Mina asks for the fourth time in the last hour.

I keep staring at the map. "Why'd you come here?"

"Pardon?"

"I'm serious, Mina. You did your job; you got me this map; you pointed me where to go. Why get on the plane with me and put yourself at risk?"

She doesn't hesitate. "Because you did the same for me, Beecher. When my brother needed you, you gave him the very best day of his life. I want to pay that back. And if I'm wrong, and this is all some big lie, well, then I guess I'm on the case of my life."

Makes sense. "Now why'd you really come?" I add.

"I just told you—"

"No. You didn't do this for some karmic payback, or even for some casework. You may be a fellow archivist and even a friend, but first and foremost, you're a Secret Service employee. Job one is reporting suspicious activity. So for you to be here with no backup, no one to help you, and no cover in case this all blows up and you're suddenly the one knee-deep in manure...? You could've called in a supervisor and watched it play out from your office. Try again, Mina. A real answer this time. Why. Are. You. Here. With. Me?"

Across the pullout desk, Mina stands up straight. With the jet's low ceiling, she's too tall. She lowers her chin toward her chest. Her voice is barely a whisper. "I don't know."

Her words, packed with a far-too-familiar loneliness, catch even her off guard. I stay right where I am. There's something about this girl. This stubborn, unstoppable girl. I know she loves the past as much as I do. But unlike me, when it comes to her personal history, she's figured out a way to embrace it...and draw strength from it. It's the only way to reach the future. "I'm glad you're here," I tell her.

"So am I," she agrees.

I can't help but grin.

"Beecher, now would be a good time to kiss me."

"I was about to."

"Sure y—"

I flip up the table, sending the map and my shoes catapulting across the cabin. She's a good two inches taller than me. It excites me even more.

My fingers slide to the nape of her neck. I pull her toward me, kissing her hard as our tongues find each other. She tastes warm and somehow familiar.

There's no such thing as a perfect kiss. But this one's definitely in the running.

"Mm," she murmurs, catching her breath. She plants a soft kiss on my cheek and whispers three words into my ear: "Do that again."

I'm facing the front of the plane, Mina's facing the back. With the momentum of the jet, she's closer than ever, pressing hard against me. Her body's so strong, her muscles are tensed. She's a thoroughbred.

"This's the reason you wanted the private jet, isn't it?" she whispers, her lips vibrating against mine.

"I'd be just as happy in the back of a Toyota."

"That's cute. You're cute, Beecher. But you really think you'd get this in the back of a Toyota?" she teases, hitting me with a dark, sly grin that I'll be thinking about for hours. This day has felt like one of the longest and shortest of my life. But I finally know what I want for my birthday.

Over our heads, next to the lights and the call button, there's another button: a red **Do Not Disturb** one. When we first got on board, I didn't know what it was for. I do now.

**Kllk.**

A rose-colored light tells me it's on. We crash into a nearby recliner. Mina starts unbuttoning my shirt, kissing her way down my neck, toward my chest.

There really is something about this girl. And right now, Something I want more of.

## 78

## Sanford, Florida

Nine hours later, Marshall woke up. It was morning and his armpit was throbbing. Clementine was still sitting there, her face swollen, the sleeping cat in her lap, watching over both of them. She hadn't moved from her spot on the edge of his fold-down bed. For a while, he just lay there in the sleeping car, lost in the train's churning rhythm.

"Why'd you save me?" Clementine finally asked, sounding in-disputably thankful.

"What're you talking about?"

"At the herbal shop. When Ezra hit me with the car. You could've turned the ignition and taken off. Instead you came back and saved me."

"You deserve to be saved," Marshall said, though he wouldn't face her.

She paused at that, unable to contain her grin.

"Don't make this more than it is," Marshall pleaded.

"I'm just saying..."

"You're making it more than it is."

"I'm just saying, people don't usually do stuff like that for me. Not without wanting something."

"I don't want anything."

"I know you don't," she said, reaching for Marshall's hand.

Marshall pulled it away, though it didn't take the joy from Clementine's scabbed face. Her hands were scraped. Her left eye was red from a broken blood vessel. "By the way, what was Ezra whispering to you?" she added.

Marshall replayed Ezra's offer to join the Knights. To become one of them. "Nothing. Kooky rambling." The train continued to churn. "Where are we anyway?"

"I think Orlando. We'll be in Miami in a few hours."

Nodding, Marshall opened and closed his fists. He'd been sleeping too long. His scars had tightened and his skin was stiff. It was the worst at his elbows, knees and knuckles. If he flexed them too fast, it felt like he was tearing open his scars.

"Does it hurt when you do that?"

Clementine asked.

"No," Marshall said far too fast. Clementine knew it was a lie, but she didn't call him on it. She looked down at his hand. He again pulled away.

"Y'know you do the same thing in your sleep," Clementine said. "I'd try to hold your hand, and each time, you'd tug it free." When Marshall didn't respond, she said, "It's really not a healthy way to live."

"I didn't realize we were suddenly sharing life advice."

"All I'm saying, Marsh, is that—"

"Marshall."

"Can you just listen? Whatever demons you carry in your life, they become more powerful over time."

Flat on his back, Marshall stared up at the fluorescent lights, still flexing his fists and stretching his skin.

"Y'know, in France, scars aren't even considered ugly," Clementine added. "They're thought of as beautiful—as signs of experience and grand adventures. It's only in America that we try to cover them up and get embarrassed by them. For the French, they're proof of a life well lived."

"I've been to France. They stared at me just as hard as people here."

"That doesn't mean you're—"

"Clementine, I appreciate the group therapy, but let me explain something. Once a year, I go back to the local burn center for checkups and whatever new grafts I need. Last time I was there, I saw this family huddling and crying in the hallway. Their son was set on fire as he was getting off a city bus. A local gang doused him with gasoline and set him ablaze. The poor kid's body was charred. His ears and whole face melted away. We're talking 90 percent of his body with third- and fourth-degree burns. That means it extends into his muscles and bones," Marshall explained. "So when the father of the family noticed my face, he pulled me aside, pointed to his son, and asked, 'How do you come through all that and survive?' I looked him straight in the eye and told him, 'He won't.'"

The train continued to churn. "You didn't have to tell him that," Clementine said.

"So you think lying and giving him false hope is a better option? Not every story gets a happy ending—and not every burn on your face is a sign of good living."

Locking eyes with him, Clementine reached into her mouth and—**tuukk**—used her thumb to unhinge something from the roof of her palate. From between her lips, she pulled out the metal bridge that held a row of fake teeth. It was still dripping with saliva as she tossed it onto Marshall's chest. "We all have our scars," she lisped, flashing a nervous jack o'lantern grin and revealing three pointy, filed-down teeth that hung like stalactites from her gums.

Marshall cocked his head. He knew he was staring, but he couldn't stop.

Clementine didn't move, no matter how much she wanted to.

"That thing you said about France, with the scars..." Marshall eventually asked. "That really true?"

"Dunno." She snapped her bridge back in place. "A therapist told it to me years ago. I choose to believe it," she explained as she scootched forward and reached out—again—for Marshall's hand.

His fist was clenched, but this time, he

didn't pull away. "What about your boyfriend Beecher?"

"He's never been my boyfriend. Not even in fifth grade. Besides, do you think Beecher knows what it's like to live like this?" she asked, pointing to his face, then her own.

Marshall stared straight at her, his fist still tight as ever.

As gently as possible, Clementine lifted his hand. His candle-wax skin was bumpy and felt stiff to the touch. Leaning down, she planted a soft kiss on Marshall's middle knuckle. He still didn't pull away.

Along the back of his hand, she eyed a fleshy white knob of skin, a spot where the burns ran deep. She put her lips on the lump and kissed him again.

She was close to him now, so close she was in his scent. He smelled like an old hardware store. On the back of her neck, she felt that familiar humming that'd been gone for so long. She wanted to be closer. Lifting her chin, she leaned toward his lips and...

"Clementine, don't—"

It happened so fast, she was still moving.

Marshall shoved the air to push her back. "I mean it. I'm not doing this."

"I-I wasn't— I just thought—"

"I know what you thought. And if it makes you feel better, I had the same thought. But I'm not doing it."

For a moment, Clementine just sat there. With each churn of the train, she felt the subtle shift from embarrassment, to anger, to pity. "Let me ask you something, Marshall: Is this how you punish yourself, or are you just terrified to be happy?"

Marshall turned toward the wall. He didn't say another word until the train reached Miami.

## 79

The pilot lets us sleep until almost 8 a.m. The problem is, this is Key West.

"They look closed," Mina says, cradling her winter coat like a football and already sweating in the Florida sun. As she plows through the parking lot, her ponytail's back in place, and she's not slowing down. Neither am I.

Our destination is directly across the street from the Key West airport: a small white modular office that looks more like a snazzed-up mobile home, complete with a canopy awning, a beat-up porch...and a **Closed** sign in the window.

Of course it's closed. Nothing in the Keys opens before nine. Or ten thirty, according to the sign.

"We should've waited in our jet," she says.

I shoot her a look. "I liked the jet too."

She grins at that, a blooming, generous grin that completely undoes me.

"Good morning, good morning," a man's

voice calls out nearly an hour later as we wait on the bench outside the office. On our left, an absurdly tanned middle-aged guy wearing an unbuttoned Hawaiian shirt comes rolling on his rusted bicycle through the parking lot. His scraggly gray hair blows behind him, and he's missing his canine tooth on the left side. "What gloriousness can I bring you today?" he asks.

He goes sidesaddle on the bike, standing on one pedal as he coasts toward the freestanding sign out front: **Key West Seaplane Escapes**.

Devil's Island is surrounded by water. There's no runway. The only path in or out is a four-hour boat ride...or the one seaplane company with clearance to fly.

"Please tell me you work here," Mina says.

"I certainly don't clean the place," he says with a pirate's laugh, pulling a keychain from his pocket. As he opens the front door, a welcome chime plays the song "Kokomo" by the Beach Boys. "Where can we take you to today?"

"Devil's Island," I say.

He nods, unsurprised. "They call it the Dry Tortugas now. Better for business," he explains as he leads us inside and steps behind a white chest-high counter. On every wall are posters with aerial views of Key West and nearby islands. "Problem is, the island—Fort Jefferson—the Park Service closed it since the last hurricane. Structural damage to the bricks—and with budget cuts, this isn't exactly a priority for federal spending. No planes—or tourists— in or out."

"We saw. Online," I say, sliding my backpack off my shoulder. Mac gave me three things for the trip. Here's the second. Unzipping the pack, I pull out two stacks of unmarked cash and drop them on the counter. "I have a reservation."

# 80

Clementine drove them the rest of the way. They arrived in Miami early. From the Amtrak station, Key West was only a few hours.

She had taken this trip before, a decade ago, when she was in her early twenties, during those hard years in Atlanta. At three in the morning, a bad boyfriend with an even worse band drunkenly declared that they should drive straight to the Keys—that if they made good enough time, they'd be there to watch the next day's sunset.

Clementine had driven then too, windows rolled down, air blowing through her hair, and a blasting Sonic Youth album that preached all the life lessons that seem so unarguable when you're twenty-two. Back then, Clementine and her boyfriend held hands—held them hard—all the way down the two-lane stretch of U.S. 1. At each bridge—and there were dozens of them— they held them even harder, rolling over the crystal blue water that winked at them as they passed.

Today, with the skinny white cat still in her lap and Marshall in the passenger seat, she knew better than to reach for Marshall's hand. From the moment they got in the car, he'd barely said a word. At first, she thought it was leftover awkwardness from the train ride. But the way he was nursing his arm, and his mouth was sagging open... He wasn't sweating—he didn't have any beard holes or sweat glands on the sides of his face; they were all burned away—but his coloring was all wrong.

"I'm fine," he said, before she could ask.

In her lap, the white cat jerked suddenly, his tail wrapping around Clementine's free wrist. Her old cat used to do tail hugs too, whenever he was anxious or fussy.

"Can you open your window some more?" Marshall added.

"Mouse won't like it."

"Mouse?"

"The cat. I gave it a name. It likes cheese," she explained. "Plus, if I open the window, my wig'll blow off."

He went quiet at that, turning away, but blinking too many times. He was definitely in pain.

"Marshall, we need to get you to a—"

"I don't need a doctor. The wound is fine. It's clean. Ezra put something on the bullet."

"What're you talking about?"

"On the musket ball. Back during the Civil War, Confederate soldiers used to coat their musket balls with poison, then cover them in wax to seal it. So even on a grazing shot, it'd still do damage. Ezra's rebuilding the Knights. He's using old Knight tricks."

"Then we should definitely get you to a—"

"I'm fine," Marshall warned, his voice rising. "If it was bad, I wouldn't be able to stand. Whatever was on that musket ball, it just needs to work its way out of my system."

Clementine wanted to argue, but in the back corner of her mouth, her tongue felt the rough edges of yet another loose tooth, one of her last original ones. She'd been bleeding for a while now, since before they left the train. For the past few miles, the salty metallic taste of her own blood had been coming faster than ever. She knew what it meant.

Gripping the steering wheel and feeling the cat's tail wind tighter around her wrist, Clementine eyed the ugly little bridge ahead of her: a gray and uninspired slab of concrete framed by telephone poles whose wires formed parallel smiles that ran along both sides and stretched the length of the bridge. Usually, she liked bridges. She'd kissed Beecher on a bridge once. So today, she tried to focus on the beauty of the bridge, to focus on the winking waves on either side of her, even to focus on the fact that she'd soon be seeing her father.

But as the wheels of the car **daduuunk-duunnk-duunnked** across the bridge's concrete seams, it was clear that, even in the morning sun, the waves were no longer winking. They probably never had winked, even a decade ago. Indeed, as Clementine's car cleared the bridge and rolled past the bright blue, yellow, and orange sign that read **Welcome to Key West**— Paradise USA, the only thing she could really focus on was the gnawing, unarguable feeling that her return to Key West would be a one-way trip.

Unbelievably, she realized, she was actually okay with it. Since the moment she was diagnosed, her deepest fear had been of suffering alone. This was the least alone she had felt in a long time.

"Make a left up here," Marshall said, pointing to a small sign just past the sandal outlet store in front of them. "The seaplane place should be dead ahead."

## 81

"So just the two of you?" our Hawaiian-shirted friend asks.

"Just us," I say, staring out the front window of the seaplane company, checking the empty parking lot and the private runway in the distance. I put down even more money so he wouldn't issue actual tickets. The other half is payable when he flies us home. Anything to keep our names from searchable systems.

"Relax. No one's coming," Mina whispers. She puts a hand on my shoulder. It doesn't help.

"How long did you say until the pilot gets here?" I ask.

"About twenty minutes ago," Hawaiian Shirt teases. Mina and I both turn around. He flashes his gap-toothed grin. "Whattya think this is, Pan Am? It's Key West; have a drink. Jamie McDonnell IV—gate agent, flight attendant...**and pilot**—at your service."

I swear to God, he's unbuttoned another

button on his shirt.

"By the by," Pilot Jamie adds, "you're going to an island, so there's no drinking water out there. If you want, head into our shed out back and grab one of the coolers and some waters. Only a dollar apiece."

I shoot him a look.

"Fine. Soda and water are free," he says, tossing me the key. "I gotta charge for alcohol, though. It's expensive."

As Jamie finishes whatever he's doing at the computer, Mina and I head around back, to a prefab vinyl shed that looks like a mini red barn.

"You think he'll keep quiet?" I ask.

"You gave him three thousand dollars. The man's not wearing shoes," Mina points out. "He's not saying anything."

Taking a final look around, I undo the padlock and tug open the shed door.

"Smells like raccoon turds," Mina says as I nod. Inside, there are two refrigerators on my left and a few mini-coolers on our right. "I'll grab the water; you grab the coolers," she adds.

Following her inside, I take yet another look over my shoulder. If I'm right, I know what's waiting for me on that island, and it's not just a file. The last thing I need is having it take a shot at her.

"Mina, I've been thinking…"

"I knew this was coming. This is where you tell me you're worried about my safety."

"That's not what I was gonna say."

"Okay, then what **were** you going to say?"

I stand there, watching her scoop armfuls of bottled water out of the refrigerator. "I want to spend even more time with you, Mina. I want to sit down, and have a nice meal, and take the time to see what an amazing woman you are. You know it's not safe on that island. If I bring you with me—"

"Let me be ultra clear: The only way you're keeping me off that island is if you lock me in this shed."

"I thought about it."

"You did, didn't you?"

I don't answer. She dumps the bottles of water in a faded blue cooler.

"So what stopped you?" she asks. "There's a padlock on the shed. Why not lock me in?"

"Because if I did, I'd be a dick."

"And why else?"

"Pardon?"

"This is your father we're talking about. How he died. Everything you've chased for. If it brought you answers and you had to be a dick, you'd be a dick. So. Did we have fun joyriding last night? Yes. Is that the reason? No. Time to be honest with yourself. Why am I still here?"

I stare up at her. "For the same reason you got on the plane," I tell her.

Grabbing the cooler under one arm and her hand in the other, I pull her into a run back to the main office.

"You won't regret this," she promises as the shed door slams behind us with a burst.

## 82

## Twenty-nine years ago
## Devil's Island

Alby had traded a week's worth of latrine cleanup. It was worth it.

"Just keep an eye out," Timothy said at the far end of the corridor, flashlight clamped by his armpit.

Alby nodded, wiping his forehead. He was sweating hard—more than usual—even though the night wasn't a terrible one. He wasn't stupid. Every week, Dr. Moorcraft gave the Plankholders new shots and new medicine.

Rechecking the dark hallway, Alby shooed away a mosquito that wasn't even there. It was well past two in the morning; most of the Plankholders were exhausted and asleep.

Timothy was down on one knee, jabbing an unbent paper clip into the lock on the wooden door. Alby had learned of Timothy's skills during their first week on the island, when he caught Timothy using a similar technique to swipe a box of peanut M&M's from the cafeteria's locked food closet.

"And as the great Houdini used to say... **I just opened the stupid thing**," Timothy announced, twisting the knob and shoving the door open.

"Don't forget—you promised you'd keep lookout," Alby said as Timothy got up to leave.

"You're joking, right?"

"This concerns you too. You should—"

"Alby, whatever you're about to say, I don't care. You know I don't like you. And I don't want to help you. But I don't like cleaning diarrhea even more."

The pain in Alby's neck knotted tighter than ever. He wanted to hit Timothy... wanted to jam his thumbs in his Adam's apple and press down as hard as he could. Instead, Alby stood there. "Five minutes," he pleaded. "Just give me that."

"Five. That's it," Timothy warned, rolling his eyes.

"If someone comes, knock." Grabbing the flashlight, Alby darted into the narrow brick room, which smelled like an old bookstore. Wasn't hard to see why. The back wall was covered with new metal shelves that were stacked with textbooks, all of them medicine-related: **Cobb's Anatomy. Developmental Biology. Abnormal Psychology. Criminal Psychology. The Science of Human Behavior.**

Another wall had metal lockers that were filled with old faded boxes marked **Survival Supplies Furnished by Office of Civil Defense**. Nuclear war leftovers from the late sixties. But all Alby was focused on was the brick wall on his right, which held a military-issue metal desk that sat between two gray file cabinets.

Dr. Moorcraft's private office. Racing for the top drawer, Alby yanked it open as the flashlight sprayed shadows across the room.

To Alby's surprise, the first...second...all three drawers were empty. Tucking the flashlight under his opposite arm, he ran to the other cabinet. Jackpot. A long row of hanging files swayed forward and back, each one marked with a typewritten label. He immediately started finger walking through them:

**Bendis, Brian...DeConnick, Matthew...**
the file for Julian Marlin was missing, but
the others were there: **Hadrian, Nicholas...
Lusk, Timothy...**and at the very back:
**White, Albert.**

Alby reached for his file, but before he
could grab it, he spotted another file folder
just behind it. **Flight 808**, the label read.

**808?** That was Alby's flight, the flight that
had crashed. **Why would they—?**

Without even thinking, Alby plucked the
file, flipping it open and spreading it on the
nearby desk. Inside were copies of airline
tickets. Dozens of them, an inch thick,
bound by a binder clip. All Flight 808.

Just behind that were fifty or so separate sheets of paper, each with names,
addresses, and personal details, along with
a square passport photo stapled in the
corner. Alby flipped through the photos.
He didn't recognize anyone, not until—

**Her.** He knew her. The woman with the
pointy face and equally pointy breasts. She
was the gate agent who'd given them the
upgrade. According to the file, her name
was Rachel Dagen. From Holland, Michigan.

Alby flipped through the next few pages.

He saw the elderly woman who'd sat diagonally behind them. And the elderly man. The woman was from Chicago. The man from Manalapan, New Jersey. Under **Marital Status**, both were listed as **Single**.

A bead of sweat hit free fall as it left Alby's nose and splattered, slowly sinking into the page. The knot tightened in the back of his neck. It didn't make sense. Alby closed his eyes, still picturing the crash of the plane...the elderly woman clutching her husband's shoulders. She had ice blue eyes and bone-colored skin. No question, they were wearing wedding bands.

More confused than ever, Alby scanned the top of the page. It was the same on all of them: three words in a delicate, swirly cursive:

## AVALON TALENT AGENCY

Alby pointed the flashlight closer, just to make sure he was reading it right. **Talent agency? Why would the army need actors?**

# 83

## Today

"Y'all set on water?" Pilot Jamie asks.

"Got plenty," Mina says, motioning to my backpack as we both eye the parking lot. Still clear.

"We should really go," I add, heading for the door and trying to nudge him outside, toward the runway. The last thing we need is him asking more questions.

"So where you guys from again?"

"Arizona," Mina says.

"Ohio," I say simultaneously.

Pilot Jamie stares at us a second too long. "You still paying me all that cash?"

"Yeah."

A smile takes his face. "Then you're the birthday boy and birthday girl. Let's start the party." Grabbing his camouflaged military knapsack, he ducks below the counter and heads for the door. His feet are still bare.

"Up, up, and away. Runway's to the far

right," he explains.

"Kokomo" starts playing as I tug the door open. But as we step out onto the porch—

**"Beecher...?"** a female voice calls out. She's wearing a brown wig, but I know that voice. I've known it since she first kissed me in junior high.

Clementine.

Her cheek is swollen and scabbed. She's cradling...**is that a cat?** Just behind her is Marshall, a homemade sling holding his arm in place. She looks bad. He looks worse.

"I take it these are friends of yours?" Pilot Jamie asks. No one answers. "So...uh...I have an idea," he adds. "Why don't I go get the plane ready?"

## 84

"You should've gone to the hospital," I say to Marshall, pointing to the white gauze covering the wound in his shoulder. "Let me see it."

He shakes his head. He doesn't like showing weakness. Glancing around, he gives a withering scrutiny to the seaplane office. Especially Mina. **Why's she here?** he asks with a glance.

"I changed my mind. She's okay," I reassure him.

"Wait. Time out," Clementine says, still lost. "How did you—?" She cuts herself off, turning to me. "How'd you know what happened to Marshall's arm? And who's she?" she asks, pointing to Mina.

"We should go," I say to Marshall, motioning toward the runway on our right. "We're running out of—"

"No. Stop talking," Clementine interrupts, sounding like she's lisping. She looks at me, then back at Marshall. "You sneaky little turds."

"Keep your voice down," Marshall warns.

"You told Beecher we were coming...and that my dad— You called from the train and plotted this little meet-up together. You've been working with each other this whole time."

"That true?" Mina asks.

Does she really think I'd come all this way without knowing what I'd be getting? I shoot a grin at Marshall. I know he won't grin back. But what catches my attention is that he's not looking at me. He's focused on Clementine, fixated on her. I shouldn't be surprised.

The two of them exchange another glance. As always, the stiffness of his skin makes him hard to read, but I know an apology when I see one.

"You're Nico's daughter," Mina blurts.

"Who're **you**?" Clementine challenges.

"I'm with the Secret Service, who would love to know where your father is," Mina says, shoving right back. She towers over Clementine and steps close enough so Clementine feels it.

A decade ago, this is where Clementine would've taken off her earrings and started throwing punches. Today, she just stands there. "Is she serious?" Clementine asks me.

I put a hand on Mina's shoulder, pulling her back and whispering into her ear. "She wants the same answers we do. She knows where the files are. She told Marshall— they're still on the island, along with something else too."

Mina glares back at me, her eyes on fire. If she wants to report us, here's her chance. For a moment, no one moves.

"The plane's waiting. We should go," Mina says, though I see it on her face. We're not done with this conversation. And she's definitely not done with Clementine.

Across from me, Clementine shoots me a look, though what she's really rolling her eyes at is my hand on Mina's shoulder.

I keep my hand where it is and glare back at Clementine, then over to Marshall, who shoots me his own look, asking me to lay off Clementine. We know each other since kindergarten. With old friends, you can have an entire war without anyone muttering a word.

"I guess this way everyone gets what they

want, huh?" Clementine says to no one in particular. She doesn't like being fooled. Neither do I, especially by her.

"You and Marshall could've told me you planned to meet up. I still would've helped," she growls at me. As she gets closer, I can see there's something wrong with her mouth. Some of her teeth are gone.

I glance over at Marshall. He told me what was on the island; he didn't tell me how sick she was.

Clementine stays locked on me, her mouth sagging open, her face softening.

**Don't fall for it**, I scold myself.

Mina rolls her eyes too.

It's what Clementine always does, preying on my emotions. Only a fool would get suckered again. I'm done being that fool. But I'd be a liar if I said it was easy. Clementine was my first real crush. My first kiss. Every time she's near, I can feel it on a chemical level. And if I'm being truly honest, I feel it even more when I see the way she's glancing at Marshall.

"My Lord, it's like being around a divorced couple," Mina says.

Clementine hits her with a look that'll

leave a dent. "Beecher, you idiot—I'm on your side," Clementine says. "I've always been on your side."

"You said the same thing the last time I saw you. Remember what happened then? You abandoned me so you could help your dad sneak away."

"He's my father. You of all people should understand what that means! But to not trust me—"

"Clemmi, if I didn't trust you, **you wouldn't be here right now**!"

She takes a half-step back, pulling her cat toward her chest. Even she can't argue with that.

"It's safer that you didn't know," Marshall reassures her.

"No. Don't you see…? By being here…" Clementine cuts herself off, her anger giving way to panic. **"This is bad."**

I roll my eyes. It's another trick.

"Beecher, when was the last time you saw Tot?"

"What're you talking about?"

"In the hospital. I know you go see him. Every day, like clockwork. Just answer the question: Did you see Tot last night?"

Mina and I both nod. "Yeah, but what does that—?"

"Ezra. Ezra's been watching you there, at the hospital. He told me," Clementine says. "He's trying to crack the Ring, so if he saw you leave—"

She doesn't have to say it. I look back toward the empty parking lot. Wherever Ezra is, he can't be far behind.

"We need to go," Marshall insists.

Three minutes later, we're out on the runway, climbing up on the wide pontoons of the blue-and-white seaplane.

"I don't mean to be a party pooper," Pilot Jamie calls out as Clementine's about to step on board, "but they don't usually allow cats out there. Part of the island is a bird sanctuary and—"

"The cat's coming," Clementine blurts, blowing past him.

The tiny seaplane is freshly painted on the outside and sorely beaten up on the inside, smelling of sand and suntan lotion. On the yoke is a faded sticker for Castronovo Vineyards. As we strap ourselves in, Mina and I sit side by side in the first two saggy green-pleather seats.

Clemmi and Marsh are side by side behind us. I swear, I feel Clementine's stare scalding the back of both our heads.

"This really is the worst double date I've ever been on," Mina says, trying to lighten the mood.

None of us respond.

**You okay?** Mina asks with a glance. She knows the answer.

"Seat belts on...though if we crash, ain't gonna matter," Pilot Jamie jokes, grabbing the yoke and flicking a dozen different switches on the console. With the turn of a key, the engine coughs to life. We put on the faded yellow headphones that dangle from the ceiling. Down on the floor, he follows a stray wire to a first-generation iPod and presses the middle button. Through our head-phones, tropical steel drum music starts playing.

"For five bucks I'll play 'Margaritaville.' For twenty bucks I **won't** play it," Pilot Jamie teases, offering the only smile on board.

"Can we just go?" I say.

"At your service," Pilot Jamie replies, pressing a worn silver foot pedal. As the plane starts shaking and picks up speed, I peer into the cockpit. He's still barefoot. "Goodbye, Key West. Next stop, Devil's Island."

## 85

"I'm guessing it'll be about fifteen minutes before the coast guard spots us," Pilot Jamie explains, tying ropes and securing the anchor for the bobbing, beached seaplane. "I can't wait much longer than that."

"We'll be quick," I promise, hopping from the plane's pontoon onto the damp sand. All around us, the water is clear and aquamarine, but there's no time to appreciate it.

Pilot Jamie watches as Mina, Clementine, and Marshall follow behind me, leaving a quick splash and deep muddy footprints as they land. Marshall's moving slowly. Clementine and Mina keep trading dirty looks. Yet no one says a word until we're halfway up the beach.

"He knows who you are," Mina eventually whispers at Clementine.

"Who? The pilot?" Clementine asks, glancing back over her shoulder. "No he doesn't."

"He does," Marshall agrees.

Running up the beach, I follow his gaze and check for myself. Pilot Jamie is still out on the pontoon, rope in hand. He looks our way, but not for long. He doesn't get the rest of the money until we get home.

"Your face has been on the news for months. He sees your wig. He's not stupid," Marshall says.

Clementine shakes her head, cradling her cat like a baby. "If he knew who I was, he'd leave right now."

"Who says he won't?" Mina asks.

Considering the point, Clementine picks up speed, following a wooden pier toward the enormous brick fortress that rises up like a beachfront ghost town in front of us. Marshall's just a few steps behind her, letting her lead the way. Like I told Mina, Clementine knows where she's going.

I try to tell myself that's a good thing, but the closer we get to the fort, the more I feel that familiar bite in my stomach. I didn't make this trip just for some old files and paperwork. I made it to find the other person I know is on this island. The one person who was here with my father, and who has all the real answers.

I reach out for Mina's hand, though it doesn't bring the calm I was hoping for. I look around for signs of life. The beach is a mess of seaweed and broken branches. Whenever the hurricane hit, it hit hard. Down on the ground, past an overturned trash can, a cracked brown-and-white sign announces:

## FORT JEFFERSON
## DRY TORTUGAS NATIONAL PARK

Mina squeezes my hand. This is it: the place that was on the flattened penny...the place that was clutched by the severed arm in the Rose Garden...the home base for the Plankholders...and if I'm right, the one place that has the information about how my father really died all those years ago.

**You ready?** Marshall asks with a glance.

I don't say a word. He knows what this means to me. And I know what this means to him.

The wooden pier takes us across a seventy-foot-wide moat and ends under a shaded brick archway, where a tall black metal gate serves as the fort's official entrance. A **No Trespassing** sign says we're not getting in.

"Gate's open," Clementine says, side-stepping through it. On the ground is the metal chain that held it shut, along with an industrial padlock that's sliced clean across the shackle. Whoever opened it has at least a pair of bolt cutters.

Marshall pats his waist, letting us know he's still got his gun. From the look on Mina's face, she's wishing she'd brought her own.

As we follow Marshall through the archway, the only sound is the steady rhythm of the ocean waves behind us. But I can't shake the feeling someone's watching all our moves.

"Which way?" Marshall asks as Clementine glances around the central courtyard, struggling to get her bearings. Like the beach out front, the whole courtyard is a dilapidated wreck. The grass is dying, sand and dead leaves are everywhere, and nearly every palm tree is bent sideways, bowing to the hurricane.

"Where'd he say he'd meet you?" I ask her.

"Just gimme a second," she says, still pissed that Marshall called me from the train—actually, before and during the train—and told me the rest. Like I said, I'm after more than just files.

"I know he's here," I tell her. In the back of my head, I replay the President's theory that Nico, for some reason, looks out for me and protects me. If I didn't believe that, I wouldn't be here right now.

Clementine reaches for her phone. She's forgetting we're in the middle of nowhere. There's no signal on the island.

"She's lost," Mina says.

"Clemmi, let me help," I add.

"How can you possibly—?"

"This is still a government building. In 1992, Bill Clinton made it a national park, which means their records, layout, and architectural drawings are all held by the Archives. I pulled their disaster relief plans last night—they always show you the hidden nooks and crannies. Tell me what you need."

She looks at Marshall, who nods an okay. Eventually, she offers, "The grouper cam."

Of course.

A decade ago, when the island first became a national park, to attract more tourists, the government installed an underwater camera deep below the main dock. Dubbed the "grouper cam," it streams a twenty-four-hour live feed of local fish. Needless to say, it didn't become the Web sensation everyone had hoped, but to keep the grouper cam running in this salt-air environment, its servers and hardware—plus dozens of extra underwater camera lenses— were locked up in one of the few secure storage rooms on the island. The perfect place to hide.

Getting my own bearings, I look for... **There**. On my left is a ruined two-story, New Orleans–style house with a blown-off porch. "This way..." I say as they fall in line, racing behind me.

## 86

## Twenty-nine years ago
## Devil's Island

**It wasn't... None of it was real.**

Hunched over the metal desk, flashlight still clamped in his armpit, Alby was frantically flipping through files. The pinch in his neck squeezed like a vise. Beads of sweat dripped from his nose, from his chin, from his forehead. But he couldn't turn away.

The funding had come from the army, something called the Division of Military Psychology. They'd been doing it for years. According to the file, one time they followed students across campus, watching surreptitiously as each student came upon someone lying facedown in a mud puddle. Would the student save the victim or keep walking? The army wanted to know whether there was a way to predict how people would react. And most important, if they could **change** that reaction.

The more Alby read, the more it all made sense. The pay stubs...the talent agency... Every person on the plane, from the elderly couple behind him to the flight attendants who'd checked up on him, they were all hired and paid for—actors playing a role.

That meant the plane crash...the gas truck that ran into them...even the black smoke that came rushing from the back... None of it was real. As he thought about it now, he had never seen real flames. Just smoke and screaming.

Based on what he was reading, it was all a test to see how they—how Nico, Timothy, and Alby—would react in a crisis. During orientation, the colonel had told all the Plankholders that they'd been selected for a reason. That much was true. But as Alby continued to flip pages, what made his stomach churn and made his colon feel like it was about to burst, were the words in front of him: **bystander apathy... narcissistic tendencies...indifference toward others... We've identified twelve of them.**

Alby clenched his buttocks, the pain

pressing from within. **Narcissistic tendencies. Twelve of them.** He reread it again and again. From what he could tell, Flight 808 was most definitely a test. But it wasn't a test to find heroes. It was a test to find cowards...to find the selfish... to find those who would run from a burning plane without helping anyone who needed it.

That's who he and his fellow soldiers were. Not the bravest. Or the most daring. In Dr. Moorcraft's words, the greatest secret of the Plankholders was simply that, to the best of the army's assessment, **they were the ones who cared about no one but themselves**.

As Alby again read the words, a thin stream of diarrhea trickled down his leg. Not because they called him a coward. But because he knew they were right.

**"Timothy, you need to see this!"** Alby hissed, clutching a stack of files.

Behind him, Timothy didn't answer. Back by the doorway, it was completely silent. **"Timothy...?"**

Alby started running for the exit. But as he turned the corner, a brand-new shadow was waiting there for him.

Colonel Doggett took a single step forward. Alby took two steps back. "I really wish you hadn't done that," Doggett offered.

## 87

## Today

With each step, my shoes fill with sand, and the waves continue to grind. Years ago, when we were all in fifth grade, we used to play a game called RCK: Run, Catch, and Kiss. We'd run from the girls. If you got caught, you got kissed. The smart ones, like me, would get caught on purpose. Marshall never did. He was the fat kid. No matter how slowly he ran, he never got kissed.

Today, though, Clementine can't take her eyes off him. Neither can Mina. He's a half-step behind us. He's fighting to keep up, but from the way he's holding his arm, this is harder than he thought. He's in real pain. Anyone else would stop. He keeps going, jaw clenched.

As we cut around a fallen palm tree, Marshall motions up with his chin. Three stories above us, half a dozen massive twenty-five-ton Rodman cannons are spread out along the top ledge of the fort, each its own vast hiding spot. I take the hint: Out here in the open, we're easy targets.

"Inside," I say, making a sharp left, then right, as I dart into one of the nearby brick rooms.

"Casemates," Mina says, well aware of the history.

Almost all of Fort Jefferson is made up of open, connected gun rooms known as casemates. Side by side, each with its own masonry archway, the casemates form a brick catacomb that weaves throughout the fortress. The whole network is filled with sand and dead leaves.

Marshall slows behind me. He spots something up ahead.

Mina and I see it too, in a small pile of sand. A footprint.

Clementine's unfazed. That's what she was looking for.

Up ahead, a brown-and-white National Park sign points us toward **Dr. Mudd's Cell**, with an arrow that sends us to the left. I ignore it, staying on the main hallway and looking for—

There. Dead ahead. A narrow corridor
with white-painted bricks snakes deeper
into the fort. According to the files, these
back rooms are called bastion magazines. It's where all the gun-powder used
to be stored—barrels and barrels of it—
in rooms with thicker walls, no windows,
and an angled, maze-like entrance. That
way, there'd be less chance for a stray
spark and a boom.

"Marshall, if the room's locked…"

He steps ahead of me, fishing through his
pockets for a lock-pick.

We make a left, then a quick right in
the white brick labyrinth when a loud roar
erupts from outside the fort. **Rrrrrrrrrrrr.**
We all stop where we are. I know that sound:
an airplane engine.

Even Clementine stops.

"Think that's our pilot leaving?" Mina
asks.

"Or a new plane arriving," I say. "Either
way—"

**Duuump.**

Marshall plows into the heavy wooden
door at the end of the hallway. The sign on
it says:

## DO NOT ENTER
## PARK STAFF ONLY

"Marshall, wait...!"

Too late. The door was unlocked. As it swings open and crashes into the wall, he's already inside.

Racing behind him, I smell mildew and wet books. There's a bright green hue from two glowing light sticks that sit atop a pyramid of boxes. On one wall is the grouper cam equipment, including an out-dated server stack, extra lenses, and piles of snorkels, wet suits, oxygen tanks, and diving gear. The rest of the brick room is a mess of rusted metal bookshelves, unmatched file cabinets, and metal lockers like you see in high school. But more than anything else, on every spare shelf, there're jugs of water, military-size jars of peanut butter, and at least fifty cans of dried fruit, nuts, corn, even baby food.

This isn't just the fort's best storage area...

"It's their hurricane shelter," Marshall announces.

Mina and I share a glance in agreement.

In almost every government building, old bomb shelters have become storage sheds.

Behind us, Clementine's still scanning the pale green room. She's not looking for some**thing**. She's looking for some**one**.

"Someone's been eating our porridge," Mina says, heading toward one of the tall, rusted file cabinets in the back. Marshall limps behind her. The middle drawer is stuck open like a tongue. On the shorter cabinet next to it, two stacks of files are piled six inches high, sagging toward each other. Most of the pages are in brown accordion folders. The rest are in hanging files, pulled straight from the cabinet.

"Beecher, you need to see this," Mina says as she starts flipping through the files.

My heart punches my ribcage. I race toward the cabinet, grabbing a fistful of files and sliding my backpack off my shoulder.

Marshall limps sideways, pulling open the other cabinet drawers. There are a few files in there, lots with pink carbon paper, but as he flips through them...

"These are from the fifties, before our fathers got here," he says.

He opens other drawers and says something else, but I'm too busy speed-reading. **Bendis, Brian...DeConnick, Matthew... Fuerstman, Alan...** Wasting no time, I flip to the back. **Pagano, Ralph.** No. Must be in the other stack. I switch piles, reaching for the last alphabetical file. It stands out like it's on fire. Even in a hurricane, everyone can find their own name.

**White, Albert.**

My father.

## 88

My hands start shaking. The waves continue to churn.

The rest of the files are pinned against my chest.

"Beecher, don't do this now," Mina warns. "Fill the knapsack. Let's go!"

I know she's right. No matter how long I've waited for this moment, this isn't the time to speed-read. There'll be time to read later. But as I flip the folder open, I swear to God, it's like I've conjured my father himself, his ghost rising up next to me, staring over my shoulder.

**Don't read it**, my father pleads.

I'm sorry, Dad. I have no choice.

The front sheet is a dark photocopy that looks like onion skin, wrinkled and wavy from the moist air. My eyes scan the top of the page, trying to put words together, but nothing makes sense. My brain's pumping too fast.

**Hair: Blond**

**Eyes: Brown**
**Ht: 5' 9"**

He was shorter than me. I stand up straight, feeling taller than I've ever felt in my life. My eyes fill with tears.

**"Are you nuts!?"** Marshall asks, smacking the stack in my hands and motioning toward my backpack. "Read it later! Time to go!"

Next to me, Mina starts pulling files from the cabinet drawer that's below my dad's.

Whacked back to reality, I hold tight to my stack of files and toss Mina the backpack, replaying each detail. **5' 9". Hair: Blond. Eyes—**

"Something's wrong," Clementine blurts behind us.

We all spin toward her. Frozen in the doorway, she's still searching the room. From the look on her face, her dad was supposed to meet her here.

"If he got here first…If he found the files…" she stutters. "Why would he just leave them?"

"Because he's a sociopath," Mina mutters.

"Watch your mouth, Giganta!" Clementine

shouts, her voice surprisingly shaky.

"Both of you, **stop**," I insist. "Maybe he wanted us to grab the files ourselves."

"Or maybe there's nothing in them," Clementine counters, swaying in place and starting to panic. I keep forgetting. She's not searching for answers in these files; she's searching for a cure.

"Clemmi, don't do that. You don't know that," Marshall says. He rushes to her side, holding her by the elbow. "Maybe he's somewhere else on the island."

"Where else would he be?"

"You tell me. Is there another place he mentioned?"

She shakes her head. "H-He told me— He said to meet him here."

"And there's no other spot he might—?"

"There's a chapel," I announce.

"A what?"

"On the second floor. I saw it on the plans. There's a chapel," I repeat. They know what I'm getting at. Years ago, when Nico took a shot at the President, he was convinced God Almighty had asked him to fire the bullet. He also thought God sent him on a mission to battle the Freemasons, murder the First Lady, and add feather after feather to his cuckoo's nest. To Nico, chapels are catnip.

"We should check the chapel," Mina agrees, still pulling files from the lower drawers. She's not leaving until she gets them all.

I follow behind Clementine as—

**Dkkkkk!**

The cat jumps from Clementine's arms. We all look to the left.

**Dkkkkk!**

The sound's coming from outside the room. It's a brutal, rasping noise, like a pounding or a hammering. Whatever it is, we're definitely not alone.

**Dkkkkk!**

As always, Marshall reacts first. He goes to race from the room, toward the source, but the way he's hobbling, he's not moving too quickly.

"He needs help. He's been poisoned!" Clementine tells me as Marshall disappears around the corner.

**"Poisoned?"**

"Beecher, just help him," she pleads. I can't tell if she's talking about Marshall or her dad. Either way, she starts to run. She barely gets anywhere. Her teeth are pale red. Her gums are bleeding.

"Clemmi, your mouth..."

She wobbles off balance. She can barely stay on her feet. "You need to help him," she insists, knowing I'll be faster. "Marshall needs you, and if Ezra's here..."

I still don't move. I want to leave her. I know I should leave her. But I—

**Dkkkkk!**

"I'm not your girlfriend, Beecher! Just go," Clementine begs, her voice cracking.

I turn back to Mina, who's still pulling the files. She's staring our way, eyes wide with sadness. **Listen to her**, Mina tells me with just a look, knowing that even Clementine can't lie about this one.

**You sure?** I ask with a glance.

"I'll get the files. Go," Mina says, pulling another stack from the drawers.

"You need to get them all. Every scrap of paper."

"You think you've got the patent on uptight archivists?" Mina says. She motions to the stack I'm holding, with Marshall's dad's file, Nico's file, and the one for my dad. "Want me to take those?"

I shake my head. No one's taking these but me.

**"We need to help him!"** Clementine shouts, already limping out the door.

"Mina, thank you for this. I mean it," I say as she starts stuffing files into the backpack.

Glancing around, I search for a weapon. Near the scuba gear, there's a skinny oxygen tank that looks like a shortened baseball bat. It's the best I've got. Still holding the files, I grab it and take off, following Clementine.

I pass her within seconds, cutting out into the brick hallway and weaving back through the white-painted maze. Clementine can barely keep up.

"Just go! Please!" she pleads as I pick up speed.

**Dkkkkk!**

The noise is a chopping sound, like someone's taking an axe to a car...or something metal.

**Dkkkkk!**

"You okay?" I call out to Marshall, who's just ahead of me, hobbling in the main alcove.

Out of breath, he points to the right, where the sound's coming from: Dr. Mudd's cell. But just as I turn, the chopping stops.

If Ezra's already here—

**"Go! Don't look at me! Go!"** Marshall hisses.

I hold the oxygen tank like a club, running faster than ever. Unlike in the rest of the fort, the floor starts slanting downward. The brick hallway narrows, then narrows again as I run though archway after archway, brick room after brick room. It's getting darker too. There're windows down here, but not many.

Back during the Civil War, this was the entrance to their dungeon, the place where they locked up all their prisoners, including Dr. Mudd and the other Lincoln conspirators.

**Dkkkkk!**

"Nico, that you…?" I call out in a whisper. No answer.

In the main parts of the fort, all the bricks look beaten and worn. Back here, they're practically falling from the ceiling and walls. A single narrow window, barely a few inches wide, tells me why. The fort is almost two hundred years old, and this is the side of the island that got hit hardest by the hurricane. Chunks of brick are scattered along the floor.

Up ahead, there's one last archway. Just above it, an antique brown plank of wood is bolted to the wall. In faded white letters is a hand-carved message:

## WHOSO ENTERETH HERE
## LEAVETH ALL HOPES BEHIND!

They've got the Dante quote wrong, but as I pass the sign and enter the actual dungeon, I see how right the warning is.

The bricks in here aren't just red. Up by the corners of the ceiling, they're sooty and black, like they've been through a fire. On the floor is a strip of bright yellow **CAUTION** police tape, lifeless on the ground. We're not supposed to be back here. And neither is he: the man with the buzzed black hair whose back is to me.

Nico.

In the corner of the wide room, he doesn't turn around. He's got a shovel in his hand, but it's like he doesn't hear me. The thing is, he hears everything.

He leans to his right, like someone's whispering in his ear. I almost forgot. His imaginary friend.

"Nico, it's me," I say. "It's—"

**Dkkkkk!**

With his back still to me, Nico wields the shovel like a battering ram, jamming it hard into the wall. Shards of red-and-black brick splinter and fall, raining across the stone floor.

"Nico, we need to get out of here," I tell him.

"Show some respect," he says, his voice a barbed-wire growl. "Don't you know where you are? Your father died in this room."

## 89

## Twenty-nine years ago
## Devil's Island

On the island, there weren't many places to keep prisoners, so they locked Alby in the dungeon.

It was the same brick dungeon and six-by-six cell that'd held Dr. Mudd over a century ago. Like they'd done with Mudd, they clamped Alby's wrist in the rusted shackle that was bolted to the wall.

They didn't want to chain him up like that, but it was the only way for Dr. Moorcraft to give Alby his shot. **To calm him down**, the doctor said.

For the first few hours, Alby was screaming and thrashing, though out here on the island, it didn't matter. By day two, he was hoarse and exhausted. Starving too. They gave him a wooden bucket for his diarrhea, but barely any food. By day three, he just sat there in the empty cell, sagging down on the stone floor, swatting at mosquitoes that weren't there. And a moth, though somewhere in his head, he knew there were no yellow moths on the island.

Just outside the cell, Dr. Moorcraft had brought in a wooden desk and even a metal floor stand that held a tall American flag, one of the few flashes of color for Alby to focus on, especially when the sun was gone and darkness arrived. He'd save the flag for night, when it stood in a pool of lamplight. During the day, he'd stare out the thin window—barely two inches wide—that looked out toward the front moat of the fort.

According to Dr. Moorcraft, during the Civil War, all the feces and urine from every latrine on the island had drained into that front moat. The goal was to send a message to approaching foreigners, and to punish those in the dungeon, who had to sleep with the reek every night.

For some reason, he also told Alby that Dr. Mudd and the other prisoners had dug an underground tunnel. Alby spent most of that day trying to pry at the stone floor. He never found the tunnel, though when he hit a certain part of the wall, a loose stone moved in the ceiling, sprinkling a few grains of fine black dust. Alby had no idea it was gunpowder that was stored in the rooms above him.

Other than the window, the only source of light was a tall halogen lamp whose plug ran out of the dungeon, all the way back to the hurricane shelter. Twice a day, Dr. Moorcraft sat at the desk and asked questions that Alby refused to answer.

Alby had only one question: **"Why am I still here!?"** he shouted as Moorcraft lowered the halogen and darkness descended. Alby had broken into an off-limits area. It was clear insubordination. The supply boat had come yesterday. So why hadn't they shipped him off the island? **"Why not send me home!?"**

As usual, Moorcraft left the dungeon, giving no answer. The waves crashed outside. A fat three-quarter moon added a silver tint through the narrow window. But otherwise, it was another night of Alby lying on the stone floor, listening to rats skitter in every direction.

That is, until two hours later, well after midnight, when the skittering stopped.

Alby's eyes popped open at the sudden lack of sound. Even when you can't see it, you still know when someone enters a room.

Sitting up, Alby swatted away a swarm of mosquitoes.

**"Who's there?"** Alby hissed into the dark.

No reply.

Alby sat up on his knees, the chain on his wrist clanging against the brick and stone. Through the bars, he couldn't see far. Past the desk, the hallway twisted around to the left. **"You trying to give me another shot!?"**

Again, no response. Something was wrong. When Dr. Moorcraft and the guards gave shots, they didn't lurk there in the darkness. Maybe he was really crazy; maybe it was all in his head.

Alby squinted hard, his breathing in perfect sync with the crashing waves outside. He knew someone was there. He felt it.

It couldn't be Timothy. Timothy hated him too much. Maybe it was Arkansas Ovalface. But again, the only reason

Arkansas sat with him, much less spoke to him, was to get Alby's extra hash browns and biscuits. No, the longer Alby knelt there, the rusty chain tugging at his wrist, there was only one person who made sense. The person he'd last seen reading Julian's book.

"Nico, I know it's you," Alby finally said.

Still nothing.

"Nico, you came here for a reason. Don't just sit there like a coward!"

Nothing again.

"C'mon, don't you wanna know what they're doing to us!?" Alby pleaded. "How many shots have they given us? You think that's normal? I saw the proof! They're putting things in us, Nico! All we are are lab rats! If you let me out of here, I can tell you! I'll show you!"

But as Alby continued to yell, the room stayed dark and the shadows seemed to shift. Whoever had been waiting around the corner, they were no longer there.

## 90

## Today

Mina had her back to the door. She was moving quickly, tugging fistfuls of files from the cabinet and stuffing them into the backpack.

In the distance, the ocean waves continued to cartwheel. She could hear Clementine running—limping really—every other footstep slapping hard against the stone floor as she chased after Beecher and Marshall. But in no time, those echoes faded too, and the storage room settled, embracing its usual silence.

Mina didn't mind the quiet. Like most archivists, she preferred it. What she didn't prefer was being so caught off guard by Clementine's arrival. Beecher had kept that one a secret. He'd known Clementine would be here—and that Nico would too— he and Marshall had set it up. Could Mina fault him for that? Not really. Beecher was being smart and cautious. On top of that, they'd kept Clementine in the dark as well.

So why was it gnawing so deeply at Mina? Deep down, she knew the answer. Had she made the wrong choice? Should she have called it in? From her pocket, she pulled out her phone. **No signal.** Same as it'd been since they boarded the plane. Yet as she finished the last file cabinet and zipped up the backpack, Mina's biggest problem was simply this: Her back was still to the door.

She barely even noticed as the island's newest arrival joined her in the room.

"Clementine, that you?" Mina called out.

She was in mid-turn. The man's hand was arced up in the air. Stabbing down, he rammed the butt of his gun into the back of Mina's head. She stumbled, but was still on her feet. She was strong, like a bull. Not that it helped.

He hit her again and again until the blood started coming. Mina fell to the ground face-first.

**How nice**, the man thought to himself as he grabbed the full backpack. Everything was all packed up for him.

## 91

"What'd you say?" I ask.

Nico doesn't answer. Jamming his shovel at the wall and scattering another chunk of the red-and-black bricks, he knows I heard him. He shakes his head, still talking to his imaginary friend.

"How do you know my father died here?" I challenge, the files still tucked under my armpit.

"This room was different back then. It wasn't empty like this; it was divided into half a dozen tiny jail cells, Benjamin," he explains, always calling me by my middle name. He thinks he's the reincarnation of George Washington and I'm Benedict Arnold. Trust me, he's got no lack of crazy. But usually, his voice is filled with the confidence that comes from that crazy. Right now, he sounds—and looks—deflated, staring off at an old memory. "Do you know who else was transformed in this place? Do you know whose cell this was?"

The ancient brass plaque on the wall tells

me this is where they held Dr. Mudd. But all I care about is my father. "Nico, tell me how you—?"

"This is where Dr. Mudd's life changed too. Mudd was a bitter racist—one of the takers of Abraham Lincoln's life. But when an outbreak of yellow fever hit the island, all four nurses on the island died. The army doctor died too. Mudd was the only one with medical training left, and here he was, shackled to the wall in this exact spot where we're now standing.

"His jailers had no choice. Four hundred people lived on this island. The yellow fever caused black vomit, and the pain from it was so brutal, once you got it, they'd bring a makeshift coffin to the side of your bed, just waiting for you to die. Then they'd bury you at the edge of the island and let the tides take you away. Without proper medical treatment, yellow fever would've consumed every-one on this island."

"I know the story of Dr. Mudd."

"Then you know that when they released him from this cell, he became a new man. A different man. One day, he was a vindictive racist who wanted blacks to be kept in chains. The next day, he was working tirelessly without sleep and without help to save everyone here, black or white. Suddenly, he was a hero. In this hole, he was redeemed. They pardoned him soon after. Don't you see?" he asks, his spirit and energy all gone. "Mudd was no different than the rest of us. We all have one body, with many versions of ourselves in it."

"Nico, how do you know my father died in this room?"

He pauses at that, putting the shovel down and cocking an eyebrow toward the door. He hears someone coming. "One, two, three, four," he mutters to himself. "Always four."

"How'd you know my father—?"

"We're on an island, Benjamin," he says, turning back to me. "Everyone heard his screams."

The words drill me like a nail gun in my chest. The oxygen tank sags to my side, suddenly weighing a ton. He has to be lying. He never tells the—

**"Nico—!"** a female voice calls out.

Behind me, Clementine bursts into the room. Marshall's limping beside her. They're shoulder to shoulder, so close that I can't tell if they're holding hands or she's helping Marshall stand. But the moment she sees her father, Clementine heads for Nico. By herself.

In life, the most complex relationship you'll ever have is with your parent. It also comes with its own secret language.

Clementine's eyes go wide, like she's asking a question.

Nico turns away, refusing to face her. He knows the cure she's looking for. And even worse, he knows the truth. Whatever was in those files, it's not going to save his daughter.

It doesn't slow Clementine down. She's not worried about her-self anymore; she's worried about her father. The closer she gets, the more Nico shrinks, like he's curling inside himself. Shaking his head, he turns back toward the wall, pressing his forehead against the brick. He's not talking to his imaginary friend. He's not talking to anyone.

"Nico, it's okay...it's okay..." she says before I even realize what's happening.

When someone starts crying, you phys-ically feel it across a room. It's an emotional gravity field that pulls everything toward it.

Nico's shoulders curve inward. His body trembles. He doesn't want to let the tears come, but he doesn't have a choice.

**"I-I'm so sorry,"** he sobs. **"I thought the files— All I wanted was to save you...!"**

"No...it's okay," Clemmi says.

**"It's not okay. Those sins that are in you— They're my sins...! They should be in me, not you!"**

"Nico, they're not sins."

**"They are! Don't you see? I prayed to God every day to make you different from me. But now, I finally** understand..." His voice is speeding now as the tears finally come.

"No. Listen. Are you listening?" she interrupts, putting a hand on his back. "They're not sins. Okay? They're not sins," she insists, her voice calm and fully in control.

It's amazing really. The more Nico crumbles, the more Clementine finds her footing.

"I'm okay," she insists. "Look at me. I'm okay."

Nico won't have it; he won't look at her.

"I know why God did this," he insists, his forehead and fingers pressing against the bricks. "These past few weeks...these months... Nothing hurts me anymore. There's no hurt I can feel. The only pain I suffer is when God punishes..." He takes a breath. **"...when he punishes you."**

Clementine clenches her jaw, fighting hard to hold it together. "You don't have to worry about me, Dad."

There it is: **Dad**.

Twisting toward his daughter, Nico collapses into Clementine's open arms. His sobs are silent huffs of air that chug in their own erratic rhythm.

"I got you. I'm here," she repeats, holding him tight. "I'm not letting go."

I glance over at Marshall, who can barely stand in the entryway. "Clementine," he calls out, leaning on the brick wall to keep him-self up, "if you want to get him out of here, we need to go. **Now.**"

I start to run, knowing Marshall's right.

Clementine agrees, following behind me and steering her dad toward the—

Nico cocks his head; I know that look. He hears something.

I toss the files to the floor and raise the oxygen tank like a baseball bat.

Marshall's about to run through the archway. He stops, then backs up, raising his hands like it's a stickup.

"One, two, three, four, five," Nico mutters. "There shouldn't be five."

But there are. Through the darkness of the archway, there's no missing the shine on our newest visitor's head. Or the jagged gash across his right cheek where Clementine shot him.

"Is this really such a shock?" Ezra asks, entering the room and pointing an antique gun at Marshall's chest. He tosses Mina's backpack, thick with files, at his own feet. "Personally, I always saw the ending coming."

## 92

"Marshall, I know you have a gun," Ezra says, cocky as ever.

Marshall stays quiet, hands still in the air as he slowly limps backward, next to me. He's on my left, looking like he's about to collapse. Nico and Clemmi are on my right.

"You really do look terrible," Ezra adds, his antique pistol still pointed at Marshall's chest. "Now toss me your gun, or you can have a far messier problem. I'm counting to two. One..."

"...two, three, four, five," Nico whispers, confused. He's on Planet Nico, barely noticing Ezra's gun.

Marshall still doesn't move. I know his gun's in the back waistband of his pants.

Ezra rolls his eyes and pulls the trigger.

**Blam!**

There's a black puff of smoke from the old pistol. Blood explodes from Marshall's good shoulder. He crashes back into the brick and lets out a grunt that sounds like a wounded animal. But somehow, he's still on his feet.

"**Marsh...!**" Clementine shouts, starting to run, then stopping as Ezra points the gun at her, then at Nico, then back at me. What catches my eye, though, is the way Ezra keeps staring at Nico, like he's a Hollywood star.

"Beecher, put the stupid oxygen tank down," Ezra warns. "Same with the shovel, Nico."

I lower the tank to the ground. Nico whispers something else to himself and does the same with the shovel. The metal clangs against the brick.

I can't stop staring at Mina's backpack. If Ezra hurt her—

"You, I'm pissed at," Ezra says to Clementine. And **you**..." he says, turning back to Marshall. "You really should've taken me up on my offer. Now. For the last time: your gun."

From the back of his pants, Marshall pulls out his gun and tosses it to Ezra. It skips across the brick, stopping just shy of Ezra's feet.

"The pain must be unbearable at this point, huh?" Ezra asks as he picks up the gun. "And when you add that to the bullet from yesterday... I assume you know about the poison, yes?"

Breathing hard though clenched teeth, Marshall doesn't answer.

"To be honest, I'm amazed you're still with us. According to the Knights' diaries..."

**"Knights?"** Nico asks, startled awake.

"...it really does a number on you," Ezra says, still locked on Marshall. "In fact, if you weren't covered in those burns, you'd see that your skin was slowly turning yellow. Know what that means? You're in liver failure, Marshall. But maybe that's the one benefit of being such an ugly mess. Your body's too stubborn to realize you're already dead."

**"I-I'm...going...to...murder you,"** Marshall warns, sagging down till his ass hits the ground. Clementine wants to run to him. Nico again whispers something to his imaginary friend. They're having a full conversation.

"See, that's why I wanted you to join me, Marshall. You would've made my grandfather proud."

**"Your** grandfather? You mean the **real**

Ezra's grandfather?" I jump in. "You realize how sick you are, Kingston?"

He doesn't even react as I say his real name.

"You hear what I said? We know you killed Ezra and took his li—"

"Oh, will you please stop with the righteousness?" Ezra asks, stealing another quick glance at Nico, whose whispering is still going. "You think a name matters? Ezra had all the money and toys he'd ever need in his life, and he didn't appreciate any of it. Last year, you should've seen the fit he threw when he realized his new car didn't come with seat warmers. And when it came to his heritage—to what his grandfather left him—he didn't understand the mission. He didn't see the potential. He saw it as an embarrassment! An **embarrassment**! Can you imagine, Beecher!? All that history—all those years of keeping the country safe—and he wanted to throw it in the trash."

"So instead you killed him."

"No, I did what the mission required— what the Knights have always required. If you want to keep this country safe, hard choices must be made," Ezra says. "And Nico, if you don't stop with the mumbling, I'm going to shoot your daughter in the face!"

I wait for Nico to attack. Instead, he's listening intently, and not to Ezra. Whatever his imaginary friend is saying, it's wrecking him. I've never seen him scared before.

"Do you even realize how little sense you're making?" I ask Ezra.

"You keep talking about this grand mission, but how does sneaking into the White House and threatening the President keep this country safe?"

Ezra's eyes roll sideways, away from Nico and back to me. "**Threatening** the President?" Ezra laughs at that, a deep **rat-a-tat-tat** laugh that cuts like a childhood taunt. "Beecher, the only reason I was at the White House was to show President Wallace how vulnerable he is. And more important, to tell him we can help."

**Help?** I look over at Marshall. He's still down on the ground, clutching his shoulder. But he's just as confused.

"You really are lost, aren't you, Beecher?"

Ezra asks.

"I thought— For you to chase us here...to be searching for my father's files...?"

Ezra smiles, his laugh long gone. "Why would I want your dead father's files? I told you before, for centuries, the mission of the Knights has never changed: We keep this country safe. So ask yourself the question: When it comes to that safety, who's the one walking time bomb who wants to slaughter the President and put us all at risk?" Oh, God.

On my right, I finally make out what Nico's whispering. **"I'm the sinner... I'm the sinner."**

Ezra points his gun at his real target. "This isn't about the Ring, Beecher. Or even about **you**."

Without another word, Ezra takes aim at Nico Hadrian. And pulls the trigger.

## 93

**"Don't...!"**

Too late. Ezra's finger squeezes the trigger.

Diving to my right, I'm still in mid-syllable as I grab the scuba tank of oxygen and leap in front of Nico. I hold the tank to my chest and shut my eyes.

**Tot, I'm sorry I won't be there for you.**

Afraid to hit the scuba tank, Ezra jerks the pistol upward just as the gunshot goes off. There's a black puff of smoke and a sulfurous smell. The musket ball whizzes above us, hitting with a deafening crack. Shards of rain down on our heads. The brick-work is so old and damaged, half the ceiling comes with it, drizzling pieces on all of us.

"Are you that much of a moron?" Ezra growls. "Get out of the way, Beecher." He aims his gun straight at me. I'm still standing directly in front of Nico.

"You know what happens if you do it," I warn, holding the oxygen tank at my chest.

"That's who you want to protect? Nico? The poster boy for lunatics who's been on a murdering tour all week? Did Clementine tell you? He killed a retired colonel! Pulled the skin from his fingers! You think he's not taking another shot at the President? Ask him yourself. Nico, do you want President Wallace dead?"

Behind me, Nico's blinking brick dust from his eyes. As Clementine rubs his back, he's staring down at the floor, muttering to himself. **"...ere should just be four. Always four. Take the sinner away... that'll leave four."**

"Are you even hearing him right now?" I ask Ezra. "There's a reason we have courts. And insane asylums. Nico may be crazy, but he has rights."

"That's what you want for him? He'll get his day in court and then **what**? Escape again?"

"So you should shoot him in the head? That's your solution?"

"I'm not having a morality debate about our judicial system, Beecher. In the Knights, we have one way to deal with things. The Culper Ring has another. But I promise you this, from Nazi scientists to Lee Harvey Oswald, the world is a far safer place with us in it."

"Then take your shot," I challenge, still holding the oxygen tank at my chest.

Ezra's jaw shifts to the side. "In the movies, when you puncture an oxygen tank, it explodes. But in real life, it's not a bomb—it just lets out a hiss."

"All I know is that at the end of **Jaws**, this is what they used to take out the big shark. So I don't care how much **MythBusters** you watch, I got faith in Spielberg. Take your damn shot."

"You think I won't?"

"I know you won't. And y'know why? Because if you were all about keeping America safe, you'd have already risked your life and pulled the trigger. But Ezra... or Kingston...or whatever the hell your name is now...you're not in this for safety. You're in it for glory. That's your flaw. This isn't about the good of the country, or doing what's right. You crave status. That's why you thought your roommate's life was so great. That's why you wanted his dead, rich grandfather for your own. And that's why you carry that dumb photo in your wallet that Clementine told us about. You're as shallow as any other spoiled shit who thinks that a photo with the President means that you're a member of the private club. So know this: The Knights of the Golden Circle weren't hunted for their philosophy. They were hunted because they're selfish elitists who think they know how to run the world better than the rest of us. And that's why you'll always lose. You're not fighting for what's right. **You're fighting for yourself.**"

Ezra presses his lips together into a thin line. "You done yet?"

"I think so."

Cocking his head to the side, Ezra lowers his gun, aims at my leg, and pulls the trigger. A puff of smoke erupts from the pistol. A bee sting bites my thigh. I see the hole—the size of a quarter— before I register the pain. Blood, charred skin, and bits of my pants run down into it. In shock, I stick my finger in it. There's a hole. He shot me, I think as time unlocks and starts rolling forward.

"**Fuuuh...!**" I shout, grabbing my thigh.

"**—eecher! Beecher!**" Marshall shouts,

still down on the ground, trying to get my attention. He points to the scuba tank. "Don't let go of the—!"

Too late. My leg's on fire. I crumple in pain. The oxygen tank tumbles from my hands.

No. It's **pulled** from my hands. I'm hunched forward, in mid-fall. Next to me, Clementine's just a blur. In one fluid movement, she races in, rips the scuba tank out of my hands, and heads straight for her target: straight at Ezra.

**Clemmi, don't!** I shout in my head.

Nico grabs at her arm, trying to hold her back.

She's already moving too fast. Barreling toward Ezra, she holds the oxygen tank out in front of her like a shield.

Enraged and without even hesitating, Ezra raises his gun, points it at her, and again pulls the trigger.

There's another puff of black smoke as the musket ball hurtles directly at the scuba tank.

The impact isn't loud. But it is devastating.

## 94

There's a vicious pop. By the time I hear it, the punctured oxygen tank is already at lift-off, the sudden release of pressure turning it into a steel-plated bottle rocket that erupts upward.

I try to yell something. Clementine and Ezra are knocked backward, floating in mid-air.

It all happens so violently and so fast. With the dungeon's low ceiling, the scuba tank has nowhere to go. In an eyeblink, it pummels into the roof, then ricochets and reverses course, pulverizing the ground, then rising back up again, zigzagging with reckless ferocity.

**Zuung...zuung...zuung...**

I was wrong before; it isn't a bottle rocket. It's a thrashing, tumbling missile. Ceiling, floor, ceiling. Each impact hits like a wrecking ball that's whipped back and forth. Up above, the ceiling ruptures and gravity does the rest. Bricks vomit from above, followed by jagged hunks of sandstone and two hundred years of dust.

Down below, it's even worse. The scuba tank hammers the limestone floor with a thunderclap, and the whole room shakes. Before I even know what's happening, the ground tilts, and Clementine and Ezra start to tumble. I hear Clementine screaming, Nico too. He's yelling, still reaching out for her, but I can't see anything. The sand and soot are too thick as they rain down from above. For half a second, the world turns ash gray. Then, in the same half-second, it's over.

Across the room, the metal scuba tank lies there, lifeless.

Up above, the ceiling continues to spew a few thin waterfalls of dust and debris that rain like an hourglass.

What the hell was—?

**"Where'd they go?"** Marshall calls out, covered in dust and coughing uncontrollably. Still on the ground, he points across the room. Clementine and Ezra are... Where are they?

Ignoring the heartbeat that's throbbing in my leg, I climb to my feet. As I blink through the dust cloud, I start running toward—

"Clemmi...?"

At first, I thought she was just knocked over. But as I reach ground zero, she and Ezra... They're not there. I wave my hand, fanning the dust. In the ground... There's a jagged hole the size of a bathtub, filled with bricks, debris, and—

"Beecher...? Beecher, I'm here!" Clementine coughs, her voice faint and far away. "Down here."

Squinting through the dust, I can barely see. The limestone floor is cracked open. I follow Clementine's voice. One of the wide slabs of limestone is snapped and broken away, revealing what looks like a shallow room underneath.

"Clemmi, listen to me. Tell me what you see!"

"I-It looks like a tunnel," she calls back.

Of course. I almost forgot where we were. Two hundred years ago, this was the dungeon. Some of the prisoners must've burrowed underneath to make their escape, all of it hidden under the slab of rock.

"I can't feel my leg! There's something wrong with my leg!" she yells, clearly in pain. She's lisping more than ever, like the impact took the rest of her teeth.

"We need to get her out of there," Marshall insists, fighting to his own feet. He can barely stand. The blood from his newest wound soaks the side of his shirt.

I look at Nico, the only one of us who wasn't knocked over. He doesn't say a word, doesn't even acknowledge I'm there. But within seconds, he's by my side, grabbing shattered bricks and chunks of rock from the pile.

"**Here.** I think she's here," I tell Marshall and Nico, pointing to the far right side of the hole.

"**Beecher, you need to hurry! Ezra's up...he's up and moving!**" Clementine yells. She's breathing heavily, like her lungs don't work. "**I can...I can see him moving! He's crawling down the tunnel... trying to get away!**"

We all furiously start trying to dig her out. Marshall races to the opposite side of the hole, using his good arm to move a hunk of the brick ceiling that's still stuck in place. His own blood drips onto the floor. As we lift the bricks away, I hear a soft clicking. Something skitters from the hole. I see the thick tail first, then shiny black eyes. There're two...three... No. There're dozens of them: fat black rats.

**"There's something else in here, Beecher! Something's touching me!"** Clementine shouts.

"It's a rat, just a little one," I tell her as a dozen of them swarm to the surface, making the whole floor look like it's moving. I jump and high-step as they scurry past us, racing out of the dungeon. Nico and Marshall barely react.

**"Ezra's still crawling! He's getting away!"** Clementine shouts.

We yank at another layer of bricks.

**"No! Not like that! It won't work!"** she screams.

We quickly see why. Underneath the bricks, there's a massive slab of sandstone —like a serrated surfboard—that's slicing diagonally down the hole. It plummeted from the ceiling, and no question, it's what's pinning Clementine in place. I give it a shove. It weighs a ton. Won't budge.

**"You're not moving it!"** she scolds.

By now, the dust is settling. I again peer into the hole, noticing the putrid smell of sulfur. I can't see all of Clementine—chunks of floor and layers of rubble form a maze of debris with no clear view—but as we tug another chunk of limestone out of the way, I see just her face. She's at least six feet down, looking up at me.

Her mouth wilts open. Her teeth are gone. It doesn't look like a single tooth is left after the explosion and the fall. Her face is black, and two streams of blood form a Y from her nostrils. But what undoes me is that look in her eyes. I've known Clementine since grade school. I've seen her giddy and excited, angry and enraged, shocked and surprised. I've seen the way her eyelids get heavy when you kiss her. And the way they'd screw tight, like the aperture of a camera, when she knew her mother was drunk. But I've never seen her defeated. Until now.

Her ginger brown eyes stay wide, trying to sell me calm. It's not working. "You need to...you need to find Marshall's gun," she tells me, fighting for each breath.

"What're you—?"

"Just find it!" she insists. "When we were falling...I saw Ezra drop it. Look around!"

Marshall, Nico, and I all glance to different parts of the room. It's a chaotic wreck, filled with loose bricks, chunks of rocks, and piles of dirt. But that means shiny metal weapons stand out even more.

**There.**

"I see it! I got it!" I call back, scooping the gun up and heading back to the hole. "You want me to lower it down there?"

"There's no time. You need to…you need to stop Ezra. **Point it here and shoot!**"

"Wha? I can't even see him. How can I—?"

**"Just shoot, Beecher! Point and shoot!"**

Confused, I squint deep into the hole. Her weight shifts and the floor seems to shift with her. Underneath the slab of limestone, she's covered in what looks like black sand. It's all over her, filling most of the jagged hole that connects with the tunnel. The sulfur smell. I finally place it.

"Gunpowder," Marshall says.

I nod. They used to store it in the bastions all around the island. Over the years, it must've seeped down to the tunnel. She's swimming in gunpowder.

I start putting the rest together. If I fire the

gun, when the bullet hits the ground and sparks, all that gunpowder will—

Clementine looks up from the hole, taking a long, labored breath that sounds like her last. "I know what I'm doing, Beecher."

Further down the tunnel, I hear Ezra scrambling, scratching through the dirt and sand.

"He's...he's already around the corner," she adds. "If this leads to the beach— It's the only way to stop him."

"By starting a firestorm? All that gunpowder in a contained space... When you light it, that whole tunnel will turn into a cannon. You'll be—"

"I'll be in the exact same place where we all know I'm headed," she lisps, her voice cracking. She's wheezing now, starting to fade. With her free hand, she pulls her wig from her head. "Look at me. Look at what little is left."

I stare down at her toothless mouth and her sweaty bald head. It looks extra pale— and even more like a cancer patient's— thanks to the blood and dirt on her face. She doesn't look like she's dying. She looks like she's already dead. "We can still get you out of there."

"No, Beecher…you can't," she wheezes. "Not this time. You rescued me enough. Now please…for once…let me do right by you. We're running out of time."

I don't move. If I've learned one thing over the years, it's that every person you encounter brings out a different part of you. From youth to adulthood, even when she was hurting me, Clementine brought out my best. Whether I liked it or not.

"I know you can't do this," she says. "Give the gun…give the gun to Marshall."

"But if we—"

**"Give the gun to Marshall!"** she screams, tears pouring from her eyes and a blood bubble popping from her nose.

Before I can say a word, Marshall tugs the pistol from my hand, staring down at Clementine. As they exchange a glance, Clementine nods, fighting for another breath. She doesn't have long.

Marshall's plastic face is unreadable as ever, frozen by his scars. But some things don't need to be seen; they can be felt. When they rode down here on that train, something happened between them.

"You don't need to do this," he says.

"I do. You saved me for a reason. Here's your reason," she insists, more demanding than ever. "This is your chance. If you don't stop Ezra now, he'll...he'll keep coming for you, hunting you."

"I can protect myself," Marshall says.

"And who'll protect Beecher?"

"I don't need protection!" I insist.

"And what about my dad? Who'll protect him?" she adds, glancing at Nico, who's still hopelessly pulling bricks from the hole. As Clementine's voice again gives way, it's the first time I realize she's not just fighting for us. She's fighting for **him**. "When they lock Nico back up in that mental hospital, you think...you think anyone will argue when Ezra comes knocking? They'll be happy to see him dead," she says. "He's my dad. Please...if I do nothing else...let me save my father."

Marshall stands there, his gun still flat at his side. "You're making a rash decision."

"I'm making the only decision I have left! The sole reason...**ahuuh**...the sole reason I came to your place was because I knew my life was over. I know I won't have years in the future. I don't even have weeks! I just want the time that I did have to count for something. Is that so bad? To want to count for something?"

Marshall still doesn't move.

She doesn't let up. "I...ahuuh...I know you understand, Marshall. I know you've been here—and I know that after all the burn treatments, and the fighting, and the pain—I know that all you really want, even now, is peace," she lisps, rubbing her hand over her own bald head. "Let me have my peace. Please. It's my time. If we stop him now, think of how many people you'll be saving from pain."

Marshall's posture shifts just slightly. It's the one thing he understands better than anyone. Pain.

"You're sure you know what you're doing?" he asks.

Clementine takes a labored breath. She forces a weak smile. "We all have a **before** and **after** to one moment," she says. "Let this be yours."

Marshall takes two steps back. Thanks to the rocks that cover Clementine, the blast should go out toward Ezra, but now Marshall has a safer angle in case some of it goes up. We still hear Ezra crawling and scratching in the tunnel. Marshall's out of time. So is Clemmi.

Marshall's hand is shaking as he raises the gun. He points it down the hole, toward the gunpowder-filled tunnel. Six feet below us, Clementine shuts her eyes. Marshall's finger curls around the trigger and—

Nothing.

"I can't. If I do it— I can't put you through those burns," Marshall says, lowering the gun.

**"You have to! He's getting away!"** Clementine pleads. **"Don't deny me this!"**

I still hear Ezra crawling, but the sound is starting to fade.

In a blur, the gun is ripped from Marshall's hands. Holding it tight, Nico points the pistol down, aiming toward his daughter.

The rest happens within seconds. For a moment, Clementine almost looks relieved. Tears flood her eyes. Nico's too. He's bobbing his head, muttering something to his imaginary friend.

**"No, I know... And this will leave three... not four,"** he whispers. His chin starts to quiver. On his free hand, his thumb taps against each of his fingers, from pointer-finger to pinkie, like he's counting. **One... two...three...four...** No question, it's ripping Nico apart. But that won't stop him from doing it.

Nico doesn't say a word to her. Clementine says nothing back. They don't need to.

Nico tries to keep his head up, but it keeps falling, like his chin is being pulled by the gravity of his crumbling body. His features contort as he asks his daughter a final silent question.

Fighting to hold it together, Clementine clenches her jaw, nodding over and over. The way she's looking up, the tears run from her eyes, to her temples, then down to the back of her bald head. She's not asking anymore. She's begging.

"I love you," Nico says, his voice breaking as he raises the gun.

"I love you too, Dad," she replies, the words strangled by her tears.

That's all he needs. His thumb taps each of his fingers one last time. **Four...three... two...one...**

Pulling hard, Nico squeezes the trigger.

Even before the gun lets out its muted pop, Marshall's running. He grabs me by the shoulder, spinning me to follow. We're both sprinting full speed toward the exit, trying to leave the dungeon through the open archway. The bullet whizzes down toward hundreds of pounds of packed gunpowder. Behind us, Nico starts running too.

The world goes silent, like we're all underwater. Still running, I don't hear the explosion or the deafening boom. A burning, scalding heat screams up from the hole and sears the back of my neck. The sheer force shoves me so hard from behind, my feet leave the ground.

The last thing I see is the look on Marshall's face as he glances at what's behind him.

## 95

Nico's the one who finds her body.

He's dealing with his own burns as he sees her. His neck and arms are swollen and blistered. The hair on the back of his head is singed away. But that doesn't stop him from going back into the room, crawling down into the hole and cradling his daughter in his arms.

He doesn't cry as he holds her. He sits there mutely, looking straight ahead—staring at nothing—as he pulls her close. Clementine's charred body is still pinned by the slab of limestone. Her jawbone's gone, so are her ears, and most of her left hand was burned so bad, all that's left are ashes. But he still holds tight, his posture back to its stiff perfection.

Next to me, Marshall can't stand anymore. His face is yellow and puffy. He keeps looking down into the hole, then has to turn away just as fast. At first, I assume it's because of her burns. He can stomach anything, but he can't stomach that. Yet rather than lying down or waiting out on the beach until the medicine he needs arrives, he stays where he is, never getting too far and always glancing back at her body.

He did the same thing with his mother's coffin when we were little. Marshall can play as tough as he wants. Of all the wounds he wears, this one's cutting deep.

The Plankholder files are burned and gone. Even the ones in the backpack. The explosion took care of that—and also shook Mina awake, rousing her from where Ezra had knocked her unconscious in the storage room. Nursing the blow at the back of her head, she's standing in the archway, still refusing to step in this room.

As for Ezra's body, the other side of the tunnel leads to a massive outcropping of rocks along the beach. When the gunpowder erupted, the entire underground tunnel was turned into the barrel of a gun, shooting everything in it out to sea. Our seaplane captain is dead—Ezra shot him for putting up a fight when he first arrived—but thanks to a radio on his plane, we called the coast guard, who are on their way. It'll take a while, but they'll find Ezra's body eventually.

Beyond that, there's nothing to do but wait. Nico knows that if he wants to escape, this is his chance. He told us he had parked a small stolen motorboat on the opposite side of the island. Truth is, if he ran, I'm not sure I'd try to stop him. Or that I could, considering how my leg is aching and how nauseous I'm feeling. But instead, Nico stays where he is, down in the hole, staring at the charred walls of the tunnel and rocking back and forth as he cradles his daughter.

Every few minutes, he whispers something into Clementine's burned-off ear. And then, out of nowhere, he stops.

"Agreed," he whispers, his head turned slightly to the side, toward his imaginary friend. He blinks a few times, his close-together eyes now keenly focused. "I know. I will."

Gently putting Clemmi's body aside, Nico stands up perfectly straight and climbs from the hole.

"Nico, you okay?" I ask.

It's like I'm not even there.

"You're probably still in shock," I tell him.

He doesn't care. He heads calmly, silently toward the back wall—the wall he was ramming with a shovel when I first found him down here. For a few seconds, he looks around. The shovel's wooden shaft is burned away. All that's left is the metal blade, buried in the corner in a pile of ash.

Doesn't seem to matter. Nico stares hard at the wall. All the brick is burnt black. Hunks of mortar are missing, leaving gaps between sections of the brick. For a full ten seconds, he just stands there, studying it.

"They're going to take me back to St. Elizabeths, aren't they, Benjamin?" he finally asks.

"I don't think they have a choice."

"I want you to bury her near the hospital. So I can visit her," he blurts, eyes still on the wall. "There's a cemetery nearby. They let patients go there for visits."

I nod, watching him carefully. "I think she'd like that."

Stepping closer to the wall, he slides his bent pointer-finger into one of the gaps where there's no mortar. He slides it sideways, like he's cleaning it out.

"I only wanted to help her. That's the only

reason I hurt those—" He slides his finger into another open gap. Then another. He's searching for something. "She's my daughter, Benjamin. I was only trying to save her."

"She knew that. She told us that when we—"

In the wall, his finger catches on something. He stops, sticking two fingers into the gap and tweezing out whatever it is. It's Something small. As he studies it in his palm, I can't see it, but he definitely—

"Nico, what'd you find?"

He turns away slightly, whispering something to his imaginary friend.

"Nico, did you hear what I said?"

He continues to whisper, still lost in his own world. His head starts bobbing. That means he's praying. **Fourteen...fifteen...** it bobs sixteen times, just as always. "Amen," he says.

"If you found something, I need to know what it is!" I demand, surprised by my own outburst. My body's buzzing. I'm still in shock too.

His left hand stays closed as he turns back toward me. Usually, his dark eyes flick back and forth. For once, they're focused perfectly on me. I get the same feeling I had earlier in the hurricane shelter, like my dad's ghost has returned.

"You came here for a reason, Benjamin. Do you want to know how your father died?"

## 96

## Twenty-nine years ago
## Devil's Island

Some people think they know when they're going to die. Alby White was one of them. His whole life, he'd thought he'd die young. Tonight, he'd know the pain of being right.

He'd been sleeping poorly as usual. Then, for no reason, he was awake. Sometimes, your body just knows when it's the middle of the night. A gob of sleep-drool soaked his cheek.

Blinking out at the darkness, Alby looked through the bars of his cell, noticing the rats were gone. Nothing else moved. Nothing made a sound. The tall American flag stood there, imperceptibly swaying.

**"Nico, that you?"** Alby called out toward the room's entrance.

There was no answer.

**"I know it's you. I know you're out there, Nico."**

Still nothing.

"If you're here, you know something's wrong. You can feel it, right?" Alby asked, his voice hoarse from dehydration. "You need to hear what they did. The plane crash …Julian…it's all fake…! **Julian's alive!**"

Alby let that one hang in the air. But again, still nothing. Until…

A shadow shifted. Tiny chunks of brick popped and cracked. "How do you know that?" Nico asked, slowly turning the corner.

Alby shot upright, the chain that bolted his wrist to the wall sounding like a tambourine. He hadn't seen a fellow Plankholder in over a week. But even as Alby got up, he was careful to make sure he felt the plastic spoon he'd tucked into the back of his underwear. Two days ago, Alby had palmed the spoon, which was the only utensil they were giving him these days.

"How do you know about the plane crash …and Julian?" Nico repeated, entering the room and so focused on Alby, he nearly tripped on the halogen lamp's long cord.

"I-I saw him…and the files," Alby explained. "From the start, they were—

Everything they do, it's all bullshit! It's all a test."

Nico blinked a few times, more than he usually did. As he got closer to the cell, Alby saw there was something in his hand. Something in a baggie. "They had peach cobbler for dessert. I know you like peach cobbler," he said.

Alby offered a silent thank-you, stretching the chain so he could reach through the bars. Nico put the baggie of mushed peach cobbler on the floor, just outside the cell. Alby smelled the sugar and caramel. He wanted it so badly. But as he reached for it, he stopped himself.

"You think I put something in it?" Nico asked.

"That's what I'd do if I were them. Send a friend. I bet they put stuff in our food since the first moment we were here," Alby said, swatting at imaginary mosquitoes.

"I wouldn't do that to you," Nico insisted, blinking over and over. "You can trust me."

"Why should I—?"

"I know about the spoon you're hiding," Nico insisted. "I was here late yesterday... and the day before that. I saw you using it to dig the mortar from between the bricks. You should look for the tunnel. In Dr. Mudd's book, he talks of a hidden tunnel that they dug to get out of here."

"There's no tunnel."

"Maybe you haven't found it yet. Either way, what you were doing... I didn't tell anyone. Not anyone."

"And that's supposed to prove your loyalty?"

"What other proof do you need?"

"Let me out."

"Alby..."

"Why'd you bring me peach cobbler, Nico? If you really want to absolve yourself of guilt, get me out of these shackles, out of this cell. Moorcraft keeps the key in the middle drawer," Alby said, pointing toward the wooden desk.

"He hides the key right **here**?" Nico asked.

"Just for the shackles. The lock for the cell, he keeps with him. But at least I'll be able to move...to climb...to do something next time they come in to give me another injection."

Nico glanced over at the desk, locking on

the tall American flag. Years from now, this would be the moment he'd forever regret. "You said the middle drawer?" Nico asked. He shoved the desk chair aside as the leg of the chair caught on the halogen lamp cord.

**"The lamp...!"** Alby called out.

Nico caught it easily, grabbing the lamp mid-fall and setting it upright. Staying focused on the desk, Nico tugged the center drawer open and quickly flipped through some papers until...

Nico pulled out an old, rusted barrel key with a tooth that was shaped like the letter E.

Inside the cell, Alby raced forward and stuck his free hand through the bars, stretching the chain as far as it would go.

Outside the cell, Nico held the key high, out of Alby's reach. "Promise me you won't hurt the colonel," Nico said.

"I don't wanna hurt anyone."

"Just promise me. You can escape...you can run...do whatever you want. But he's still— You can't hurt him."

Down the hallway, there was a clicking sound, like someone was coming.

"Nico, I swear on my kids. I just want out of here."

Blinking twice in quick succession, Nico let go of the key, dropping it in Alby's open palm. In a blur, Alby raced back to the wall, stuffing it into the lock at the base of his wrist.

"Does it fit?" Nico asked, slowly stepping backward.

Alby didn't answer, still fighting the lock. Behind them, the clicking got louder.

"You need to hurry," Nico added.

**"I'm trying!"**

As Nico backed away from the cell, something tugged at his foot. The cord from the halogen light... His heel kicked it. Like a cleaved tree, the lamp fell fast, right at him. Nico tried to hunch forward as it crashed into his shoulder. At the impact, the lamp bounced sideways, hitting the American flag and smashing into the brick wall, where it—

**Fwoosh!**

The halogen bulb exploded. A burst of white light blinded them. Within seconds, the American flag was on fire, kicking embers in every direction, toward the desk, toward the chair. But what froze Nico midstep was the way the fire instantly spread out in two zigzagging tendrils. One tendril crawled along the stone floor; the other climbed the wall, popping and sparking as it snaked almost purposely toward the prison cell.

**"Alby, move!"**

The flames zigzagged across the wall, like the handwriting of God. Stray gunpowder had seeped down from the rooms above and was sprinkled along the bricks.

Alby twisted the key. The shackle clicked and unlocked.

**"Let's go! Kick it open!"** Nico shouted, gripping the rusted bars and tugging on the door in hopes of letting Alby out.

For a moment, Alby was ready to run free from the shackles. They still had to figure out how to open the jail door. But as Alby turned and saw the flames slowly engulfing his cell...as the black smoke took his lungs and he began to cough... It was just like—

The airplane. This was the exact same setup as the airplane. Alby stood there a moment, frozen in his cell. Without a word, he grabbed the arm shackle and threaded his hand through it. He squeezed the shackle hard. It clicked and locked around his wrist, like a handcuff.

**"Wh-What're you doing!?"** Nico yelled from outside the cell. The door was still locked.

"You think I'm stupid? Don't you see? It's another test...like the plane."

**"Alby, this isn't a test!"**

"They didn't even tell you, did they?" With a smile on his face, Alby took the key and headed for the narrow window.

**"Nonono! Don't...!"**

With a flick of his wrist, Alby tossed the key out the window. As it hit the moat water, it made an unheard plink.

**"Someone help! We need help!"** Nico screamed up the main hallway. The wooden desk was on fire, flames dancing along the top. Nico could've left, could've run, but instead— Outside the cell, Nico pulled out all the drawers, looking for something... anything to pry open the jail door and free Alby.

Inside the cell, chained to the wall, Alby refused to move. The fire continued to spread. He was still trying to smile, but the smoke was getting to him. "You'll see. They're just— **Kafff...kafff...** They're doing it again. Another fake fire to see if they can make us...make us...**I know what you're doing! I'm done being your guinea pig!**" he shouted at the sky. He sat down on the ground, arms crossed at his chest.

**"Alby, please... You have to get out of here!"**

"No. You'll see. This is what they do. Just like they did with the elderly couple...and with Julian. Watch... Go get the colonel. They're not letting me die."

The flames were tall now, crawling up the walls toward the ceiling. The wooden pole holding the American flag snapped in two. The flag was gone now, consumed. Outside, Nico grabbed what was left of the lower half of the pole and tugged it from its base. Racing to the door of the cell, he wedged it between the bars, a makeshift wooden lever.

**"HEEELP! SOMEONE HELP ME GET HIM OUT!"** Nico screamed, getting ready to ram his shoulder into the lever. **"Alby,**

get up! Please! You need to fight!"

"And prove them right? Prove that they can fool us again? Someone needs to stand against them!" Alby said, coughing through smoke that was so thick he could barely see. All the walls were on fire. The heat seared against his face, his arms, his ankles. **"They're not gonna let us die,"** he cried as the room began to shake.

At full speed, Nico rammed his shoulder at the bars. The wooden pole was so thin, it snapped in two. It was no use. The only way to open the door...

**"Timothy! I can get Timothy to pick the lock!"** Nico shouted, though Alby wasn't listening.

**"That's right, Colonel! Make it as hot as you want!"** Alby shouted as the fire began to roar. **"You'll see, Nico. They have hoses! They'll come racing in! You'll see!"** he snarled. He was in pain now. The heat was unbearable. A stray ember popped from the wall and hit his neck, just behind his ear. Another hit the back of his hand. His skin bubbled and blistered. He refused to yell, refused to give in.

"**I'm not leaving you! I'm getting Timothy! I swear I'll be back!**" Nico shouted, starting to run.

"**You don't need to! You'll see...**" Alby coughed, the smoke burning his lungs. The pain in his throat, it was just...just like the airplane, he told himself. Exactly like the airplane. "**You'll see...they won't let us die!**"

Nico was gone now. By the time he got back, it would all be over.

Swatting smoke and imaginary mosquitoes from his face, Alby could no longer open his eyes. He smelled his own burnt hair before he felt the pain or even realized his skull was on fire.

"**Do your worst! I can take it!**" he shouted again, the last few syllables shifting into an animal wail. "**I can!**" he howled, still refusing to get up, though he couldn't have even if he'd wanted to.

His whole life, Alby thought he knew when he was going to die. He thought it'd be when he was young. But as always, just because you know something's coming, doesn't mean you're prepared for it.

"**I know you hear me, Colonel! You**

can— You can—" A high-pitched hum filled the air. The mosquitoes were gone. So was the knot in his neck. For Alby White, the worst part wasn't the pain. It was the speed with which the realization hit. Life takes time. Death, however, reveals itself in an instant.

As his skin melted to the stone floor, Alby was done yelling, done making predictions. In the end, all he had left were apologies.

**I'm sorry,** he thought, picturing his wife... his girls...and his little newborn, his only son. **I'm sorry I failed you, Beecher.**

## 97

## Today

My whole life, I thought this would be the part where I felt good.

"That's a bullshit story," Marshall says with a cough.

"Think what you want," Nico says, his voice flat as ever. "It's what happened."

I stand there, the heartbeat in my leg pumping over and over, as I try to digest it. The wide dungeon feels smaller, like it's shrinking around me. I didn't even see Mina enter the room, but I feel her behind me, her hands on my shoulders. I pull away and glance around, trying to imagine where the metal bars used to be, where my father's cell was. But all I see are the Rorschach-shaped scorch marks that haunt every wall. They look like shadows screaming.

"Beecher, go outside. You need fresh air," Marshall tells me.

I stay where I am. I've spent my life away

from my father. But now, to have him this close... My soul feels like it's been shoveled out of my chest. My body tells me to cry, but the tears won't come. "I-I always thought he died a hero. I **wanted** him to die a hero," I say. "Instead, he died uselessly."

"He died because he was tricked," Nico says. "I was there. He died because of their tests. Their lies. Their manipulations."

I know that's right. I understand how it happened, but all these years, the one consequence of not knowing my father was simply that...he could be **anyone**. The CFO of a start-up...a scientist who studies the therapeutic use of plants. When we were little, my sisters said he was a teddy bear repairman, whatever that was, while I pictured him as a water slide and roller-coaster designer, making them extra twisty just for me. Whatever dream I had, no matter how absurdly big, it was easily projected onto him. But now, instead of seeing my father's potential, all I see is his limits.

"Why'd you tell me that?" I ask Nico.

He blinks, confused by my sudden anger. "Isn't that what you wanted?"

"That's not why you told me, though! You knew it would hurt me! You could've told me something **good** about my father... you could've given me a moment I could treasure! Instead you—!"

"I told you the truth, Benjamin."

"No, you took that truth and used it like a blade! You knew that when I heard about his suffering— You did it on purpose, knowing all the pain it would bring! **You— You should've died instead of him, you selfish ass!**" I race forward, fist cocked.

Pulling me back, Mina steps in front of me, trying to block my way.

Doesn't matter how big she is, I practically plow over her. I don't see Marshall move, but he's on me too, grabbing my chest and shoulders, both of them tugging me back. **"You should be the dead one!"** I explode at Nico. **"Not him! They should've killed you!"**

I pull out of Mina's grip, nearly knocking her over. Marshall's injured. He can't hold on much longer. Nico sways just slightly. He won't fight back. He wants me to do it.

**"Enough,"** Marshall growls. He presses his fingers into my armpit. My right arm goes numb as well as my thigh. Like a puppet with cut strings, I tumble from the momentum, nearly falling on my face. Marshall falls with me. That's all he has left.

When I was in twelfth grade, our anatomy class dissected a dead cat. I refused since we had a cat of our own.

"Just pretend it's a dead frog," my teacher told me.

"I like frogs," I told him.

"Then pick an animal you don't like. Pretend it's a snake. Or a worm. Everyone hates worms. Or take the F for all I care."

I pretended it was a rat. But today, as I crash on my knees, palms shredded by the rough stone, all my rage gives way to one inescapable fact: That's what they did to my father. For their tests...for their experiments...for everything that caused his death... They saw him as a rat, a worm.

My tears push out from behind my eyes and rain from my nose. My body shatters, fragmenting along the floor. My fingers, my hands, I can't stop them from shaking. I'm in shock. I kneel down on all fours. How could they—? **How could anyone—? "Oh, God, Dad!"** I cry, still picturing his final terrified moments as the burn marks sear into my brain. **"They did this! They took him apart!"** I shout, not even sure who I'm yelling at.

Marshall collapses on the floor. Mina kneels next to me, pulling me close. "It's your father," she says. "He deserves to be mourned."

For me, that's all it takes. At just her embrace, something cracks inside me. I break into uncontrollable sobs. For two minutes, she stays there, keeping me close and rubbing my back. Snot pours from my nose, all over her shirt.

"You owe me a shirt," she teases.

I laugh and cry in the same huffy breath. It takes another full minute for my breathing to settle. As I wipe my eyes, she knows there's nothing to say.

"You shouldn't have told me," I finally whisper, looking up at Nico. "I wish you wouldn't have told me."

Nico continues to sway, standing above me. "My daughter is dead, Benjamin. She's gone. So don't complain to me how much your past hurts. Don't you see? You got what you asked for. And so did I." He starts to say something else, but as our eyes lock, his body...he's shaking too. I keep treating him like he's made of armor, but it's clear...he was a rat. Just like my dad.

"Nico, listen... I'm sorry for— Clementine was— She was—" I stop myself, pulling away from Mina and finally admitting the other thing I secretly hoped to find as I searched for these files. A cure for Clemmi. "I loved her too."

Marshall looks over as he hears the words. So does Mina. And Nico.

Outside, there's a familiar whine in the distance. An approaching seaplane.

Wiping my eyes, I climb to my feet and head outside to meet it. Nico grips me by my shoulder. "With your father, I wasn't trying to hurt you, Benjamin."

"I know. And again, I'm sorry for—"

"Stop talking," he insists. As usual, he takes an extra step too close, invading my personal space. "There was a reason I came here. To this room. The First Lady... the...the woman I speak to..." He takes a breath. "She told me your father wanted you to have this..."

Nico sticks his hand out, palm-up, his fist squeezed tight. I almost forgot, when I first found him here...with that shovel... he was pulling something from the wall. With no fanfare, he opens his hand. In his palm is something round and metal. It's so rusted and corroded, at first, it looks like an old bottle cap. But as he tips his palm and dumps it in my hand...

I pull it close to get a better look. It's a pin. At the center of it, underneath the orange rust flecks, there's a black-and-white picture. It almost looks like—

**"Charlie Chaplin?"** I ask. I look up at Nico. "I don't get it."

"When we were on this island, your father carried that pin with him everywhere we went."

Right there, the rusted old pin feels heavier in my hand. "He—? This belonged to my dad?"

"I don't know what made it such a treasure. Maybe it was just his way of proving he was here. But in those hours before he died, I saw him hide it. I was watching him back then. He didn't know I was there. He must've spent days digging the mortar out. And whatever the meaning was, this was what he chose to hide. He chose **this** to protect. I thought you'd want it back."

I tilt the old pin. Through the rust, my reflection bends and warps off a dent in it, like a fun house mirror. Even at a convention of Charlie Chaplin superfans, I couldn't sell this thing for more than a nickel. But it reminds me of what someone once told me during one of my very first days in the Archives. We were hunting through the stacks, surrounded by literally millions of useless old pages. Pulling a single yellowed file off the shelf, he said the words that I now share with Nico as I stare down at my dad's old metal button. The ultimate archivist mantra: "Everything's worth Something. To the right person."

Nico stares at me, fighting to prop up a crooked smile that keeps trembling and splintering. His rush of emotion catches me off guard. "I think that's how Clementine saw **me**," he says, his own tears pooling in the bottoms of his eyes. "I was important just to her. Loved by...loved by one."

**"Nico, hands up!"** a deep voice yells

behind us. **"No movements!"**

As we turn, two massive coast guard officers point guns at Nico's face. Racing into the room, they slam Nico to the ground, cuffing his hands behind his back. Another two race to Mina. She points them to Marshall, who's unconscious.

Nico doesn't fight back, doesn't say a word. I try to mouth him a quiet thank-you, but he doesn't see it. His eyes never leave the charred remains of his daughter.

One body, with many versions in it.

As they drag Nico from the room, I limp behind them and say my final goodbye to my dad, my fist clenching Charlie Chaplin's rusted face.

## 98

## One week later
## The White House

This time, they bring me in the front door.

"You're in luck. Hear that clinking?" the square-faced middle-aged woman asks, sounding far too excited. She's the secretary for the most powerful man on the planet. She doesn't get excited much. "The valet just delivered fresh lemonade," she adds. "He's in a good mood. Get it? Lemons into lemonade?"

"I get it," I say, shifting uncomfortably in the wingback chair across from her desk.

Throughout the history of our relationship, President Wallace has met with me in a private office of the Residence, an underground bunker below Camp David, and, just last week, a laundry room in one of the White House's subbasements.

On each of those visits, he was worried that the Culper Ring had proof of what he did all those years ago back in college. It's the only thing that scares him, if such a thing is possible. For that reason, they brought me through a back entrance, so no one saw me coming. Today, they told me to come to the northwest gate, a public entrance. The **most** public entrance, since it's right by the press office. Whatever Wallace is up to, he's done hiding me, and hiding from me.

Still, I saw how the marine guard was staring my way as I came up the front walk. Same with the suit-and-tie agents who brought me through the West Wing. White House security isn't made to be welcoming. They're even less welcoming when they see someone doing their job.

"He's just finishing up a call," the most powerful secretary in the world adds.

On my left, through the curved door to the Oval, I see President Orson Wallace in profile, sitting at his desk. He's not on the phone. He's reading from a file.

On the wall behind the secretary, there's a framed, enlarged photograph of the President pitching a Wiffle ball to his eight-year-old son. It's a candid shot out on the lawn, though Wallace is in a full suit.

For some who get this close to the commander in chief, it's an unsubtle message about the President's priorities. To others, it's a reminder that since they're not family, they need to be careful what they ask for. Yet for me, while of course it reminds me of my own dad and the maudlin father-son catch we'll never have, the real meaning of the photo is far more simple: When you come to the Oval, you're not playing Wiffle ball anymore. This is a big league game.

"He's waiting for you," the secretary announces, making me feel like I'm suddenly late.

I hop from my chair. Stepping though the curved door and into the Oval, I work hard to hide my limp from where Ezra shot me. My leg's still healing, though the President doesn't need to know that.

"Still can't walk, huh?" Wallace asks, sounding truly sincere. He's already headed my way, towering over me. I always forget how tall he is.

"If you need one of our doctors, say the word. We have the best," he offers, his gray eyes widening and making me feel like he'd evacuate an entire medical center for me. "Come. Sit. We can't have you hurting yourself."

He points me to one of the dark brown velvet sofas at the center of the Oval. But he doesn't head back to his desk or to the matching sofa that's opposite mine. Instead, he joins me on my sofa, right next to me, both of us facing the antique grandfather clock that I know has been in the Oval Office with every President since Gerald Ford.

I've seen this trick before. Men communicate side by side, shoulder to shoulder, which is why they like walking and talking, or sitting together in a car or at a sporting event. Women prefer face-to-face communications, which men tend to use only when there's a conflict or a need to show rank. Wallace usually sits behind his big desk. Right now, he wants me to know we're on the same team.

"You gotta try this lemonade—they put a hint of cranberry in it," the President of the United States tells me, pointing to the crystal pitcher on the nearby coffee table.

"I don't like cranberries. Too sweet," I say.

He fakes a grin at that, leaning forward

and pouring himself a glass. The ice pings in a high pitch off the fine crystal. As he sits back on the couch, the only sound in the room is a soft **wrrr** from the grand-father clock.

"I didn't bring you here for a fight, Beecher. This was a big win. For all of us."

"Not **all** of us."

He nods and stays silent, letting the air come out of that one. Eventually, he offers: "I'm sorry about Clementine. I know she—"

"Please don't turn this into a pep talk where you pretend to find good in her life. You brought me here for a reason. Just tell me what it is."

He lets the air come out of that one too. The **wrrr** of the clock seems to grind even louder. "I made a promise to you, Beecher. I intend to keep it."

I glance to my left, directly at him. The most powerful man in the world is swirling his pink-tinted lemonade, creating a tiny whirlpool in his glass. What a President does more than anything else is seduce.

"I'm not sure I follow," I say.

"You stopped Ezra. You helped us bring

in Nico. That's why Tot picked you. You did the Ring proud." He turns to his own left, and it's the first time I notice the thick accordion file folder that's still sitting at the center of his meticulous desk.

"Both the FBI and the Service combed through Ezra's apartment," he explains. "For the past week, we've been scrubbing his computer and phone records. From what we can tell, he paid off one of the delivery men in the White House flower shop. That's how he got inside. Otherwise, he was working alone. No contact with Riestra or anyone in the Service. And though Ezra was hoping to rebuild the Knights, he hadn't gotten anywhere yet. Thanks to you."

"What about his body? Did the coast guard…?"

"They've been picking up pieces all week. They found his arm five days ago. They said some of the other parts were probably eaten by sharks. That far out from the mainland, no way anyone survives." He takes a sip of the lemonade, his eyes closed as he drinks it.

"Can I ask you one last question?" I stay

locked on him, watching his reaction. "You knew Ezra's real mission, didn't you?" I ask. "From the very start, you knew he wasn't going after you. You knew his real target was Nico."

Wallace continues to sip his lemonade, eyes still shut.

"So when Ezra buried those arms..." I continue. "He really was just trying to make a point. He wasn't trying to kill you—he was showing you the flaws in your security."

Lowering his glass, the President never turns my way. He stares straight at the grandfather clock. "When Ezra first got inside the White House, he said he wanted to make me an offer. He wanted my help rebuilding the Knights. His first mission would be hunting and killing Nico—to make the country safe."

"So the buried arms..."

"The arms—and the penny and codes inside—were never about your father. They were Ezra's way of showing just how many holes Nico could sneak through. Naturally, our real fear was: Who else was helping him?"

I think on that, replaying our very first

conversation in the underground laundry room. "I knew you weren't telling the full story."

"I knew you wouldn't have helped if I was," the President challenges.

Now we're both staring at the grandfather clock.

"We both did what we had to, Beecher. I just need you to look at it from our perspective. At that point, we didn't know who Ezra was working with: you...Nico... Riestra and the Service. We didn't know who was with whom," Wallace explains. "But when it was clear that the Ring might be the best solution, and we saw that penny in there, well...Francy said you wouldn't jump in without some personal incentive." He looks back at the file on his desk. "I'm sorry we had to mislead you. I truly am. But I meant what I said about keeping my promise."

I follow his glance back toward the accordion folder. There's almost nothing else on his desk. Even the phone is stored in a drawer. On the right of the desk is a wooden box that holds the red buzzer for the President to call his aides. On the front corners, there're silver picture frames with photos of Wallace's family, a childhood one of him and his mom, and one of him with the previous four Presidents. Every frame is faced out, which means he can't see them when he's sitting at the desk. It's the same with the two tall flags that sit behind his chair and therefore show up in every photo. Everything in the Oval is meant to be seen by someone else.

"So that file…"

"Beecher, whatever else you think of me, I'm a man of my word. You did your part with Ezra. Now it's up to me to bring my part of the bargain."

Still holding the lemonade, the President gets up from the sofa and reaches for the thick file. "I know you saw some of it. Here's the rest," he says, handing me the accordion folder. "The real story of what happened to your father."

## 99

The first pages in the file are the same: my dad's hair and eye color, his height and weight. Each word on the page is marked with an indentation from a typewriter. These aren't old copies like on the island. They're originals.

After that is page after page of handwritten reports. Some are medical and show my father's heart rate and blood pressure. Others are behavioral, filled with descriptions like "exhibiting a strong response to angry and threatening stimuli."

One of the last pages is a death certificate. Under **Cause of Death**, it says the same thing they told my mother thirty years ago: accidental drowning from automotive accident on military bridge.

Unlike last time, my hands aren't shaking as I read this one. "Nico told me how he really died," I say to the President.

He stays quiet as I flip through the rest. The accordion folder has a few files in it. The one after my dad's is marked

**Operation: Plankholder.**

I pull it out, slowly thumbing through it. These are copies, but nearly every page is covered with black horizontal lines—all redacted.

The next folder in the file is labeled **Sagamore, Wisconsin**. My hometown, where Clementine, Marshall, and I all grew up. The pages in there are redacted too. It makes no sense. What's our town have to do with all this?

I look over at Wallace, who's leaning on the front corner of his desk and staring down at the cream-colored carpet. He's taking no joy from this.

"Why's there a file on Sagamore?"

The President shifts his weight, still staring down.

"I appreciate the dramatic pause," I tell him. "But we both know you read the un-redacted version."

"Beecher, does the name Dr. John Karlin mean anything to you?"

I shake my head.

"Dr. Karlin passed away a few years back. He had a doctorate in mathematical psychology, trained in electrical engineering, and was a professional violinist."

"Is he the one who did the experiment on my dad?"

"He had nothing to do with your dad. Or your town. He was a social scientist who worked at Bell Labs. After World War II, as they were developing phones, Dr. Karlin was the person who figured out how numbers should be arranged on the keypad of a phone: 1-2-3 in the top row, 4-5-6 below that..."

"I know how keypads look."

"But do you know **why** they're set up like that? It's because Dr. Karlin studied people's limits. He figured out that the 1-2-3 setup creates the most accuracy when people dial. Back then, they were worried people wouldn't be able to remember even seven digits for a phone number. So Karlin looked at round and square buttons...and whether to put the numbers in a circular or rectangular pattern.

"To this day, that 1-2-3 setup is an internationally accepted design, used on calculators, ATMs, door locks, and vending machines across the world. And it all came from this modest guy out in New Jersey.

He even figured out the optimum length of a phone cord by secretly cutting down his coworkers' cords each night to see what length it was when they finally complained. And you know what he proved? That studying human factors and limits always beats market research. Forget our strengths. If you want to know us, learn our **limits**."

"I assume there's a reason you're telling me this."

The President hits me with the kind of look that forced the leaders of Pakistan back to the peace table. "Dr. Karlin's research wasn't just used by Bell Labs. Folks in our military were paying attention too. You have to understand, for over a century, the army had spent a few billion trying to answer one simple question: Out of a thousand soldiers, how do you identify which one will step up and be the true leader? We still don't have a definitive answer. But thirty years ago, knowing that our weaknesses are as important as our strengths, a small group within the military asked a different but related question: Could they identify which soldiers were likely to be the weak ones? Could they recognize and detect our bad soldiers? And—most important—could they take that bad soldier and turn him into a **great** one?"

"You're telling me my father was the bad soldier they studied?"

"Forget good and bad. We all have heaven and hell in us. Y'know who said that?"

"Oscar Wilde."

"And he was right," the President says. "So with an eye on Dr. Karlin's telephone research, this group began studying the limits of our own soldiers. The injections that your father and the Plankholders got were supposed to bring out the truest version of themselves. It was just an amplifier."

"An amplifier of what?"

"Of who they already were. Think about it, Beecher: What's more valuable to a standing military? Knowing how to find the strongest of us, or knowing how to weed out the weakest?"

I shake my head, knowing the rest. Nico told me about the shots and what they did on the island. But as I look down at the folder marked **Sagamore**... "I still don't understand what this has to do with my hometown."

Wallace glances to his left, at the oil painting of Abraham Lincoln. "Beecher, this is just you and me now. Just us," Wallace says. "You hear me?" He's not trying to cover his ass. For the very first time in our relationship, the President of the United States seems absolutely concerned.

I nod, holding tight to the file folder. I try to take a breath, but it feels like my chest won't expand. There are four curved doors in the Oval Office. It's the first time I notice all of them are closed.

"These weren't good people," Wallace explains. "What they were doing with the Plankholders...the early reports saw it as a success. Even the death of your father, sick as it sounds, convinced them they were on the right track. From there, the program grew in scope. Instead of just identifying weakness, they started wondering if they could **predict** it. Is selfishness a learned trait? Is it traceable? Could it even be hereditary? To find answers, they needed more than just a few weeks on an island. For the true science behind it, they needed a place to observe repeated actions over time. Over a long time," the President explains, a deep crease burrowing between his eyebrows. "Like decades."

I glance down at the folder marked **Sagamore**. "Wait. You're telling me—?"

"Haven't you ever wondered how your family…and Clementine's family…**and** Marshall's family all wound up in the same small town? That's a hell of a coincidence, don't you think, Beecher?"

I try to take another breath. My lungs are punctured, deflating.

"The big secret wasn't your father," the President says. "The was the town itself."

I shake my head in disbelief.

"On the lives of my children, I wish it weren't true," he adds. "But ask your mother how she found Sagamore. If I had to guess, she'll say that one of the army's grief counselors told her about this great new community in Wisconsin. They probably helped her get the loan for your house, calling it a military death benefit. Then within those next months, when Marshall's dad and Nico were done with their service, they were steered there too. The first pastor at your church was a former army chaplain. He wrote weekly reports. I read the file, Beecher. There were three towns used, all in the Midwest. Yours was focused on troublemakers and rule-breakers."

I clench my jaw.

"Within a year, in one of the other towns, some kid from Arkansas started finding pustules around his anus. Soon it developed into a cancer no one had ever seen before. By the time Nico started hearing those voices in his head, the program was shut down and defunded, though one of the doctors—someone named Moorcraft— always filed an annual report that gave updates on the offspring."

**"Offspring?"**

Tightening his gaze, Wallace explains, "For a while, it looked like he might even be right. Before Clementine and Marshall left high school, they both had arrest records. Marshall even managed to get kicked out of the marines. Maybe it was nature, maybe it was nurture, but at the extremes, the genetics predicted all of it— the apples had fallen right next to the trees. Except for one thing, Beecher: They were wrong about **you**."

The President sits there, still leaning on the edge of his desk. He's waiting for me to yell or scream in shock. Instead, I sit there, with newfound calm, taking in every detail, every syllable. He's not stupid. I'm too quiet.

"You already knew all this," the President says.

I shoot him a look. He shoots one back. Like all Presidents, he doesn't like not being in charge.

"Who told you?" he challenges.

"When the Archives sent you the files, they had to digitize them," I explain.

"So your Culper Ring— You had the Ring's hacker break into our system?"

"Your system's a fortress. The Archives was much easier."

I wait for him to lash out. Instead, he looks uneasy. "Beecher, if you've known all this for a week, why didn't you say Something?"

"Believe me, I will. What those scientists did to Nico and my father...even to me and those in our town...You can't do that."

"I didn't do it."

"I know you didn't. But right here...at this

moment...I needed to know what you **would** do."

"So this was **my** test?" Wallace asks. "You wanted to see if I'd tell you the truth?"

"Do you have any idea how many lives were cratered by these experiments? Clementine died! Nico went insane! My own father was made so sick and paranoid, he locked himself in a burning jail cell! So excuse me for being pessimistic, but this government I've been fighting so hard for— What the hell kind of government does something like that?"

"The same kind of government it's always been: one comprised of the people, by the—"

"No. I've heard your stump speech. All I care about now is making this right."

"We'll never make it right. I know you know that. Families were ruined. We didn't take care of those who trusted us with their lives. No matter how much restitution we give—and we will give it—money doesn't make this right. There is no making it right. All we can do is make it **known**."

I shoot him a doubtful look. I thought for sure he'd bury it.

"Beecher, remember when President Clinton apologized for the WWII Tuskegee syphilis experiments? Or when Obama apologized for when, during the 1940s, we purposely gave hundreds of Latin Americans sexually transmitted diseases? Whatever else happens, we'll take our rightful responsibility. If you want, I can make you one of the founders on the independent investigative committee that's being put together. The announcement is being written as we speak. And the apology. I just thought you'd want to hear it first."

I hear the words, but they don't make sense. It'll create a shit-storm for his office. "You're really going public with this?"

"Don't look so surprised. Sometimes we actually do the right thing around here. Like saying thank you to those who helped us when we needed it." He motions my way, never looking more serious. "I mean it, Beecher. What you're building with your life and with the Culper Ring... I told you last week: There's a reason Tot picked you. We all have heaven and hell inside us. But what you have, is something **more**."

I sit up straight, confused.

"I'm telling you the truth. You did good here, Beecher. You always do good. And you always will."

It's the perfect speech delivered by the perfect speaker. In this town, people would kill for flattery like that. But as I fit the final pieces in their respective places, there's still one thing running through my brain. "Can I ask you a question?" I finally add.

"I'd be surprised if you didn't."

I look past the President and out the windows, where the morning sun lights the Rose Garden on fire. "Why'd you send me to stop Ezra?"

"Beg pardon?"

"When Ezra was first here...when he first snuck inside...you said Ezra made you an offer. He was all ready to kill Nico, which is great for you, since Nico's the escaped sociopath who wants you dead. So if that's the case, why not let Ezra do the job?"

Wallace cocks his head, like I'm speaking Cantonese. "Because it's **wrong**," he insists.

"I know it's wrong, but—"

"But what? You know what I did back in college, so you think I'm still that much of a monster?"

Even I have to admit, it sounds silly as he says it.

"None of us are who we are on our very worst days," he adds. "I know you know that."

I think of my own dad. I know it all too well. Just like I know we'll all have regrets we can never make up for.

"Listen," the President says, though for the first time, it doesn't sound like a command, "a few months back, when Nico escaped St. Elizabeths, my daughter wouldn't leave the third floor of the Residence for a week because she thought he was coming here to put bullets in us. On every single one of those days, I wanted Nico dead. The Knights would've made it even easier. But that's not how we do things here. We don't bury old military experiments from thirty years ago. And we don't let citizens execute other citizens—regardless of how much they deserve it."

I stay still, eyeing the Rose Garden. He doesn't move from his corner of the desk. But that doesn't mean there's no movement.

"Beecher, when I was twenty years old, I did a horrible thing that I still regret every day of my life. I mean it: **every day**. But that doesn't mean I'm the bogeyman you think I am. Tot, Marshall, even you...show me who's perfect."

I replay Clementine screaming at us, sacrificing herself at the bottom of the hole.

The President stands up and heads my way. "I was right about your defining characteristic: You always do what's right, at least you try to. I want you and the Culper Ring to keep trying."

"So now we're supposed to have a team-up?"

"Despite what you think, I respect what the Ring stands for. I respect what George Washington designed. What you did with Ezra proves that. I'm just trying to make your life easier, Beecher. You know what my job is. Like Washington himself, when you need something, I can get things. And by things, I mean **anything**."

It's a hell of an offer. With his help, the Ring can help people in a way I never thought possible.

"We can do amazing things together," he

adds. "With you in charge, the Ring will—"

"You're about to give me an inspirational speech, aren't you? I really don't need one."

"Have you heard my inspirational speeches before? I'm really good at them. I mean, **really** good."

I laugh at that. A real laugh. "I think I'll be okay."

"Then how about I just give you **this**?" From his pocket, he pulls out and offers...a handshake.

"There's no way you just made up that handshake thing right now," I say.

"It's an old JFK trick. Helluva pickup line, though, huh?" the President of the United States asks with a warm smile. "Sometimes we don't know that the most significant moments in our life are happening. It's time to decide, Beecher. What's your purpose in life: fighting me or helping others?"

I stand from the sofa, still considering the offer. My whole life, I thought if I knew who my dad was, I'd know who I was. Now that I have the answer, all I know is this: We may have heaven and hell in us, but we choose who we are. And who we fight. "You can't put us on assignments," I warn him. "We decide which cases we take— the ones best served by the Ring— without interference."

"No interference. It's your show," he agrees. "When you need help, you'll call. If not, I'll be cheering from here. So what do you say, Beecher?"

I don't say anything. I stare down at his extended hand. And I shake it.

## 100

## Waupun, Wisconsin

"Phone and keys go in the lockers. Wallet too," the guard at the X-ray called out. "No money allowed inside."

"They told me I could bring a movie," Marshall said, holding up a DVD case, then putting it on the conveyor belt.

As Marshall and his DVD headed through the metal detector, he could feel them all looking at him: the X-ray guard, the guard at the main visitors desk, plus the sergeant who was stationed behind the bubble of bulletproof glass. For once, though, their stares weren't about his face. Prison guards stare at everyone.

"Wait there," a voice squawked through an intercom. A metal door slammed behind him. In front of him, a sliding door was still shut, locking him in a narrow hallway. If there were any problems, here's where—

**Klik**, the door announced, sliding open.

"Welcome    to    Dodge    Correctional

Institution," a female guard with a heart-shaped face announced. "You're here for inmate 619216?" She shined a special flashlight on the back of Marshall's hand to make sure he had the glow-in-the-dark check-in stamp from the front desk.

Marshall nodded, knowing better than to give her any more information. Prison walls always have ears.

"You been here before?" she asked, opening another door and leading him outside, through the frozen courtyard.

"First time," he said, eyeing the electrified gate and braids of barbed wire along the top. Even on a state budget, they could do better than that.

At the large main building, the guard pulled out a ring full of keys for yet another metal door. Marshall noticed that on her left wrist was the faded green remnant of a laser-removed vine tattoo. If only all regrets went away as easily.

"Just remember," she said, tugging the door open as the stale smell of piss, rust, and body odor hit them in the face, "no talking to strangers."

Up the gray hallway, inmates in forest

green scrubs checked Marshall out and headed to the left, following signs to rec and to the gym. "This way," the guard said, leading him to the right, up a small ramp toward the only sign Marshall cared about:

## INFIRMARY

Even before the door **kllked** open, Marshall smelled it: Silverol, the burn ointment.

"Y'okay?" the guard asked as they stepped inside. "If you're claustrophobic, prisons can be—"

"I'm not claustrophobic," Marshall insisted, counting the hidden cameras and fighting to stay focused. Unlike the prison's gray hallways, the rooms here were pale yellow, designed to provide some needed cheer.

The sign out front was marked **Infirmary**. But even with guards at a small desk, and bulletproof glass that protected the nurse's station, it really looked more like a hospital. Medical carts, linen carts, and food carts were scattered throughout the hallway. Indeed, when an inmate becomes ill in the Wisconsin prison system, they're sent here.

"Bed number?" a black nurse wearing Smurfette-covered scrubs asked through a speaker in the bulletproof glass.

"Bed two," Marshall said.

The nurse lowered her chin, giving him the kind of look that goes with a funeral. "Samara, he's in—"

"I know where he is," the guard replied as Marshall followed behind her. Turning back over her shoulder, she told him, "I lost my uncle last year. Colon cancer."

Marshall ignored her, in no mood for pity.

As they passed room after room, every patient was locked behind a closed metal door with a tiny square window in it. At the far end of the hallway, two metal doors were propped wide—for the pair of rooms dedicated to hospice.

Marshall's sweat glands were gone, but he felt his internal heat starting to scorch. He told Beecher most everything. But not this.

"He's waiting for you," the guard said, pointing to the open door.

Marshall stepped over the threshold, then

glanced back at the guard, waiting for her to leave.

"They make me stay in the hallway," the guard apologized. "I know. It's not like he's going anywhere."

Giving one last look to the security camera in the corner, Marshall stepped inside, where the smell of Silverol wafted over him.

In the bed was a sleeping older man—he was in his fifties, though looked at least seventy—with a big barrel chest and thick arms. No question, he'd been strong in his day. At the foot of his bed, the way his covers were tucked, it was clear that below his knees, his legs were gone. Double amputee. White medical tape covered the hole in his neck where the breathing and feeding tubes used to be. They'd pulled those a few days ago. According to the nurses, he wouldn't make it to the end of the month.

Stepping closer, Marshall studied the man's face: the lumpy, sagging texture of his skin, like melted candle wax that streamed down toward his chin. He was covered with burns.

Like father, like son.

"Dad, can you hear me?" Marshall said, knowing he wouldn't get an answer. In Beecher's mind, Marshall's dad had died a long time ago. It wasn't that much of a lie. "Dad, it's me."

Still nothing.

Unlike Marshall's, his father's nose was mostly gone, whittled down to a soft muddy nub that looked like a dented thimble with a hole in the tip. Without the feeding tube, he breathed hard through his nose, each labored breath forcing the flap of skin that hung from his nose to wag back and forth like a minuscule leathery flag. His ears were worse, two jagged open holes on the sides of his head. His right hand was missing two fingers. His forearms were shiny and lumpy, like his face, and had no hair whatsoever.

Like Marshall's, none of his burns were red—they were pale and old, from years ago. But as the guard with the removed tattoo instinctively knew the moment she saw them together—Marshall and his father had been burned at the same time. And the older man definitely got it worse. Much worse.

"How do you like the new place?" Marshall

asked, noticing the bright yellow paint on the cinderblock walls and the matching yellow curtains that were supposed to make prison hospice feel less like prison hospice. There was even a TV, along with a few out-of-date movies. Sure, there were bars on the windows, and the sink and toilet were one metal unit, but it was still fifty times better than the rathole in Ohio where he'd been rotting. True to his word, the President had had him transferred here with no problem. Marshall would forever owe Wallace for that.

"I brought you a DVD. Your favorite," Marshall added, holding up the case with Tim Robbins standing out in the rain. **The Shawshank Redemption.**

In the bed, his father's head was turned sideways, his mouth hanging wide open, like he was forever in mid-scream.

"By the way, I met a girl. A good one this time," Marshall added, trying to sound upbeat as he turned on the TV. Stuffing the disc into the DVD player, he collapsed in the wheelchair next to the bed.

From his pocket, Marshall took out a photo—a childhood one, from twenty years ago. It was an old class picture, part of the big group shot, from when he, Beecher, and Clementine were all in seventh grade. In his hand was just a jagged piece of the photo, which he'd cut out after Clementine died. It was the only shot he had of her— young Clemmi looking more bucktoothed than he remembered, and him looking exactly as pudgy and scared as he remembered. But there they were, standing in class-photo pose: smiles wide, proudly next to each other. It took everything he had to not see the rotted teeth falling from her mouth.

"She's definitely something special," Marshall said to his dad, whose heavy breathing caused the flap of skin on his nose to wave back and forth.

"You'd like her for sure," Marshall added as the DVD swirled and the movie began. On instinct, he went to shut the bright fluorescent lights. Then he remembered: no light switch. Even in hospice, the lights always stay on in prison. "She's a hustler, Pop, just like you."

Once again, Marshall gave his father a chance to answer. Once again, all he got was heavy breathing and the waving flap of skin on his nose.

Settling in, Marshall turned the wheelchair toward the TV, where Morgan Freeman's magnificent baritone welcomed him to Shawshank. For years, Marshall knew it would end like this. He knew he'd never be able to reverse what happened to his dad. That didn't stop him from trying. And thanks to Beecher, he knew all there was to know about the Plankholders, the town, and the island where they'd experimented on their fathers. In the coming weeks, when the info went public, he'd even get some money from the government, though it was never about money. Otherwise, Marshall had everything he wanted, including an offer from Beecher to join and help rebuild the Culper Ring.

Marshall hadn't given him an answer, but he knew. He was done fighting. At least for now.

For the next hour and a half, he sat there in his dad's wheelchair, stealing glances at Clementine's old photo and bathing in the full irony of watching a prison break movie in the one cell where the prison door was wide open.

**"Remember, Red, hope is a good thing, maybe the best of things— and no good thing ever dies,"** Andy Dufresne said onscreen.

Marshall loved that line, even though he knew how wrong it was. Good things died all the time.

As the music swelled and the camera rose above Andy and Red's reunion, Marshall stood from the wheelchair and bent toward the bed.

"Dad, I'll see you soon," he lied.

His father was breathing heavier now, the skin flap on his nose still moving. His eyes were closed; he was sound asleep.

Leaning down toward his father's missing ear, Marshall whispered the two things he knew his dad needed to hear. One of them was true. The other was, "You were a good father."

With that, as the credits for **Shawshank** began to roll, Marshall tucked Clementine's picture into his father's fist and headed out the open door.

## 101

## St. Elizabeths Hospital
## Washington, D.C.

It took nearly a week for Nico to be transferred back.

First, there was that jail cell in Miami, then on to the hospital with all the news crews outside and the Hispanic orderly who snuck cell phone photos of him that she thought he didn't notice.

Nico noticed. He just didn't say anything. Not to anyone.

It was the same on the plane ride, and with the doctors who were waiting for him, watching with clipboards as they brought Nico back to St. Elizabeths and put him— and the skinny white cat he'd taken from the island—through the delousing shower. They tried to take the cat away, but when they saw Nico's reaction... The cat stayed. Pet therapy, one of the doctors called it.

Even during Nico's two days in the Quiet Room, with the glass walls so they could

keep him and the cat under extra obser-
vation, he barely uttered more than the
few syllables he needed to get the attention
of the guy who ran the juice cart.

It was the same with the dead First Lady.
Neither of them was in a talking mood.

**"At least they gave you your old room
back,"** the dead First Lady pointed out,
eyeing their sparse room on the NGI floor.
Not Guilty by reason of Insanity.

Sitting Indian-style in bed and watching
his cat walk in circles in the corner, Nico
didn't respond.

**"They even let you keep your Bible.
And your rosary. Not to mention your
favorite,"** she added, eyeing the Washington Redskins calendar above his desk.
Nico wouldn't look at it.

**"C'mon, Nico. Say something. I'm
starting to get bored."**

More silence.

The dead First Lady looked at her watch.
Ah. It was nearly 4 p.m. The scheduled
time.

**"I'm sorry they didn't let you go to her
funeral,"** the First Lady added.

Nico looked up, then back down again.

"I know how much Clementi—"

"Please don't talk about her. Please," Nico pleaded, his voice fracturing.

The dead First Lady had been by his side a long time. She knew not to push, not about this. She took a seat on the bed, next to him. **"Nico, last week, when we were back on the island...I saw those files. I read some of them too. The science was pretty amazing,"** she said, hoping he'd take the bait.

He didn't, but he was listening.

**"One of their studies focused on a group of firefighters,"** she explained. **"This social scientist was trying to analyze so-called heroes. He looked at people who rush into burning buildings, or who, when there's a tsunami, race back into the ocean to save someone else. According to the study, heroes like that can be impulsive and argumentative—they don't like authority and they'll break the rules, especially when they think they're in the right. But if you met that person in real life, you probably wouldn't like them, though they have the largest potential to do good."**

"Why are you telling these things to me?" Nico asked.

**"Just listen. In that same study, when they looked at the genes and physical brains of those brave heroes, you know who had an almost identical genetic map?"** She paused, watching his reaction. **"Sociopaths."**

Nico sat up and turned.

**"That's right,"** the First Lady said with a grin. **"Impulsive, argumentative, hates authority, and will put their own life at risk when they think they're right. The only difference between the two groups is their levels of empathy. Otherwise, you and the brave hero? You're basically twins."**

Nico sat there a moment, trying to process. "I still don't understand. Why're you telling me this?"

**"Because you need to hear it. It's like you told Beecher: Our souls have missions. Missions that we repeat over and over, until we conquer them. It's time, Nico. Time to realize who you really are. And time for me to take my leave."**

Nico glanced over at the clock on his

nightstand. It was exactly four. Always four. The funeral was about to start. He was missing it. "Whattya mean **leave**?" Nico looked back across the room.

For the first time in years, the First Lady was gone.

"Ma'am...?" he called out.

No answer.

"Ma'am, you there?"

Confused, he hopped off his bed, which sent the white cat darting under the desk. Nico looked under the bed. Nothing but lint. His mouth went dry; his heart felt like it was being folded in half. He turned toward his desk, then his unbreakable window. No. Can't be. He frantically yanked open his armoire. Empty.

**"MA'AM!"** Nico shouted. **"MA'AM, WHERE ARE YOU!?"**

By now, the silence was a high-pitched dog whistle, piercing his brain.

**No, this isn't— This can't be happening.**

Lunging for the door, Nico went to rip it open as —

There was a muted noise behind him. That sound of the air moving when some- one's standing near you.

Spinning backward, Nico froze as he saw her. He sucked in hard, letting out an audible gasp. **Dear God.** Blinking over and over, he couldn't believe his eyes. The First Lady was gone. Instead, he was staring at...at...

**"Hiya, Dad,"** Clementine said, flashing a wide smile with shining, perfect teeth.

Tears rose in Nico's eyes, blurring everything in front of him. He couldn't stop them. "How did you—? How can—?"

**"You earned this one,"** Clementine said, her short black hair back again. She looked so beautiful she practically glowed.

**"Prrrd,"** the skinny cat trilled, poking his head out to look.

"Thank you, God, thank y—"

The door burst open. "Nico, you okay?" the nurse with the yogurt breath challenged. "I heard screaming."

"No, we're— Everything's fine. It's great," he insisted, wiping his eyes with the backs of his hands. Some tears come from sadness. Others come from truth.

**"She can't see me, can she?"** Clementine asked, standing right where the First Lady used to, at the center of the room.

Nico shook his head, glancing back at the clock. 4 p.m. Always four. Just like God promised.

"I was thinking about my daughter's funeral," he told the nurse. "It just— The funeral's starting right now."

The nurse with the yogurt breath stared at him. She had nothing to say. "Indoor voices, okay? I'm sorry about your daughter. I read the write-up online—the way she gave her life to catch that guy. She sounded like one awesome badass bitch."

The door slammed shut and the nurse locked it from the outside. Nico had lost his grounds privileges. Mail, phone, and visitor privileges too. Didn't matter. He kept studying his daughter. Her eyes flickered with something he thought he'd never see again.

**"She's right, y'know,"** Clementine said. **"I am an awesome badass bitch."**

"Of course you are," Nico replied, smiling so wide his gums went dry. "You're my daughter."

## 102

## The White House

"I don't care who else is going."

"Dad, it's just a sleepover," the twelve-year-old girl challenged, the ringlets in her brown hair bouncing with tween rage.

"It's **not** a sleepover," the President told his daughter. "Not when there are boys invited."

"So if it was all girls, it'd be okay?"

Wallace pinched the bridge of his nose. He had come up here—to the Solarium on the top floor of the White House—for the same reasons George W. Bush used to come up here: He could get away from staff, and he could sit on this couch, watch sports, and relax. The plan wasn't working. "Nessie, you'll make a great lawyer one day. That day is not now."

His daughter crossed her arms in that same way her mother did. DEFCON 1 was coming. "I know why you're worried. You think I don't know about sex."

"Do not say those words again. Not in this argument."

"Jacob's mom—"

"And if you mention Jacob's mom, or Jacob, or even one of Jacob's pets, I'll have their whole family deported. I can do that. Three hundred million Americans gave me that power."

"You wish they did. No one votes any-more."

The President started to yell and laugh all at once, getting ready to say something that, no matter how much he fought against it, would make him sound as ridiculous as his own father.

A knock on the door saved him. "Sir...I'm sorry to interrupt this late..."

Across the room, a Secret Service agent with thick black hair stuck his head inside. Christian Deutsch. Christian was new, though well aware of the punishment that came from interrupting the President with his kids.

"He's here? Send him in," Wallace said, thankful for the distraction. Christian opened the door wider, ushering A.J. into the room. "Nessie, I need a few minutes.

**In private.**"

Nessie didn't move. "If I do, will you think some more about the sleepover?"

"I'll absolutely 100 percent pretend to," the President of the United States promised.

"I'll take it," Nessie said, racing for the door. "Hey, A.J.," she added, knowing her dad hated when she knew the agents' names.

As his daughter left the room, the President nodded at A.J., who tugged the door shut and locked Christian out. Even in the Residence, there were always people listening.

"Sir, I know it's late, but—"

"Don't apologize. I invited you," the President said, pointing him to the wicker chair next to the sofa.

In this room, the most casual in the White House, the Clintons, the Bushes, and the Obamas had all watched TV. Wallace was no different.

"Michigan still winning?" A.J. asked of the Michigan-Iowa basketball game, but never taking his eyes off the President.

"They **were**—right before my daughter came in and asked me if she can sully the family name at Jacob's house. Am I crazy—at this age should there be co-ed sleepovers?"

"I take it Jacob's parents don't have a daughter?"

"Exactly. **Exactly!**" the President said, starting to laugh.

A.J. forced a grin. This was the first time he had seen Wallace since the night Francy tested him at the crypt. Laughing was a good sign. "So…you said you wanted to see me, sir?"

"I just wanted to see how you were doing. And to tell you that in two weeks, after Riestra gets his due, you're being transferred back to my detail. We want you back in the one-spot."

A.J. leaned forward, nearly bursting with excitement. "Th-That's amazing. Thank you…thank you so much, sir. I won't let you down."

"You won't let me down **again**."

"I won't let you down again," A.J. agreed. "I swear to you."

The President said nothing, staying locked on the Michigan game.

"Sir, I know I screwed up. It's just that

Director Riestra—"

"Director Riestra is a pain in my ass. But based on what we now know, he was just doing his job. This is me doing mine," the President insisted. "You know how vital it is to be surrounded with people you trust."

A.J. nodded, feeling the words like darts in his chest.

"So I take it things will be smoother from here on in?" the President asked, though it wasn't a question.

"Sir, I know how things looked, but when I let Beecher go—"

"You think I care about Beecher? What I care about is how you got us into this mess. You went out on your own! You ignored everything we said!"

"You told me to be proactive."

"Yes. Proactive. As in—" The President cut himself off, knowing the dangers of his own anger. Pressing his lips together, he studied the TV. "A.J., see these basket-ball teams here? Every player on these teams is expected to be proactive. That's how you win. But even when these players feel like they've got a hot hand, you don't see them flinging the ball in wild half-court shots. Now why do you think that is?"

A.J. sat there, smart enough to stay quiet.

"It's because there's a playbook," Wallace explained. "And in that playbook, there's one unwritten rule: Every shot needs to be **smart**."

"Sir, I swear to you, I was trying to be smart. Back when Ezra first broke in, you said you didn't trust the Service anymore —that if someone here let him in, we should loop in Beecher and the Ring. Coming to the rescue is exactly what the Ring's been doing for centuries. But even you agreed Beecher would never help us…"

"…not unless he had a personal reason. I remember. But that doesn't mean you take two severed arms and bury them in the damn Rose Garden and Camp David! Forget about nearly giving my wife a stroke —how can you possibly think the best solution is one where the highest levels of the Secret Service are now putting a microscope on everything we do?"

"You said last time, the Knights had infiltrated the Service. Wasn't that the priority: trying to figure out how deep Ezra had burrowed?"

Wallace couldn't argue with that. When Ezra got inside the White House with his Lee Harvey Oswald fake ID...they didn't know if he'd single-handedly sidestepped security, or if someone inside the Service had been holding the door open for him.

"With the buried arms, I just— I thought it'd tell us what side Riestra and everybody else was on," A.J. explained. "And then...like you wanted...we'd get Beecher and the Ring back on our side instead of against us. And that's what happened, isn't it?"

Onscreen, one of the Iowa players went in for an easy lay-up. "A.J, you're a good investigator," the President finally said. "You were able to track Ezra from the moment he first broke in here. You dissected his life; you found his dead roommate; you even figured out where he had buried him. But when it came to Beecher, the only reason he decided to join us was because I lied and said that an old penny was in your overdramatically buried hand."

On TV, one of the Michigan players sank a beautiful three-pointer. "Do you understand what I'm saying?" the President added. "The goal was to stop Ezra from rebuilding the Knights. The goal was to learn who else Ezra was working with. And yes, the goal was to stop Beecher from biting at my ass instead of being on my leash. But in the end, that 2.5-gram, copper-plated penny did far more to get me what I wanted than you recklessly going out on your own, stupidly digging up a dismembered corpse, and putting the top tier of White House security on high alert."

"We needed them on high alert. What if Ezra and his Knights decided to come for you? We had no idea who he was working with! You want to call in Beecher, that's fine. Again, that's what the Ring is there for. But I still don't understand why you thought the Culper Ring could protect you more than I could. No offense, sir, but you asked me to solve an aggressive problem. I thought it needed an aggressive solution."

The President didn't say anything, still locked like a laser on the TV.

For a moment, A.J. sat there, glancing around the Solarium. "Sir, not to change the subject, but do you remember what the last emergency in this room was?"

Again, Wallace didn't answer.

"It was when George W. Bush choked on a pretzel. Remember that? He was here in the Solarium, watching baseball and throwing back pretzel nuggets like they were peanuts. Suddenly, one of the pretzels goes down too fast and Bush falls to the ground, purple and unconscious. Just imagine: We've got dozens of terrorist groups who want to cut his throat, and the leader of the free world is about to be taken out in the private Residence by some Rold Golds."

"Make your point, son. Quickly."

"My point, sir, is that in the weeks following, the Secret Service did a vast months-long investigation about how to stop something like that from ever happening again. And y'know what their solution was? That," A.J. said, pointing to the wall, at the small button that looked like a doorbell. "They installed a push-button alarm system. If a President feels like he's getting sick, he goes and pushes the button. But what's the problem with that?"

"It doesn't stop someone from choking

on a pretzel."

"Exactly," A.J. said. "That's all I'm trying to say, sir. With some problems—especially human problems—there's no easy solution. I humbly apologize for putting Mrs. Wallace through that."

"She wanted to kill you. I mean it. She's still not sleeping right."

"And that's on me. It was an unforgivable error. But that doesn't mean I'm not killing myself to make sure that you and your family are safe."

On TV, the Iowa coach was screaming at one of the referees as Michigan began pulling away. "A.J, why do I treat you differently than everyone else?" the President asked.

"Pardon?"

"I have thousands of agents. Why do I treat you differently?"

"Because you trust me, sir."

"Because I trust you. So if you go off the playbook again—"

"I won't."

"But if you do—"

"I promise you, sir. I **won't**."

The President nodded, still watching the

game. "I'm glad we understand each other. Welcome home."

Getting up from his wicker chair, A.J. thanked the President, quickly leaving the room. For a few minutes, Wallace sat there in silence, until it was halftime in the game.

From his pocket, the President pulled out his phone and headed for the Solarium's wide glass windows. Ignoring the perfect view of the Washington Memorial, he looked straight down, focused on the now-dark South Lawn.

Unlike the White House itself, except for the fountain, the lawn wasn't lit at night. But as the President dialed one of the few phone numbers he knew by heart, he couldn't help but squint down toward the Rose Garden.

From this angle, he couldn't see it, but he could feel it. His wife was kneeling there in the dirt, once again working on her garden. Things were back to normal. On all fronts.

"How'd it go?" Francy asked, picking up before the first ring was done.

"He said everything right. He was doing his best. I just wish he had never buried the arms."

"So you're worried he'll share the story elsewhere?"

"It's the one thing I can't ignore," the President of the United States said, squinting down toward his wife. What were the words A.J. used? **An unforgivable error.** "If he does, it would be the end of us."

Francy didn't say anything else. She just hung up the phone.

## 103

## Two hours later
## Old Town Alexandria, Virginia

"So they gave you a promotion?"

"Not a promotion," A.J. said, propping his phone on his steering wheel and talking into the speaker as he blew past the bars in Old Town. "More like a reinstatement. In a good way. Worth celebrating."

"Ah. So that's why you're calling?" Angela asked. "To claim a celebration and see if I'll let you take me home?"

"Don't be so jaded. I'm a modern man. If you want, you can take **me** home."

On the other end, Angela was silent.

"Angie, that was a joke."

"...he said, realizing he hadn't called this beautiful and oh-so-patient decorative painter in two weeks."

She was right about that. With everything going on, A.J. had made the one mistake every White House employee makes: He let the President's life become his own life.

Tonight, though, he was determined to change that. "I'm not gonna make an excuse. All I'll say is this: The Basin Street Lounge has live jazz, and we can go make fun of everyone there wearing a turtleneck. Then I've got a pint of raspberry chocolate chip custard from the Dairy Godmother. I rest my case."

Pulling into the garage of his apartment building at the end of Fayette Street, A.J. didn't have a pint of custard. He also had no idea if there was live jazz at the Basin. But if he'd learned anything during his year with Wallace, it was that there was no better way to get what you want than by helping someone else get what they want.

"I'll eat your ice cream," Angie said. "That's a literal statement, not figurative."

"I see your ice cream weakness, and I second it," A.J. said, pulling into an open parking spot. "I just got home. Let me change out of my suit. Want to meet me at the Basin?" he added, shutting his eyes and hoping she didn't call his bluff.

"I'm in no mood to count turtlenecks. You bring the Dairy Godmother; I'll supply the hot fudge. Again, literally. I have fudge. We can microwave it."

"Deal. Done. See you soon," A.J. said, allowing himself a small fist pump. Shutting his phone and his car, he was still replaying his conversation with the President. Was it hard at times? For sure. But Wallace sat there; Wallace listened; and in the end, even Wallace couldn't argue with the results. Ezra was stopped, Beecher was neutered, and for at least a day, there was actual peace. Best of all, A.J. was coming back to the one-spot. "Welcome home," the President had said. **Welcome home.**

Elbowing open his door and still hearing those words in his head, A.J. took a deep breath, so lost in the garage's familiar gasoline smell he didn't even notice the young man with the thick black hair who was waiting for him, syringe in hand.

It was the last breath A.J. would ever take.

Stabbing the needle straight into A.J.'s chest, Secret Service Agent Christian Deutsch pressed on the plunger.

A.J.'s right arm went numb. His body went into spasm. Then the light left his eyes. That's all it took.

The chemical was fentanyl. Even an experienced medical examiner, unless they're looking for it, will never find a trace of it. But they will find something that looks like a sudden heart attack. "Too much pressure at work," his closest friends would say.

Lowering A.J's body back into the driver's seat, Christian wasn't proud of the decision. But he knew they wouldn't have asked—and they especially wouldn't have asked him—if there were another way. Christian's father had gone to high school with the President, was **like family** with the President. Indeed, when Christian first applied to the Service, he'd never told anyone about his connection. He wanted to rise on his own. Just like A.J. all those years ago.

Even now, Christian was replaying their words. There was no other choice, they'd explained. Christian understood. Peace wasn't possible without loyalty.

Pulling out his cell phone, Christian dialed the number that Francy made him learn by heart. It rang three times before someone picked up. The person didn't say hello.

Christian said nothing back. The message was clear. For now at least, their secrets were safe. And so was President Wallace.

# 104

## Washington, D.C.

"How's he doing?" I ask the nurse who likes poppy-seed bagels.

"Same," she replies, well aware it's too late for bagels. "You okay?" she adds as I head for my usual spot in the ICU. "You look tired."

Sometimes I forget—nurses spot pain like no one else. "I'm good. Just one of those weeks at work."

"You're a terrible liar, Beecher. But if it makes you feel better, I'm sure he appreciates you coming."

Nodding my thanks, I stop at the sliding glass doors of Room 355. Inside, Tot's eyes are closed, his skin is gray, and as his palms face upward, his mouth is still open like a urinal: right where I left him. Taking a deep breath, I touch my Kenny Rogers belt buckle and...

"Okay, who's ready for the single greatest moment in country music history—and yes,

I'm including the Dixie Chicks being naked on the cover of **Rolling Stone**," I call out, marching into the room and approaching his bed.

Tot's only response is the automated hiss from his ventilator. A spitball of air shakes the accordion breathing tube in his neck.

"No, okay, you're right—this may not be better than Billy Ray deciding we needed an 'Achy Breaky Heart Part 2,' but just wait...this is up there," I tell him. "For your listening pleasure: Kenny Rogers and Kris Kristofferson—together—**in concert**. It's like **A Star Is Born** with two guys and no Streisand. It's country music heaven." From my pocket, I pull out an old silver iPod. I'm about to switch it with the black iPod in the sound dock on the rolling cart, but at the last minute, I stop myself.

I look over at Tot. The pale purple scar that curves down the side of his head looks as gruesome as ever.

Stuffing the iPod back in my pocket, I pull out my phone and swipe to my own music. Enough with the Gambler. Time for Something new.

"Oh, stop complaining, you old fart. Just

give it a chance," I tell Tot.

The ventilator pumps back his usual response.

"And now…presenting the true fearsome four—the outlaws from Detroit who like to rock loud, like to wear makeup, and are prepared to melt your face off… I give you: KISS, live from the Los Angeles Forum— **the 1979 Dynasty Tour!**"

With a cheering crowd and a steady haunting drumbeat, the song "Rock and Roll All Nite" begins to thunder from my phone's tinny speaker.

"You're judging now, aren't you?" I ask Tot. "Don't. When they were getting inducted into the Rock and Roll Hall of Fame, someone said that KISS was never a critics' band; they're the people's band. In fact, at this concert, Ace Frehley shot rockets from the neck of his guitar. Real rockets—**from a guitar**! At one point in the show, a guitar would rise into the air, and then Ace would grab his rocket guitar and shoot the first guitar down! Let's see the Gambler do that! It may be loud and childish, but sometimes you unapologetically need to be who you are."

**"You drive us wild, we'll drive you craaazy,"** KISS sang from my phone.

"You feel that? That's not just nostalgia. That's your heart pumping, screaming that you're alive. Feels great, right?" I ask, sitting in the vinyl chair next to his bed and grabbing Tot's open palm. "C'mon, Tot, this is your chance. I need you to squeeze my hand."

Tot doesn't squeeze back.

"You can do it. I know you can," I tell him, gripping him a little harder.

His hand feels dead in my own.

"Fine, you leave me no choice. I bring you **this**..." From my coat pocket, I hold out a photo of a woman in a black sweater. "Verona. From Human Resources. Sweater tighter than ever," I explain, wedging the photo into the faux paneling on the guard rail of his hospital bed. "I took it secretly with my phone, and I swear to you, there are four Archives employees who would pay for this picture. If you open your eyes right now, it will greet you like a big-bosomed sunrise."

Tot's hand just sits there.

Can't say I expected any different.

However long it takes, I'll be here. "By the way, I met with Wallace today. As usual, he's awful. His ego's awful. He'll always be awful. He even thinks he actually fooled me, as if I didn't know he snuck that penny into the dead hand. But by playing along, at least for now, he's done coming after us." Leaning in close to Tot, I whisper, "Big secret? I'll never stop hunting him."

The automated blood pressure cuff tightens around Tot's arm. The rest of the monitors sing a song of beeps and pings.

"Best of all, we stopped the real bad guy: Ezra and his so-called Knights," I say, though as the words leave my lips, all I see is Clementine's coffin from today's funeral. No question, the Culper Ring has the potential for so much good. I just wish Tot had warned me it could also bring so much bad.

"I know," I tell him, still holding his hand. "And I do realize that the longer I talk to you, the more I'm like Nico with his imaginary friend."

In the middle of the KISS song, there's an explosive boom. "Here we go...**pyrotechnics**!" I call out. The crowd erupts with raucous cheers that turn me into my twelve-year-old self, when Marshall and I used to listen to this in his treehouse.

Back when Tot was first shot and the doctors told me to play him his favorite music, they explained that the reason people like old songs is because they know what's coming. When that classic song starts playing and you know all the words, you mentally start singing along. According to neurologists, that feeling provides a true sense of safety that doesn't exist in real life. In real life, there are so many unknowns.

"Imagine it this way," the doctor told me. "When you go down a slide, it's usually a fun ride. But if I blindfolded you, and you didn't know you were at the top of that slide, and I suddenly gave you a push, you'd scream, **'Whoa! Hey! What the hell's going on!?'** Same ride. Two different reactions," the doctor said.

Yet the longer I sit here and hold Tot's cold hand, the more I realize that, whether it's through song or anything else, there's no getting rid of the unknown. The bumps will always be there. And so will those who love you.

Taking out a ballpoint pen, I turn Tot's hand palm-down, getting ready to press the point into his nail bed to test his reflexes.

For months now, I've been searching through history, sifting through the most complex and screwed-up history of all: family history. I thought that finding the truth about my dad would bring me certainty and wipe away the unknown. But now that I have it, it doesn't make me feel any better. In fact, during all the time I was searching for the father I **didn't** have, I'm not sure I fully appreciated the one I **do** have.

I press the point of the pen into Tot's nail bed. At the pain, he jerks his hand back. He's definitely still in there.

"You think I'm done with my bribes, old man? Father's Day is coming, and until the day they die, KISS will still tour. Verizon Center. This August. You and me, third row. We'll throw our panties onstage—or maybe some obscure historical documents."

The ventilator hisses in agreement. The machines ping. And KISS continues to rock and roll all night.

As I hold Tot's hand, his fingers convulse and jerk slightly, which always happens after I press the pen into his nail bed. It's a reaction to the painful stimulus. But as I grip his hand tighter, I feel something. His fingers move more than before. Not by much. But by enough.

"It was throwing the historical documents that got you in a tizzy, wasn't it?" I ask.

Tot still doesn't answer. Not yet. But eventually, he will.

"You really know the most romantic spots," a female voice calls from the hallway. I turn just as Mina enters the room, twisting out of her winter coat. She's wearing a great charcoal knit sweater and black boots that make her look even taller than she is.

"Sweet mother of Abraham Lincoln! Are you playing **KISS**?" she asks. Before I can even answer, her smile lights the room. "I used to **love** this song!"

"Used to?" I challenge.

She glances over at Tot. "He looks better than last time."

"He does, doesn't he?" I say, still sitting in the vinyl seat, holding his hand.

BRAD MELTZER

"If you want, we can stay."

"No, it's okay. He knows I'll be here tomorrow. Besides, he told me never to refuse a dinner date with a beautiful woman."

"Dinner? I thought you said you had something special planned."

"I do. When we're done, I'm taking you on a brand-new tour of the Archives. The lights in the Treasure Vault have a dimmer. I'll read you Lincoln's early draft of the Emancipation Proclamation, and we'll figure out what changes he made."

She looks at me, standing there. "Beecher White, you are the nerdiest, sexiest man I've ever met in my life. You know how to turn a girl **on**!"

Laughing out loud and getting up from my chair, I give Tot a soft kiss on his forehead. "Toldja, right? You can fake boobs—you can't fake brains."

"By the way," Mina asks as I follow her out of the room and into the hospital hallway, "why's there a picture of me in my black sweater on the armrest of Tot's bed?"

I grin at that. "I have no idea what you're talking about."

Nico was right about one thing: Our souls have missions. Missions that we repeat over and over until we conquer them. For so long, I thought I knew what my mission was: to uncover my family's history. I spend every day showing people the power of history. But history only has the power you give it.

Heading for the elevator, I turn and take one last look at Tot, then another at Mina. You may never make peace with your father. But you can always make peace with yourself.